Praise for
A Death in Vienna

"[An] elegant historical mystery . . . stylishly presented and intelligently resolved." —*The New York Times Book Review*

"[*A Death in Vienna* is] a winner for its smart and fin-de-siècle portrait of the seat of the Austro-Hungarian empire, and for introducing Max Liebermann, a young physician who is feverish with the possibilities of the new science of psychoanalysis." —*The Washington Post*

"Frank Tallis knows what he's writing about in this excellent mystery. . . . His writing and feel for the period are top class." —*The Times* (London)

"An engrossing portrait of a legendary period as well as a brainteaser of startling perplexity . . . In Tallis's sure hands, the story evolves with grace and excitement. . . . A perfect combination of the hysterical past and the cooler—but probably more dangerous—present." —*Chicago Tribune*

"Holmes meets Freud in this enjoyable . . . whodunit." —*The Guardian* (London)

Vienna Blood

Vienna Blood

A Novel

Frank Tallis

VOLUME TWO OF THE
LIEBERMANN PAPERS

RANDOM HOUSE TRADE PAPERBACKS
NEW YORK

2007 Random House Trade Paperback Edition

Copyright © 2006 by Frank Tallis
Dossier copyright © 2007 by Random House, Inc.

Published in the United States by Random House Trade Paperbacks,
an imprint of The Random House Publishing Group.
A division of Random House, Inc., New York.

RANDOM HOUSE TRADE PAPERBACKS and colophon are trademarks
of Random House, Inc.
MORTALIS and colophon are trademarks of Random House, Inc.

Originally published in the United Kingdom by Century Books in 2006.
Published in paperback in the United Kingdom by Arrow Books,
an imprint of The Random House Group, Ltd., in 2007.

ISBN 978-0-8129-7776-9

Printed in the United States of America

www.mortalis-books.com

6 8 9 7

Part One

The Ideal Suspect

I

THE ITALIAN LUNGED FORWARD. He was a small, lean man, but very muscular. Any disadvantage he suffered because of his lack of height was amply compensated for by his sharp eye and astonishing speed.

Liebermann successfully deflected the foil's thrust but lost his balance. He was unable to produce a counterattack and his opponent advanced yet again. The tip of the Italian's foil came perilously close to the protective quilting over Liebermann's heart. Recovering his footing, Liebermann chose to make a *passé*—darting behind the Italian and taking a few steps backward. A trickle of sweat slid down his hot cheek. The Italian shrugged and walked away, flexing his foil in a gesture of indifference. After a few paces he swung around and adopted the preparatory stance, his chin tilted upward in an attitude of arrogance. Liebermann edged forward.

The Italian seemed to relax, his foil wilting a little in an apparently weaker grip. Liebermann noticed the subtle change and struck. A violent brassy clang was followed by the shriek of scraping metal: the Italian's foil yielded, offering no resistance. Liebermann congratulated himself, believing that he had taken his opponent by surprise—but the concession was merely tactical. The Italian's blade deftly flicked around Liebermann's, displacing it with a powerful grazing action, and, once again, the tip of his opponent's foil effortlessly penetrated Liebermann's defenses. Liebermann retreated, executing a series of deflective maneuvers that barely contained the Italian's renewed fierce attack.

They circled each other, occasionally touching blades in glancing contact.

"You should have anticipated my *froissement*, Herr Doctor," said the Italian gruffly. He tapped his temple and added: "Think, Herr Doctor! If you do not think, all is lost."

Liebermann examined the blank oval of Signore Barbasetti's mask, eager to observe some mark of humanity—a conciliatory expression or the glimmer of a smile, perhaps. The mesh, however, was impenetrable.

Their foils clashed again—blades flashing in a shaft of early-morning sunlight. A swarm of lazy dust motes was sucked into a miniature cyclone of displaced air.

Barbasetti produced a feint, switching from one line of attack to another, forcing Liebermann to draw back. However, the young doctor retained his composure and made a move that he intended should fail, thus provoking a predictable and powerful thrust from Barbasetti. Liebermann dodged and struck the forte of the Italian's foil as he stumbled past—Barbasetti almost lost his grip.

"Bravo, Herr Doctor," Barbasetti said, and laughed. "An excellent *falso!*"

"Thank you, signor."

Barbasetti came to a halt and lifted his blade, scrutinizing it closely. "Please excuse me, Herr Doctor."

Barbasetti walked to the other side of the drill hall and pressed the hilt of his foil against the surface of a battered wooden table. He then hung a small iron weight from the tip and watched the metal blade bend. Its gentle curvature elicited an equivocal grunt from the watchful Italian.

"Is everything all right, signor?" Liebermann asked.

"Yes, I think so," Barbasetti replied. The Italian raised himself up, marched back, and warned his student: "*En garde.*"

Immediately they were engaged, Liebermann's foil sliding along his opponent's blade until the hand guards crashed together. The fencing master pushed and Liebermann was thrown back: he landed awkwardly, but was nevertheless able to execute an impressive flying parry.

Barbasetti disengaged. "Much better."

Liebermann noticed that the button at the end of his foil was trembling—he was feeling tired. After his lesson, he would have coffee and croissants in the little coffeehouse close to the Anatomical Institute. He would need something in his stomach to keep him going. . . .

"*En garde!*" Barbasetti barked again. The Italian had noticed that his student's mind had begun to wander. Liebermann was astonished by the fencing master's insight.

Again their blades connected, and the plangent clatter of contending steel filled the hall. Liebermann thought that Signore Barbasetti was tiring too. His pace had slackened slightly and his movements were less balletic. The Italian deflected Liebermann's lunge, but failed to resume his guard. Observing the exposed chest protector, Liebermann recognized a rare opportunity. Excited by the prospect of victory, he raised his foil, ready to strike.

But the blow was never delivered.

His body froze, paralyzed by the inexplicable pressure that he felt against his heart. Dropping his gaze, he contemplated the tip of Signore Barbasetti's foil, which had found its home precisely above the intercostal space separating ribs five and six.

Barbasetti pushed, and the cold steel curved upward.

"I don't understand," said Liebermann.

"You were not concentrating, Herr Doctor," said the Italian. "Such an error would certainly lose you a competition . . . and of course, in some circumstances, your life."

Barbasetti lowered his foil and then raised it in salute.

Liebermann returned the gesture politely. In spite of the fencing master's dramatic declaration, the young doctor was ashamed to find that he was still thinking of the little coffeehouse near the Anatomical Institute: crisp flakes of buttery pastry, a pot of plum jam, and a cup of very strong black coffee.

2

Detective Inspector Oskar Rheinhardt followed a path that led upward through wooded parkland. He glanced over his left shoulder and saw part of the Schönbrunn Palace through the trees. It was a bright cold morning and the rotting leaves were crisp with ice. They made a satisfying crunch beneath his boots.

Rheinhardt had not been to the zoo in years. As he progressed, he was reminded of the time when his daughters were very little—a time when he had been a frequent visitor. He remembered Mitzi's eyes widening at the approach of a lion, and Therese, laughing at the chattering monkeys. The memories flooded back, happy memories, as bright and colorful as a picture book. Rheinhardt smiled inwardly, but his recollections were shadowed with guilt and regret. Being a detective inspector was encroaching more and more on his personal life. If he wasn't investigating, there was always the paperwork—the endless form-filling and report-writing. How could he possibly find time to take his daughters to the zoo?

A cast-iron gate loomed ahead. As he approached, he recognized the spindly wide-spaced gold lettering that curved over the archway: *Tiergarten*. Beneath it stood a stout man in a long winter coat. He was smoking, pacing, and occasionally stamping his feet. When he caught sight of Rheinhardt, he stopped and waved—a somewhat redundant signal as Rheinhardt was in no danger of missing him.

"Thank God you've come," the man called out, stepping forward and taking a few steps down the slope.

Rheinhardt smiled and felt obliged to quicken his pace.

"Herr Pfundtner?" The man nodded. "Inspector Rheinhardt."

They shook hands.

"Thank you for coming so quickly," said the zoo director. "Please, this way . . ." He set off at a brisk pace and immediately started talking.

"I've never seen anything like it. I can't think who would have done such a thing. It's appalling. So utterly senseless that I can hardly believe it's happened." Pfundtner raised his hands in a gesture of incomprehension and shook his head. "What am I to do? We'll never be able to replace Hildegard. We'll never find such a fine example of *Eunectes murinus* again! She was a favorite of the emperor's, you know. He'll be devastated."

The two men marched past the tiger enclosure. One of the beasts lumbered toward them, pressing its nose up against the bars.

"What time did it happen?" asked Rheinhardt.

"Seven o'clock," said Pfundtner.

"Exactly?"

"Yes. It was feeding time."

"A keeper was present?"

"Yes. Herr Arnoldt. Cornelius Arnoldt. He was knocked unconscious."

"While feeding the animal?"

"No, while preparing the food in an adjoining room."

The tiger's throat rattled. A deep, gurgling sound, like water pouring down a drain.

"Do you know Herr Arnoldt?"

"Yes, of course. I'm familiar with all of my keepers. He's an excellent fellow."

"So the intruder struck Herr Arnoldt and took the keys?"

"Yes."

"Then he let himself into the pit?"

"Quite so," said the director.

The Tiergarten was arranged like a bicycle wheel, with pathways radiating like spokes from a central hub. All the buildings were painted mustard-yellow, just like the adjacent palace, a consistency of color that commemorated the zoo's earlier existence as the royal menagerie. They were heading in the direction of the central octagon, an elegant structure decorated with ornamental urns and braided bas-relief.

"What time do you open?" asked Rheinhardt.

"I'm not sure that we should. Not today. My staff are too . . . distraught."

"It would be a shame to disappoint your visitors."

"Quite so, Inspector, quite so. Like you, we too have a duty to perform."

"And a very important one. My family and I have spent countless happy afternoons here in the company of the animals." Rheinhardt continued: "I have two young daughters." His addendum hung in the air.

The director turned to look at his companion and, smiling faintly, said: "We do our best, Inspector."

"Quite so," Rheinhardt replied, mischievously appropriating the director's verbal tic. Somewhere, in a distant corner of the zoo, an unidentified creature, most probably an exotic bird, cawed loudly. Beyond the central octagon the two men veered to the right, finally approaching their destination.

They entered the reptile house through a door at the rear of the building. The atmosphere was warm and humid, in sharp contrast to the icy air outside. A tall zookeeper was standing in the narrow hallway next to an open door.

"This way, please," said Pfundtner. The keeper pressed his back against the wall, allowing the director and Rheinhardt to pass. The door opened out from a small room, the occupants of which formed an odd tableau. A second keeper, with a bandage around his head, sat on a wooden chair. Next to him stood a sober-looking gentleman in a dark suit (clearly the doctor responsible for the bandage), and to their left was a white slab on which several animal carcasses were laid out. Rheinhardt was dimly aware of an arrangement of pelts—one of them lying in a circular pool of blood.

"How is he?" asked the director, nodding toward the injured keeper.

"Much better," said the doctor, resting a hand on his patient's shoulder. "A little concussion—but that's to be expected. A few days' bed rest and he'll be in fine fettle."

Rheinhardt stepped into the room. "May I ask Herr Arnoldt some questions?"

"Of course," replied the doctor. "But I'm not sure he'll be able to tell you very much. He's suffering from retrograde amnesia."

"Which means?"

"Memory loss," the doctor explained. "Most people lose some memory after a head injury—usually the memory of events leading up to the point where they lost consciousness."

"But how much?"

"It varies, but Herr Arnoldt can't remember much more than getting up this morning and eating his breakfast."

"Is that so?" asked Rheinhardt, directing his question at the keeper.

Herr Arnoldt attempted to stand.

"No, Herr Arnoldt," said the doctor, applying a gentle pressure to the keeper's shoulder. "Please remain seated."

Herr Arnoldt dropped back into the chair and looked up at Rheinhardt.

"I can remember getting up this morning . . . eating some eggs and pickled cucumber."

"And anything else?" asked Rheinhardt.

"No. . . . The next thing I remember is waking up here . . . on the floor. And Walter . . . Walter helping me."

"Walter?"

"That's me," said the keeper outside. "Walter Gundlach. I was on my way to the hyena enclosure when I noticed the door at the back had been left open. It's usually locked, so I stuck my head in to take a look. Herr Arnoldt was lying on the floor."

"Where?"

"Half his body was where you're standing, the other half sticking out into the hallway."

"There's no blood on the floor," said Rheinhardt. "Has someone cleaned it up?"

"There was no blood," said the doctor. "There were no lacerations. It seems that Herr Arnoldt was struck on the back of the head with considerable force—but not with a weapon."

"Then with what?"

"A clenched fist . . . the forearm, perhaps." The doctor pointed at his patient's neck. "The cervical area is tender and badly bruised."

"You didn't notice anything else?" Rheinhardt asked Gundlach. "Anything unusual?"

The keeper shook his head.

"No. . . . I made sure that Herr Arnoldt was comfortable and then I called the director."

Rheinhardt turned to face the doctor again.

"Is Herr Arnoldt's memory loss permanent?"

"It's difficult to say. Some people recover their memories—others don't. We'll just have to wait and see."

"But what is the likelihood?" asked Rheinhardt insistently.

The doctor looked down at Herr Arnoldt, narrowed his eyes, and pressed his lips together.

"There is a fair chance," said the doctor.

Like most medical men, he seemed reluctant to give a definite answer.

Rheinhardt surveyed the circle of faces surrounding him: the doctor, the director, the unfortunate Herr Arnoldt, and his gangly colleague who was looking in from the corridor. They all seemed to be expecting him to say something important. Feeling slightly uncomfortable, Rheinhardt said: "Where is the . . ." He found himself unable to articulate the word "body" and hesitated as he searched for a more appropriate alternative. "Herr Pfundtner, where are the remains?" It seemed a reasonable compromise, neither too anthropomorphic nor too disrespectful.

The director gestured toward a second door, next to the heap of furry carcasses.

Rheinhardt turned the handle and pushed it open. The air that escaped was laden with a strange pungent odor. He stepped over the threshold and examined his surroundings. He had stumbled into a primeval world. The pit resembled a large bowl, one with earthen sides that were scattered with rocks and tropical vegetation. A single stunted tree leaned its crooked trunk out over the depression, which was filled with dark stagnant water. Colonies of algae floated on the surface, creating an emerald archipelago. On the other side of the pit was a featureless wall, over which members of the public might peer.

Rheinhardt could hear the director standing behind him, breathing heavily.

"Who has been in here this morning?" asked Rheinhardt.

"Myself," said Pfundtner, "and Herr Gundlach."

"What about you, Doctor?" Rheinhardt called back. "Have you taken a look in here."

"No, Inspector," said the doctor. "I've been rather preoccupied with the health of my patient." He sounded irritated.

Rheinhardt looked back at the director. "Where do we go?"

"Over there," said Pfundtner, pointing.

"Please follow me very closely, Herr Pfundtner. Try to tread on the rocks rather than the soil."

"Why?"

"Footprints."

Rheinhardt negotiated the shallow slope, using the rocks like stepping stones. He felt them sink a little under his weight, making his progress unsteady. The pit was horribly humid, and beads of sweat had begun to trickle down his cheek. As he rounded a large sandy boulder, he caught sight of the animal. Even though he knew what to expect, he found himself surprised by the bizarre spectacle.

The snake was enormous—a mythical beast, a sea serpent or basilisk. But its dimensions were exaggerated still further by the odd way in which the creature had been mutilated.

"Hildegard," said the director.

Rheinhardt thought that he detected a slight catch in the director's voice. He did not find it difficult to sympathize with his companion.

The snake had been cut into three sections: head, trunk, and tail. These body parts were ordered correctly, perfectly aligned, and separated by gaps of approximately one yard—they had been arranged in a curve that followed the arc of the water's edge. The effect was striking and curiously aesthetic. Taken together, the three segments were longer than a streetcar. The central section had a diameter wide enough to accommodate a small child.

When the two men had completed their descent, Rheinhardt clambered onto a large rock near the snake's head. Hildegard's eyes and nostrils were set high up on her flat pointed skull, and a delicate forked tongue protruded from between powerful jaws that had been propped open with a small stone. The device seemed to serve no purpose other than artistic effect. Her skin was green—the same shade as the water—and mottled with black egg-shaped patches. Rheinhardt was fascinated by the textured surface, each scale a tiny blister of jet or obsidian. The snake's innards were revealed in vivid cross section where the central segment had been cleanly sliced.

"Extraordinary," said Rheinhardt. "Quite extraordinary."

"It must have been a madman," cried the director. "A lunatic escaped from Am Steinhof."

The soil around the water's edge was light brown and stained with dark splashes of ophidian ichor.

"Is it a python?" asked Rheinhardt.

"Good heavens, no," said the director. Hildegard is—was—an anaconda, a water boa."

"Nonvenomous?"

"Quite so. *Eunectes murinus* is a constrictor. In the wild, *murinus* lies submerged underwater and grabs prey as it arrives to drink."

"Then it kills by asphyxiation?"

"Yes, or by drowning. The jaws are very strong. It can hold a large animal down with relative ease."

"How large?"

"An adult deer would not escape those jaws. Large anacondas like Hildegard have even been known to kill big cats—like jaguars."

"What about human beings?"

"Some attacks have been confirmed, but it is an exceedingly rare occurrence."

Rheinhardt contemplated the snake's enormous size. He only just stopped himself from uttering *What a monster!* fearing that he would hurt the director's feelings.

"How long is Hildegard?"

"Nearly thirty feet. Pythons grow longer, though they are not so heavy."

"Even if one knew that anacondas rarely attack human beings, entering her domain would still have been a daunting prospect."

"Quite so," said the director yet again. "But the villain would never have been in any real danger. This pit has been Hildegard's home for more than twenty years. She is—" The director corrected himself. "She *was* accustomed to human company—which almost always signified the arrival of food. In spite of appearances, she was a very docile creature."

Rheinhardt scratched his head.

"Herr Pfundtner, have any of the keepers reported seeing anything irregular—a patron acting suspiciously, or showing excessive interest in Hildegard?"

"No. Besides, Hildegard had so many devoted admirers that it would be difficult to say."

"What about persons who might bear the zoo itself some grudge? Do you know of any?"

"Inspector, we are the most well-loved institution in Vienna."

"Indeed, but I was thinking that perhaps you might have dismissed a keeper, who—"

"No!" interrupted the director. "No one has been dismissed. And relations between the board of governors and the keepers have always been excellent. You mark my words, Inspector," said Pfundtner, pointing his finger at the mutilated anaconda. "This abomination is the work of a madman!"

"You may well be right, Herr Director," said Rheinhardt, taking his notebook from his pocket. As he did so, the door to the snake-pit opened and Walter Gundlach appeared.

"Inspector—your assistant is here."

Rheinhardt called out, "All right—I'm on my way." Then, turning to Pfundtner, he added more softly, "Remember, Herr Director, tread only on the stones." Then he dropped his empty notebook back inside his coat pocket.

The two men made their way back up the slope, occasionally stretching out their arms to keep their balance. When they reached the door, the director politely allowed Rheinhardt to go through first. The doctor was still standing next to his seated patient. Walter Gundlach gestured Rheinhardt toward the hallway, where young Haussmann, the inspector's assistant, was waiting. He looked flushed and was breathing heavily as though he had been running. Without saying a word, Rheinhardt joined his junior, and they walked along the corridor until they could speak without being overheard.

"Please accept my apologies, sir. There was a—"

Rheinhardt did not want to hear any excuses. Haussmann was only a little late. Rheinhardt was disinclined to reprimand his assistant and so cut his apology off with a question: "Do you know what's happened here?"

"No, sir. I left the security office as soon as I learned of your whereabouts."

Haussmann took out his notebook and waited for the inspector to speak. His pencil hovered over the blank paper. Rheinhardt's baggy eyes suddenly sparkled with a playful light.

"The victim is a thirty-foot female—approximately five hundred fifty pounds. She is known only as Hildegard and is said to be a personal favorite of the emperor."

The young man stopped writing and looked up at his superior.

"You *are* joking, sir?"

"It's a snake, Haussmann—a snake!"

"A snake?"

"An anaconda, to be precise. Death was probably instantaneous after decapitation. Subsequently the intruder mutilated his victim by cutting off her tail. He gained entry into the snake-pit after knocking out one of the keepers, Herr Arnoldt. He's the poor fellow with the head bandage. Get a police photographer down here at once and prepare a floor plan. Take impressions of the director's shoes and those worn by the two keepers—Herr Arnoldt and Herr Gundlach—then see if you can get a cast of any prints in the snake-pit. Herr Arnoldt has lost his memory, but the doctor says that there's a fair chance it will return. I'll try interviewing him in a couple of hours: he might have more to say by then."

The assistant looked up from his notebook. "This is all very unusual, sir."

"Haussmann, you have a gift for understatement."

Rheinhardt turned and began walking toward the exit.

"Sir?"

"Yes, Haussmann?"

"Where are you going?"

"To inspect the perimeter fence for damage." Rheinhardt paused for a moment and then added, "Oh yes, and see if you can find a murder weapon. If it's here, it'll be easy to find. Something large, I suspect—an axe or some sort of sword."

After the stifling heat of the reptile house, the fresh morning air was a delight.

3

THE DINING ROOM WAS large and grandly decorated. An ornate chandelier hung from a high ceiling, and one of the walls was dominated by an intricately carved Biedermeier chest. It was a massive piece of furniture that stood almost as high as the cornicing. Liebermann—a man whose aesthetic preferences were decidedly modern—found its involutions too fussy and its stolid virtues dull. On the opposite wall was a large canvas by a popular landscape artist depicting trees and a distant horizon of snowcapped peaks. It was blandly titled *Vienna Wood*.

Since his engagement to Clara, Liebermann had found himself eating with the Weiss family at least once a week. Whenever he chose to visit Clara, Jacob or Esther (Clara's parents) would invariably insist that he stay for supper. Dining with the Weisses was not as exacting as dining with his own family—which was always a somewhat tense affair—but it represented, nevertheless, an obligation that was beginning to pall. In addition to Clara and her parents, several other members of the Weiss family were present: Clara's adolescent sister, Rachel, her older brother, Konrad, and his wife, Bettina. Konrad and Bettina's two infant sons—Leo and Emil—were asleep in a bedroom upstairs.

The company had just finished the main course, which consisted of boiled beef with green vegetables, and the servants were clearing the plates.

Clara was in full spate.

"You will never guess who I saw yesterday—Fräulein Stahl. Outside Lobmeyr's. I haven't seen her for ages—apparently she went to Franzenbad this year, although she didn't have a single good thing to say about the place."

"Where did she stay?" asked Esther.

"The Hotel Holzer. She said that the people there were very stuck-up."

"Yes, I'd only go to Meran now," Jacob proclaimed. Turning to Liebermann, he spoke more softly. "We went there in the summer, of course." Then, addressing the table at large, he added, "A much nicer atmosphere. I don't know why we've never been before. The grapes were particularly good."

"Fräulein Stahl said the water in Franzenbad tasted disgusting," said Clara. "Even so, she was made to drink buckets of the stuff because her doctor—what's his name—Rozenblit—thinks she has a weak liver and he believes the waters of Franzenbad are particularly good for such complaints. Do you know him, Max? Rozenblit?"

"No," said Liebermann. "I'm afraid I don't."

"Max," said Clara, a trace of exasperation creeping into her voice. "You never know any of the society doctors!"

"He will," said Jacob, smiling. "Given time—won't you, my boy?"

Liebermann smiled patiently at his host. "Perhaps, Herr Weiss."

"Rozenblit advised Fräulein Stahl to consult the doctors at Franzenbad," continued Clara, "who prescribed a special diet of cabbage and dumplings, and she had a mineral bath every day. But she said the evenings were very boring. The main street had one hotel after another and the whole place was lifeless after eight o'clock."

The conversation stopped as the cook arrived with a monumental emperor's pancake. Soft lumps of fragrant batter had been piled high to form a massive yellow pyramid, the slopes of which were sprinkled with generous snowdrifts of castor sugar. A kitchen maid followed, carrying two bowls: one filled with a thick maroon plum stew and the other with a spiraling conch shell of stiff whipped cream. Jacob complimented the cook, a sentiment that was echoed around the table.

When the conversation started again, Bettina inquired if Fräulein Stahl was still being courted by Herr Bernhardt, the famous entrepreneur, and slowly, talk flowed from incipient romances, through society engagements, to the forthcoming wedding of the couple present.

"Have you decided where the ceremony will take place?" asked Bettina.

"The Stadttempel," said Clara.

"How wonderful," Bettina exclaimed, "I love the Stadttempel—the ceiling . . . with its gold stars."

"Very romantic—and we're having the dress made by Bertha Fürst," said Esther.

"Clara," said Bettina, "you'll look stunning."

"And me . . . ," said Rachel. "I'm going to have one made too."

"Well," said Jacob, "we'll see—"

"But you promised, Father!" said Rachel, her face beginning to color.

"I promised you a new dress. I didn't promise you a Bertha Fürst dress."

"Oh, Father," said Clara, appealing to him with wide eyes. "Rachel must look her best on the day too."

Jacob groaned.

"Oh, very well then—a Bertha Fürst." He leaned toward Liebermann and said under his breath, "See what I have to put up with."

Rachel clapped her hands together and her face radiated joy.

"Thank you, Father," she cried. Then, getting up, she ran around the table and threw her arms around Jacob's neck, kissing his cheek.

"Enough now," he said, theatrically shaking her off in mock high dudgeon.

Rachel skipped back to her chair.

"You won't regret it, Father," said Clara, more seriously. "She'll look like a princess—won't you, Rachel?"

Rachel nodded and slipped a fork full of whipped cream into her mouth.

Further discussion of the wedding was continued after coffee had been served. Herr Weiss was quick to declare, "Gentlemen, perhaps we should retire to the smoking room?"

When Liebermann stood, Clara looked up at him, took his hand, and pressed it to her shoulder. It was a small gesture, but one that was full of affection. Her eyes glittered in the candlelight and her lips parted a little, showing a row of straight white teeth. Unusually, Clara had let her hair down. It was dark and undulated in glossy waves around her face. Liebermann's fingers lingered in her gentle grip as he left the table.

In the smoking room, Jacob Weiss distributed cigars and brandy. He stood by the stately gray-marble fireplace, an arm resting on the mantelpiece. Occasionally he would flick the ash from his cigar into the fire's flames. The two younger men occupied deep leather armchairs, facing each other across a Persian rug.

They discussed politics for a while: the appalling cant to be found in the columns of the *Deutsches Volksblatt*, the mayor's vanity, and how the deep cultural divisions in the empire seemed to be getting worse rather than better.

"I heard a good joke the other day," said Jacob. "You know that the parliament building has chariots on the roof—and they all point in different directions. Well, some wag I was talking to said that they are becoming increasingly recognized as a very good symbol. Everyone inside the parliament building wants to go a different way. And, you know, it's true—things are falling apart. I don't know what's going to happen."

"People have been saying much the same thing for years, Father," said Konrad. "And nothing changes."

"Ah, but things *do* change. And not always for the better."

"You worry too much." Konrad stubbed out his cigar and consulted his pocket watch. "Excuse me. If you don't mind, I think I should check the children."

"And you say it's me who worries too much?"

Konrad smiled at his father and left the room.

"Another cigar, Max?" Jacob offered.

"No, thank you."

"Then another brandy, surely."

Jacob moved away from the fireplace, filled Liebermann's glass, and sat down in Konrad's vacant chair.

"I saw your father the other day," said Jacob. "We met for coffee at the Imperial."

"Oh?"

"We had a long talk." Jacob exhaled a stream of blue smoke. "He wants you to take over his business one day. You know that, don't you?"

"Yes."

"But you're not keen."

"No. Unfortunately, I have no interest in textiles or the retail industry. I intend to remain in medicine."

Jacob pulled at his chin. "He seems to think that you'll find it difficult—financially, that is. After you're married, I mean."

Liebermann sighed.

"Herr Weiss, it's true, my position at the hospital is a very junior one at present. However, one day I hope to gain an academic position at the university, and I am confident that I will be able to build up a large practice."

Jacob laughed. "God only knows there are enough mad people in Vienna to keep a man in your profession busy."

"My father is always—" Liebermann was about to say something indelicate but he changed his mind. "I fear that in some ways I may have disappointed him."

"Who? Mendel? No, he's very proud of you, very proud. It's just . . . he wants you and your family, God willing, to be safe." Jacob rapped his knuckles on the chair arm to underscore the virtues of security. "Our generation is less . . ." He searched for the right words. "*Less at ease* than yours—less confident that we can rely on the world to treat us kindly, or fairly." Liebermann shifted uneasily at Jacob's use of the word "us." "That's all it is. No, my boy, he is very proud of you—and so are we."

Whereas Liebermann's father, Mendel, wore a long beard, giving him the appearance of a hierophant, Jacob sported only a small curled mustache. His hair had receded a little, revealing a high forehead, and a pair of small oval-lensed glasses rested on the bridge of his nose. He could still be described as a handsome man.

"You know, Max," Jacob continued, "we've never had a *professional* in the family before." Again, he drew on the cigar and exhaled a nimbus of smoke. "I had hoped that Konrad might be a doctor or lawyer, but, to be honest, I don't think he's got the brains. That's why he ended up with me, in the same business. There it is, none of us are satisfied with what we get—isn't that always the way?" He smiled benignly and took a sip of his brandy. "The thing is, Max, I wanted you to know that I understand how important medicine is to you. And after you and Clara are married . . . should you experience any problems—financial problems—you can always come to me if you require help. I'd much rather see my daughter married to a distinguished university professor than to a fellow tradesman, if you know what I mean."

"Herr Weiss, that's very kind of you, but—"

Jacob Weiss held up his hand—an abrupt and decisive salute.

"Please don't mention our little discussion to Mendel, or to Clara for that matter. This is just between me and you."

4

The desk was covered with papers and official forms. On one side sat Rheinhardt and, on the other, Haussmann. Although it was only early in the afternoon, the light was already failing.

"You couldn't get a cast?"

"No, sir."

"Strange. . . . The soil was quite soft."

"He obviously trod on the stones, sir."

"But when he was arranging the snake's body parts, he must have stood in the soil at the water's edge."

Rheinhardt examined a close-up photograph of the dead anaconda.

"The only impressions I found were those of the director and the two keepers; however, these marks here . . ." Haussmann pointed to a curving ridge close to the snake's head. "They suggest that the perpetrator may have tampered with the soil."

"He erased his tracks?"

"Yes, sir."

Rheinhardt turned one of the sharp points of his mustache between his thumb and forefinger. "Which, if true, implies that our villain is familiar with our new detection methods."

Haussmann nodded.

The ensuing silence became prolonged as the two men puzzled over the evidence.

"Sir?"

Rheinhardt looked up.

"Did Herr Arnoldt's memory return?"

"No. I interviewed him at the zoo and paid him a visit yesterday evening, but he had nothing new to add. The doctor still thinks there's a possibility something might surface, given time. But I'm not optimistic."

Icy flakes had begun to settle on the windowpanes.

"It's started snowing," Haussmann said softly.

Rheinhardt turned and glanced at the taupe-and-ash sky before confirming Haussmann's observation with a staccato grunt. Conscious of the fact that he may have seemed less than fully attentive, the assistant detective asked his superior a question. "Do you think there was a motive, sir? Or is this just the handiwork of a madman?"

"The latter, I imagine."

"Then perhaps we should consult your friend Doctor Liebermann?"

"Indeed. It's certainly odd enough to arouse his curiosity."

Rheinhardt cleared a space on his desk, opened a drawer, and removed a form, which he placed in front of him. Smoothing the paper with the palm of his hand, he sighed and said, "Well, Haussmann, I now have the unenviable task of writing my preliminary report. You will excuse me."

Haussmann stood. As he did so, the telephone rang. Rheinhardt answered and identified himself, but said little as the attenuated voice of the caller crackled in the earpiece. The inspector's expression changed from disgruntlement to concern, and then to shock.

"Good God!" he whispered.

Haussmann sat down again.

Rheinhardt reached for his pen and scrawled an address on the report sheet.

"I'll leave immediately," he said, and replaced the phone's receiver.

He did not, however, get up. Instead, he stared at the address, his eyebrows knitting together.

"Sir?"

Rheinhardt stirred, and looked across the desk at his assistant.

"Haussmann, something terrible has happened in Spittelberg." His voice was tight with suppressed emotion.

"A murder?"

"No," said Rheinhardt. "A massacre."

5

THE CARRIAGE CROSSED A STREETCAR rail and veered off in the direction of Spittelberg. Rheinhardt and Haussmann were preoccupied with their private thoughts—neither of them had been very talkative.

Out of the window, Rheinhardt saw briefly the impressive neo-Renaissance edifice of the Justizpalast. He silently implored the gods of jurisprudence for assistance. A maniac capable of performing such appalling acts of violence must be stopped immediately.

The carriage turned sharply along a narrow cobbled street.

"Spittelberg," said Haussmann.

The contrast with the palatial law courts, only a short distance away, could not have been more marked. Although the houses had a certain antique charm, they were mostly dilapidated after generations of neglect. The buildings were of uneven height and size and the stucco paintwork was faded. But vestigial streaks of pink, ocher, and blue betrayed a more colorful and prosperous history.

The carriage negotiated a tight corner and rattled down a gloomy alley that was hemmed in on both sides by ramshackle dwellings. Washing lines hung overhead like oversize threads of spider's silk. Rheinhardt imagined a giant arachnid, its legs folded around its fat abdomen, waiting to pounce. The carriage escaped the squalid street and entered a small square. On one side was an inn, and nearby was a corner of plain walls around which ran a continuous undecorated metal balcony. In front of the inn was a melancholy fountain—a stunted black spire out of which feeble jets of water spurted into separate basins. The carriage turned again, but within moments the horses began to slow.

The driver had had no trouble identifying the detectives' destination. It was a low two-story house, squashed between larger buildings and guarded by two constables. The men were blowing into their hands and stamping their feet on the ground, trying to stay warm. On the other side of the road, an elderly gentleman in a threadbare coat, scarf, and Bohemian hat had stopped to observe. He leaned on a knotted stick, his crooked back bent at a cruel angle. Apart from this solitary tatterdemalion, there were no other members of the general public present.

The carriage wheels ground to a halt.

Rheinhardt opened the vehicle's door, stepped down, and looked at the houses. The relics of more salubrious times were now clearly visible: relief cherub heads stared out blankly into space from below several window ledges. One building had a domed recess above the front door that was occupied by a figure of Saint Joseph, his aureole represented by radiating metal strips. A plump but weather-beaten infant Jesus was balanced in the crook of his left arm.

The snow was getting heavier: the air was growing dense with feathery flakes. A curious hush seemed to have fallen over Spittelberg, a magical stillness somehow enhanced by a vague impression of constant, mesmeric descent. The horse snorted and shook its bit. One of the constables advanced, his sabre dragging over the cobbles.

"Security office?"

"Yes. I am Detective Inspector Rheinhardt, and this is my assistant, Haussmann." The constable bowed and clicked his heels. "I presume you and your colleague are from Neubaugasse?"

"Yes, sir."

"Have you been inside yet?"

"Worst I've seen, sir," said the constable. "God only knows what happened in there." He jerked his head toward the half-open door.

"I understand that the landlord's agent discovered the bodies. Where is he?"

"At the station, sir. He gave us the key and refused to come back. Be careful as you go in—he was sick in the hallway."

A snowflake landed on the constable's eyelashes.

The inspector moved toward the door but then halted suddenly. He turned and marched over to the old man who was still watching.

"Good afternoon, sir," said Rheinhardt.

The old man's eyes were bloodshot. He moved his head backward and forward, trying to bring the speaker into focus. Finally he asked a question in heavily accented German. "What happened?" His mittens were fingerless and he raised a fossilized digit. "In there."

"Are you acquainted with the householders?" Rheinhardt asked in turn.

"Not at my age," said the old man. His lips parted to form a gummy smile, the curve of which was broken by a single black tooth. "It's a whorehouse!" He couldn't sustain his laugh. It fractured, turning into a hacking cough. Fluid crackled in his lungs.

Rheinhardt rested a hand on the old man's arm.

"It's cold, my friend. There's nothing for you to see here." The old man shrugged. "Go home and light a fire," Rheinhardt urged him.

The veteran lifted his stick and stabbed the cobbles with unexpected violence. Dragging his feet, he created two parallel tracks in the snow as he negotiated the slippery incline.

Rheinhardt walked back to where Haussmann was standing with the constables.

"All right, let's go in."

The hallway was dim, claustrophobic, and smelled of vomit. A thick soup of half-digested food had been disgorged onto the floor. Haussmann's features twisted, showing his disgust.

"I think we can expect worse than this," said Rheinhardt stiffly.

To the left was a sparsely furnished room containing a sofa, an armchair, and a small table by the window. On the table was a paraffin lamp, the upper cylinder of which was made of red glass. A potbellied stove stood in the center of the room. Rheinhardt tested the iron with his fingers and found it to be cold. The floor was littered with ashtrays, most of them overflowing with cigar stubs. Three empty champagne bottles stood in the corner.

The unnatural quiet was suddenly disturbed by the sound of ordnance. Outside, the horse began to clop restively on the cobbles.

"The barracks," said Haussmann.

"Yes. How very convenient."

They crossed the hall to a second room that faced the first. As they entered, both men recoiled. Haussmann turned his head away sharply. Only by degrees did he then reverse the movement, and slowly, as if the atrocity that confronted him could only be properly apprehended piecemeal.

The victim was a middle-aged woman with slate-gray hair that hung in lank strands around her swollen, bruised face. Her body was sprawled out on the floor with her hands either side of her head, the palms open, suggesting an attitude of submission. She was wearing a blue bathrobe, which had ridden up her legs, exposing the varicose veins of her calves, bony ankles, and dainty feet in embroidered silk slippers. Her throat had been opened with a clean, deep slice, and a vast quantity of blood had escaped from her arteries. The floor around her head was a black lake of coagulated gore. Some cartilaginous material was clearly visible protruding from the wound. The unfortunate woman had been almost decapitated.

Rheinhardt stepped closer and squatted next to the body, making sure that his coat did not make contact with the blood. He pinched the material of the bathrobe and tried to lift it up, but the garment was stuck. Eventually it came away, making an unpleasant ripping sound.

"She was stabbed in the heart too," he said quietly.

Haussmann did not reply.

"Are you all right, Haussmann?"

"Yes, sir. I think so, sir."

"Good man."

Rheinhardt pushed down on his thighs, stood up, and looked around the room. It contained very little furniture: a writing bureau, a tallboy, and a simple bed with a plain headboard. The blanket was pulled back, and the undersheet was rucked up. Beyond the bed was a half-open window. Rheinhardt walked around the bloody pool and pulled the curtains aside. A dim, cramped passage ran between the brothel and its neighbors.

"This is where he made his exit," said Rheinhardt. "There are bloodstains on the frame and sill. I'd like you to comb the area in due course."

"Yes, sir."

Making his way back to the writing bureau, Rheinhardt turned the key and let the lid down. Inside were some papers, a few silver coins, and a locked cash box. The papers were promissory notes of payment addressed to Madam Borek—almost all of them were signed by military men.

"Lieutenant Lipošćak, Captain Alderhorst, Lieutenant Hefner, Private Friedel . . ."

Rheinhardt took out his notebook and scribbled down their names.

Haussmann lifted the cash box and shook it. "Full, sir."

"Indeed. The motive for such wanton carnage is rarely theft."

Haussmann replaced the cash box and Rheinhardt closed the bureau.

"Come, Haussmann. I fear that even greater horrors await us."

The two men left Madam Borek's room and climbed the staircase at the end of the hallway. Rheinhardt noticed a trail of dark spots on the bare boards. As they ascended, the smell of vomit receded, only to be replaced by more ominous odors. As they neared the top of the stairs, the landing wall came into view. Rheinhardt stopped, his attention captured by a curious emblem that had been crudely painted on the bare plaster.

"Look, Haussmann."

"A cross of some kind?"

They finished their ascent slowly. Dark runnels, striping the wall, dribbled down from the strange crooked cross. Rheinhardt reached out and rubbed his forefinger into the dried liquid. Even in the poor light he could see that the gritty particles he had collected were crystalline and rust-colored.

"It's blood, Haussmann. The cross has been painted in blood!"

Rheinhardt, taking pity on his tallow-faced companion, said quietly, "Now might be the time to examine the passage behind Madam Borek's room."

The assistant detective raised a hand to his mouth and coughed.

"Yes, sir, I think it might be better . . ."

Rheinhardt nodded. Haussmann, relieved, ran down the stairs.

The inspector withdrew his notebook and sketched a simple equilateral cross. He then added opposing horizontals to the vertical line, and opposing verticals to the horizontal line. He looked again at the original. This strange daubing, and its bizarre method of execution, seemed to indicate the existence of a greater level of evil than Rheinhardt had ever before encountered. Satisfied that his sketch was accurate, he replaced the notebook in his coat pocket and braced himself.

On the first floor, a baleful light filtered through a grimy window.

Three doors could be seen from his vantage point—two to the left and one to the right. Rheinhardt moved forward, his footsteps sounding a funereal beat on the bare boards. He pressed his fingertips against the nearest door—the one to his right—and pushed. It swung open and the receding edge revealed—inch by inch—the Grand Guignol tableau within. It was of such unspeakable depravity that Rheinhardt was forced to bow his head.

"Dear God . . . ," he muttered at his shoes.

The remnants of his childhood faith stirred.

The dusty interior of a provincial church.

Cassocks and incense.

The protective potency of holy water. . . .

Something close to instinct made him want to touch his forehead and cross himself.

A young woman with thick brown hair was lying on a large bed that took up most of the available space in the room. The front of her bloodstained nightdress had gathered in a sopping heap beneath her breasts. As with Madam Borek, her throat had been cut; however, her body had been arranged so that her legs were wide open, exposing the genital area. She had been viciously mutilated. Where her thighs met, a ragged crater had replaced the expectation of a tidy vertical line. An incontinent eruption of gore had flooded the mattress and splashed onto the floor. A flap of skin, covered in matted pubic hair, hung precariously from where it seemed to have stuck on the bedspread.

Rheinhardt felt an involuntary spasm in his gut. A wave of nausea made him feel unsteady. His rational everyday self struggled to comprehend such depravity—such unspeakable savagery.

The scene in the second upstairs bedroom was even more sickening. Another woman, young like the first, had been laid out in a similar fashion. Again, her throat had been cut, but in addition her belly had been sliced open and her intestines scooped out. A bulky segmented length of colon had been looped around her head like a garland. The smell was so revolting that Rheinhardt's head began to swim. He rushed to the window and forced it open. Leaning out, he saw two faces staring up at him.

The senior constable called out, "Unbelievable, isn't it, sir?"

Rheinhardt nodded. There was nothing he could add.

The street was now covered with a thick carpet of snow. In the recess opposite, Saint Joseph and the infant Jesus had acquired an attractive white mantle. The winter weather was cleansing Spittelberg, concealing its poverty beneath a garment of vestal purity. Rheinhardt could not reconcile such beauty with what he had just seen. It seemed impossible that a single world could accommodate such disparities. In the distance, he saw a figure trudging up the incline: it was young Haussmann. Rheinhardt reluctantly resolved to continue with his own ordeal.

In the final bedroom he found the fourth body: a woman lying facedown on the floor. It appeared to Rheinhardt that she had stumbled and had grabbed the bedsheets as she fell. Her right hand, adorned with cheap jewelry, was still closed around a blanket. She was wearing a nightdress, but unlike those of her housemates, its material was relatively clean. There were no bloodstains, splashes, or trails of grume.

Suddenly it occurred to Rheinhardt that the girl might still be alive. He hurried over to the prone body and fell to his knees, anxiously resting a hand on her back. She was cold—very cold—and perfectly still. Refusing to accept that this newly kindled hope should be so precipitately extinguished, Rheinhardt snatched a small hand mirror from a chair by the bedside and wedged it close to the woman's nose and mouth. There was no misting. She was, all too clearly, dead.

Rheinhardt sighed and sat back on his heels. As he did so, he noticed a crusty deposit on the woman's crown. He systematically teased her hair apart, burrowing down toward her scalp. The perfumed fibers became increasingly matted with blood. She had obviously received a fatal blow that had been delivered to the back of the head.

As Rheinhardt rose, he caught sight of an object sticking out from beneath one of the pillows. He flipped the pillow over, exposing a small book bound in worn red leather. He picked it up, opened it, and discovered an inscription on the first page. The spidery scrawl was written in a foreign language, but he recognized the name *Ludka*. On the next page there were a Star of David and some Hebrew characters. Rheinhardt flicked through the thin, almost transparent pages, and surmised that the item was some kind of prayer book. He placed it in his pocket and sat down on the edge of the bed.

Resting his elbows on his knees, Rheinhardt placed his head in his open hands. He remained in this position for some time, eyes closed, unable to think, and feeling strangely numb, impressions of carnage flaming in the darkness behind his eyelids.

6

Liebermann occupied a window seat in the small coffeehouse near the Anatomical Institute. He dabbed his lips with a starched napkin, and examined the remains of his breakfast: a few croissant flakes and a mauve smear of plum jam. Raising his cup, Liebermann swirled the dark liquid and savored its aroma. It was strong and pungent. When he finally tasted the coffee, he found it to be curiously medicinal—bitter but fortifying.

On the street outside, the pedestrians were mostly men, somberly dressed in hats and long winter coats, carrying black leather bags and wearing severe, determined expressions. The exception was an animated young man with astonishingly clear blue eyes, who peered through the window and rapped on the glass. He pointed at himself and then at Liebermann while mouthing the words: "Can I join you?" Liebermann responded by gesturing toward an empty chair.

Stefan Kanner entered the café and sat down without removing his coat. He beckoned a waiter and ordered a *brauner*.

"I've just had my fencing lesson with Signore Barbasetti," said Liebermann. "The second this week. As a result, I am now in dire need of sustenance."

"How did it go?"

"Yet again I was roundly thrashed."

"Should I commiserate?"

"No, not at all. I learned a great deal." Liebermann took another sip of coffee and examined his friend more closely. "What are you doing here so early?"

"I musn't be late for Professor Pallenberg's ward round."

Liebermann glanced at his wristwatch. "Well, there's no danger of that."

"There was hardly any traffic. . . ."

"Why are you so anxious to be on time?"

"Pallenberg wants me to take notes. He's examining a new patient—a rare example of Cotard's syndrome."

"*Le délire de négation.*"

"You know of it?"

"I read Cotard's *Maladies Cérébrales et Mentales* when I was a student."

"Sometimes, Maxim, you can be very irritating." The waiter arrived with Kanner's coffee and a small glass of water on a silver tray. "The patient is a fifty-six-year-old shop owner," Kanner continued, adopting the clipped style of a case presentation. "A few years ago he began to complain of feeling like death. His wife arranged for him to stay in a sanitorium—Bellevue, I think—which made him feel better, but after returning to Vienna, he became very depressed. He has since been under the care of a general physician. Recently he caused his wife and children considerable alarm when he claimed that he not only felt like death but actually *was* dead. A few days ago he requested burial."

"I believe that when the Cotard delusion reaches its apotheosis, the patient not only denies his own existence but that of the entire universe."

"It will be interesting to see how Professor Pallenberg deals with such a challenging patient. I wonder what treatment the old boy will favor?"

"Morphine and chloral hydrate. Like he always does. I fear that Professor Pallenberg has yet to learn that a sleeping patient is not necessarily a cured patient."

Kanner laughed, throwing back his head to reveal the pink-ribbed roof of his mouth.

Liebermann peered over the rim of his coffee cup at the bustling street outside. Among the many pedestrians, he observed a young woman. She was wearing a simple gray pillbox hat, which rested on a cushion of fiery red hair. Her coat was olive green, with black velvet trimmings. She was walking quite fast, and passed out of view almost immediately.

"Excuse me, Stefan," said Liebermann, quickly rising.

"What is it?"

"I'll be back in a moment."

He rushed to the door and, leaving the coffeehouse, ran a few steps.

"Miss Lydgate!" he called.

The young woman turned. Her face was pale and her expression intense. She did not smile, but a subtle change in her features suggested pleasure.

"Doctor Liebermann."

"I was in the coffeehouse and saw you passing by."

"I am on my way to the Anatomical Institute."

"For a class?"

"Yes." Her German was perfect, but modulated with a slight English accent.

"Is everything well?"

Miss Lydgate hesitated, then replied, "I believe so." But the hesitation was enough to raise a splinter of concern in Liebermann's mind.

"Are you quite sure?" he asked solicitously.

A characteristic furrow appeared on Miss Lydgate's brow. "Actually, Doctor Liebermann, a certain matter has arisen—it is of no great consequence, and I am reluctant to trouble you—but . . . I would very much value your opinion."

"Is it a matter connected with your studies?"

Miss Lydgate paused again before saying hesitantly, "In a manner of speaking."

"Then, I am at your service."

"Could we meet for tea, perhaps—later in the week?"

"Yes, of course."

"Thank you. I well send a note." With this, Miss Lydgate turned and walked away. For a few seconds, Liebermann stood in the middle of the sidewalk, watching the receding back of Miss Lydgate's olive-green coat until it disappeared behind a group of students and medical men.

"Where have you been?" asked Kanner when Liebermann returned.

"I saw Miss Lydgate," said Liebermann. "You remember Miss Lydgate?"

"Of course. How is she?" asked Kanner.

"Very well," Liebermann replied before adding more cautiously, "as far as I know." He sipped his coffee, which was now a little too cold to be palatable. "She is studying medicine now."

"Really?"

"Yes, she was accepted with a recommendation from Landsteiner—who, incidentally, has also agreed to supervise her thesis on blood diseases."

"Remarkable," said Kanner. "Considering . . ."

"Yes," said Liebermann, slightly discomfited by the implications of Kanner's unfinished sentence. Liebermann had become very fond of Miss Lydgate and did not like to think of her as a former patient. "She is an extraordinary woman," he continued. "Her grandfather was a physician to the British royal household, you know, and something of a savant—I believe she must have inherited some of his gifts. . . ."

The door of the little coffeehouse creaked open and a large man with a ponderous gait made his way to a shadowy recess at the rear. The two doctors watched him with the same kind of muted and detached pleasure that might accompany observation of a great sea vessel arriving at its berth. There was something utterly engaging about the man's stately progress. After he had settled, Liebermann's and Kanner's gazes met—each of them was a little embarrassed but also amused that the other had been equally distracted.

"So," said Kanner, rousing himself from his state of abstraction. "You must be very excited."

"Why do you say that?" Liebermann's response sounded a little strained—almost querulous.

"Your wedding!" said Kanner. "When is it to be? Have you decided yet?"

Liebermann's fingers worried the edge of the table. "Clara would like us to get married in January." His voice was curiously flat. "However, I think that perhaps it would be better if we waited until the spring. My situation could be better—and the weather will be more clement, should we decide to travel."

"Well, Max," said Kanner, "among your many admirable qualities, self-restraint must rank very highly."

Liebermann scrutinized the dregs in the bottom of his coffee cup. When he looked up, he did not respond, and his fidgeting fingers conveyed a certain unease.

Kanner's smile faded and he leaned closer to his friend.

"What is it, Max?" His voice softened. "You seem preoccupied."

Liebermann waved his hand in the air. "It's nothing, Stefan—I'm tired, that's all. I'm not sure these early-morning fencing lessons are such a good idea."

7

THE WALLS WERE DRAPED with brightly colored tapestries depicting a fairy tale world of Gothic castles and jousting knights. In the flickering torchlight certain characters became more vivid: a group of gossiping ladies wearing high wimples, two huntsmen and their hounds, a lovelorn page contemplating a volume of poetry. Others faded into shadow. One of the hangings was sinuously undulating in the thermals rising from a nearby stove. Even so, the air was cold and smelled faintly of damp earth. There were no windows, and a low vaulted brick ceiling made the cellar overwhelmingly oppressive.

Pews, arranged in the shape of a horseshoe, faced a wooden throne that had been placed on a small dais. The throne was carved from oak and possessed heavy volute arms. The backrest tapered like a bishop's miter, and close to its top the runic character known as "Ur" (resembling the Greek capital pi) had been crudely carved within a raised circle. Behind the throne, purple curtains suggested holiness and majesty.

Gustav von Triebenbach had aged beyond the middle years of life, but he was still spry and stood head and shoulders above his companions. His thick eyebrows curled upward, giving him the severe, startled expression of an owl. When he wasn't talking, his shaggy mustache covered his mouth completely.

"I received a note from Counselor Hannisch this afternoon," said Von Triebenbach. "He was very optimistic."

"The invitation has been accepted?" asked Andreas Olbricht, unable to conceal his excitement.

"Our good friend the counselor spoke to the great man's wife yesterday . . . and my understanding is that it was *his* intention—at that time—to honor us with his company this evening."

"Excellent," said Olbricht. The bridge of his nose was sunken, making his eyes look as though they had been set unusually far apart. As he smiled, he revealed two rows of peculiarly stunted teeth, the ends of which were somewhat rough and uneven. Deep lines fanned out from the corners of his mouth, making him look considerably older than his forty-two years.

"What backbone, what fiber!" said Von Triebenbach's other companion.

"Indeed, Professor," Von Triebenbach replied.

"Why do you say that?" asked Olbricht, looking from the professor to Von Triebenbach and back again. "The weather could be better, I agree, but none of the roads are blocked."

"No, no, my dear fellow," said the professor. "You misunderstand me. I wasn't referring to the weather. You see, our distinguished guest has only recently undergone a very major operation. For cataracts." The professor glanced at Von Triebenbach. "I know the surgeon." Then, addressing Olbricht again, he added, "And *he* is still recovering. . . ."

Professor Erich Foch was a medical man. Yet he looked more like an undertaker. He was gaunt in appearance and seemed to have nothing in his wardrobe that wasn't funereal.

"It is truly a token of the esteem in which he holds us," said Von Triebenbach, "that he sees fit to rise from his sickbed—on such a night as this—so that he might give us the benefit of his wisdom and learning."

"Very true," the professor concurred. "Among the sympathetic brotherhoods in Vienna, our order must occupy a special place in his affections."

"Have you read his latest pamphlet?" asked Olbricht, looking up at the medical man.

"I regret to say that I haven't," said the professor, looking a little ashamed. But he excused himself by adding, "Onerous duties at the university . . . onerous and interminable."

"It is a preliminary work on the origins of our glorious language," said Von Triebenbach, stealing the initiative from his junior companion. "A wonderful piece of scholarship."

"In which case, I very much hope that we shall be hearing more on the subject this evening," said the professor. With that, he turned and walked to the nearest pew. He was wearing an old-fashioned frock coat, and clasped his hands behind his back. His gait was distinctly avian, which, combined with his choice of clothing, made him look like a great stalking crow. When he reached the pew, he sat down and took an envelope from his pocket. He opened it, withdrew a single sheet of paper, and began reading the letter.

"I believe that congratulations are in order?" said Von Triebenbach, leaning toward Olbricht. It was, perhaps, a conciliatory gesture, the older man having just deprived the younger one of an opportunity to demonstrate the breadth of his reading.

"Oh?" said Olbricht, staring at Von Triebenbach with his wide-eyed, froglike gaze.

"The commission."

Olbricht smiled, revealing again his square little teeth. "How did you hear about that?"

"I am a business associate of Herr Bolle," Von Triebenbach replied.

"Ah," Olbricht said. "I see. Yes, Herr Bolle requires a large canvas for his country house. I received the commission on account of the kind ministrations of my patron, Baroness von Rautenberg. She plays cards with Herr Bolle's wife."

"And the subject of your new work? What will it be?"

"I haven't quite decided yet. Although, Herr Bolle has stipulated that it must be a scene from *The Ring*." Von Triebenbach nodded with satisfaction. "The gods engulfed by fire, the ride of the Valkyries, or Siegfried's funeral pyre, perhaps."

"Outrageous!" cried the professor.

Von Triebenbach and Olbricht were at first astonished, because it seemed that the professor was—quite unaccountably—objecting to Herr Bolle's aesthetic preferences. The misunderstanding was swiftly resolved, however, when Foch raised the letter he had been reading and with small, jerky movements, tore it from top to bottom.

"It is from the dean of the medical faculty," he huffed. "I don't believe it! I have been reprimanded for my treatment of the female students."

Von Triebenbach and Olbricht were still unsure how to respond.

"The faculty should never have allowed it!" the professor continued. "Women doctors! Who ever heard of such nonsense? I told them that women were ill-suited to the demands of a medical training, and they ignored me. Women are weak, squeamish. . . . How can they be expected to open up a man's chest without swooning! And how can it be correct for a young woman—from a good family—to be exposed to those parts of the male anatomy that should by rights be of no concern to her until her wedding night?"

The professor quartered the letter and, rising to his feet, marched to the stove, where he posted each of the four pieces through the grill.

"I could not agree with you more, Herr Professor" said Von Triebenbach. "I would never subject myself to the humiliating experience of examination at the hands of a woman, however qualified. But for what—exactly—have you been reprimanded?"

"It has been my great misfortune," continued the professor, "to have, in my demonstration classes, several of these new female students. They are a confounded nuisance! At the first sight of blood they become pale, distraught, and a distraction to the young men. Subsequently, I have had to insist—on no less than five occasions—that they leave. Typically, these women—these *girls*—claim that they were not overwhelmed, and that I have misjudged their condition. I—a doctor for some thirty years—am supposed to be in error. And those fools, the dean and his cronies, are stupid enough, idiotic enough, to countenance this despicable calumny."

"Appalling," said Olbricht, "that a person of distinction, such as yourself, Herr Professor, should be treated with such little respect."

"Damned hypocrites!" cried the professor. "In actuality, the dean and his cronies are as opposed to women being admitted into the faculty as I am. But, being spineless sycophants, they are less inclined to resist political pressure."

"I tell you," said Von Triebenbach, shaking his head. "This city is courting catastrophe and ruin. I pray and hope that we are not too late. Otherwise, I fear that all shall be undone."

Von Triebenbach's words gave way to a low, thrumming sound, a hollow reverberation of increasing magnitude. Someone was descending the stairwell. As each hurried step became more distinct, the three men tensed slightly, adopting frozen, expectant postures. The latch lifted, and the door at the back of the chamber burst open, revealing a young man. He was wearing a brown suit, and a yellow-and-green checked scarf was wrapped loosely around his neck. His hair was long, swept back, and so blond as to be almost white. Under his left arm he carried a portfolio. On entering the chamber, he lifted his right arm and called out, *"Heil und Sieg!"*

Salvation and Victory.

In unison, the company returned the ancient greeting and battle cry.

The young man then marched aaround the pews and entered the central open area of the horseshoe. Nodding at Olbricht and the professor, he turned questioningly to Von Triebenbach and said, "Is it true? He's coming? Tonight?"

Von Triebenbach placed an avuncular hand on the young man's shoulder. "We hope so."

Hermann Aschenbrandt raked a handful of platinum strands back from his forehead.

"That is wonderful news. Wonderful." He looked at Olbricht and the professor. "We are most fortunate. Truly." Then, addressing Von Triebenbach again, he added, "Herr Baron, I beg you, when the meeting is adjourned—may I play him the overture to my opera? It is based on his great novel *Carnuntum*. It would be such an honor. Such an honor."

The young man's eyes were a clear powder-blue—and they positively flashed with eagerness. He was breathless with excitement.

Von Triebenbach, amused—as always—by the energy and zeal of his young favorite, threw his head back and laughed heartily.

"We can but ask him, my dear friend. And perhaps he will condescend to hear your work. He is a man of generous spirit."

Aschenbrandt inhaled deeply, and his chest expanded. "Such an honor," he repeated, his thin lips curling to form a slightly lopsided smile.

8

Rheinhardt tested the upper register of his voice with an ambitious arpeggio. He held the top note for a few moments and winced.

"No," said Rheinhardt. "There's definitely something wrong. My pitch is off when I go above middle C."

"Perhaps it is the cold?" said Liebermann.

"Cold?"

"Yes—cold. Surely the weather hasn't escaped your attention, Oskar?"

"No, it hasn't," said Rheinhardt, again worrying his refractory high E. "Even so, I should have warmed up by now."

"There is no instrument more sensitive," declared Liebermann, "than the human voice."

"I suppose you're right," Rheinhardt muttered.

"Perhaps we should finish with something"—Liebermann allowed his fingers to find a simple C-major triad—"undemanding. Something that will be kinder to your vocal cords?"

"*An die Musik?*" Rheinhardt suggested.

Liebermann's expression changed: a slight, almost imperceptible tensing of the jaw that showed reluctance. This was not because Liebermann disliked Schubert's setting of Von Schober's paean to the "blessed art" of music-making—rather the exact opposite. The words expressed sentiments that he felt so deeply, so profoundly, that for him the song had the qualities of a prayer. Playing *An die Musik* was like a personal affirmation of faith. If Rheinhardt's voice had been affected by the cold, he didn't want to squander a performance. To do so would be almost sacrilegious.

"Very well, then," continued Rheinhardt, responding to his friend's hesitation. "How about . . . *Litany for the Feast of All Souls?*"

This was another Schubert setting, similar in atmosphere to *An die Musik*, but with words by the poet Johann Georg Jacobi.

Liebermann rearranged the songbooks on the music stand and brought a Schubert collection to the front. He flicked through the volume in search of the right page.

"The Feast of All Souls . . . ," he said, abstractedly. "That's around this time of year, isn't it?" He could barely remember the dates of Jewish festivals, let alone those celebrated by the Catholic Church. However, he had some vague notion that All Souls fell around the beginning of winter.

"Yes," said Rheinhardt, "it's in a few weeks, in fact. The second of November."

"Here it is," said Liebermann, smoothing out the page. The piano part had been annotated in pencil where Liebermann had changed some of the fingering and phrasing.

The young doctor looked up at his friend to see if he was ready, and then began. The music immediately suggested majesty and gentle progress. Rheinhardt opened his mouth and, crossing his hands over his heart, sang softly:

> *"Ruhn in Frieden alle Seelen."*
> Rest in peace all souls.

The accompaniment drifted through some artful changes of harmony, making the melody more poignant. Even though the music was peaceful, the chord changes seemed to reveal the presence of an underlying aching sadness. Rheinhardt's voice became more confident, more controlled, and he accomplished the higher notes with little trouble. Liebermann was surprised by the sudden improvement of tone. He was even more impressed when Rheinhardt's baritone floated above the accompaniment and enjoyed a moment of near-unbearable sweetness—seemingly removed from all worldly suffering. But, as was so often the case with Schubert's composition, this moment of transcendent vision was all too brief, and the demands of the score forced Rheinhardt to surrender one note, then another, then another, until the descending sequence arrived at a prolonged, empty caesura. It was Schubert's genius to place a beat of chilling silence—as still as death, as cold as eternity—within the first verse.

When Liebermann looked up to see if his friend was ready to begin again, he noticed that Rheinhardt's eyes were brimming. The inspector was oddly transported, but he was also sufficiently aware of his surroundings to register Liebermann's attentiveness. Once more, pressing his hand against his heart, Rheinhardt filled the room with plaintive melody.

> *"Ruhn in Frieden alle Seelen."*
> Rest in peace all souls.

Rheinhardt's rendition of the next verse was even more powerful. When Liebermann had played the final chord, he lifted his hands from the keyboard and respectfully bowed his head. Rheinhardt sniffed once, and Liebermann allowed his friend sufficient time to wipe the tears from his eyes. It was not unusual for Rheinhardt—or Liebermann, for that matter—to be moved to tears by music, but on this occasion the outpouring was so sudden, and so unexpected, that the young doctor could not help speculating about why this should be.

"Well, Oskar," said Liebermann, closing the songbook and still not looking directly at his friend, "You certainly found your voice in the end. That was exquisite. . . ."

"Thank you, Max," said Rheinhardt. "It seemed to just . . . come back."

The inspector sounded a little bemused.

As was their custom at the end of every musical evening, the two men walked through the double doors leading to the paneled smoking room. Liebermann's manservant, Ernst, had discreetly performed his duties. The fire was roaring, and on Liebermann's new, very modern-looking Moser table the servant had laid out a decanter of brandy, crystal glasses, and two freshly cut cigars. The table, a hollow black cube with an ebony top, was flanked by more traditional armchairs. Rheinhardt lowered himself into the right-hand one, and Liebermann the left. Their respective seating preferences, never negotiated nor commented upon, were—like the sleeping positions of a long-married couple—invariant.

Liebermann poured the brandy and offered his friend a cigar. A few small pleasantries were exchanged before the two men settled down and stared into the fire. Several minutes passed and the room filled with pungent cigar smoke. Finally, Liebermann spoke.

"I am in no doubt, Oskar, that tonight you intend to consult me with respect to a murder inquiry. In spite of your many years at the security office, I think it fair to say that corpses still cause you considerable distress; however, on this particular occasion, I am convinced that you witnessed a scene that was unusually disturbing. In fact, it may be that you have had to examine not just one but two murder scenes. If not, then you have certainly been exposed to more than one body. The exact number is difficult to ascertain, but I think . . . two. I am very confident that these bodies were, first, female, second, young, and third, that these young women met with deaths remarkable for their violence."

Rheinhardt sipped his brandy and said, "Not bad, Max. Not bad at all."

"I was wrong in some detail?"

"The number of bodies."

"I see. There were more than two, then?"

"Indeed. There were four."

"*Four?*" Liebermann cried out in disbelief.

"Yes—and although you were correct in deducing that most were young, the first was, in fact, middle-aged."

Liebermann exhaled a cloud of cigar smoke. He looked mildly disappointed.

"Come now," said Rheinhardt. "You were right in all respects bar a few particulars. I *have* visited the scene of a vicious multiple murder, and the victims *were*—as you determined—all women. How did you do it?"

"Well . . . ," Liebermann replied. "It was the sudden improvement in your singing that attracted my interest. You claimed to be experiencing some problems with pitch in the upper register, but— with the greatest respect—every aspect of your performance this evening was deficient or strained."

"I couldn't agree more," said Rheinhardt, shaking his head contritely.

"It was as though your throat were too tight," continued Liebermann. "I had attributed this loss of tone to the cold weather, but your rendition of Schubert's *Litany for the Feast of All Souls* was so wonderful, so magnificent, so perfect, that I was forced to question my previous thinking. If your voice had really been impaired by the cold, it would not have recovered so dramatically. I subsequently wondered whether this *tightness* might be due to some psychological factor? Now, you must have noticed how when people become anxious or are placed under duress their voices become thin? Well, I surmised that something very similar was happening to you. By paying close attention to the music, you were able to keep a memory—an upsetting memory—out of your conscious mind. But it was still exerting an influence, still creating levels of tension sufficient to affect the quality of your voice.

"To end our little concert you chose to sing Schubert's *Litany for the Feast of All Souls*, the subject of which is, of course, souls—plural—leaving the world behind to be granted *eternal rest*. From this I inferred that you had recently seen more than just one body, and that these unfortunate individuals had been the victims of some great violence. Why else would you be so anxious that they should be granted *eternal rest*?

"The combination of Schubert's music and Jacobi's words allowed you to give expression to feelings that were hitherto repressed, and as a result, the song was cathartic and your voice was immediately restored to its former glory."

Rheinhardt looked perplexed. "But you seem to have based your deductions on an erroneous supposition: that I am able to remember all of Jacobi's words, and the fact is that I can't. *Rest in peace, all souls who, a fearful torment past* . . . *and*—No, you see? I can't do it. Now, I accept that the song itself is uncannily appropriate, given my recent experiences . . . but when I made the choice, there was nothing on my mind save the *apparent* technical limitations of my voice."

"How many times must I remind you, Oskar?" said Liebermann. "The unconscious never forgets. Just because you can't remember the words right now does not mean that they are not in there"—he jabbed his cigar at Rheinhardt's head—"somewhere!"

Rheinhardt squeezed one of the tips of his mustache. "What made you think there were two bodies?"

Liebermann took a sip of brandy and leaned closer to his friend. His expression was solicitous. "I could not help but notice how deeply moved you were by the song. . . ."

"I was," said Rheinhardt. "My chest was swollen with emotion."

"Which made me ask myself: what might arouse such strong feelings in my dear friend? And I concluded that the murder scene must have resonated sympathetically with something of great personal significance. And I assumed that nothing could stir the feelings of a father of two daughters more than the demise of two young women. But in this respect, of course, I appear to have strayed." The look of dejection returned, but was almost immediately dispelled when Liebermann cried, "But perhaps I can redeem myself—a little. The song you chose was a litany for the Feast of All Souls. *All* souls, note. *All* souls. The word 'All' would suggest a desire to include all of humanity in your prayers— humanity in the round, humanity in its entirety. Which makes me think that the bodies you saw belonged to individuals commonly excluded from society. Pariahs of some description? Out of pity, you wanted to welcome them back into the fold. . . ." Rheinhardt nodded, but said nothing. "In which case," continued Liebermann, "it is very likely that these murders took place in a brothel!"

"Extraordinary!" exclaimed Rheinhardt. "Exactly right! The bodies were discovered in a brothel in Spittelberg."

Liebermann, his confidence somewhat restored, rewarded himself with another tot of brandy. "Have the bodies been identified?"

"Yes," said Rheinhardt. "The man who owns the property where the bodies were found has an agent. We managed to get him to visit the morgue. He did so reluctantly, and I don't blame him—the injuries inflicted on these women were unspeakable. The madam was a woman called Marta Borek. The three girls were Wanda Draczynski, Rozalia Glomb, and the third was called Ludka. The agent didn't know the third girl's full name. At present, we know nothing more about them."

Rheinhardt rose from his seat and went to the bookcase, where he had previously deposited his bag—a large brown leather case. He released the hasp, opened it up, and took out a small book and a handful of photographs and papers. He returned to his seat and passed the small book to Liebermann.

"I found this in the girl Ludka's room."

Liebermann examined the inscription. "It's in Yiddish."

"Yes: *To dearest Ludka from your loving grandfather*. It's a prayer book."

Liebermann flicked through the pages. "Are there any other inscriptions?"

"No," Rheinhardt replied. "She was undoubtedly one of a growing number of Galician women who are routinely sold into prostitution. White slavery has become an international business. Galician girls can be found in the brothels of Alexandria, New York, Buenos Aires, and London. There have even been reports of trafficking operations taking Galician women to Africa, China, and India."

"She was Jewish," said Liebermann—his brow furrowing slightly.

"Indeed—most . . ." Rheinhardt hesitated. "Well, let's say many of these poor girls are."

"I didn't realize . . ." Liebermann did not finish his sentence. Instead, he waved his hand, saying, "No matter," and placed the book next to the ashtray.

"Now," said Rheinhardt. "I have to warn you. These are extremely unpleasant images."

"I *am* a doctor," said Liebermann.

"Even so—you have never seen anything like these before, I can assure you."

Rheinhardt handed the photographs to his friend. Liebermann looked at the first image: the madam, Marta Borek, lying in her pool of blood. He then examined the second image: a close-up of the deep cut in her neck. Liebermann worked through the stack mechanically, not dwelling on any one image for very long. He did stop once, however, in order to rotate a particular photograph—to establish whether or not it was the right way up. He showed it to Rheinhardt.

"What's this?"

"Some kind of cross. It was painted on the landing wall—in blood."

"Whose?"

"Well, we can't say for certain, but it was most probably Marta Borek's. We found her body first, in a room downstairs. There was a trail of blood going up to the landing. The monster must have brought a brush with him specifically for this purpose!"

Liebermann nodded, drained the remains of his brandy, and continued to inspect the photographs. His face was rigid, his jaw tense.

Lacerations, slashes, mutilated pudenda, a thick rope of intestine . . .

When he had viewed all of the photographs, he placed them on the table next to the prayer book and said softly: "I don't know what to say."

Rheinhardt passed Liebermann a large sheet of paper, on which the floor plan of the Spittelberg brothel had been sketched. The walls were shaded, and each room was filled with symbols: a quarter circle to show the arc of an opening door, a large rectangle to show a double bed, and so on. Each object was lettered, and each letter was included on a key: D = Door, B = Bed, F = Fireplace. A narrow barred rectangle showed the staircase, which was transected by an arrow marked "up."

"Marta Borek's body was found in this room here," said Rheinhardt, pointing out the location on the plan. "The room on the opposite side of the hall is a rather squalid waiting room. The three girls were found upstairs. Wanda Draczynski was in the first room— she's the one with the . . ." He suddenly faltered.

"Genital mutilation," suggested Liebermann.

"Yes," Rheinhardt continued. "Genital mutilation. Rozalia Glomb was found in the second room. She's the one who had the contents of her belly strewn over the bed. And Ludka was found here." Rheinhardt tapped the plan.

Liebermann rifled through the stack of horrific images until he came to the photographs of Ludka: a slender girl in a nightdress, her right arm extended and her fingers closed around a blanket that she had almost pulled off the bed.

"She doesn't appear to have been mutilated."

"No. She was struck on the back of the head. But it was enough to kill her."

"When did this happen?"

"On Tuesday."

"And at what time?"

"Late morning or early afternoon."

"Why were all the women in bed?"

"That is when prostitutes sleep, Max."

"Yes . . . of course." Liebermann was momentarily embarrassed, but he continued. "I wonder how he, the perpetrator, succeeded in committing these atrocities. Surely he would have made some noise? Why didn't one of the women wake up and raise the alarm?"

"I think Ludka did," said Rheinhardt. "That was why she was struck on the back of the head. She met him at the door, turned, and then received the fatal blow."

"But I don't see how he—"

"Allow me to explain," said Rheinhardt.

Liebermann settled back in his chair and adopted a characteristic pose: his right hand pressed against his cheek, three fingers clenched, thumb cocked, and the vertical index finger resting against his temple.

"I believe," continued Rheinhardt, "that the perpetrator arrived at the front door, confident that only the women were inside. I suspect that he had been observing the house and did not act until he had counted out all those patrons whom he had previously counted in. Then he knocked on the door—which was answered in due course by Marta Borek. He stabbed her in the chest and dragged her limp body to the room in which we found her. After ascending the stairs, he entered Draczynski's room and slit her throat while she slept before doing the same to Glomb. By this time, Ludka was most probably awake and out of bed. . . . After dispatching Ludka, the perpetrator went down the stairs and slit Borek's throat. When he climbed them again, it was with a brush dipped in Borek's blood. He then set about mutilating Draczynski and Glomb, but was disturbed before he reached Ludka."

"What by?"

"I don't know. Another caller perhaps. . . . The perpetrator then descended the stairs for the last time and made his exit through Borek's window. There's an alleyway at the back of the house."

"Where does it come out?"

"It divides before joining roads at either side of the brothel."

Liebermann poured himself and the inspector another brandy.

"He must have been covered in blood," said Liebermann. "Drenched. He could never have left the apartment in such a state, even if Spittelberg is relatively quiet. He must have changed his clothes before leaving."

"There were no discarded items of clothing in the area."

"In which case he would have arrived and left with some kind of receptacle."

Liebermann picked up the photographs again and found the close-up of Borek's throat.

"The cut is so deep: she's almost been decapitated. The perpetrator must have wielded a large knife or even a sword. During the autopsy Professor Mathias suggested a sabre, which might prove to be a highly relevant observation. Spittelberg lies between two barracks, and Marta Borek's bureau was filled with promissory notes from military men."

"If it transpires that this carnage is the work of one of His Majesty's soldiers . . ."

"The emperor will be appalled!"

Liebermann flicked through the images once more and shook his head. "Surely, only a man who had some prior experience of killing would have dispatched so many bodies with such ruthless efficiency." Liebermann's finger tapped against his right temple. "This is certainly the work of an individual inured to the sight of blood."

"I am reminded," said Rheinhardt, "of the famous Whitechapel murders."

"Oh?"

"You are too young to remember—but they created a worldwide sensation. They took place in one of the poorest districts of London and were attributed to a man whom the English call Jack the Ripper."

"Ah, yes," said Liebermann—the name was not unfamiliar to him. "I believe the case is included in the latest edition of Krafft-Ebing's *Psychopathia Sexualis*."

"The Ripper's victims," Rheinhardt continued, "were also prostitutes and it was his habit to mutilate and remove their internal organs. The identity of the killer was never discovered, but I can remember some commentators proposing that his victims had died at the hands of a surgeon."

"He was never discovered, you say?"

"No."

"And when did these murders take place?"

"Let me see." Rheinhardt did some mental calculations. "About thirteen or fourteen years ago."

The two men looked at each other, raised their eyebrows, and simultaneously shook their heads.

"No," said Liebermann, smiling awkwardly. "Nevertheless, one cannot help wondering what might have become of such a creature. . . ."

The young doctor offered his friend another cigar, which Rheinhardt gladly accepted. They sat in silence, staring into the flames, both of them deep in thought. Occasionally Liebermann selected from the stack a single photograph, which he examined more intently. After some minutes had passed, he turned to Rheinhardt and said, "Clearly, this is no ordinary murder. Our perpetrator's heinous acts are much removed from the common criminal well-heads of greed, envy, and revenge. His motives are twisted and obscure, yet he is not entirely beyond the reach of modern psychology."

Liebermann stubbed out his cigar in the ashtray.

"Your perpetrator hates women or, perhaps more precisely, the sexual power of women. This explains his choice of prostitutes as victims. He also chose to mutilate those areas of their bodies associated with reproduction: the genitals and belly. He was not content simply to murder these young women. He needed to annihilate their sex— utterly. I suspect that he is sexually inexperienced—possibly impotent—socially inept, and has at sometime in his life suffered greatly on account of being attracted to, or rejected by, a woman. However, even as I say these words, my account seems woefully incomplete. There is much, much more here. . . ."

"Go on," said Rheinhardt.

"Such ferocity," Liebermann continued, "seems to betray a far deeper motivation—the influence of primal memories. Something happened to him in his childhood, something traumatic, that touches upon the erotic instinct but that also shaped his character. Whatever that event was—he blames women."

Rheinhardt took out his notebook and jotted down a few of Liebermann's comments. Before he had finished writing, he said, "What do you make of that crooked cross? Why on earth did he bother to paint such a thing on the wall?"

"At first, it occurred to me that the perpetrator might be on some kind of religious crusade, working under the delusion that he is God's instrument, empowered to cleanse Vienna of moral impurities. However, if this were the case, then I would have expected him to have executed a more conventional crucifix—a long vertical line transected by a shorter horizontal one. I think, therefore, that this symbol has more personal than religious significance. It is, as it were, his calling card. It is also why I think that he is socially inept or ineffectual. In the absence of real status or achievement, the inconsequential person is often minded to leave his mark—his initials, or some other identifier—carved in a public place. It is his only method of leaving an impression on the world, his only claim on posterity. You will find several examples of such graffiti in the tower of the cathedral. . . . In his sick mind, this atrocity"—Liebermann tapped the photographs—"has acquired the properties of an accomplishment, a proud creation for which he craves and desires recognition. He could not leave without first signing his 'art.' The strange cross is his signature."

Rheinhardt placed the stub of his cigar in the ashtray and took the photographs back.

"Oskar," said Liebermann, "with so much blood, were there no footprints on the floor? No impressions?"

Rheinhardt shook his head.

"So he is someone who is perhaps aware of police procedures?"

"It would seem so."

Rheinhardt felt a nagging *something* at the back of his mind—a vague memory that he could not quite place. His brow furrowed and he twirled his mustache again.

"What is it?" said Liebermann, noticing his friend's mental effort.

"Nothing," said Rheinhardt. Then, fixing Liebermann with his melancholy sagging eyes, he said, "He will do something like this again, won't he?"

"Yes," said Liebermann, with economic bluntness. "And very soon, I expect."

9

THE CHAMBER WAS FULL and the air hummed with the low drone of conversation. Those present were well dressed (tending toward sobriety) and were seated in the horseshoe arrangement of pews. The atmosphere was similar to that in a theater just before the curtain rises, but it was also ecclesiastical: an odd combination of excitement and reverence. In the front pew, close to the wooden throne, stood Professor Foch, Andreas Olbricht, and Hermann Aschenbrandt. The professor removed a watch from his fob pocket, flicked open the case, and observed the time.

"He's late," said Olbricht.

"Yes," replied the professor, dryly.

The door at the back of the chamber creaked open, and a short plump man entered. His cheeks were glowing and he was evidently in good spirits. The smile on his face was broad and radiant. He stopped to shake hands with one or two members of the assembly and was seen to nod vigorously in response to their inquiries.

"Hannisch looks happy," said Olbricht.

"Then *he* must have arrived," said Aschenbrandt.

Soon the monotonous drone that had filled the chamber was replaced by the rustling sibilance of subdued voices. Certain words and phrases became distinct:

"He's here. . . ."

". . . genius . . ."

"*. . . greatness . . .*"

"*. . . reputation . . .*"

The plump man took a seat that had been reserved for him on the other arm of the horseshoe and gestured a greeting toward the professor, who replied with a brief downward jerk of the head, like a bird pecking.

Suddenly the door opened again, and a voice called out, "All rise for the first steward of the Order Primal Fire."

The assembly stood up. Gustav von Triebenbach, wearing a ceremonial red cloak with ermine trim, entered the chamber. He was carrying an ornate staff, which he used to propel himself like a gondolier punting his boat. Von Triebenbach was followed by a liveried servant, whose right arm was linked through the left arm of an extraordinary companion—a man in his fifties, with a long unruly gray beard and an enormous, incongruously dark bushy mustache. He was wearing a rather shapeless velveteen flat cap, which would not have appeared out of place on the head of a Renaissance courtier. However, the most striking feature of his appearance were the lint bandages that had been wound around the top half of his head. Nothing of his face could be seen above the tip of his nose.

As the three men walked to the front of the chamber, the congregation began to clap, and soon the enclosed vaulted space was reverberating with the noise of an enthusiastic reception.

The liveried servant helped the bandaged man onto the wooden throne, but his progress was faltering: the sudden movement of his hands—plunged desperately into empty space—suggested a moment of anxious uncertainty. Eventually, however, he was able to lower himself between the volute chair arms, and the liveried servant bowed and withdrew.

Von Triebenbach stood at the head of the chamber and lifted his right arm.

"*Heil und Sieg!*"

The company returned the gesture and repeated the battle cry.

As the applause petered out, the men sat down, and silence soon prevailed. Von Triebenbach bowed and proclaimed, "O primal light, grant us thy consolation, consecrate our hearth, and purify our blood. Deliver us from the hindrances and snares of our enemies and clothe us with the armor of salvation."

The assembly responded with a softly spoken "*Heil und Sieg.*"

Von Triebenbach raised his head.

"Brethren . . . tonight, we are most fortunate." The blazing torches made the repeated motif of griffins on Von Triebenbach's red cloak glimmer. "Among the societies who have sworn to preserve and protect our glorious heritage—our language, our art, our values—the name of Guido Karl Anton List has become familiar and much respected. He is to be counted among the great thinkers of our age. However, for the benefit of our most recent members, it is incumbent upon me to say a few words of introduction. . . . Most of you, I am sure, will have read our distinguished guest's masterpiece, *Carnuntum*—a novel of great power and elegance. It has been some fourteen years since the publication of this great work, which has played no small part in inspiring its many readers to rediscover, and take pride in, the legacy of our ancestors. It was *Carnuntum* that also brought its author to the attention of many politicians, who have since shown an enlightened interest in promoting traditional values. . . . Our distinguished guest has been responsible for the formation of two literary societies, the Free German Society for Literature and the Danubian Literary Society, both of which have provided a safe haven for many writers who would otherwise have found no platform for their work in a city obsessed with degenerate fashionable trivia. . . . Some of you here will remember with great affection, as I do, a wonderful performance—sponsored by the German League—of our distinguished guest's dramatic poem *The*

Wala's Awakening, which was attended by an audience of over three thousand." There was a low murmur of agreement. "Although our distinguished guest is recovering from a surgical operation—the outcome of which is still, sadly, very uncertain—he has generously agreed to address us this evening, for which we are truly grateful." Turning to the man on the throne, Von Triebenbach proclaimed, "I, Gustav von Triebenbach, first steward of the Order Primal Fire, welcome you, our most honored guest, scholar, and skald."

The man nodded, and Von Triebenbach took a seat (next to Professor Foch) at the very end of the pew nearest the throne.

"First steward of the Order Primal Fire, friends, and brothers, I thank you," said the bandaged man, his voice sounding a little dry and hoarse. He raised his palm.

"*Heil und Sieg.*"

"*Heil und Sieg,*" came the response.

"My dear friends," said List, opening his arms as if in supplication. "You look upon a man diminished. I am blind—and may never see again. But do not be deceived. To be sightless is not to be without vision. And although my body may be weak, in truth I have never felt so strong, so powerful, and so much in command of my faculties. I have never been more certain of the fundamental truths that must guide our thinking. . . ."

List's head moved from left to right, as if he were surveying the scene and taking in—one by one—the attentive expressions of his audience.

"There is a theme which many of our great stories share." His voice became a little louder. "The promise of redemption, through suffering. I have been cast into darkness. But I have also been redeemed. I have been granted such revelations . . ."

Olbricht and Aschenbrandt leaned forward; the pew creaked.

"When I was still a boy," List continued, "in my fourteenth year of life, I experienced a presentiment of my destiny. My father permitted me to join him and a party of friends on a visit to the catacombs under St. Stephen's. We climbed down, and everything I saw excited me with a strange galvanic energy.... When we descended to the fourth level, we discovered a ruined altar. I was overwhelmed by an emotion that, even now, I can barely find the words to describe. I proclaimed, 'When I am a man, I will build a temple of Wotan.' Of course, I was laughed at ... and in truth, I knew nothing more of Wotan than I had read in Vollmer's *Wörterbuch der Mythologie*. But the atmosphere of the catacombs had aroused in me a religious sentiment, and my instinct was to turn not to Christ but to the gods of our fathers. The old gods ..."

The speaker paused. Once more, his head movements gave the eerie impression that he could see through the bandages and was inspecting his audience. Olbricht and Aschenbrandt both leaned back, as though repelled by some strange power, when they came into the purview of his hidden, sightless eyes.

"I am indebted to the first steward," List began again, "for his kind and generous words concerning my novel *Carnuntum*. I am often asked, *'From where did such a work come?'* In some respects, I feel it fraudulent to claim authorship, because I was nothing but a vessel through which *Carnuntum* came into the world. The work grew, however, from a seed, and I can attest to when that seed was planted. . . ." A faint smile hovered around his lips. "When I was a young man, about twenty-seven or so, I traveled—some twenty-five miles east of Vienna—with a small group of companions, to celebrate the summer solstice at the ruined Roman city of Carnuntum. It is a place of great significance for the German people. For it was at Carnuntum that the Quadi, a Germanic tribe, brave and morally pure, conquered the decadent Roman garrison and, in the fullness of time, pressed on to establish a new Teutonic empire. The Quadi were not barbarians but a noble race, reclaiming lost territories.

"Our so-called scholars have paid scant attention to the script of our German ancestors—the runes. They have based all their works on a false and baseless assumption that the Germanic peoples had no script of any kind, and that their writing signs had been imperfectly copied from the Latin script. But they are woefully wrong!"

During this pedagogic digression, List's voice had become whiny and querulous. Perhaps realizing that he had departed from his intended narrative, he sighed, and resumed his story.

"It was an arduous journey, but we persevered. We climbed steadily until I could see the Heathen's Gate in the distance, black against the horizon—a great arch, towering above us. When we had accomplished our goal, I lit the solstice fire. We stood, united, and drank toasts to the long-forgotten heroes of the Quadi . . . and in the glowing embers of that holy fire, I arranged our bottles in the shape of the eighteenth rune. The stars glittered in a clear sky, as lamps in heaven."

As he said these words, List raised his hands as though beseeching a deity. He remained in this position for a moment before allowing his hands to slowly descend. When he spoke again, his voice was less reverential.

"In the weeks after the removal of my cataracts, I was confined to bed, the only comfort being the press of my dear wife's hand, and I experienced . . ." His sentence trailed off. "I experienced a kind of . . . waking dream. Again, I found myself approaching the Heathen's Gate . . . where I lit not a solstice fire but an invocatory fire. I stared into the dancing flames, which began to suggest certain forms— fleeting patterns that sprang into being before vanishing. Among the twisting ropes of fire, I could detect a certain regularity of shape—the curvature and intersection of lines, the emergence of a luminous female figure that, by degrees, achieved permanence. What followed was an experience that is almost impossible to communicate. . . .

Words, ordinarily so potent, seem utterly inadequate; however, after many hours of intense reflection, I could only conclude that my experience was one of mystical revelation."

The assembly stirred, and a few puzzled glances were exchanged.

"Long hours of interminable lonely darkness have liberated my spirit. It has soared through the abyss, and communed with the *weltseele*, the world soul. . . . I have become a channel, through which sacred knowledge flows. . . . I speak to you this evening not as a blind scholar but as a prophet. The thousand-year twilight of the German people is coming to a close. We will see, in our epoch, the dawn of a new golden age of heroism. Let our enemies mock and scoff—let them deride the old ways . . . for their days will soon be at an end."

Unexpectedly, two men in the middle of the assembly stood up and raised their hands.

"*Heil und Sieg!*" they cried. Soon the battle cry had been taken up by everyone present.

10

AFTER THE MEETING HAD been brought to a successful close and the vote of thanks given, Von Triebenbach issued discreet invitations to his most trusted deputies. He was delighted to report that their distinguished guest had consented to attend an informal party, upstairs in Von Triebenbach's apartment. They climbed up the stone steps that ascended from the basement—with its honeycomb of chambers—to the ground floor, where they negotiated a further flight of stairs leading to the first floor. At Von Triebenbach's door they were welcomed by servants wearing cockade hats and were escorted through two anterooms into an impressive parlor.

A mountain of glowing coals burned brightly under the arch of a large black-marble fireplace. On the mantelpiece was a substantial clock, the intricate workings of which were visible through a glass cover. The furniture—consisting of display cabinets, a bureau, three couches, and several chairs—was early-eighteenth-century. Striped burgundy wallpaper adorned the walls, and classical figures—almost life-size—made silent music on pipes and lyres. The center of the room was dominated by a rosewood-veneer grand piano, the castors of which were buried in a thick Persian carpet.

Aschenbrandt was eager to show List his work, and as soon as the great man was settled on one of the couches, he begged the baron to introduce him. List accepted the young man's proffered hand, and Von Triebenbach—always kindly disposed to Aschenbrandt—

explained that the young musician was eager to perform the overture of a work in progress: an opera based on the author's novel *Carnuntum*.

List graciously consented and Aschenbrandt, excited beyond measure, sat down at the Weber grand and opened his piano score.

The room fell silent.

Aschenbrandt brushed thin wisps of platinum hair behind his ears and his pale face grew solemn. He raised his hands and allowed them to fall onto the keyboard, striking three dramatic opening chords—his celluloid cuffs rattled. An ostinato bass conjured images of marching soldiers, over which an oscillating figure of open fourths and fifths suggested a brassy clarion call. The music was literal, but it was also evidently to the taste of the audience, who nodded appreciatively at the transparent programmatic references. The music ended with a triumphal theme in the relative major key, played fortissimo. Even before the showy coda had come to its predictable conclusion, Von Triebenbach was on his feet. The ovation lasted for several minutes, with List participating as enthusiastically as anyone else present. It was an endorsement that Aschenbrandt had hardly dared dream of, and when List congratulated the young composer personally, he felt as though he had been crowned with a laurel wreath.

After the concert, servants supplied guests with champagne and frosted cubes of crystallized fruit. For a short while there was a general mingling, during which Von Triebenbach circulated among his friends. Eventually the company separated into small groups—some sitting, others standing, but all engaged in animated conversation.

Von Triebenbach and Professor Foch were seated at either side of List, who was expounding his views on the writings of Houston Stewart Chamberlain—an Englishman who had made Vienna his adoptive home. Chamberlain's idea of a great northern alliance, in which all the old Germanic peoples—the Germans, Austrians, English, Netherlanders, and Scandinavians—might join forces, was indeed very appealing. Such an alliance would, as Chamberlain suggested, be invincible; however, List queried Chamberlain's inclusion of the French as Teutons—a position that he considered untenable. Even so, the Englishman's work was certainly worthy of the utmost respect.

Hannisch, Aschenbrandt, and Olbricht were standing in a close group by the piano.

"Well," said Hannisch to Aschenbrandt, "you must be feeling very proud. What did he say to you?" The counselor's gaze darted toward List.

Aschenbrandt leaned forward to ensure privacy.

"He said that he was deeply moved . . . that my music had captured perfectly the heroic spirit of the Quadi."

"High praise indeed," said the counselor, popping a cube of sugared plum between his bright red Cupid's-bow lips. "You are a very lucky young man."

"Indeed, and I believe, sir, that we are all indebted to you, for—"

Hannisch killed the compliment with a hand gesture and began to make dismissive puffing sounds. "Not at all, dear fellow, not at all. It was my pleasure." He sucked some sugar from his fingertips. "Your overture reminded me a little of *Rheingold*," he added. "The entry of the giants."

"You are too kind," said Aschenbrandt.

"And when do you think the opera will be completed?"

"In a year or so, perhaps. Now that I have the approval of the author, I feel completely inspired. I will work day and night on the score."

"Tell me, Herr Hannisch," said Olbricht, capturing the counselor's attention, "does the mayor intend to proceed with the Mozart memorial?"

"Yes, I think so," Hannisch replied. "If I've understood the minutes correctly."

"I submitted some drawings to the mayor's office. . . ."

"Oh?"

"Unfortunately, they were rejected. Although, to be frank, I was in two minds about such a project."

"Did you ask your patron to use her influence?"

"Yes, of course—but alas, her efforts were wasted."

"What's this?" asked Aschenbrandt, emerging from a fog of self-satisfaction.

"The district chairman has been pestering the mayor for a Mozart memorial to be erected just outside this building."

"Might I ask," said Olbricht, "the name of the artist who was awarded the commission . . . in the end?"

Hannisch looked into Olbricht's widely spaced eyes. There was something quite pitiful about his attempt to feign indifference.

"I'm really not sure, my dear fellow," Hannisch replied.

A servant approached and refilled their glasses, while another offered more pieces of crystallized fruit. Hannisch picked up two cubes and immediately pressed one between his lips.

"What will it look like? This memorial?" asked Aschenbrandt.

"Mmm . . ." Hannisch seemed to be distracted by the taste of the sweetmeat—he was clearly engaged in the important task of determining its flavor. "I beg your pardon?"

"What form will the memorial take?" said Aschenbrandt, a hint of tetchiness creeping into his voice. "What will it be?"

Hannisch swallowed.

"Well, as far as I know, it will be a fountain, decorated with bronzes that represent a scene from *The Magic Flute*."

"Mozart! Mozart!" Aschenbrandt growled. "Why not Beethoven? Or Richard Wagner, for heaven's sake! We already have a Mozart monument!"

"I couldn't agree more," said Olbricht. "And why have they chosen to commemorate the most ridiculous of his operas?"

"It is little more than an entertainment for children . . . ," continued Aschenbrandt.

"Yes, yes—he is a superficial composer in many respects," Hannisch continued. "However, he is becoming increasingly popular."

"Well," Aschenbrandt interjected, "I blame Mahler. He's always scheduling Mozart. In fact, a new production of *The Magic Flute* is planned for this season."

The three men looked glum at the prospect.

"The sooner we're rid of him the better," muttered Olbricht.

Hannisch bit into the second cube of fruit. "They say it is a Masonic opera—*The Magic Flute*—full of their secrets."

"Quite so," said Aschenbrandt. "Mozart is supposed to have raised the ire of his Masonic brothers by incorporating many of their treasured symbols in the text and set. It was regarded as a betrayal of trust, and could have cost him his life."

"Mmm . . ." Hannisch's reply was delayed by a protracted episode of mastication. "Mozart may have fallen foul of his fellow Masons on account of his indiscretion, but surely it was the composer's intention to *celebrate* their doctrine in *The Magic Flute*?"

Before Aschenbrandt could answer, Olbricht muttered, "He's probably one of them."

Hannisch and Aschenbrandt turned to look at their companion.

"The district chairman," Olbricht continued. "He's probably one of them—a Mason. And Director Mahler, too."

"Well," said Aschenbrandt. "That wouldn't surprise me in the least."

11

BEFORE LEAVING HIS OFFICE the previous evening, Rheinhardt had received a visit from Commissioner Brügel's adjutant. The self-important underling had handed him an envelope and proclaimed, "The commissioner will see you tomorrow morning." It was not necessary to reinforce Brügel's summons with a command (Rheinhardt knew better than to neglect a communication from the commissioner), but the adjutant was typical of that class of men who, when given a modicum of authority, never fail to abuse it. Although the note was rendered in an ornate Gothic script, it had the modern virtue of brevity, having been composed in the unmannered style of a telegram: *Spittelberg. Progress report. My office. Seven o'clock tomorrow morning. Brügel.*

Rheinhardt sat patiently while the commissioner examined photographs of the Spittelberg massacre. Brügel didn't look horrified, or stunned—merely irritated. Occasionally he grunted in a curmudgeonly fashion. A considerable period of time elapsed before he finally raised his blockish head and asked, "What did the soldiers say?"

"I beg your pardon?" Rheinhardt responded.

"The soldiers!" barked Brügel. "Lipošćak, Alderhorst, Hefner . . ."

"You are referring to the promissory notes?"

"Of course."

"I haven't discovered their whereabouts yet."

"Why? Is there a problem? Is their posting classified?"

"No, sir . . ." Rheinhardt's collar suddenly felt tight. "I have not, as yet, had an opportunity to visit the barracks. I intend to—"

"Rheinhardt," Brügel interrupted, "today is Friday. This atrocity took place on Tuesday. What on earth have you been doing?"

"With respect, sir, if I might explain . . ." Rheinhardt took a deep breath. "Professor Mathias was indisposed on Tuesday. He suffers from a respiratory illness and the cold weather affects his lungs. The good professor—although an inspired pathologist—works slowly, and it was not until late Wednesday evening that the fourth autopsy was completed. On Thursday I worked on my preliminary report, and later in the day I consulted Herr Doctor Liebermann. I have arranged to visit the barracks this morning."

Brügel did not look impressed. "You didn't have to wait for the autopsy results. You could have contacted the military police straight away."

"Indeed, but—"

Brügel slapped his hand on the desk.

"Spare me your excuses, Rheinhardt!" The commissioner grumbled something under his breath and began to fulminate again. "Two days, Rheinhardt. You have wasted two days. The brothel is a short walk from the barracks, three of the women were clearly killed with swords, and in Madam Borek's bureau you found the names of eight soldiers who owed her money. Isn't it obvious what you should have done?"

Rheinhardt, not wishing to lock horns with the commissioner, conceded the point. "Yes, sir. It is obvious. It was a mistake to wait for the autopsy results."

In fact, Rheinhardt thought nothing of the sort. He always preferred to initiate an investigation after consulting Professor Mathias. Moreover, he was well aware that had he not completed a preliminary report by Thursday afternoon, the commissioner would have been equally disgruntled. Even so, he was sufficiently acquainted with Brügel's explosive temper to forgo the modest and perilous pleasure of drawing such arguments to the commissioner's attention.

Brügel opened a buff file and removed the floor plan of Madam Borek's brothel. He unfolded the stiff paper and smoothed it out on his desktop, tutting over some minor aspect of its detail. Then, examining Rheinhardt's preliminary report, he proceeded to question the detective minutely. Brügel's inquisition was not intellectually demanding, but his relentless, bludgeoning style of inquiry made Rheinhardt's head throb.

There was a moment of reprieve when the adjutant arrived with the commissioner's tea. Rheinhardt ruefully observed that the beverage was accompanied by a small pile of *Manner Schnitten*—wafers filled with hazelnut cream—a new type of biscuit for which the inspector had developed a particular fondness. The commissioner managed to consume all of them without showing any signs of enjoyment, a fact, thought Rheinhardt, that revealed even more about Brügel's deficiencies as a human being than did his habitual rudeness.

The commissioner sipped his tea and dabbed his muttonchop whiskers with a napkin.

"Nothing in your report about Liebermann," he grumbled.

Rheinhardt explained that this was because he had only consulted the young psychiatrist after submitting the preliminary report. He set about summarizing—as best as he could—his friend's psychological portrait of the perpetrator. But before he had finished, Brügel was impatiently waving his hand in the air. "Yes, yes, I see what he's getting at. But it's all speculation—isn't it?"

Because Rheinhardt was tired, he soon found himself halfway through a sentence the aim of which was to remind Brügel that Liebermann's psychological insights had been of considerable use to the security office on more than one occasion in the past. However, recognizing his error by the minatory ascent of Brügel's left eyebrow, he allowed his explanation to dissolve into an incoherent burble.

"Remember, Rheinhardt," said Brügel sagely, "there is no substitute for good, solid police work. Look for clues. Interview suspects. And never neglect your paperwork."

The inspector thanked the commissioner for his sensible advice.

"Now," said Brügel in a more friendly tone. "Let's get this investigation under way!" He clapped his hands and rubbed them together as though enthused by a prospect of punishing manual labor.

"Yes, sir," said Rheinhardt, rising up from his chair.

He executed a curt bow and marched toward the door.

"Rheinhardt?"

"Sir?"

"One of His Majesty's aides called yesterday. He wanted to know if there was any news concerning that curious incident at the zoo. That business with the snake?"

"Hildegard."

"Yes. I was led to understand that the animal was a personal favorite of the emperor's."

Rheinhardt swallowed. "I'm sorry, sir. But what with the Spittelberg incident . . . I have not had the time to . . ." He shook his head and made an appeasing gesture with his hands.

The commissioner sighed. He seemed disinclined to chastise Rheinhardt a second time. Rheinhardt imagined that this was probably due to fatigue rather than sympathy.

"So be it," said the commissioner. "I will inform the palace that the investigation is progressing, but that no new facts have come to our attention."

"Indeed, sir. Thank you, sir."

Rheinhardt closed his hand around the door handle and silently gave thanks for his deliverance.

12

THE MAID ADDRESSED BETTINA in a hushed voice. "It's Herr Fränkel. He won't go without seeing you. He said that he has some very important documents for Herr Weiss."

Bettina rolled her eyes, glanced up at the ceiling, and addressed Liebermann and Clara.

"One of Konrad's business associates, Moritz Fränkel. I don't know what's wrong with him. He insists on delivering contracts in person and won't leave anything with our servants. He's always worried about things getting lost or stolen. I'm sure it's an illness. Perhaps you should see him as a patient, Max?"

Liebermann shook his head. "I think not."

Rising, Bettina touched her little son's nose. "Leo, Mutti's going outside. Be good for Uncle Max and Auntie Clara." She then glided toward the door, veering sideways to avoid baby Emil's head. "This shouldn't take too long," she added, glancing back at her guests.

As soon as the door had closed behind Bettina, Clara looked from Leo to Emil and back again. Her face was shining with joy and mischievous excitement. She seemed to be in a quandary, unsure of which nephew to play with first. Gleefully casting the customs of gentility aside, she jumped up from her seat, lowered herself to the floor, and began crawling on all fours toward Emil.

"I'm coming to get you," she announced, extending the syllables and dropping her voice an octave to achieve a hint of menace. "I'm coming."

Leo, who was seated on a high wooden chair, was so impressed by the irregularity of his aunt's behavior that he could not stop himself from emitting a high-pitched squeal. The toddler was dressed rather formally in a red-striped coat with gold buttons, a velvet hat, and a diminutive bow tie. Clara looked up. "That's it, Leo, warn your little brother. . . . I'm coming, I'm coming."

Liebermann was humbled by Clara's insouciance, her natural capacity to derive intense joy from such innocent pleasures. She was a woman with many faults—she could be superficial, preoccupied by social trivia, and prone to worthless gossip—but emotional dishonesty was not one of them. Her love was simple and direct, free of unnecessary cerebral complications.

"I'm coming to eat you up," Clara panted.

As Liebermann looked on, tender feelings gave way to desire. The sway of Clara's hips, the pointed heels of her leather boots, and the glimpse of a silk undergarment soon destroyed the fragile purity of his reverie.

"Max?"

"Yes?" He shifted uncomfortably.

"Quick. Get me the Perzy."

"The what?"

Clara turned. "The snow globe! It's on the mantelpiece. Next to your elbow."

Liebermann picked up what appeared to be a crystal ball mounted on a black gypsum base. Inside the globe was a minute replica of the Riesenrad—the giant Ferris wheel on the Prater.

"This?"

"Yes."

"What is it?"

"Shake it and you'll see."

He did so. Suddenly the enclosed world was animated by a violent snowstorm—thousands of white flakes whirled around within a cyclone of invisible turbulence.

"Ha!" cried Liebermann. "Ingenious."

"Haven't you seen one before?"

"No."

"You must start taking an interest in the *real* world, Max! They've become very fashionable. Herr Perzy started making them a few years ago. He has a shop in Hernals."

Liebermann handed Clara the globe. She shook it and placed it in front of Emil's face. The infant was lying on his stomach, the upper half of his body raised on thick, stocky arms, the extremities of which were lost in a pillow. He was wearing a long white lacy smock and little woollen shoes. His enormous round head bobbed up and down, supported precariously by a thin neck.

"Look, Emil. Snow!"

The infant continued to survey his surroundings in an unfocused state of wonderment and confusion. Then, suddenly catching sight of the glittering ball, his mouth opened, allowing a thin but unbroken line of dribble to fall slowly to the floor, where it fed an expanding pool of transparent saliva.

"Oh, good heavens!"

Clara handed the snow globe back to Liebermann, produced a handkerchief from nowhere with the dexterity of a stage magician, wiped Emil's mouth, mopped the floor, and scooped the child up in her arms. Liebermann found the artless ease with which she dealt with the predicament curiously affecting.

Liebermann bent his knees and squatted down beside her.

Clara's eyes were closed, and her lips were pressed up against Emil's plump red cheek. The child gurgled and produced the immature throaty music of infant laughter. Liebermann had never seen Clara looking so content, calm, or beautiful. When she opened her eyes, something passed between them. Unspoken, but powerful: the promise of intimacy and children of their own.

Liebermann swallowed, and felt an uncomfortable lump in his throat.

Clara reached out and touched Liebermann's face. The contact was as gentle as the brush of a falling leaf.

"What is it, Max?"

The door opened and they both turned toward the sound. It was Bettina. "What are you two doing on the floor? You're worse than the children—I can't leave you alone for two minutes!"

13

RHEINHARDT FOLLOWED COLONEL PÁL Kabok through the dimly lit corridor of the barracks building. Kabok was a short-legged stocky man with a heavy, ponderous gait. Unlocking one of many identical doors, the colonel gestured that Rheinhardt should enter.

"No one will disturb us here."

Rheinhardt was surprised to find himself in the colonel's private room. It contained an iron camp bed, two colored prints—one of the emperor and the other of the late Empress Elisabeth—and a few poorly mounted photographs of regimental inspections and dinners. On the wall above the bed hung a pair of crossed swords and a finely decorated Turkish pistol. There was nothing else in the room: no wardrobe, no table, not even a chair. It was uncompromising in its austerity. The colonel turned to face Rheinhardt. He stood squarely, arms akimbo.

"Yes, Inspector?"

Rheinhardt had not expected to conduct his interview standing in the middle of a cold half-empty barracks room.

Outside, a bugle sounded, followed by the clatter of hooves. Rheinhardt suspected that the colonel was content to dispense with pleasantries.

"I am investigating the Spittelberg murders."

The colonel's low oxlike brow creased.

"Murders? In Spittelberg?"

"Yes. You have perhaps read about them in the *Zeitung*?"

"The *Zeitung*? Inspector, I haven't read a newspaper in twenty years."

"Oh . . ."

"Like His Majesty, the imperial commander-in-chief, I favor the military gazette. What isn't in the military gazette, I don't need to know."

Unperturbed, Rheinhardt continued. "On Tuesday, four women were murdered in a Spittelberg brothel. A madam and three house girls believed to have recently come to Vienna from Galicia."

The colonel rotated his bullet-shaped head on his thick bull neck. His rigid expression changed slightly. "Ah yes, the men were talking about this in the mess."

"You overheard something?"

"Yes."

The colonel didn't care to elaborate. He remained perfectly still, his eyebrows bristling.

"The women," continued Rheinhardt, "were horribly abused—their genitals had been mutilated, their throats cut. The incisions were deep. It is possible that some of these injuries were inflicted with"—he glanced down at the colonel's weapon—"a sabre."

Kabok's crude rustic features remained fixed. His face reminded Rheinhardt of a potato that he had once used to amuse his daughters. After a long silence, the colonel said bluntly, "You wanted my assistance."

Rheinhardt handed him a sheet of paper. On it were written the names of several military personnel.

"All these men were patrons of the Spittelberg establishment."

"Where did you get these names?" barked the colonel.

"They were found on promissory notes in the madam's bureau. Do you know any of them?"

"Yes. Lieutenant Lipošćak, Lieutenant Hefner . . ." Kabok's eyes moved from side to side. "Renz and Witold."

"I must speak to them."

For the first time Kabok moved. He lumbered over to the twin prints of the emperor and the late empress, his spurs producing a dead jangling in the closed space. With his eyes fixed on the image of the imperial commander-in-chief, he said, "In this world, Inspector, nothing is more important to me than the uhlans, and nothing more sacred than regimental honor. I know these men. . . ." He flapped the sheet of paper in his hand. "No one knows them better. You will not find a spot of rust on their swords, a button badly polished, or a single scuff mark on their boots. They are a credit to His Majesty, a credit to the empire. None of them would ever disgrace the regiment. If—as you imply—the abomination you described was perpetrated by one of my men, then I would have failed His Majesty. I would take that pistol from the wall and blow out my brains."

Rheinhardt shifted uncomfortably.

The colonel looked up. His cheeks had reddened slightly, and a vein on his temple had started to throb.

"I will arrange for you to meet these men. But believe me, Inspector, you are wasting your time."

14

RHEINHARDT WAS ESCORTED TO a room located in an outbuilding some distance from the barracks. On the wall hung the obligatory image of Emperor Franz Josef; however, the old print was not a good likeness and the paper was mildewed around the edges. A small stove heated the room, but it was miserably inadequate. Rheinhardt's fingertips were almost numb. He had finished interviewing Lieutenant Harry Lipošćak (a polite but somewhat taciturn Hungarian) and was now in the process of interrogating Lieutenant Ruprecht Hefner.

Slim, handsome, pale, with blond curls peeping out from under his peaked cap and with a downy, carefully combed mustache, Hefner was the kind of young officer whom Rheinhardt would have expected to encounter on the pages of a romantic novel. His uniform was, as Colonel Kabok had promised, immaculate. The blue of his tunic and breeches was as vivid as a summer sky. His buttons glowed with a lustrous aura, and his fine leather top boots produced a satisfying creak every time he moved. A gold-yellow tassle hung from the pommel of his sabre. The other lieutenant, Lipošćak, had also sported a pristine uniform, but there was something about Hefner's posture, the straightness of his back, the projection of his chin, the relaxed attitude of his shoulders, that gave him a definite sartorial advantage.

"Where were you on Tuesday morning?" Rheinhardt asked.

"In bed. I wasn't very well." Hefner's voice was clear and steady, but he spoke with a certain languor. He seemed to be affecting a world-weariness that would have been more appropriate in a man twice his age.

"What was wrong with you?"

"I don't know—I was just sick."

"Did anyone see you on Tuesday morning?"

"Yerik, my batman."

"Anyone else?"

"No."

"Why didn't you call the regimental doctor?"

"I did, later in the day."

"And what did the doctor say was wrong?"

"He said I had an inflammation of the gut."

"Which was caused by?"

"I have no idea, Inspector. I'm not a doctor."

Rheinhardt produced a sheet of paper, which he shunted across the table.

"Do you recognize this?"

"Yes," said Hefner, calmly. "It is a promissory note, signed by myself. I owed Madam Borek ten kronen."

"How often did you visit Madam Borek's establishment?"

"Quite often."

"Why?"

"Isn't it obvious, Inspector?" Hefner's bloodless lips curved slightly. He seemed mildly amused.

"There are many brothels in Spittelberg, Lieutenant. Why Madam Borek's?"

"I was rather fond of one of the girls. She was new there. . . ."

"What was her name? This new girl?"

"Lucca? Something like that."

"Ludka?"

"Yes, that's it, Ludka. Very pretty. . . ." Hefner smiled again. "And very compliant—if you follow my meaning."

He lifted his chin a fraction higher in order to clear his stiff high collar. The material was decorated with two gold embroidered stars.

"Madam Borek's establishment did not possess a government trade license," said Rheinhardt.

"Why should that be of any concern to me?"

"The establishment was illegal."

Hefner shrugged. "I did not break the law."

"State-registered prostitutes receive a medical examination twice a week. What precautionary measures do you think Madam Borek took?"

Hefner's lip curled again. "There are always risks, Inspector, wherever one goes in pursuit of pleasure. I am sure that a man of your"—Hefner looked Rheinhardt up and down—"*experience* appreciates that fact."

It was an insolent remark, which Rheinhardt did not wish to acknowledge with a response. Instead, he jotted down a few lines in his notebook. When he looked up again, a supercilious smirk was still hovering around Hefner's lips.

"Did Madam Borek have any enemies?"

"How should I know?"

"Did you ever hear of anyone being violent with the women at Madam Borek's?"

"No."

"Did you ever see anyone there who behaved oddly? Anyone you suspected of being mentally unbalanced?"

Hefner laughed. "Inspector, when I visited Madam Borek's establishment, the behavior of the other patrons was the least of my concerns. Besides, I hardly ever saw them."

"Did you see Lieutenant Lipošćak at Madam Borek's?"

"No."

"What about Renz and Witold?"

"I saw Renz there once . . . a few weeks ago."

"Do you know who Captain Alderhorst is?"

"I've never heard of him."

"Private Friedel?"

"Who?"

"Friedel."

"I've never heard of him, either."

Rheinhardt looked toward the window. The day was overcast and the clouds radiated a putrid gray-green light.

"Lieutenant Hefner," said Rheinhardt, "Ludka—the Galician girl you claim to have been fond of—Madam Borek, and two other women, Fräuleins Draczynski and Glomb, were subjected to the most appalling violence."

"I know."

"Yet you do not seem"—Rheinhardt searched for a diplomatic phrase—"*moved* by their fate."

"Inspector," said Hefner, "I am an officer of the eighteenth. What do you want me to do? Weep like my grandmother? Bang my fist on the table and rail against heaven?" Hefner crossed his legs slowly and his spurs rattled. "I am a representative of His Majesty's army. A cavalryman. I wear this uniform with pride. We have a reputation to consider. I will not disgrace the regiment with some unseemly display of emotional incontinence. If you want to see that, go and interview an Italian corporal!"

15

Liebermann looked up and into the dome. Sixteen cherubs danced above eight circular windows, and the whole edifice was supported on gilded archways.

He adored the Natural History Museum. It was a place in which one could marvel at the diversity of life and contemplate the extraordinary power of science to unlock the secrets of the universe. Charles Darwin had dispensed with a Creator and replaced Him with a simple principle: natural selection. In his masterpiece *The Origin of Species by Means of Natural Selection, or, The Preservation of Favored Races in the Struggle for Life*, the great biologist had succeeded in describing the evolutionary process in a single, simple sentence: "Multiply, vary, let the strongest live and the weakest die." It was at the same time terrifying and beautiful, and it explained everything: eyes, ears, birds, and desire—nothing was beyond the reach of Darwin's awesome theory.

"Where are we going now?" asked Clara.

"To see our relatives."

"Did you invite them?"

"No—they're already here."

"What!" Clara was quite obviously miffed.

The couple entered an immense hall filled with glass display cases, all of which were occupied by stuffed animals. Liebermann gestured toward one in which a troop of gorillas—a male, a female, and two young—languished beneath a scrawny tree.

Clara poked a finger into Liebermann's ribs and cried, "Max!"

"Well," said Liebermann, "strictly speaking we *are* related."

"*You* may be . . ."

"Indeed, I am perfectly happy to concede that the Liebermann bloodline carries with it certain characteristics that are decidedly pongid. Look at that male—he looks a little like my father, don't you think?"

Clara stepped closer to the glass, and immediately her expression brightened with an astonished smile. It was true. The gorilla *did* look a little like Max's father. There was something about the creature's heavy brow and rigid jaw that reminded her—albeit only vaguely—of Mendel Liebermann's disapproving mien.

"Max . . . ," Clara said, raising a hand to her mouth, at once both shocked and amused. "You shouldn't be so disrespectful . . . but"—she began to giggle—"it *is* an uncanny resemblance."

"There you are, then. Indisputable proof of Mr. Darwin's hypothesis."

Clara's expression changed. Her lips pressed together and she began to pout.

"What is it?" asked Liebermann, stepping forward and letting her lean back into his chest. There were no other visitors present—but Liebermann nevertheless kept a judicious eye on the doorway. A public display of intimacy would not be countenanced in a royal museum.

"Do you really believe it, Max? That we have—what is the word . . . evolved, yes? That we have evolved from apes?"

"Well," Liebermann replied, "I certainly don't believe that Adam and Eve begat the human race after being banished from the Garden of Eden."

Clara looked up. Her red lips were too inviting to resist, and Liebermann stole a quick, dry kiss.

"But apes . . . ," she said softly.

Liebermann kissed her again, on the cheek this time. Clara did not respond, and her expression became increasingly fixed in an attitude of seriousness. She seemed inordinately discomfited by the idea.

"Maxim . . . ," she began hesitantly.

"Yes?"

"If we evolved from apes . . . could we not—one day—become apes again?"

"There are a number of scientists and doctors who fear such a thing. They have suggested that civilized societies must be vigilant for signs of what they call *degeneration*. These include unrefined physical features and certain mental traits. But such a descent into chaos would take many generations. Thousands or perhaps even millions of years . . ."

Clara's mood lifted in an instant. It was as though her moment of dejection had never been. Her lips parted and she produced a brilliant flashing smile.

"Let's go into town, Max. Mother said that the jeweler's on Kärntner Strasse has some garnet earrings in the window—just come in from Prague." She pulled away. "I think they will go well with my new crepe-de-chine dress: you know the one, I wore it at the Weigels' party? It cost one hundred florins—you *must* remember it."

16

RHEINHARDT HAD FINISHED CONDUCTING his interviews. He was bid an indifferent farewell by Colonel Kabok, and given explicit directions to expedite his departure. He wended his way through the assorted collection of outbuildings and soon found himself trudging along the edge of a frozen parade ground. He followed a low perimeter wall of dirty sludge and ice that had been shoveled aside earlier in the day.

A regiment of uhlans seemed to be practicing a complex drill that required considerable skill and concentration. Each horse's head was inclined at an identical angle, and all the riders were pointing their swords upward. An officer, seated on a beautiful chestnut gelding, was obviously displeased with one of his command and cantered up to the unfortunate miscreant. He opened his mouth and bellowed a torrent of foul invective. In response, the rider seemed to make a few small adjustments, but Rheinhardt was unable to detect just how his comportment had improved. To his untutored eye, horse and rider looked just the same. The officer, however, appeared to have been appeased, and he withdrew from the squadron column.

Rheinhardt walked under an arch above which projected two sculpted horses' heads; on closer inspection, he saw that the smaller of the pair represented the living horse, while the larger one depicted its protective headgear or armor.

It had not been a particularly productive morning. All the cavalrymen had been subtly uncooperative, and Rheinhardt was left with the impression that, simply by making routine inquiries, he was—in their eyes—questioning the integrity of His Majesty's army, and therefore, by implication, conducting an unpatriotic investigation. Perhaps it was this feeling of having accomplished so little that urged Rheinhardt to walk quickly past the welcoming steamy windows of several coffeehouses, with their blue uncovered gas jets flickering inside, to head off in the direction of Spittelberg. He was not sure what he hoped to achieve by making this detour, but he was of the opinion that action—*any* action, in fact—would remedy the sense of frustration that had been building up inside him since his first encounter with Colonel Kabok.

Rheinhardt raised the collar of his coat and made his way through a series of backstreets that led to his destination. Entering Spittelberg, he found that he had to take more care on the slippery cobbles. Although it was relatively early in the afternoon, the light was already beginning to fail. A woman, her head wrapped up in a voluminous scarf, was slowly ascending the narrow road. She was clutching a wicker basket, the contents of which were covered by a grubby napkin. Behind her a little boy followed, dragging a toy sword made from two pieces of wood joined by a rusty nail. Rheinhardt winked, but the diminutive soldier was too cold to respond.

As Rheinhardt neared Madam Borek's, he spied a figure who looked familiar: an old man, bent over his stick, wearing a broad Bohemian hat. It was the same old-timer who had been waiting outside Madam Borek's when the inspector had first arrived with Haussmann. Rheinhardt waved, and the old man responded by lifting his hat.

"So," said Rheinhardt. "You are still waiting here." The old man worked his jaw and smacked his lips. He looked at his interlocutor with a quizzical expression. "We've met before," Rheinhardt added.

"Yes," said the old man. "You're the policeman who told me to move along. You told me to go home and light a fire."

"That's right. And today is another bitterly cold day. Why, my friend, are you standing here again? You'll get pneumonia!"

"I'm waiting for my daughter," the old man replied. "Sometimes, when she's late, I get worried. I come here, and stand under Saint Joseph." He pointed up at the little statue with its aureole of metal strips. "From here I can see her coming around the corner." The old man gestured up the street.

"What does she do? Your daughter?" asked Rheinhardt.

"She sells glasses of pickled gherkin juice to schoolboys at the bread market. She's a bit simple." A gust of wind whipped up a cloud of powdered snow, which made the old man close his eyes. When he opened them again, they were moist and glistening. "Have you caught him yet?" he croaked.

"Caught who?"

"Krull—the man who killed them . . . Frau Borek and the three girls." The old man pointed his stick toward the abandoned brothel.

"What did you say?"

"Krull. Have you caught him yet?"

"Who is Krull?"

"The man who killed them all."

"Why do you say that? Why do you think that this Herr Krull is responsible for their murder?"

"He was always loitering aaround here."

"Outside Madam Borek's?"

"Yes."

"Doing what?"

"Waiting."

"Waiting for who?"

"One of the girls—he used to go on about how beautiful she was, and that he wanted to give her something. . . . I don't know."

"Did you ever see her, this girl?"

"Yes. The small one. Like a child, she was."

"And what did Krull do? Did he enter the house with her?"

"No. He never went in. Just used to wait outside. He was biding his time, waiting for the right moment."

Rheinhardt took out his notebook and began to write. "What does he look like?"

"Well, he's short. Not much taller than me."

"What color is his hair?"

"I don't know—he always wears a hat."

"And how old is he?"

"Twenty, thirty . . ." The old man pulled at his beard. "Forty . . . perhaps."

Rheinhardt sighed. "Young or old?"

"Young—but then, everyone seems young to me. Oh yes, and he has a limp."

"Why didn't you tell me any of this before?"

"I didn't know they were dead. *You* never told me. My daughter told me."

"Yes, of course," said Rheinhardt apologetically. "However, once you suspected Herr Krull, you should have got your daughter to contact the police."

The old man shrugged. "She's simple."

"Do you know where I can find Herr Krull?"

The old man returned a vacant expression.

"My friend," said Rheinhardt, trying to keep calm. "It is extremely important that I find this man. Do you know where he lives?"

"Go to the inn and ask the landlord. Herr Jutzet—he knows where everybody lives."

17

THE STAIRCASE WAS MADE of rough-hewn stone squeezed between two high windowless walls. As it went up, the stairs became both narrower and more uneven. At the very top was an alcove, which contained a plaster cast of Christ on the cross. The scene was bathed in a sickly yellow light that pulsed out of a faulty gas lamp. To reach the first step it was necessary to step across a pool of frozen water, which had collected in a depression where some paving stones were missing.

Rheinhardt tested the ice with his shoe, and watched a dendritic pattern grow from the point of impact. He applied more pressure. The liquid that welled up between the cracks was more like oil than water.

"Are we going up, sir?" asked Haussmann.

"I suppose this must be the address."

Herr Jutzet—a big-bellied, red-cheeked publican—had been most obliging.

Yes, I know Herr Krull. A loner, with a gammy leg. Owes me four krone. Here's his address—I'll write it down for you. You see him, you tell him I want my money. Four krone. And if he doesn't pay soon, I'll be around to collect it myself.

The two detectives began their ascent. On either side, large nails had been driven into the walls, and from these a gallery of grim detritus hung: a cracked old mirror, some lengths of string, and an assortment of dirty rags.

Almost immediately, Rheinhardt slipped. It was difficult to find reasonable purchase on the raked stairs. He reached out and touched the wall to steady himself.

"Are you all right, sir?" asked Haussmann.

"Yes, thank you," Rheinhardt replied—but he was not altogether confident that they would reach their destination without sustaining serious injuries. They progressed slowly, pausing on each step before attempting the next. Finally they reached the top, where they both stopped to inspect the crucifix, which was housed in an ambry and protected by an iron grill. The effigy itself was chipped and faded; however, it looked as if Christ's crown of thorns and the spear wound in his side had been recently retouched with generous amounts of red paint. A number of candle stubs lay at the foot of the cross, and Christ's legs had been blackened with soot. Red and white wax had spilled over the lip of the ambry and congealed in runnels that had stuck to the plaster.

"It's rather ugly, isn't it?" said Rheinhardt.

"Yes," Haussmann replied. "And this is a horrible place."

The younger man's shoulder shook with an involuntary shiver.

"What's that?" Rheinhardt lowered his head and peered into the aumbry. The light was extremely poor, but he could see something small and pale inside. He searched his pocket for a box of Vestas and lit a match. In the flare the object became more visible.

"Do you see it?" Rheinhardt was whispering now.

"Yes, sir."

"I'll light another match. See if you can get the thing out."

In the phosphorescent glare Haussmann thrust his long fingers through the grill and caught the object with a scissoring movement. He slowly dragged it out, and lifted it up. The fitful gaslight provided just enough illumination.

"My God," said Rheinhardt.

"It looks like . . ." Haussmann did not finish his sentence.

"It's a bone."

The younger man shuddered again. "Human?"

"It could be."

"Sir?"

"Yes?"

Haussmann lowered his voice again, so much so that Rheinhardt needed to lean closer in order to hear him. "Do you think it is wise for us to be here like this—just the two of us? We haven't notified the security office of our whereabouts. If Krull is responsible for the terrible things we saw . . ."

Rheinhardt took the bone from his colleague and turned it between his thumb and forefinger. He slid it into his coat pocket. When he withdrew his hand, he was holding a revolver.

"I would not place your life in danger, Haussmann," he said firmly. Then, putting the revolver back into his pocket, he placed a hand on his companion's shoulder. "Come, Haussmann. We have work to do."

The two men walked into the shadows and found a door. Rheinhardt felt for a knocker but could not find one. Instead, he clenched his fist and hammered against one of the panels. They waited.

"Who is it?" came a muffled voice.

"Police. Open the door," said Rheinhardt.

There were a number of sounds. Bolts being drawn back, chains rattling, and a key turning. Finally the door was unlocked. Rheinhardt could not see the features of the man who'd opened it. The only significant source of light was coming from a paraffin lamp behind him.

"Herr Krull?"

"Yes."

"Detective Inspector Rheinhardt—and my assistant, Haussmann. May we come in?"

The man's head moved quickly, looking at Rheinhardt first, then at Haussmann, then back again to Rheinhardt.

"You're not wearing uniforms. How do I know whether you're with the police or not? You could be anybody." Krull's accent was rough and hard-edged. There was no music in his German, which was spoken largely from the back of the throat. He could have been hawking rather than speaking.

Rheinhardt sighed and took out some identification documents. Krull examined them for a few seconds and nodded.

"Very well, then—come in. You can't be too careful here, believe me."

Krull ushered them in. The room was little more than a hovel. A table, a chair, and a small stove. On the table was a large leather-bound volume—it looked like a Bible. Through an adjoining door could be seen a shadowy bedroom: a pallet lay on the floor and there was an oversize wardrobe. The air was fetid. Rheinhardt noticed a figurine of the Virgin Mary in the recess of a tiny square window. Krull limped to the chair and sat down.

"What is the matter with your leg?" asked Rheinhardt.

"Clubfoot," said Krull.

"Is it painful?" asked Rheinhardt.

"Can be," said Krull.

Rheinhardt took a step forward and made sure that there was nothing that Krull might use as a weapon in easy reach.

"So what's this about, eh?" Krull demanded.

Observing the irate little man, Rheinhardt could not determine whether it was more appropriate to feel disgust or pity. Among the variety of human types, Krull was a most unfortunate specimen. A criminologist sympathetic to Galton and Lombroso's ideas would immediately identify Krull as a murderer. His features were entirely atavistic: low forehead, ears like jug handles, and a bony ridge over the orbits of his sunken eyes. A flat nose and prognathous jaw completed the simian ensemble.

"We are conducting a murder investigation, Herr Krull."

"I don't know anything about any murders." He shook his head.

"Perhaps not, but I believe that you may be able to help us with our inquiries."

"Believe what you like—but I know nothing."

Haussmann slipped discreetly behind Krull's chair; however, he was not sufficiently discreet to escape Krull's notice. The little man glanced over his shoulder, and looked anxiously back at Rheinhardt.

"What are you dong here? What do you want with me?"

"Herr Krull—I am sure you are aware of the recent atrocity that took place in Spittelberg."

"I keep myself to myself."

"Well, not entirely. I understand that you are well acquainted with Herr Jutzet."

Haussmann had discovered another religious image and he held it up briefly behind Krull's back. It was a small woodcut of Saint Francis of Assisi offering his benediction.

Krull's jaw seemed to project out even farther.

"Herr Jutzet sent you?"

"It was he who gave us your address. Incidentally, the good landlord is also somewhat anxious that you should pay him a visit in order to abrogate your pecuniary embarrassment."

"What?"

"The matter of your debt, Herr Krull. The sum of four krone was mentioned."

"Three krone. He's added another krone as interest. The man's worse than a Jew. He probably *is* a Jew."

Rheinhardt looked over Krull's shoulder. Haussmann had stepped backward into the bedroom.

"Herr Krull," Rheinhardt continued. "Earlier today I spoke to a gentleman of your acquaintance, a certain Herr Chalupnik."

"Who?"

"Herr Chalupnik. An old gentleman. He often waits for his daughter under the statue of Saint Joseph."

Krull sniffed. "I don't know his name. I presume you mean the old Czech."

"Yes. Big hat, long beard—walks with a stick. You *do* know him."

"I wouldn't pay much attention to what he says."

"Why not?"

"He's senile."

"He might be old, and his memory might be failing, but you, Herr Krull, seem to have made quite an impression on him."

Haussmann opened the door of the wardrobe. He had tried to do it quietly, but the door emitted a loud creak.

Krull turned around abruptly.

"What are you doing? Get away from there. Get away from there at once."

The grotesque little man raised his arm and started for the bedroom.

"Herr Krull," Rheinhardt called, "remain seated."

Krull ignored the inspector and advanced toward the younger detective; however, by the time Krull reached Haussmann, a bundle of clothes had already tumbled out of the wardrobe and now lay on the floor. Even in the half-light, stains were clearly visible.

"Sir . . . ," Haussmann called.

"You don't understand," said Krull. "You're making a mistake. You're making a big mistake."

Rheinhardt entered the bedroom and hunkered down next to the stinking pile of clothes. He lifted a shirt. The material was stiff and gritty with crystals of dried coagulated blood.

18

KRULL HAD BEEN ESCORTED from his cell by two constables who now stood guard outside the specially prepared room. On arrival, Liebermann had instructed Krull to lie down on the divan. The little man immediately protested.

"Herr Krull," said Rheinhardt, "judges are not kindly disposed toward defendants who have failed to cooperate with the police. This is something you might care to consider before making a stand."

Krull swore under his breath and gracelessly mounted the divan. His apelike features were not matched by any simian agility.

Liebermann drew up a chair and placed it at the head of the divan—out of Krull's sight. Krull jerked his head back.

"Please, Herr Krull," said Liebermann. "Do not attempt to look at me. I want you to look straight ahead, or close your eyes—whatever you find more comfortable."

"Comfortable?" Krull repeated. "You must be a comedian, Herr Doctor."

Liebermann crossed his legs, placed his elbow on the chair arm, and allowed his head to rest against his right hand. He began by taking a history—just as he might with a patient being admitted to the hospital.

Krull had been born and raised in the country, but had come to Vienna to seek his fortune. Like many before him, he had soon discovered that the great city distributed its bounty capriciously. Not everyone found employment and amassed wealth. Krull spent his first winter in a charitable shelter, and the next three years in a men's hostel in Brigittenau. His companions were mostly laborers and handymen. Like him, the majority of them came from lower Austria, but Krull was also compelled to share a dormitory with several "lying Croats," "greedy Hungarians," and the odd "filthy Russian." He moved first to Landstrasse and then to Ottakring, before eventually securing the comparative luxury of his dismal apartment on the edges of Spittelberg. During his many years of abject poverty, he had come under the influence of a Catholic priest called Father Anselm, who had become his spiritual mentor.

"You should find him!" Krull cried. "He'd speak up for me. He'd tell you what a big mistake you've made!"

Liebermann's index finger stirred. He tapped his temple three times and asked, "Why did you visit Madam Borek's brothel, Herr Krull?"

The little man grumbled something inaudible and finally replied, "I never visited Madam Borek's brothel."

"You were seen outside on several occasions. What were you doing?"

Krull rolled his head back. "Why must I lie here like this—are you going to do something to me?"

"No," said Liebermann patiently. "Now, could you please answer my question? What were you doing?"

"I wanted to see the girl," snapped Krull.

"Which one?"

"The young one, Ludka."

"Why did you want to see her?"

Krull squeezed his thick lower lip. Dark crescents showed where dirt had collected beneath his nails.

"I wanted to talk to her." Liebermann allowed the subsequent pause to lengthen. "I wanted to *save* her."

The young doctor raised his eyebrows and glanced at Rheinhardt.

"Save her?" Liebermann repeated.

"Yes, from a life of sin."

"I see," said Liebermann. He uncrossed his legs and leaned forward. "Did you ever speak to Ludka?"

"Only once."

"When was that?"

"The first time I saw her: the first time we met. About a month ago—it was by the fountain."

"And what did you say to her?"

"I had a cold and was sneezing. She gave me her handkerchief. I asked her where she lived and she pointed down the street. I knew the house. . . . That's to say, I knew what sort of house it was. I promised to return the handkerchief. Thing is, her German wasn't very good—I'm not sure she understood what I was saying."

"And did you keep your promise? Did you return her handkerchief?"

"No, I didn't get the chance to."

"Where is the handkerchief now?"

Krull appeared to tap his heart—a gesture which Liebermann took to mean that the handkerchief was in one of Krull's pockets.

"May I see it?"

The little man slid his right hand under the left lapel of his jacket and pulled out a small square of white cotton. It was embroidered around the edges with a tiny motif of linked roses.

"Thank you," said Liebermann.

Krull held the handkerchief up to his nose, sampled its fragrance, and stuffed it back into his jacket pocket.

"I went to the house," Krull continued. "I don't deny it. I used to stand outside for hours, waiting for her to come out—which was how I got talking to that old gossip Chalupnik."

"Why didn't you knock on the door?"

"I don't know . . . embarrassment . . . shame. I ended up in the inn more often than not, warming myself up with one too many slivovitzes."

"Are you saying that you never saw her again after that first meeting?"

"No. I *did* see her again, but only once more. Chalupnik was there. She came out with a cavalryman. Blond tall chap—I suppose you'd call him handsome. They were laughing. . . . I think he was drunk. I felt . . . I don't know . . . churned up inside. I turned my back on them and spoke to the old man. She didn't see me."

"Herr Krull, were you in love with Ludka?"

"Don't be ridiculous! I felt sorry for her. I wanted to help her get out of that place. Those soldiers . . . I've heard what they get up to. If the emperor knew the truth, eh?"

Liebermann produced a small white object, which he proceeded to hold above Krull's head.

"Do you recognize this, Herr Krull?"

"No."

"The third metacarpal, I believe—probably belonging to a woman aged around nineteen or twenty years."

"Meta what? What are you talking about?"

"It's a woman's finger, Herr Krull. And do you know where it was found? In the recess just outside your apartment—among the votive candles."

"People are always throwing things in there. It probably belongs to the medical student downstairs. . . ."

Liebermann removed the bone from Krull's line of vision.

"Herr Krull, why were the clothes in your wardrobe covered in blood?"

"You know why—I've told the inspector."

"Yes, but I want you to tell *me*."

"My clothes were covered in blood because I work in an abattoir. It's pig's blood."

"Do you normally leave bloody clothes in your wardrobe?"

"Yes. There's nowhere else to put them. If I don't get to the bathhouse, then my clothes don't get washed."

19

THE SMALL COFFEEHOUSE near the Anatomical Institute was a short walk from the Schottenring police station. Liebermann found himself once more by the window seat, observing the passing traffic. Across the table, Rheinhardt was admiring the involuted structure that occupied his plate. It was a generous portion of *tiroler strauben*—crisp, freshly fried curls of pancake mixture, flavored with schnapps and sprinkled with sugar. Rheinhardt sliced off a coil of the light brown confection with his fork and lifted it to his mouth.

"Oh yes," he said, chewing vigorously. "Very good indeed—just like I had in the Tyrol last summer."

Liebermann sipped his *schwarzer* and drummed a five-finger exercise on the edge of the table.

"Well?" said Rheinhardt, finally.

"I'm thinking," said Liebermann.

"My dear fellow," said Rheinhardt, "I had already guessed that you weren't counting streetcars. Perhaps you would be so kind as to share your thoughts?"

Liebermann sighed and looked toward his friend. "I am deeply troubled by Herr Krull's appearance."

"Indeed. When I saw him for the first time, I thought to myself, Here is a face that proves Lombroso's theories. I know you do not hold with Lombroso, Max, but the man looks like—forgive my incivility—an ape. I once saw an illustration showing an artist's impression of the

creature from which *Homo sapiens* is said to have evolved. It could have
been Krull's brother."

"And therein lies the problem," Liebermann said. "We see his face
and are prejudiced immediately. Moreover, the brute does little to
dissuade us otherwise. His manners and toilet are appalling. Did you
see his fingernails?" Liebermann gave a mock, theatrical shudder.
"Yet," he continued, "that is precisely why one must be cautious."

Rheinhardt stopped eating his *strauben* and placed the fork down on
his plate. "With respect, Max," he said slowly, "I'm not altogether sure
what you mean."

Liebermann steepled his fingers. "It is all too easy to see how a
pathetic figure like Krull might come to commit an atrocity: lonely,
impoverished, and disappointed, a man rejected by his peers—and by
women—because of his misbegotten appearance. Embittered, he
angrily rejects society and embraces God, becoming the hapless acolyte
of a fanatical priest. He preys on prostitutes, his violent feelings
vindicated by a religion that urges him to eradicate corruption from
the world. He is well equipped for such a mission, his sensibilities
having been blunted by the daily slaughter of animals. Each murder is
dedicated to his redeemer during a private ceremony—a trophy
having been removed from the corpse and laid among votive candles."

Rheinhardt leaned forward, the skin around his eyes growing
hatched with lines of interest. Liebermann allowed his hands to open.

"Now imagine, if you will, the following: into this dark, desolate,
cold existence comes a vision of compassion. He encounters a woman,
Ludka, who is beautiful and bestows on him an act of kindness. It is a
rare and exquisite pleasure. Her smile is like vernal sunlight. Our man
is torn. He knows that Ludka is a prostitute—an anathema—but for
the first time in years the balm of pity has been applied to his psychic
wounds. He is deeply disturbed: vacillates, ruminates, procrastinates,
and attempts to anesthetize his pain with drink. Eventually he finds a

way to resolve the dreadful conflict, and the psychological defense of rationalization comes into play. He will liberate the poor child from earthly suffering and deliver her to the gates of heaven. He will, in effect, *save her* from a life of sin. When he dispatches Madam Borek and the other two women, his anger is undiluted. He kills them without mercy and mutilates their bodies. Ludka, however, he cannot profane. . . . Her act of kindness sticks in his soul. Her handkerchief will never be far from his heart."

"And what was the trophy, this time? The bodies were mutilated, but none of the body parts were missing."

"Blood," said Liebermann. "He took their blood. Conveniently absorbed into the clothes in his wardrobe."

Liebermann drained his coffee cup.

"Good heavens! It all fits," cried Rheinhardt, suddenly scooping the honey-colored remains of the *tiroler strauben* into his mouth.

"Indeed," continued Liebermann, "such a man might even consecrate his dreadful act by sanctifying the brothel with a cross."

Rheinhardt clapped his hands together. "Yes, of course, that too, that too! It all fits!" However, his excitement could not be sustained in view of the young doctor's sour expression. "Whatever is the matter, Max?"

"It's too obvious. Krull is the . . . *ideal* suspect: a perfect example of Lombroso's *L'uomo delinquente*, whose personal history and psychological conflicts seamlessly correspond with the crime."

Rheinhardt leaned back in his chair and pushed his plate aside. "And what, in God's name, is wrong with that?"

Liebermann shrugged. "Of course, all my theorizing would amount to nothing if we were to discover that Krull had told us the truth about those stains—if the blood isn't human."

"Indeed," said Rheinhardt. "But how on earth could we establish that? Blood is blood—isn't it?"

"Not exactly."

"There is a test?"

"I am not familiar with one—but we both know someone who might be."

"We do?"

"Yes. Miss Lydgate."

Rheinhardt raised his eyebrows. "The Englishwoman. . . . I did not realize that you were still in contact with her."

"She is now conducting research into diseases of the blood with Landsteiner—at the Pathological Institute," Liebermann continued. "If any procedure exists that can distinguish animal blood from human blood, I can assure you that she will know about it."

20

AMELIA LYDGATE POURED THE tea and offered Liebermann some English biscuits.

"My mother sent them from London. She purchased them in Fortnum's."

"Fortnum's?"

"Yes, Fortnum & Mason—a shop of quality in Piccadilly. They are suppliers to the royal family."

"Thank you," said Liebermann, biting through the plain, crisp circle, and cupping his hand to collect the crumbs. The biscuit was flavorless and extremely dry—nothing like the rich, fruity, sugar-coated creations that could be found in any Viennese bakery. Even so, he smiled politely and took a sip of Earl Grey to moisten his mouth.

"It was kind of you to respond so quickly to my note," said Amelia, sitting down on the other side of the gateleg table.

"Not at all," said Liebermann. "You said that you wished for an opinion?"

"Yes," Amelia replied. "Are you familiar with Professor Foch?"

"The surgeon?"

"Yes. I have attended several of his lectures and practical demonstrations—which, on the whole, are highly informative. However, some weeks ago he insisted that I should leave a class because I was clearly about to swoon. This was not the case, but Professor Foch was very determined and I was eventually obliged to comply with his request. We met the following day: he suggested that his lectures might not be suitable for young ladies and proposed that I make alternative arrangements. After making further inquiries, I discovered that Professor Foch has been ejecting women from his classes since the medical faculty began admitting female students two years ago. I subsequently made a formal complaint to the dean." Amelia paused and her brow furrowed. "Dr. Liebermann, do you think my response was appropriate? Or have I behaved rashly?"

"Oh, without a doubt it was the correct thing to do . . . but . . ."

"Yes?"

"A man like Professor Foch wields considerable power among Viennese doctors, and if you decided, on graduation, to specialize in his discipline, I daresay he could make life very difficult for you. However, given that your interests lie elsewhere—and that you already have a well-placed friend in the person of Landsteiner—I suspect that the registration of your complaint will have few, if any, adverse consequences. The dean will now be obliged to reprimand Professor Foch, which one hopes will have the desired effect. But I doubt very much that the dean can be counted on to deliver sanctions. Unfortunately, he too is a misogynist. He once told a colleague that women could never be doctors because they are handicapped by their smaller brains."

Miss Lydgate's hand covered her mouth in horror. "If that is his view, then why should he respond to my complaint at all?"

"Oh, he has no choice. The emperor is very keen on the idea of female doctors. Only an absolute idiot would risk the emperor's displeasure. Miss Lydgate, in Vienna promising careers have been utterly destroyed by a fleeting look of dissatisfaction on the emperor's face, a fleeting look that might—in all likelihood—have been nothing more than a touch of indigestion!"

"Then perhaps I should petition the emperor himself."

Amelia said these words calmly and seriously.

"Well, you *could* do that," said Liebermann, suppressing his surprise. "But I would advise you to delay such a bold course of action. First, let us see how things develop. Even the likes of Professor Foch cannot resist progress indefinitely."

"Thank you, Dr. Liebermann," said Amelia. "You have been most helpful. Could I interest you in another biscuit?"

Liebermann raised his hand a little too hastily. "No, thank you. Most kind—but no, thank you."

"Then, more tea?"

Amelia filled the young doctor's cup and offered him the milk jug.

For some time they discussed Amelia's life at the university and the projects she intended to initiate with Landsteiner at the Pathological Institute. Although her manner was—as always—cool and detached, Liebermann could tell that she was excited by her new life. She enthused, in muted but expressive tones, about the courses she had chosen, a full scientific curriculum including anatomy, botany, chemistry, microscopy, physics, and physiology. She was even attending a few nonscientific lectures in philosophy (having recently been exposed to—and become intrigued by—the writings of Nietzsche).

When they had exhausted these topics, Liebermann asked, "Miss Lydgate . . . I was wondering if you would be willing to assist again with respect to a police matter?"

"Of course. I would be glad to. Is Inspector Rheinhardt well?"

"Yes, very well, thank you. He sends his best wishes."

"You will do me the small service, I hope, of returning the compliment."

Liebermann paused and placed his hands together.

"Miss Lydgate," he began. "Are you aware of what happened in Spittelberg this week?"

"Yes," said Amelia. "Four women were murdered. I read about it in the *Zeitung*."

"Indeed. An atrocity, the likes of which Inspector Rheinhardt and his colleagues at the security office have never encountered before. A man—suspected of the crime—has already been apprehended. Blood-soaked clothes were discovered in his wardrobe but he works in an abattoir and claims that the blood is only pig's blood. Is there any way we can determine the truth or falsehood of his assertion?"

"Yes," said Amelia plainly.

"But how . . ."

"There is a test," said Amelia. "It was developed a few years ago by an assistant professor at the University of Greifswald. I believe he is Viennese by birth: his name is Paul Uhlenhuth."

"The name is not familiar."

"A brilliant man. The procedure requires the production of an antiserum, which can then be used to determine the presence of characteristic precipitates. It has come to be known as the precipitin test."

Liebermann had not really grasped Amelia's short explanation; however, he was too excited to stall his next question on a point of scientific curiosity.

"Miss Lydgate, I imagine that Professor Uhlenhuth must have conducted his work in a laboratory, using samples of fresh blood. Could the same test be used to establish the provenance of blood that is almost a week old?"

"Yes. One simply dissolves the crystals of dried blood in salt water. The test would be just as accurate."

"Could you . . . Can you . . . ?"

"Perform the precipitin test? I would have to reread some of Uhlenhuth's publications, but yes, the fundamental procedures are simple enough."

"What will you need?"

"Some syringes, some test tubes, some human blood, the stained clothing—and . . ." Amelia touched her lips and, looking into the distance, added, "A rabbit."

"I beg your pardon?"

Amelia turned to face Liebermann. There wasn't a trace of humor in her expression. "A rabbit."

"What . . . any rabbit?"

"Yes. Providing it is alive, any rabbit will do."

"Could you conduct the test tomorrow?"

"I could begin the test tomorrow—but producing an antiserum will take two weeks or thereabouts."

"And the results will be conclusive?"

"Absolutely. Now come, Dr. Liebermann—you have had only one biscuit. You really must have another."

Compelled by shame and guilt, Liebermann lifted a pale disc from the proffered plate and, smiling weakly, bit through the dry, thin biscuit with saintly forbearance.

21

THE SEATS IN THE Bösendorfer-Saal were not separated by armrests, and as the music became more turbulent, Clara edged closer to her fiancé. Liebermann bowed his head, catching sight of the hem of her skirt and Clara's small black boots. She casually extended the toe, revealing—as if by accident—the roundness of her ankle. He imagined the appearance of her diminutive feet—which, in fact, he had never seen—the delicate fanning of metatarsal bones beneath translucent, pale skin. Taking her hand, he felt her fingers squeezing tighter with each musical culmination—and their exhausted release when the tension ebbed away. By the time the pianist had brought the recital to its dramatic conclusion, and the audience was responding with applause, the young couple was breathless with excitement.

Liebermann took Clara's arm and followed the other members of the audience out of the Bösendorfer-Saal and onto the busy thorough-fare of Herrengasse. A few gently falling flakes of snow glinted in the beams of the carriage lamps. Liebermann raised his arm to hail an approaching cab.

"No," said Clara. "Let's walk for a while."

"Walk? It's very cold."

"Yes, but I feel like walking."

Clara smiled uncertainly.

"Very well. Which way shall we go?"

"Toward the Volksgarten, then we can cut across to the Burgring. There'll be cabs outside the Court Theater."

They set off slowly, passing a street vendor with a brazier covered in scorched *käsekrainer* sausages.

"Well, did you enjoy it?" asked Liebermann.

"It was wonderful," Clara replied. "I was amazed. She is not a very large woman, yet she produced so much . . . noise!"

"Her technique is faultless. But I suppose that is to be expected from the pupil of such an illustrious teacher."

The pianist—Ilona Eibenschütz—had been a pupil of Clara Wieck. Eibenschütz's program had included a poignant *Romanze* by her mentor, the *Sonata Number 2 in G minor* by her mentor's husband, Robert Schumann, and the *Paganini Variations* by their mutual friend Johannes Brahms. All of the works had been played with extraordinary passion, but Eibenschütz's rendition of the *Paganini Variations* had been truly astonishing: bravura playing of the highest calibre—the virtuoso's hands had become a barely visible blur as they leaped around the keyboard with infernal speed.

"He went mad, didn't he?"

Clara's voice sounded distant. The principal theme of the *Paganini Variations* was still occupying Liebermann's mind, providing the accompaniment to a dark ballet of strange fleshy images. It was like viewing one of Gustav Klimt's paintings through a wineglass.

"Max?"

"I beg your pardon?"

Liebermann realized that Clara had been talking while he had been lost in self-absorption.

"Robert Schumann. Herr Donner told me that Schumann went mad. . . . He—that is, Herr Donner—has been teaching me *Einsame Blumen*, or trying to, at least."

"A charming piece," said Liebermann. "And yes, Herr Donner is quite right. Poor Schumann died in an asylum."

"What was wrong with him?"

"That is a very interesting question. His symptoms have been the subject of much debate in medical circles. He became violent—he suffered from uncontrollable rages—and expressed grandiose ideas. At one point, I believe, he claimed to be in conversation with angels."

They turned into a side street and left the sounds of Herrengasse behind them.

"But why did he go mad? How could such a great mind become so . . . disturbed?"

"Some have suggested that he never went mad at all—and that he was nefariously incarcerated by his wife."

"But why would she do that?"

"In order to facilitate an illicit liaison with Brahms."

Clara's eyes widened with interest. "Is that true?"

"Who knows? I doubt it. There are many independent accounts of Schumann's demise. He was certainly very ill. As to the exact cause . . . well, I did hear a rumor once."

"Oh?"

"A few years ago I met a psychiatrist from Bonn. His father was also a psychiatrist and had once worked in the very same asylum where Schumann died. The old fellow was of the opinion that Schumann had paid the ultimate price . . ." Liebermann broke off and frowned, before continuing, "For an indiscretion of youth."

Clara sighed. "Max. We are to be married. I am to be a doctor's wife. I assume you are referring to syphilis?"

Liebermann smiled.

"Yes, syphilis." He said the word emphatically, but still felt uncomfortable naming the disease in Clara's presence.

"And syphilis causes madness?"

"Yes. It can do."

"But wouldn't his wife . . ."

Liebermann anticipated the obvious question. "Syphilis has a long latency stage. Schumann and Wieck were married many years after the danger of infection had passed."

Their conversation continued in a similar vein for some time. It was unusually muted and measured. So much so that Liebermann was inclined to reflect on the significance of Clara's little admonishment. Was the prospect of their pending marriage making her more thoughtful? More mature? And had he—again—been guilty of treating her like a child?

They entered the Volksgarten. The park had become an enchanted enclave, glittering with frost and moonlight. Low, heavy clouds passed overhead, like enormous sea creatures, and against the yellow luminosity of the city sky loomed the pitch-black classical edifice of the Theseus Temple—an exact replica of its original in Athens. As the couple drew closer, the structure grew more austere and uncanny. They veered toward it as if drawn by some mysterious, compelling charm. Silently, they ascended the steps.

For a moment, they paused and viewed their surroundings. Then they slowly turned to face each other. Clara leaned back against one of the great Doric columns. Her eyes seemed to feed on the darkness, becoming larger. She tilted her head back.

"Max . . ." She said his name softly and reached out. Her fingers found his and she pulled him forward.

They kissed. A prolonged, languid kiss that became—by degrees—more agitated. Clara, ordinarily the passive recipient of her fiancé's amorous advances, responded with an unprecedented hunger, a greedy, sucking osculation. Liebermann's hands swept over her body, eventually discovering a vent through which he explored the warmth and softness beneath her coat. Clara moaned with pleasure.

They pulled apart—both of them shocked by their mutual abandon.

To conceal her shame, Clara buried her head in Liebermann's chest.

"I am sorry," said Liebermann. "Forgive me . . ."

He looked up to the heavens but saw only the underside of the great architrave, from which massive icicles were suspended. He was reminded of the unfortunate Damocles, whose fate it was to attend a banquet seated beneath a sword hanging by a single hair.

"We are to be *married*," said Clara softly. "If you wanted . . . I . . ."

"No," said Liebermann. "No, it would be inexcusable. I will not take advantage of you. I will *never* take advantage of you."

Clara nestled closer. Liebermann lifted his chin to accommodate her head. He could feel the hot pulse of her shallow exhalations on his bare neck. It was intolerably exciting. Even so, he did not move. Instead he stood still, gazing over Clara's hat at the locked, frozen world—his consciousness attenuated painfully between polarities of fire and ice.

22

ANDREAS OLBRICHT STOOD IN the middle of his studio. Condensation had frozen onto the windows, making them opaque and subduing the light. Propped up against the walls were some wooden frames for stretching canvases, some finished paintings, and a large full-length mirror. Olbricht studied his reflected image: a short man, wearing a soft cap and a brown, paint-spattered smock of coarse material. He affected a dignified pose.

The artist embarks upon the act of creation.

His gaze lingered on a smear of vermilion.

Turning, he walked across the bare floorboards to his table, where he examined his array of pigments: ocher, malachite, madder lake, raw sienna. The malachite caught his attention. He tipped some of the emerald powder into the mortar bowl and ground it with a wooden pestle. As he worked, he remembered his conversation with Von Triebenbach about Herr Bolle's commission. What scene from *The Ring* would he choose? The gods engulfed by fire, the ride of the Valkyries, Siegfried's funeral pyre? At that time he had been almost certain that the subject of the commission would be something heroic. Yet, as he worked on the preliminary sketches, another, quite different scene kept entering his mind—the tableau with which *The Ring Cycle* opens: the three Rhine maidens—Woglinde, Wellgunde, and Flosshilde—and the dwarf Alberich. This scene had kept on returning, asserting itself with something close to willfulness.

Eventually he conceded, content to assume that a great work of art was struggling to be born.

Olbricht mixed some linseed oil into the powdered malachite and poured the mixture onto his palette. Then he turned and looked at the large canvas on his easel. The work was in its very early stages. Only the top left-hand corner had been colored with brushstrokes; the rest was still in sketch form. The figures had been executed using a red crayon, and Olbricht congratulated himself that the effect was not unlike a well-known Leonardo da Vinci cartoon.

On the table, next to the pestle and mortar, was a notebook in which he had copied out some of Wagner's original stage directions.

In the depths of the river Rhine.

A greenish twilight, brighter toward the top, darker toward the bottom. The upper part is filled with swirling waters. . . . In all directions steep rocky reefs rear up from the depths. . . . There is a reef in the middle of the stage that points a slender finger up into the denser water where the light is brighter. . . .

Olbricht diluted his malachite with a few more drops of linseed oil and mixed it in with a stiff hog's-hair brush.

He was pleased with his Rhine maidens. They looked like good-natured, big-hearted German girls. Healthy, buxom, and carefree—possessed of an innocent charm. If the same scene had been treated by one of the Secessionists, it would have looked very different indeed. Someone like Klimt (or one of his degenerate associates) would have transformed the Rhine maidens into emaciated, orgiastic water nymphs, naked, with tiny breasts and exposed genitalia. The modernists were incapable of dignifying the female form—they could only degrade it. Their work was obscene.

Herr Bolle was a sensible man—a man who cherished traditional values. He would want his Rhine maidens to be stolid, chaste, and pure.

In a rocky hollow, Olbricht had sketched what would eventually become a giant nugget of gold. He considered the pigments he would use: lead-tin yellow, lead white, and iron oxide. He imagined how the amber glow would penetrate into the dark green depths. He let his gaze drop and allowed it to settle on the figure of Alberich—the Nibelung dwarf—climbing out of a dark rift in the riverbed.

The Rhine maidens were the guardians of the *Rheingold*, sacred treasure from which might be fashioned a ring that would give the wearer ultimate power. But, so the legend ran, such power could be achieved only by first renouncing love. The Rhine maidens were negligent in the exercise of their duty, because they believed that no thief would be prepared to pay such a high price. Who would possibly forswear the joys of love in exchange for earthly power?

Olbricht took a step closer to the canvas and squatted to look more intently at the dwarf who was clawing his way out of the crevice like a venomous reptile—his bulging-eyed stare fixed on the giant nugget.

Was it so remarkable that a creature spurned, taunted, and considered misshapen should have any difficulty making such an exchange? Love for power?

It was not *so* remarkable.

23

HERMANN ASCHENBRANDT SAT IN a wicker chair next to the piano, listening intently. The prospective pupil had written to Aschenbrandt after he had heard the composer's D minor String Quintet ("The Invincible") performed at the Tonkünstlerverein. The letter had been full of enthusiastic praise, and the young man had expressed a keen desire to begin composition lessons as soon as possible. Aschenbrandt agreed to an initial meeting, but now that his admirer was seated next to him at the piano, Aschenbrandt was not altogether sure that Herr Behn's musical instincts and his own were similar after all. It had been a very misleading letter.

The young man was halfway through his Fantasia in B-flat Major. The piece had begun with an improvisatory first movement, vaguely reminiscent of Chopin. But then it had evolved—through some tortured key changes—into a torpid, directionless adagio. The melody meandered over a muddy bass, and its fussy turns and grace notes suggested the east: not the East of the Arabs or the Chinese but the more local east of Hungary, Galicia, and Transylvania. Aschenbrandt was finding it slightly irritating, like a mosquito complaining in his ear.

"Yes, yes . . . ," he said impatiently, pushing back a fine strand of white-blond hair. "I understand. Perhaps we could now hear the final movement?"

Behn's fingers slowed and he took his hands off the keyboard.

"Oh, there is an interesting modulatory passage—in just a few bars." He began to turn the sheets of manuscript nervously.

"Herr Behn," said Aschenbrandt tartly. "The last movement, if you would."

"Yes," said the young man. "I'm sorry. Of course."

Behn found the appropriate page and began playing. Again, the music sounded like Chopin. However, Aschenbrandt could not help noticing how the melody persistently struggled to escape from its harmonic ground. It pitched and tumbled around the very edges of tonality—like the undisciplined and frantic scrapings of a gypsy fiddler! Aschenbrandt made a closer study of Behn's physiognomy.

Behn was a small, thin man, with sloping shoulders. His complexion was definitely swarthy, and those eyebrows . . . the way they almost touched in the middle. Yes, it was all beginning to make sense.

Aschenbrandt listened for a few more minutes and found that he could no longer tolerate the dissonances. He clapped his hands together.

"Thank you—thank you, Herr Behn!"

The young man stopped playing and, assuming that Aschenbrandt wanted to hear more examples of his work, lifted another score from the pile that he had deposited on the piano.

"Three romantic songs?" he said, his voice rising with expectancy.

Aschenbrandt smiled coldly, and let the clenched fist of his right hand land gently in the cupped palm of his left. Behn realized that his suggestion had not been warmly received and silently replaced the manuscript.

"Tell me, Herr Behn," said Aschenbrandt slowly. "Which composers do you admire?"

"Well . . . apart from yourself, Maestro Aschenbrandt, I very much enjoy the music of Karl Prohaska. I heard his *Fourth String Quartet* last year, performed by the Fitners. I thought it was an excellent piece—so accomplished. And Woss—I adore his symphonic poem *Sakuntala*."

"But, Herr Behn, these are not, by any stretch of the imagination, significant composers."

Behn paused for a moment, adjusted his spectacles, and said, "Goldmark, Alexander Zemlinsky, and Director Mahler, of course. His second symphony is surely a masterpiece."

Yes, the position was becoming increasingly clear.

"I am afraid, Herr Behn, that I must disagree with you on both counts. None of these gentlemen are composers of significance, and I can assure you that the director's second symphony is no masterpiece. If you think so, you are very much mistaken."

"Oh . . . ," said Behn.

"It is not a symphony but an incoherent, poorly structured ragbag of ideas linked by an infantile program. As Wagner wisely pointed out, Beethoven took the symphony to its absolute eminence. Only the most stupid—or immodest—individual would seek to advance the symphony beyond Beethoven!"

"I see," said Behn, tugging nervously at his cuffs.

"Herr Behn," Aschenbrandt continued, "I must be frank with you. I am not overly impressed by your work. You are a competent musician, and some of your harmonic progressions show ingenuity, but you do not possess that indefinable quality, that vital spark, that *gift*, which distinguishes the true composer, the true artist, from the tunesmith, the dilettante."

"But . . ." Behn's cheeks flushed. "Maestro Aschenbrandt, surely, under your tutelage, I could—"

"No," Aschenbrandt interrupted coldly. "I cannot accept you as a pupil." Behn raised his foliate eyebrows. "Please understand, Herr Behn, I would be doing you a great disservice if I encouraged you to pursue a career in music that was destined to fail. You are at present studying law, and if you apply yourself diligently, I am sure you can look forward to a lucrative career in the Justizpalast. Let music be your pastime, your pleasure. . . ."

"But music is my *life*." Behn raised his hands helplessly. "I want to compose."

"I am sorry, Herr Behn. I cannot accept you as a pupil."

Behn shook his head and, gathering his scores together, slipped them into his leather briefcase.

Aschenbrandt stood, picked up a small handbell, and rang it loudly.

"Elga will show you to the door."

A few moments later a serving woman appeared.

"Good-bye, Herr Aschenbrandt. I am—you will understand— very disappointed. But I am also of the opinion that men of talent must be true to their calling. I respect your honesty."

"Indeed," said Aschenbrandt.

The rejected pupil walked to the door.

"Herr Behn," Aschenbrandt called out.

The student stopped and looked back into the room.

"You could always try Zemlinsky. . . ."

Behn nodded and left the room.

Aschenbrandt wiped the piano stool with his handkerchief, sat down, and began to play the opening chords of a new baritone aria— *Victory shall be ours*. It was to be the main set piece in the first act of *Carnuntum*. When Aschenbrandt lowered his hands, a charm bracelet appeared from beneath the sleeve of his jacket. Among the small objects attached to the silver chain was an effigy of a man in a kaftan suspended from a gibbet. It represented a hanging Jew.

24

CAFÉ IMPERIAL: FRETTING WAITERS, gesticulating patrons, and the peal and crash of cutlery.

The pianist had just finished playing a Strauss polka, and after a moment's rest he began a breezy popular melody.

"What's this?" asked Mendel.

"*The Skaters' Waltz*," said Liebermann. "Waldteufel."

"See?" said Mendel to Jacob Weiss. "He knows them all."

Liebermann was sitting opposite his father and future father-in-law. Their conversation had briefly touched upon the subject of wedding arrangements—but not for very long. The three men were content to leave such matters in the hands of their wives (and the bride-to-be).

A waiter arrived with a tray full of coffee and cakes: a Viennese walnut-and-apple torte topped with waves of cream and sprinkled with cinnamon and silver pearls, some poppy seed strudel, and a thick spongy wedge of *guglhupf*.

"Thank you, Bruno," said Mendel.

The waiter deposited the order on the table, clicked his heels, and excused himself.

Mendel was soon talking business. "I've been thinking about another factory for some time. Now that our families share a common interest"—he nodded toward his son—"perhaps, Jacob, we should consider a joint venture."

"Are you still talking to Blomberg?" Jacob asked, digging his fork into a moist pillow of strudel.

"Yes," said Mendel. "His department store is still doing very well. He's been trying to interest me in a partnership for a while now, but I'm not sure. Redlich says he can't be trusted."

"Redlich?"

"Owns the sugar refinery in Göding."

"Oh yes, *that* Redlich!"

"Even so, a department store on Kärntner Strasse couldn't possibly fail—whatever you think of Blomberg."

Herr Weiss nodded and asked a few questions about ground rent, surcharges, and interest rates.

Liebermann scooped the cream off his torte, tilted his fork, and let the silver pearls catch the light. They were perfect spheres of different sizes and flashed like stars. When he became aware of his father's voice again, he realized that he must have been distracted for some time.

". . . A cousin of mine, Selma, married a Pole called Kinsky." Mendel speared a chunk of *guglhupf* and raised it. "They emigrated eight years ago, to a place in England called Manchester. We still correspond regularly. They have two little boys, Peter and Robert, and their import-export business is thriving. Now, the thing is, they want to expand, and they need a large capital investment. I'm sure I could negotiate favorable terms." Mendel placed the cake in his mouth and chewed vigorously. "I don't know about you," he continued, speaking with his mouth full. A few crumbs tumbled into his long beard. "But I'm very keen to get a foothold somewhere else—somewhere less volatile. Every time the politicians mess things up, the people go looking for a scapegoat. . . ."

"You sound like Herzl!" said Liebermann.

"Well, what if I do?"

"When Herzl visits the theater nowadays," said Liebermann, "he's greeted with cries of 'Welcome, Your Majesty!'"

Jacob Weiss looked puzzled.

Liebermann leaned a little closer and said, "It's because of Kraus—the journalist. He described Herzl in *Die Fackel* as the king of Zion."

Mendel shook his head and began tutting loudly. "Herzl has a much better grasp of the *situation* here than you realize."

"Father . . . ," said Liebermann. "Vienna is our home. Our language is German, not Hebrew, and I don't want to live in Palestine!"

Mendel glanced at his old friend. "We can remember Schönerer's thugs marching up Taborstrasse. . . . That's something you don't forget, my boy. Believe me!"

Liebermann reached across the table and squeezed the old man's hand. "I know there are problems, Father. But we are living in better times." He looked at Herr Weiss, smiled, and then looked back at his father. "You worry too much." They were the same words that Konrad had used a few weeks earlier.

"The younger generation," said Weiss, shrugging his shoulders. Although these words were offered as nothing more than neutral observation, they seemed curiously explanatory.

"Eat your cake," said Mendel, pointing at his son's walnut-and-apple torte. "You've hardly touched it."

25

CAFÉ HAYNAU WAS ONLY a few minutes' walk from the barracks and as a result was much frequented by military men. The landlord, who had developed a weakness for vodka since the death of his wife, was rarely present; however, his two dutiful daughters were always prepared to take charge in his absence. Neither of them could be described as pretty, but both possessed generous figures and showed a willingness to flirt, albeit playfully, with the soldiers. The elder of the two daughters, Mathilde, fancied herself a chanteuse and would often sing mawkish ballads, accompanied by an old accordion player.

Lieutenant Robert Renz and Second Lieutenant Christian Trapp were seated at their usual table, playing a drawn-out game of taroc. Through an archway they could see a billiard table around which a large crowd of cavalrymen had gathered. An ensign was creating something of a stir by beating the regimental doctor, a man who had not been defeated for a month. A cheer went up as the ensign sent another ball into a pocket. The doctor looked on, pulling at the sharp point of his neatly trimmed beard.

Ruprecht Hefner burst through the door and marched directly over to the table occupied by Renz and Trapp. He sat down on one of the spare chairs, took a slug of schnapps straight from his comrades' bottle, and said, "I am glad you're here. I need you to do something for me."

Renz and Trapp looked at each other and laid down their cards.

"What?" asked Renz, slowly.

"A favor," Hefner replied. "Do you know Freddi Lemberg?"

"No."

"Alfred Lemberg's son. Lemberg—the industrialist!" Renz showed no sign of recognition. "Oh, it doesn't matter. I ran into Lemberg junior at the opera—*Siegfried*, a very good performance conducted by that ape Mahler. They say Jews can't understand Wagner, but he makes you wonder. Anna von Mildenburg was wonderful. I think I'm falling in love with her! They say she had an affair with him, you know?"

"Who, Lemberg?" asked Renz.

"No, Mahler, you fool!"

"So what's all this about Lemberg?"

"Yes, right. I ran into him after Act Two, and he was most disagreeable. Having been stirred by the drama, I was in no mood for his nonsense and our exchanges became somewhat heated. The outcome of which was that Lemberg demanded satisfaction. Of course, I said that I was happy to oblige. Tarnoploski was with him and begged us both to reconsider. But Lemberg had clearly made up his mind. What could I do?"

"You could have quoted the Waidhofen manifesto," said Trapp. "A Jew is born without honor, and therefore is not entitled to demand satisfaction."

Hefner dismissed Trapp's counsel with a disdainful wave of the hand. A gasp came from the billiard room, and Renz was momentarily distracted.

"Pay attention," said Hefner, tapping the surface of the table. "I want you to go to Café Mozart."

"What, now?" asked Renz.

"Yes, now," said Hefner. "There you will find Lemberg's seconds." Hefner produced a scrap of paper and read some names. "Fritz Glöckner and Gerhard Riehl. I want you to accept whatever conditions they propose: sabres, pistols—it's all the same to me. He'll be incapable of handling either—although he's supposed to be a very good violinist, so I'm told."

"But what was it all about? Your quarrel?" asked Trapp, pouring himself another schnapps.

"Oh, something . . . something I'm supposed to have done last summer."

Hefner removed his cap and ran a hand through his thick blond hair. Mathilde noticed him from the other side of the room and waved. Hefner inclined his head and smiled graciously.

"Go on," said Renz.

"He thinks I took advantage of his wife," Hefner continued. "I was staying at Schloss von Triebenbach on the Kammersee, as a guest of the baron. The Lembergs had rented a villa just outside the village. His wife was convalescing from some kind of nervous illness. . . ." For a moment Hefner played with the gold-yellow tassel hanging from his pommel. "She was often left on her own. Freddi and his friends used to take the steamer across the lake to Weyregg. I paid her my respects a few times, that's all. . . ."

An ambiguous smile flitted across his handsome face.

There was a sudden round of applause from the billiard room. Cavalrymen were congratulating the regimental doctor, who had—to the ensign's dismay—secured another victory.

"I'd better have a word with him too," said Hefner, gesturing toward the medical man. "I'll catch him now—while he's in a good mood. Then I'm off to bed, where I will no doubt dream of Mildenburg carrying me off to Valhalla!" Rising abruptly, he called out, "Doctor, Doctor! Well done! You are in danger of becoming a legend. Please, could I trouble you for a moment—in private?"

26

THE SCHOTTENRING POLICE LABORATORY was a spacious rectangular room with high leaded windows. Outside, the dense cloud cover had broken and the air was suffused with bright winter sunshine. Amelia Lydgate was standing by a long workbench, holding a test tube up to the light. Her hair had been pulled back and arranged in a large reticulated bun. Yet even this drastic measure could not diminish the reflective power of those densely compressed copper strands. A reddish spectrum revealed itself as she tilted her head.

She was wearing a plain white high-collared blouse and a long gray skirt that almost touched the floor. Liebermann allowed his gaze to drop down her spine and linger around her hips. A feeling of excitement flared in the pit of his stomach, followed by a hammer blow of shame. He looked away and found himself staring at the twitching nose of a plump brown rabbit.

"Well, Miss Lydgate?" asked Rheinhardt.

Amelia turned and stood facing the two men. As usual, her expression betrayed no sign of emotion.

"A precipitate has not formed."

"Which means?" asked Rheinhardt.

"The blood on Krull's clothes is not human."

Rheinhardt puffed his cheeks out and let the air escape slowly. "I see."

A lengthy silence ensued and Liebermann laid a consoling hand on his friend's sleeve.

"Forgive me, Miss Lydgate," Rheinhardt continued, "but are you absolutely sure?"

"I am quite sure, Inspector."

"There is no chance that this test could produce an erroneous result?"

"No."

Her perceptive gaze registered the detective's disappointment.

"Inspector, allow me to explain the procedure again." Although Amelia Lydgate's manners were faultless, a hint of impatience had crept into her voice. "If human blood is injected into a live rabbit over a two-week period, then the rabbit's blood acquires a specific property: it will react with any human blood to form a precipitate. This is because these frequent injections of human blood have promoted a defensive response in the rabbit's blood. I have been injecting this rabbit"—she gestured toward the cage—"with samples of my own blood for several weeks, and the animal's blood is now an antiserum. It will recognize the unique proteins in human blood and react with them to form a precipitate."

Amelia approached Rheinhardt and held the test tube up in front of his eyes. The contents appeared to glow in the bright light of the laboratory.

"It is clear, Inspector. If the blood on Krull's clothes had been human blood, the serum would have become cloudy. Professor Uhlenhuth's precipitin test may be simple, but it is entirely reliable."

Rheinhardt nodded. "Thank you, Miss Lydgate, thank you. Once again, the security office is indebted to you."

"My pleasure, Inspector Rheinhardt."

The detective took a deep breath and walked over to the rabbit cage.

"Of course," said Liebermann softly, "this doesn't mean that Krull is innocent."

"No," said Rheinhardt, "but the evidence is certainly stacking up in his favor. The medical student who lives below Krull has confessed to being a member of a fraternity whose initiation practices involve the theft of body parts from the morgue!"

"Explaining the presence of the metacarpal bone."

"It would seem so." The inspector leaned forward, poked a finger through the grill of the cage, and scratched the rabbit's furry head. "And it's a bad day for you too," he said to the creature, in a somewhat distracted fashion.

"Oh?" exclaimed Amelia. "Why is that, Inspector?"

"Commissioner Brügel asked me to notify him when the test was completed. He fancied his cook could make this poor fellow into a fine stew."

Amelia Lydgate's brow furrowed. "With respect, Inspector, I would ask that the commissioner reconsider his position. That rabbit is the *only* animal in Vienna whose blood serum reacts with human proteins. With regular injections he will continue to be reactive. You should retain him as an invaluable member of the scientific staff."

Rheinhardt almost smiled, but recognized—just in time—that Miss Lydgate was deadly serious.

"Of course," he said. "I will see if there is a relevant form. Perhaps I could register him as a junior technician."

Amelia Lydgate's brow lost a furrow or two—as demonstrative a sign of satisfaction as could be expected, given the peculiarities of her temperament. Rheinhardt stole a quick glance in Liebermann's direction and rolled his eyes. The young doctor tried not to laugh, but found to his great embarrassment that his shoulders were shaking.

* * *

By early evening Rheinhardt had finished writing his report—to which he appended an official "registration" document. It identified Miss Lydgate's rabbit as a new member of the security-office staff, occupying the position of laboratory assistant. His little joke had proved prophetic. In Austria-Hungary, nothing was deemed so insignificant or inconsequential that it did not warrant recording, licensing, or an official stamp of some kind.

One day this empire will disappear under an avalanche of paperwork!

Rheinhardt stretched, yawned, rose from his desk, and switched off the light.

He was feeling tired, and he decided to clear the fug from his head by walking home instead of taking a cab. The sky had remained cloudless all day, and now the temperature was plummeting. A sharp wind scoured his cheeks, but Rheinhardt was determined to persevere. He passed a streetcar stop, where several gentlemen were waiting in a line, and turned onto the concourse in front of the town hall. It was a broad, open space, divided by an avenue of gas lamps. The flames emitted a yellow sulfurous glow, which was sufficient to illuminate the town hall itself—Rheinhardt's favorite building in Vienna.

"Magical." He spoke the word aloud, while slowing to admire the prospect.

It was like something out of a fairy story: a Gothic palace consisting of a massive central structure—as big as a cathedral—and five spires. The central spire rose much higher than its companions, and on its summit stood a statue of a medieval knight in full armor. He was barely visible on his lofty perch, but Rheinhardt could determine his shadowy presence against a background of glittering, spiteful stars. The overall impression of the building was one of great intricacy. One could see lanterns, finials, arched mullioned windows, buttresses, and several pitched roofs. It was a glorious sight—made even more glorious by a dressing of niveous garlands. Rheinhardt enjoyed having it all to himself.

He bid the knight good evening, walked around the town hall, and headed off into the backstreets of Josefstadt.

It had been a disappointing day.

If only that test had proved positive . . .

If only, if only . . .

When Rheinhardt arrived at his apartment building, he climbed the stone steps leading to the first floor. His heavy footfall announced his arrival. Before he reached the top of the stairs, the door of his apartment flew open, revealing his wife, Else.

"There you are!" she cried. "Where have you been?"

"At work," said Rheinhardt.

"The security office called. . . ."

"But I've only just left Schottenring!"

"They said you'd been gone for some time."

"Well, that's true, I suppose. I decided to walk home."

Else's expression vacillated between anger and relief.

"I was worried," she said finally.

"Well, there was no need to be," said Rheinhardt, ascending the last few stairs and planting a kiss on his wife's forehead. "What did they want?"

"You must go to the Ruprechtskirche."

"Now?"

"Yes. There's been another murder."

27

THE VENERABLE WAS SEATED on the master's chair, a beautiful throne of carved oak. It was thought to have been made in Scotland around 1690 and given as a gift to one of the earliest Viennese lodges—perhaps even Aux Trois Canons, the very first. He ran his fingers over the carved arm and traced the lines of a raised pentalpha, the Pythagorean symbol of perfection. The five-pointed star was held between twin compasses.

From his vantage, the venerable could look through the body of the Temple toward the entrance. Two great bronze doors were flanked by Corinthian pillars, denominated J and B for Jachin and Boaz—evoking the two columns built by Hiram at the gates of the Temple of Solomon. Above these was a relief equilateral triangle, from within which a single all-seeing eye coldly contemplated the empty pews. On the east wall a mural awaited completion. When finished, it would show the Ark of the Covenant, and Jacob's ladder ascending toward the Hebrew symbol Yod. *There is no rush*, he thought. *We still have plenty of time to prepare.* . . .

The venerable raised himself from the chair and walked down the center aisle. Stopping to turn off the gas lamps, he slowly made his way toward the entrance. He pushed one of the bronze doors open and took one of two oil lamps that were hanging from hooks in the wall. The vestibule was relatively small, with two adjoining staircases: one ascending, the other descending. The venerable took the stairs going down—a tight spiral of stone wedges that sank deep into the earth. When he reached the bottom of the stairs, he found himself in another antechamber, illuminated by light that was spilling from a half-open door.

"Ah, still here, brother?" the venerable called out.

"Yes," came the reply. "Still here."

The venerable pushed the door, which emitted a loud creaking. It opened by degrees to reveal a rectangular room, considerably smaller than the Temple. The walls were almost totally obscured by bookcases, although much of the shelving was unfilled. In the middle of the room were several crates. Two of them were empty and the third contained a collection of leather-bound volumes. A man—seated at a desk nearby—was leaning over and lifting books from the half-full crate, examining them, and carefully entering their details in a large register.

"All of them have arrived safely?" asked the venerable.

"Yes, I think so."

"Good." The venerable looked down at his pocket watch. "It's getting late, brother. You should go home."

The librarian lifted his head, placed his pen on the table, and stretched his arms. "It's the last crate. I may as well finish."

The venerable smiled and approached the desk. He picked up the book that the librarian was in the process of recording, and examined the spine. It read: *Journal für Freymaurer, 1784–1786, Volume IV.*

"Do we have all twelve volumes?" asked the venerable.

"Of course," said the librarian.

"Excellent," said the venerable, stroking the binding. "All of the *Truth and Unity* papers. It will be an invaluable addition to our collection."

The librarian picked up his pen again and began to scratch another entry into his register. The venerable was about to leave, but was momentarily distracted by a book lying open and facedown on the desk. He picked it up and glanced at a mezzotint illustration. Beneath the picture was a caption: *Schaffer's design reproducing Schikaneder's staging.*

The illustration showed a snake cut into three sections.

Part Two

The Realm of Night

28

Rheinhardt did not feel comfortable in the morgue. Even when its hollow emptiness was enlivened by the sound of human voices it remained a forbidding, misanthropic place. For the umpteenth time he curled his finger into the fob pocket of his vest and tugged the chain. The hands on the watch face had hardly moved.

Where is he?

Suspended from the ceiling was an electric light. Its beam was directed by means of a low conical shade onto sheets, the topography of which suggested a recumbent human form. Beyond this concise column of illumination was an impenetrable expanse of darkness.

The cold was excruciating but Rheinhardt had given up blowing into his locked fingers. He had accepted that the nagging ache in his joints would in due course become a singing pain. Thereafter, he could only hope for the unsatisfactory solace of an anesthetic numbness.

The dense silence—so compressed that it had become tintinnabulary—was ringing in Rheinhardt's ears. He began to whistle a jaunty spirit-rallying tune of his own devising. When he reached the end of the second phrase, the caesura was filled by a long, protracted groan. Disconcertingly, it came from nearby. The faint yet disturbing rise and fall of the mortuary sheets confirmed that it was the corpse who had produced this mournful sound.

Rheinhardt was gripped by a paralyzing jolt of fear. His head pulsed and his heart knocked against the wall of his chest.

Is he still alive?

Impossible!

Rheinhardt ripped the uppermost cover off, revealing the face of a man in his fifties. It was a broad Slavic face, with high cheekbones and swept-back greasy hair. The blue lips were parted. Rheinhardt nervously placed the palm of his hand over the corpse's mouth but felt nothing.

"What on earth do you think you're doing, Rheinhardt?"

The inspector jumped. "Oh, Professor Mathias."

The pathologist shuffled in and took off his hat and coat. "What's the matter? You look like you've seen a ghost!"

"He groaned," said Rheinhardt, gesturing toward the body. "I swear it. He *groaned*—like this." Rheinhardt produced a plaintive moan.

"It's the gases, Inspector—the compounds released as the bacteria get to work on his last meal. They rise up and stimulate the voice box."

Mathias hung up his coat and hat and took an apron down from a row of pegs. After slipping the top loop over his head, the old man tied the dangling side cords behind his back and shuffled over to the table.

"Good evening, sir," he addressed the corpse. "And who—might I ask—do I have the pleasure of addressing?"

"His name is Evzen Vanek," Rheinhardt replied.

"A Czech?"

"Yes. He was carrying his papers. He sold chickens at the meat market."

"Where was he found?"

"Near the Ruprechtskirche."

"New to Vienna?"

"Arrived two months ago."

"Ah, Evzen." The professor brushed the man's hair with his fingers.

"You should have stayed at home. . . . *Was not our citadel long undermined/Already by the Realm of Night?*" The professor, his rheumy eyes bulging behind thick lenses, looked up at Rheinhardt. "Well, Inspector?"

"I don't know."

"It was Schiller, Rheinhardt. 'Melancholy.' That should have been child's play!"

Mathias tutted and hobbled over to his cart, where he began a ritual with which Rheinhardt was all too familiar. The professor rolled up his shirtsleeves and proceeded to arrange and rearrange his instruments. A scoop was transferred from the bottom to the top shelf, via the second and third. A clamp was demoted. The largest drill was raised, examined, and then put back in exactly the same place.

"He was stabbed in the chest," said Rheinhardt.

"Shhh!" Mathias pushed a vertical palm toward Rheinhardt as though repelling the interruption. He contemplated his array of instruments, and carefully placed a chisel next to a line of scalpels. "There we are," he said—as if the elusive solution to a long-standing problem had suddenly presented itself. Turning to Rheinhardt, he added, "What was that you said?"

"He was stabbed in the chest."

The professor turned the sheets back, revealing the upper half of the body. Vanek's shirt was dark, but the bloodstains were clearly visible. A vent showed where the blade had entered. The acrid smell of ammonia rose from the corpse's nether regions.

Mathias tried to undo the top button but the task was impossible. It was embedded in a crust of congealed blood. The old man inspected the gritty stains on his fingertips and lifted a giant pair of scissors from the cart. With workaday efficiency he cut the shirt from collar to hem and pulled the stiff cloth away. Two strips of chest hair were removed in the process. Rheinhardt averted his gaze. The sight and sound of the depilation was quite nauseating.

"Was he married?" asked Mathias.

"No."

"Then let us thank God for small mercies," said the pathologist.

Beneath the uncompromising light Vanek's wound was vivid: an angry red ellipse caked with a granular black excrescence.

Without looking back at the cart, Mathias reached out and snatched a magnifying glass from the second shelf. He leaned over the corpse and peered through the wide steel hoop.

"Interesting . . . ," he muttered. "Very interesting. Could you please step back a little, Inspector—you're stealing my precious light." Reinhardt complied with the pathologist's request. "A stab wound— of course," continued Mathias, "but somewhat irregular. The blade of a knife—properly so called—has a back and one cutting edge. The weapon used upon this gentleman had *two* cutting edges."

"A sword?"

"Patience, Rheinhardt: *festina lente*."

The old man carefully insinuated his fingers into the wound— a maneuver that was accomplished with the knowing sensitivity of a young lover. He closed his eyes and seemed to be entering a necromantic trance. Mathias swayed gently and mumbled to himself. In the sharp electric light, his exhalations became rolling white clouds that gathered over the corpse. He was like a medium, belching ectoplasm. Between each breath the old man's mumbling was disturbed by his asthmatic lungs, which produced an eerie harmonium-like accompaniment as the freezing air tormented his constricted bronchi.

"A sabre wound," he said softly. "A common sabre, not a Turkish one—which has a much more pronounced curvature. The blade was pushed through the sternum, through the pericardium, and reached the back of the heart." The professor opened his eyes and withdrew his fingers. They trailed a gory mucoid residue.

"The same as in Spittelberg." Rheinhardt's voice was flat.

"What?"

"The Spittelberg murders. The women . . . you said that their wounds were most probably inflicted with a sabre."

"Did I?"

"Yes."

Mathias seemed distracted—unwilling to make eye contact.

"Do you think it was the same weapon?"

"Poor Evzen," said Mathias, looking up at the Czech's solemn, almost noble mask of repose. The pathologist's movements were now less fluid, and his limbs seemed to have become ossified. He froze in an awkward attitude, as if—by some strange fluke of nature—he had contracted rigor mortis from the corpse.

"Professor Mathias?" Rheinhardt ventured.

"How many more times?" snapped the old man. "Always trying to rush me!"

Mathias's expression slowly changed. The lines of his face created mosaics that shifted to suggest first compassion, then surprise, and finally curiosity.

The pathologist edged up the table and peered more closely at the dead man's face. His head swung over the corpse, and immediately traced a large figure of eight. There was something feral about his sudden agitation—like a forest animal sniffing out a buried winter hoard.

"Professor!" Rheinhardt insisted. "I would be most grateful if—"

"Look there," Mathias interrupted, completely indifferent to Rheinhardt's rising impatience. "Some slight bruising around the neck." Then, more quietly, to himself, "But he hasn't been strangled."

In a louder voice he added, "There is also something wrong with the cervical region. The laryngeal prominence is somewhat distended."

Rheinhardt did not possess a great deal of medical knowledge but he knew enough to try. "Goiter, perhaps?"

Mathias responded with a disdainful look and returned his attention to the corpse. "Pardon me, sir," he excused himself, and proceeded to feel under the dead man's stubbly chin. He pressed the throat on both sides and suddenly withdrew his hands as if he had been burned. "Good heavens!"

Not wishing to invite yet another admonishment, Rheinhardt suppressed the urge to ask the professor what he had discovered.

Mathias removed a rubber stop from the cart and handed it to Rheinhardt. Then he pried open Vanek's mouth, an action that produced a loud, liquid "clop." Holding the maxilla and mandible apart with both hands, Mathias said, "Inspector, could you please wedge the jaw open?"

The dead man's rotting teeth appeared as his lips retracted. Rheinhardt could see the pink roof of his mouth and a pendulous uvula. He did not want his fingers to make contact with the lifeless flesh.

"Come on, Inspector!" huffed Mathias.

As it was the professor's frequent habit to chastise Rheinhardt for being hasty, the Inspector's impulse to make an acerbic comment was almost overwhelming. Fortunately, good sense prevailed, and Rheinhardt obediently pushed the rubber stop between the Czech's teeth.

"Thank you," said Mathias.

"My pleasure," said Rheinhardt, producing a profoundly disingenuous smile.

The old man shuffled over to his cart and found some oddly shaped forceps. Then he returned directly to the head of the table and peered down Vanek's throat.

"So . . . ," he said, producing a puff of condensation. "Let us solve this mystery."

Mathias inserted the forceps into Vanek's mouth and tutted a few times, seemingly frustrated by the complexity of the action he was trying to perform. After a few abortive attempts, his expression relaxed and he began to withdraw the instrument.

"Extraordinary," said Mathias, raising the forceps up to the light.

Rheinhardt blinked. He could not have been more surprised. Not even if he had been standing in an exhibition tent on the Prater bearing witness to a particularly impressive piece of prestidigitation. For there, gripped between the closed bills of Professor Mathias's forceps, was a common padlock.

"Well, what do you make of that, Rheinhardt?"

The inspector was speechless.

"I dare say," continued Mathias, "that the presence of this object might explain the phenomenon you described earlier. Perhaps it allowed the gases to pass more freely past the vocal cords."

"What on earth does it signify?" Rheinhardt gasped, a note of panic shaking every syllable of his exclamation.

Mathias shook his head. "Of course, if the murderer were deranged enough to secrete one object . . ."

The pathologist raised his eyebrows, pursed his lips together, and produced a long interrogative "Mmm?"

"I'm sorry?" said Rheinhardt, recovering just enough firmness of purpose to simulate composure. "What are you suggesting?"

"Merely," said Mathias, "that it would be prudent to examine our unfortunate friend more thoroughly. We should take a look in his stomach—and inspect the contents of his rectum, of course."

Rheinhardt coughed. "If you don't mind, Herr Professor, I would prefer to take a cigar outside while you . . ."

"Complete the autopsy?"

"Indeed."

"Do as you please—it's all the same to me. I'll call you if I find anything interesting."

Rheinhardt walked across the stone flags, but before leaving, he stole a quick glance back into the morgue. There was Mathias, standing in his circle of icy light, preparing to embark upon a bizarre corporeal treasure hunt. Misty exhalations poured out of his mouth like dragon's breath. The pathologist had become quite animated, his movements quickened by an eagerness—a childlike enthusiasm and excitement—that made Rheinhardt feel distinctly uncomfortable.

In the corridor outside the mortuary, Rheinhardt rested his back against the damp wall and took out a Trabuco cheroot. He struck a match and allowed the end to burn.

Sabre wounds . . . a crooked cross . . . a padlock.

This is the work of the same man.

Karsten Krull is entirely innocent, and the maniac is still at large.

For the first time, Rheinhardt worried about the safety of his family.

29

THE ROOM WAS OPULENT: chandeliers, heavy drapes, gilt furniture, and a selection of Biedermeier oils. Gustav von Triebenbach was standing by a plinth, which supported a white marble bust of Richard Wagner. There were many guests—not all of them fully fledged members of the Richard Wagner Association but all committed to the cause. In the far corner of the room was a gleaming Steinway piano. Behind it sat Hermann Aschenbrandt and another young musician. They were playing a four-hands arrangement of Strauss's *Morgenblätter*.

Von Triebenbach sipped his champagne and surveyed the scene. He recognized several important dignitaries, including some close associates of the mayor and a minister belonging to the Christian Social party. Standing by the fire was a tall, distinguished-looking lady wearing a long black dress and a ruby necklace. This was Baroness Sophie von Rautenberg—Olbricht's patron. Von Triebenbach made a mental note that he should pay her a compliment by the end of the evening. Though in her fifties, she was still an attractive woman. To his knowledge, since the death of Von Rautenberg she had never taken a lover. He wondered whether he might one day persuade her to consider him as a possible candidate. Close to the baroness sat the Englishman, Houston Stewart Chamberlain. He was an honorary member of the association and was addressing a small group of admirers. Von Triebenbach had read Chamberlain's books and essays on "the great composer" and had enjoyed them immensely.

On the opposite side of the room, Von Triebenbach spotted Ruprecht Hefner. The lieutenant stood out from the crowd on account of his bright blue uniform (an Austrian officer was not permitted to wear mufti off duty). Hefner was talking to a pretty young lady in a dress made of yellow silk. Von Triebenbach did not recognize her but strongly suspected that she was the minister's daughter.

The cavalryman leaned close and whispered something in her ear. She blushed, looked nervously around the room, and marched away—lifting her skirts slightly in order to facilitate a nimble escape.

One day that boy will get into serious trouble.

Von Triebenbach caught Hefner's attention and raised his champagne flute. The officer smiled and crossed the floor, allowing the golden tassel to swing conspicuously from his pommel. A few people stopped talking in order to enjoy the Uhlan's magisterial progress.

"Baron!" said Hefner, bowing. "So good to see you again."

"And you, Hefner—how long has it been?"

"Too long."

"Indeed, I can't remember the last time I saw you at one of our little gatherings."

"Ah yes, Baron, forgive me. I have been otherwise engaged of late. There was a rumor circulating around the barracks that His Majesty intended to inspect the eighteenth. Well, you can imagine the effect that had on a stickler like Kabok! We've been drilling day and night!"

"Of course—but you really must come again soon. We've had some very interesting guests, you know. At our last meeting we were honored by no less a personage than List."

"Really? I was under the impression that the old man was dead."

"Not Liszt, dear fellow—Guido List! The famous writer?"

"Oh, yes . . ."

The soldier's response lacked the brightness of tone associated with genuine recognition, but Von Triebenbach was not inclined to press the matter. "Never mind. Just come when you can."

The music stopped and the room resounded with enthusiastic applause. The musicians half-rose from their seats, bowing and grinning in all directions. As soon as they sat down again, a stealthy staccato introduction preceded a fortissimo chord, which was in turn followed by a weightless, swinging accompaniment. When the melody of the *Liebeslieder Waltz* trickled down the keyboard—liquid and delicate—some of the audience began to clap again.

Von Triebenbach leaned closer to the handsome cavalry officer and lowered his voice. "Speaking of rumors, I heard that you had a set-to with Freddi Lemberg—at the opera?

"Did you?"

"Yes—and I understand too that he demanded satisfaction."

"Who told you that?"

"Hefner, you cannot expect such an exchange to pass unnoticed." The officer shrugged. "My dear boy," Von Triebenbach continued, "you must be more discreet." He nodded then toward the girl in the yellow dress, who had just reappeared. "With respect to *all* matters."

Hefner grinned. "As usual, Baron, I am indebted to you for your wise counsel. However, I must beg to be excused—the matter that you *now* refer to is still unresolved."

Hefner bowed and slipped into the crowd, clearly in pursuit of his quarry.

Von Triebenbach shook his head.

Oh, to be young again! To feel invincible!

Wistfully remembering the conquests of his own youth, Von Triebenbach edged toward the alluring Rautenberg widow. As he drew closer, he was distracted by the group seated around

Chamberlain. Von Triebenbach could not hear his every word but he soon perceived that the Englishman was discoursing on his compatriot Sir Francis Galton. The thin but clear voice floated above the general hubbub. His German was perfect: "He has been petitioning the British government since the sixties . . . must sponsor competitive examinations in hereditary merit . . . those of superior stock might be invited to marry in Westminster Abbey and be encouraged by postnatal grants to produce strong and healthy progeny." The crowd parted and Von Triebenbach got his first clear view of the Englishman.

Chamberlain's complexion was pale, and his hair and mustache displayed a variety of tawny shades. Below an extremely high forehead his face was curiously elongated. Indeed, his general appearance suggested attenuation—as though his whole body had been stretched. His lips were too full, almost feminine, and his eyes were large and reminded Von Triebenbach of those of a nocturnal mammal. Yet there was something distinctly aristocratic in his demeanor; perhaps it was his stillness, or the precision of his speech.

Von Triebenbach could now hear Chamberlain's every word.

"It is impossible to estimate the genius and development of our north European culture if we obstinately shut our eyes to the fact that it is a *definite species* of mankind which constitutes its physical and moral basis. We see that clearly today; for the less Teutonic a land is, the more uncivilized it is. He who at the present time travels from London to Rome passes from fog into sunshine, but at the same time from the most refined civilization and high culture into semi-barbarism—dirt, coarseness, falsehood, poverty."

A waiter offered the baron a salmon canapé, which he refused, eager to hear the Englishman.

". . . On the one hand depth, power, and directness of expression as our most individual gift, and on the other, the great secret of our superiority in so many spheres, namely, our inborn tendency to follow nature honestly and faithfully."

"Very true," said one of his acolytes, which roused a rumble of general approval.

When the time comes, thought Von Triebenbach, *we shall certainly be able to depend on the English.*

30

PROFESSOR FREUD WAS ALMOST hidden in a dense cloud bank of cigar smoke. He had been talking at length about the psychological differences between conscious and unconscious processes. As the exposition proceeded, Liebermann was distracted by a curious fantasy. It was playing, like a Greek drama, in the penumbral outer circle of his mind. In this fantasy, he—or someone very much like him—was a neophyte in an ancient sect, consulting a spirit oracle that was made manifest in the semi-opaque twisting veils that floated up from a gold incense bowl. . . .

"Everything conscious is subject to a process of wearing away, while what is unconscious is relatively unchangeable. Look at these antiquities." Freud passed his hands over the figurines that stood guard on his desk, among which Liebermann spied a winged Sphinx, a brachycephalic dwarf, and a falcon-headed deity. His fantasy receded.

"They are, in fact," continued Professor Freud, "objects that were found concealed in the tombs of Egypt. The oldest here is nearly three thousand years old. Yet their burial has been the cause of their preservation. So it is with an unconscious memory—it is protected beneath the superficial sedimentation of the psyche. Think of Pompeii. Was it really destroyed by the eruption of Mount Vesuvius in AD 79? Not at all. The destruction of Pompeii is only just beginning, now that it has been discovered and dug up!"

Freud cut another cigar and offered it to his companion, but

Liebermann declined. If he attempted to keep up with the old man, then they would both be rendered invisible by the intensifying dun fog.

Freud's extemporization had been detailed and extended. Liebermann was reminded of the professor's Saturday lectures: it was Freud's habit to deliver them without notes, yet they were always intricately argued and perfectly structured. Realizing that the great psychoanalyst might start discoursing again and continue for at least another half hour, Liebermann thought it wise to take advantage of the interruption. The old man struck a match and drew on his corona.

"Professor?" Freud's penetrating eyes peered out from a tawny cloud. "You have written a great deal about the appearance of symbols in dreams, and I was wondering whether you would be willing to examine a certain emblem that I have chanced upon in the course of my . . . my work."

"Of course," said Freud. "Although in the matter of dream interpretation, as you will appreciate, symbols do not occur with a permanently fixed meaning like the grammalogues in shorthand."

"This symbol did not occur in a dream," said Liebermann impassively. Freud's stare remained constant—his eyes were two points of fixed concentration. "I suspect," Liebermann continued, "that it is a sacred image of some description—an ideogram. Given your extensive knowledge of the ancient world and its cultures, I hoped that you might be able to identify it."

The professor assumed a transparently counterfeit expression of modesty and muttered, "Well, perhaps."

Liebermann stood and walked to the desk. "May I?" He gestured toward a fountain pen.

Freud nodded and took a sheet of headed notepaper from his top drawer. Liebermann drew a simple cross and added ninety-degree "arms" at each extremity. When he had completed the drawing, he pushed it toward the professor, who considered the design for a few moments and exclaimed, "Yes, I *have* seen it before. It appears on certain Egyptian artifacts, but I believe it is more commonly associated with the Indian subcontinent."

"And what is it, exactly?"

"I don't know. But I have in my possession a very informative volume on the Indo-European script that will probably tell us." Freud rose and moved over to his bookcase. He ran a tobacco-stained index finger along a row of large volumes on the subject of archaeology. "Where is it, now? I'm sure it's here somewhere." He reversed the movement. "Ah! Here we are—tucked away between Evans and Schliemann." The book that he removed was small, thick, and somewhat battered. Its spine was broken and the cover boards flapped open like a double door.

Freud's whole appearance suddenly changed. He emitted a heavy sigh and an invisible yoke settled onto his shoulders. He seemed to shrink in on himself.

"Professor?" Liebermann inquired solicitously.

The old man stroked the distressed binding of the book and shook his head. "This book—it belonged to a dear friend." Freud pointed at a photographic portrait on the wall: a handsome young man, with dark hair and soft, shadowy eyes. "Fleischl-Marxow."

Liebermann had often wondered who the young man was and had assumed, wrongly, that he must be a distant relative.

"We worked together in Brücke's laboratory at the Physiological Institute. He had a first-class mind—truly brilliant. We had such conversations: philosophy, art, science, and literature! We discussed everything. And he was such a generous soul. . . . When I ran out of money (which was all too often in those days), Fleischl always came to the rescue. During the course of his laboratory work he contracted an infection, which necessitated the amputation of his right thumb. The operation wasn't a success. He subsequently suffered from neuromas and required more surgery. But it was no good—the pain got worse and worse. In the end it proved quite intolerable, and he became addicted to morphia.

"At that time I was undertaking some research into the medicinal properties of cocaine, the alkaloid that Niemann isolated from the coca plant. I chanced upon a report in *The Detroit Medical Gazette* suggesting that addiction to morphia could be treated by substitution with cocaine—which was supposed to be less harmful. I was overjoyed. Can you imagine? What a discovery! I encouraged Fleischl to try this new treatment. And he did. Indeed, my friend clutched at the drug like a drowning man. . . ."

Freud shook his head again

"He simply replaced one addiction with another. In three months he had spent eighteen hundred marks—a full gram a day! A hundred times more than the recommended dose! He became delirious, suffered from hallucinations, and became suicidal. He could not sleep, and occupied himself through the long and painful hours of every night making a study of Sanskrit. I don't know why, but he made me promise that I would never betray his secret passion. I suppose this was just paranoia—another side effect of my wonderful treatment! Before he died, he suggested that I take this book, so that others would not know of his activities. Well, what does it matter now? I'm sure he would forgive me this small betrayal of his confidence."

The professor's head was bowed. He stroked the book again, and attempted to press the split spine together.

"You were only trying to help your friend," said Liebermann.

Freud lifted his head. "But I made him worse."

"You were acting in good faith. In reality, isn't that all that can be asked of any doctor?"

Freud smiled weakly. "Yes, I suppose you are right." He shook his head. "Forgive me, I did not mean to—"

Liebermann raised his hand, halting the apology.

Freud nodded. It was a simple, almost imperceptible movement but it expressed a great deal. Respect for his young colleague, the acceptance of good counsel, and the need for all people—even the father of psychoanalysis—to beware the subtle snare of self-indulgent guilt.

The professor opened the book and flicked through the thin discolored pages. Many of them were inscribed with comments and marks made by his old comrade. Occasionally, Freud stopped to read an inscription before continuing his search. Reading these notes seemed to raise his spirits. Once or twice the professor even laughed— caught up, perhaps, in some happy memory of his friend.

"There it is!" cried Freud. He immediately held the book up for Liebermann to see. "Now, where is your drawing?" Freud put the book down next to Liebermann's sketch. "Very similar—but not quite the same. Look, notice how your figure is arranged to the right, whereas this is arranged to the left. It is a symbol known as . . ." Freud peered more closely at the minutely printed text. "The swastika."

"The swastika?" Liebermann repeated the word, savoring the novel, alien syllables.

"Yes," continued Freud. "From the Sanskrit *su*, meaning 'well,' and *asti*, meaning 'to be.' The literal translations are 'good luck,' 'well-being,' or . . . 'it is good.' " He scanned the text. "The symbol first appeared in the Vedas—the holy text of Hinduism. I suppose it is the Asiatic equivalent of our own medical standard—the snakes and rod of Aesculapius. You discovered this symbol in some ancient medical work?"

"Indeed. I am researching an essay on the history of symbols associated with health and healing."

Freud looked mildly surprised.

"Really? I wasn't aware that you were particularly interested in such things."

Liebermann did not hear the professor's comment. He was remembering a fragment of conversation. Something that Rheinhardt had said about the notorious Whitechapel murders.

The identity of the Ripper was never discovered, but I can remember some commentators proposing that his victims had died at the hands of a surgeon.

"I must say," Freud persisted, "you surprise me. I am usually a very perceptive judge of character—yet I had no idea that you were a budding historian!"

31

RHEINHARDT OPENED THE DRAWER of his desk and slid the unfinished report inside. It landed on a pile of official forms, most of which were only half-completed.

I'll attend to it when I get back.

The thought lacked conviction. So much so that Rheinhardt was obliged to castigate himself: *You really must!*

He pushed the drawer to, took out his watch from the tight fob pocket of his vest, and gasped.

"Haussmann!" he called out to his assistant. "We'd better get going. Otherwise we'll be late."

Reluctant witnesses rarely waited long.

The younger man, who had been earnestly copying the contents of his notebook into a bulky dossier, obediently rose from his seat. At that moment, there was a knock on the door, and another young officer—distinctly ursine in appearance—lumbered into the room.

"Sir," he addressed Rheinhardt. "A man from the zoo—outside. Says he's got to see you straight away."

"A man from the zoo?" Rheinhardt repeated.

"Zookeeper. Herr Arnoldt."

Rheinhardt, still thinking about his backlog of unfinished paperwork and the meeting for which he would very soon be late, did not properly register the young officer's announcement. The inspector's expression changed from perplexity through vacancy to puzzlement.

"Herr Arnoldt," said Haussmann helpfully. "The one who looked after the snake—Hildegard."

"Ah yes," said Rheinhardt. "*That* Herr Arnoldt—whatever can he want?"

The young officer at the door decided that a little detail might encourage the inspector to be more decisive.

"Very anxious to see you he is, sir—very anxious."

Rheinhardt grimaced. "I can't see him now. Tell him to come back later. Or, even better, tell him to come back tomorrow."

The young officer was suddenly jostled out of the way and the door was flung open. Herr Arnoldt stumbled into the office. He was obviously in a state of great excitement. His hair was disheveled and his arms were raised, jerking in the air as if they were in the control of a crazed puppeteer.

"Inspector, Inspector," said the frantic zookeeper. "Thank God you're here! Something remarkable has happened. My memory has returned. I would like to make another statement."

The ursine officer lifted a large paw and made a sign, communicating that he was very willing to remove the zookeeper if his superior so wished. But Rheinhardt shook his head and said calmly, "Thank you, that will be all." The young man looked disappointed as he closed the door.

"Herr Arnoldt," said Rheinhardt. "Perhaps you could return tomorrow. I am due to interview a gentleman in connection with a murder investigation. We have arranged to meet in twenty minutes. I really cannot delay."

"Murder investigation!" cried Herr Arnoldt. "What about Hildegard? Wasn't *she* murdered?"

Rheinhardt winced. "Yes, of course she was; however, I am afraid—"

"The emperor's favorite, she was!"

An image flashed into Rheinhardt's mind: Commissioner Brügel, leaning across his desk and scowling. *It is my grave duty to inform you of a complaint, delivered to the security office this morning by one of His Majesty's personal aides, concerning . . .*

"Very well, Herr Arnoldt," said Rheinhardt. "Please sit down. You have already met my assistant." He nodded toward Haussmann. "He is a capable fellow and will take down every word you say. On my return, I will have sufficient time to give your statement the careful attention that it deserves. If there are any issues arising that require further clarification, I will contact you via Herr Pfundtner at the zoo. Good morning."

Rheinhardt bowed and, before the zookeeper could object, opened the door and left.

Haussmann, somewhat bemused, repeated the inspector's invitation for Herr Arnoldt to sit.

The zookeeper pulled a chair right up to the desk and leaned forward.

"It's remarkable. My memory, it came back."

"Just one moment," said Haussmann, adjusting his chair and removing a blank form from one of the drawers. "I'm sorry—please continue." He showed that he was ready to write by raising his pen.

"My memory," said Herr Arnoldt breathlessly. "You remember that I'd lost it, after that scoundrel thumped me on the head. I couldn't remember anything . . . just having my breakfast in the morning. Well, slowly, things began to come back, all in the correct order. First there was breakfast, but then I recovered a memory of catching the omnibus. Then—after a while—I remembered getting off the omnibus and walking past the palace. Nothing more came back for a while, until about an hour ago. It was like . . . it was like . . . the sun rising. In a single instant, everything I had lost was restored." Herr Arnoldt grinned broadly. "I can remember entering the zoo, unlocking the door to the snake-pit. I can remember preparing Hildegard's food—the carcasses, on the slab in front of me. . . ."

Haussmann's scratching pen came to a halt. He lifted his head.

"A little slower, please, Herr Arnoldt?"

"Of course," said the zookeeper. He took a deep breath, composed himself, and continued his narrative. "The carcasses—they were on the slab in front of me. I know it was that *particular* morning—and not another morning—because one of the dead mice had a distinctive pelt—white, with an orange spot. And it was then . . . then that I heard footsteps. I assumed it was one of the other keepers. You see, they weren't stealthy footsteps, not like you'd expect from someone who intended to creep up behind you and do you some mischief. No, they weren't like that at all. This fellow had a brisk step. Like a march. One two—one two. And not only that, he was whistling . . . he was whistling this tune."

Suddenly, Herr Arnoldt burst into song. "Pa, pa, pom, pom, ta-ta-ta-ta, pom, pom pom . . ."

He completed two phrases and stared, eyes wide open and shining rather too brightly, at the assistant detective. Haussmann began to wonder whether Herr Arnoldt's injury had affected more than just his memory.

Haussmann was not a very musical young man but he judged the tune to be vaguely familiar. It was quite well known, but not as famous as a work by Strauss or Lanner. He wrote "pa, pa, pom" down on the form and then crossed it out, resolving the problematic transcription with a simple worded description: *Herr Arnoldt sings a melody.* This sentence seemed too brief and after a further moment of reflection Haussmann amended his note, adding (*Jolly*).

"Well," said Herr Arnoldt. "What do you think of that?"

Haussmann was not overly impressed by this new intelligence; however, the zookeeper's expression was expectant and Haussmann had learned, by observing his mentor, the value of a diplomatic response.

"Very interesting," said the assistant detective. "Very interesting indeed."

The zookeeper smiled, and sat back in his chair. He was obviously relieved.

32

They were sitting in the Budweiser beer parlor—a favorite haunt of homesick Czechs. Jiri Zahradnik was nervous. He sat hunched over his tankard, stealing quick glances to the left and right.

"What's the matter?" asked Rheinhardt.

"Nothing."

"You think that the person who killed your friend will come after you—if you're seen talking to me?"

"I don't know. Maybe."

Rheinhardt shrugged and took out his notebook.

"Please, Inspector," said Zahradnik. "Not in here."

"Very well." Rheinhardt slipped the notebook back into his coat pocket and sipped his drink. "I am a great fan of your Czech beers— Budweiser particularly."

Zahradnik ignored the inspector's small talk.

"Forgive me, Inspector, but I mean to be brief. Before Evzen was murdered, he said that someone had been bothering him at the market. This man, he was always questioning Evzen's prices. He called Evzen a swindler and a thief. Of course, Evzen wasn't charging any more for his birds than the next man. But this—"

"Just one moment," Rheinhardt interrupted. "What did he look like? Did Evzen say?"

"He wore good clothes."

"That isn't terribly helpful."

"And he was a German."

"How do you mean? A German?"

"Like you."

"A German speaker, you mean?"

"Like I said—a German."

Rheinhardt did not insist on qualifying the terms of their discussion. "Go on."

The Czech was distracted by the arrival of three musicians: a clarinettist, an accordion player, and a man struggling with a double bass. They were soon joined by an attractive young woman in a rustic dress who was carrying a tambourine. There was a smattering of applause, an inebriated cheer, and one or two gentlemen called out in Czech.

"*Hej Slovani* . . . Where is my home? . . . *Hej Slovani.*"

Rheinhardt assumed that they were making requests. The clarinettist caught Zahradnik's eye and smiled.

"You know him?" asked Rheinhardt.

"An acquaintance. That's all. Sometimes we play *mariás* together."

"What?"

"The card game!"

"Did he know Evzen too?"

"Maybe—I don't know."

The woman with the tambourine counted out a four-beat introduction and the band started up. The double bass thumped out a simple two-note figure over which the other musicians played intricate ornaments. The woman raised the tambourine high above her head and shook it violently. Then, waving the ample folds of her dress with her free hand, she opened her mouth and produced a gloriously raw sound, untrained but powerful. Some men at the bar began cheering. It was obvious to Rheinhardt that the musicians had chosen to begin with a patriotic crowd-pleaser.

Zahradnik jerked his head around, almost like a tic, and continued his account: "So this German, he started to threaten Evzen. Told him to go back home—and said that if he *didn't* go back home, he'd be sorry."

"Why didn't Evzen call the police?"

"The police! Why would Germans want to help him?"

"Because this is Vienna—and the *Germans* who live here have a very different attitude from those whom you may have encountered in Bohemia."

Zahradnik smiled and pointed toward a boarded-up shattered window.

"Not that different, Inspector."

When Rheinhardt returned to the security office, Haussmann was still at his desk. Thankfully, there was no sign of the agitated zookeeper.

"Ah, Haussmann," said Rheinhardt, warming at the sight of his junior attending to the kind of paperwork that he himself so assiduously avoided. "I do apologize for my precipitate departure."

Haussmann turned the pen in his hand, unsure of how to respond to a penitent superior (inspectors at the security office were not renowned for treating their assistants with anything more than the minimum amount of respect).

"I trust the meeting with Zahradnik went well, sir?"

Rheinhardt took off his coat. "It seems that Herr Vanek was threatened by a gentleman who did not think Vienna should extend a warm welcome to Czechs. Moreover, the gentleman in question wore *good clothes*. And that, in essence, is all that I have learned."

"Not very productive, then, sir?"

Rheinhardt hung his hat and coat on the stand. "No, although the beer was excellent. How about you? How did you fare with Herr

Arnoldt?" The assistant detective offered Rheinhardt the completed statement. The inspector shook his head. "Just summarize, Haussmann—the key points will suffice."

Haussmann placed the statement neatly on top of a folder marked *Hildegard.*

"Very good, sir," said Haussmann. "First: it would seem that Herr Arnoldt's memory has returned. Second: he can now remember that the assailant who struck him from behind approached with a quick step and was whistling a tune."

Rheinhardt leaned back, resting his rear on the edge of his desk. "And?"

Haussmann looked at the statement again, hoping that something might have escaped his attention. "No. That's it, I'm afraid. There is no third point—or any other material point to follow, sir."

Rheinhardt twirled his mustache. "Why on earth did he think that was so important?"

"I don't know, sir."

"Did he recognize the tune?"

"No, sir, but he could remember it—in fact, he insisted on singing it to me. It *did* sound quite familiar."

"How did it go?"

"What—you want *me* to sing it, sir?"

"Yes."

"I'm afraid that I don't have much of a voice, sir."

"It doesn't matter, Haussmann. You're not auditioning as a principal at the Court Opera!"

The assistant detective coughed, and produced—in the thinnest tenor imaginable—a melody that leaped and jerked between at least three keys.

"No, no, no. That isn't how you do it!" Rheinhardt went over to Haussmann, letting his hands fall on the young man's shoulders. He gave them a little shake. "Relax. Now breathe deeply." The inspector demonstrated. "And let your whole body resonate. Like this." He produced an ascending scale of one octave. "Now *you* try."

Haussmann, wholly mortified but constitutionally unable to disobey his chief, produced a weak and tonally insecure imitation. At which point the door opened, revealing the stocky figure of Commissioner Brügel. He fumed silently for a few seconds, his complexion darkening through several shades of purple before he erupted. His opprobrium fell on the unfortunate inspector like scalding volcanic ash.

"Rheinhardt! In the last month this city of ours has been visited by the worst carnage in living memory. I had assumed that you would be applying yourself tirelessly to the task of bringing the maniac responsible for the Spittelberg and Ruprechtskirche murders to book. Now—if I am not very much mistaken—you seem to be giving your assistant a singing lesson. Would you care to explain yourself?"

33

Oɴ ʜɪs ʀᴏᴜᴛᴇ ʜᴏᴍᴇ it was Haussmann's luck—or misfortune, depending on his state of mind—to pass a number of beer cellars. He had been looking forward to a Budweiser and had felt cheated when the opportunity was denied him because of Herr Arnoldt's inconvenient arrival. Having been so far frustrated, the prospect of a restorative draft seemed particularly appealing. By the time Haussmann reached Mariahilf, he had persuaded himself that it would do no harm—indeed, it might even do him some good—to stop off at a little place he knew on Stumpergasse. So it was that, shortly after eight o'clock, he found himself sitting next to a large open fire, nursing a tankard of Zwickel beer. It was just what he needed: smooth, full-bodied, and slightly cloudy.

As he relaxed, he mulled over the day's events. The business with Commissioner Brügel had been most embarrassing; still, Rheinhardt had explained the purpose of their vocal gymnastics with remarkable forbearance. When Brügel finally departed, the old curmudgeon had been appeased—but he'd still been unimpressed by Rheinhardt's conduct. The commissioner was a difficult, irascible man, and Haussmann was glad that he did not have to report to him directly. In due course, though, if he were promoted, he too would have to lock horns with Brügel. Consideration of this likelihood prompted the assistant detective to drain his tankard.

He gestured to the landlord (by tilting an invisible drinking vessel in the air) that another Zwickel would be most welcome.

Haussmann allowed his thoughts about work to subside and began to take note of his surroundings. The relatively confined space of the cellar vibrated with conversation. Most of the tables were occupied and the atmosphere was thick with cigarette smoke. The patrons were male and working-class: the sole exception being three students from the university who were seated in a shadowy nook under a bricked arch. They were clothed in the blue of the Alemania dueling fraternity.

It was not uncommon to see young men of their type wearing bandages. Indeed, among the fraternities the medical dressing was proudly displayed as a badge of honor. A strip of lint was often visible on the left cheek—where a right-handed opponent could more readily land his blow. One of these Alemanians, however, had had his head completely wrapped up in bandages—save for a narrow "window" created for his spectacles. He had obviously been involved in a particularly violent exchange. His jaw was drawn tight above and below the mouth. Haussmann understood that this was to prevent the inadvertent ripping of cuts while eating. Even so, this Alemanian's predicament did not prevent all forms of consumption. A small hole had been made in the bandages, through which he was able to imbibe by using a straw. A Viennese student could survive without food—but not without beer.

The landlord arrived with Haussmann's second Zwickel. He banged the tankard on the table, allowing a fair amount of beer to splash over the sides.

"There you go," he roared in rough-edged rural German. "Get that down you." His big red face lowered. "You won't find a better Zwickel anywhere—not nowhere!"

Haussmann noticed that a pamphlet had been discarded close to the tankard. As a river of beer began to run down a wide groove in the tabletop, he moved the pamphlet aside to ensure that the paper would not get wet. As he did so, something printed on the front page caught his attention.

Before the landlord could leave his table, Haussmann grabbed the man's arm.

"What?" The landlord was evidently surprised by the strength of the slight young man's grip.

"This pamphlet. Who left it here?"

"I don't know."

"Who was sitting at this table—before me?"

The landlord thought for a moment. "Now you're asking. No . . . no, I can't remember."

"Was it someone who comes here regularly?"

"S'pose it could have been. I tell you what, my friend: how about letting go of my arm?" Haussmann had been unaware that he was still restraining the landlord. He nodded and pulled his hand away.

"That's better," said the landlord, smiling broadly. "Ain't it?" He was obviously used to pacifying drunks.

"What did they look like?" Haussmann asked.

The landlord shrugged. "I told you, I can't remember. Why do you want to know, anyway? People leave stuff like that in here all the time—political types. It's all nonsense. I wouldn't bother with it if I were you."

Haussmann picked up the pamphlet and stared at the front page. The crooked cross was identical to the one that he had seen painted on the wall in Madam Borek's brothel.

34

THE STREETCAR WAS APPROACHING through hazy darkness.

Like all of the new streetcars circling the Ringstrasse, it had no obvious source of power. The emperor had objected to the installation of overhead cables on the Ringstrasse because he believed that they would mar its beauty. But Liebermann, like many of his contemporaries, was fully cognizant of the real reason for the royal edict. Old Franz Josef (ever suspicious of scientific advances) had become obsessed by the idea that an electric cable might fall on his carriage, causing him a serious (if not fatal) injury.

Neurotic, thought Liebermann. *Quite neurotic.*

As the streetcar rolled to a halt, Liebermann peered through the steamed-up windows and saw that all the seats were taken; however, standing room was available on the back platform. As Liebermann took his place, the bell rang out and the streetcar jolted forward: this sudden precipitate motion made a young woman standing in front of him lose her footing. She stumbled but prevented herself from falling by allowing her open palms to land squarely on Liebermann's chest. The doctor found himself looking down at a pretty, open face—and into a pair of peculiarly arresting green eyes.

"I'm so sorry," the woman apologized in a husky contralto. "I couldn't stop myself."

Although her accent betrayed humble origins, Liebermann observed that her gloves were rather expensive: red doeskin and the wrists were trimmed with sable. The rest of her clothes were plain but tasteful: a long dark coat, French-style ankle boots, and a wide-brimmed hat with no decoration—not even a ribbon. She was not perplexed by her predicament and seemed, in no hurry to extricate herself. Liebermann, assuming that she was waiting for some gallant gesture, gently lifted her hands from his body.

"Thank you," she said, righting herself and smiling. "You're very kind."

"Not at all," said Liebermann. Then, looking over his shoulder, he raised his voice and added, "Perhaps, fräulein, one of the gentlemen inside would be willing to offer you his seat."

"No!" the woman protested. "No. I'm very happy to stand here."

"As you wish," said Liebermann.

The conductor jostled onto the back platform, took a few fares—including Liebermann's—and returned to his post. As Liebermann was pocketing his ticket, he recognized the same pleasant contralto. "You're a doctor, aren't you?"

The young woman was smiling at him again.

"Yes," said Liebermann. "How did you know?"

"The way you're dressed."

She reached out and touched his sleeve.

Liebermann looked down at his astrakhan coat and could detect nothing in its appearance that declared his profession. Perhaps she was teasing him? Before he could formulate a playful riposte, the woman had introduced herself.

"My name is Ida Kainz."

"Ah," said Liebermann. "Kainz. Like the actor?"

"What actor?

"Josef Kainz."

She shook her head and pursed her lips. "I don't go to the theater much." She pulled a pathetic face that recalled the pitiful melancholy of a disappointed child. "I have no one to take me."

The streetcar stopped and more people climbed on, forcing Ida Kainz to renew her intimacy with Liebermann's chest. She did not appear distressed by her situation, and Liebermann once more found himself looking down into her eyes, which had narrowed slightly. Her perfume was sweet—like apple blossom.

"My father is a postal employee," she said in an airy voice, as if she were picking up the thread of a prior interrupted conversation. "We live in the tenth district: three of us. Father, mother, and myself. I have a sister, but she is married." Then she boldly took Liebermann's hand and squeezed his fingers. "You need new gloves, Herr Doctor . . . ?"

The bell sounded and the streetcar rolled on.

"Liebermann."

"A nice name, Liebermann. Yes, you definitely need new gloves, Herr Doctor Liebermann. And I think . . ." Her smile widened to reveal her teeth. "I could help you there."

She produced a small business card and handed it to Liebermann. It showed the address of a glove shop on Wahringerstrasse. "Kleinmann's. Währingerstrasse 24. That's where I work. You should pay me a visit. Just ask for Ida."

They were passing the Court Theater. All of its windows were aglow with a welcoming yellow light.

"I suppose you go there often," the shopgirl continued.

"When I can—although my preferences are musical."

She nodded and assumed an ambiguous expression. "A doctor should have better gloves."

The streetcar was approaching Liebermann's stop. He signaled his imminent departure with a bow, and the young woman responded by extending her hand. He pressed the red doeskin to his lips.

"Good evening, Fräulein Kainz."

Although he had intended to perform this small courtesy in a perfunctory manner, the kiss that he delivered was lingering.

Liebermann got off the streetcar but did not walk away. Ida Kainz was staring back at him, a neutral expression on her face. The streetcar bell sounded, and her figure began to recede. As she faded into the smoky gloom, he saw her gloved hand rise—a conspicuous spot of carmine in an otherwise colorless world.

Liebermann looked at the card.

Kleinmann's.

Währingerstrasse 24.

He lifted the card to his nose. It, too, smelled of apple blossom.

A doctor should have better gloves.

Liebermann sighed heavily. Life was already becoming far too complicated. He allowed the card to slip from his fingers.

35

Director Mahler's Lieder eines fahrenden gesellen—*The Song of a Wayfarer*—was better known as a concert work for full orchestra. But the piano arrangement, stripped of distracting colors and effects, revealed a musical essence of extraordinary power and intensity.

Such is the greatness of "German" music, thought Liebermann. *So poignant, so stirring, so effortlessly superior!*

Rheinhardt was in excellent voice. The apex of every phrase seemed to weaken, yield, and sink beneath an excess of sentiment.

"O Augen, blau, warum habt ihr mich angeblickt?"
O blue eyes, why did you look at me?
"Nun hab ich ewig Leid und Grämen."
Now pain and grief are with me forever.

The rejected wayfarer bids farewell to his distant sweetheart, and in the dark of night sets out across a desolate heath, his mind filled with the tormenting memory of falling linden blossoms. . . .

Liebermann found that the words had produced in his mind an image, not of Clara (whose eyes were brown), not of Ida Kainz (whose eyes were green), but of Miss Lydgate. This ephemeral portrait, fleetingly sketched and vaporous, aroused in him a complex set of emotions: desire, shame, and a pang of something that came close to physical pain. Liebermann bowed his head and, without looking at the notation, allowed his long fingers to search out the final, inconsolable bars. These were feelings with which Liebermann was not ordinarily familiar; however, their occurrence was becoming increasingly commonplace.

When the music-making was over, the young doctor and his guest retired to the smoking room. They sat in their customary places and enjoyed a preliminary cigar with some pale Hennessy cognac. Liebermann swirled the liquid in his glass and savored the subtle, penetrating aroma. Then, leaning to one side, he made a languid gesture in the direction of Rheinhardt's case.

"Photographs?"

"Yes," replied the inspector. "The Ruprechtskirche murder."

"I read the report in the *Neue Freie Presse*."

"Not very informative, I'm afraid," said Rheinhardt, lifting the case onto his knees. He released the hasps and removed a bundle of photographs. "The victim's name was Evzen Vanek. He'd been in Vienna only a few months but he managed to find himself a stall in the meat market where he sold chickens."

Rheinhardt handed the photographs over to his friend. The first showed Vanek's body sprawled out on a cobbled street—a long shot with the Ruprechtskirche in the background, its steeple covered in snow.

"He was something of a loner," Rheinhardt continued, "but he was known to a few of his countrymen at the Budweiser beer parlor. I met with one of them last week—a chap called Zahradnik. He wasn't able to tell me much. Well . . . apart from one thing."

"Which was?"

"Vanek had been harassed by someone who didn't like Czechs."

"What kind of harassment?"

"Taunts, jibes. He was accused of pricing his birds too high. And then told to go back to his own country."

"Not so remarkable."

"Indeed. Although, I must confess that I had no idea that anti-Czech feeling was so strong in some quarters."

"Was Vanek politically active?"

Rheinhardt shook his head. "I doubt it. He had to streetcar out to a supplier in Ottakring to collect his chickens every day. He wouldn't have had much time for politics."

Liebermann examined the next image: a close-up of Vanek's chest wound. Rheinhardt returned to his exposition. "He was stabbed through the heart. Professor Mathias said that the fatal blow was delivered by someone using a sabre." The young doctor's head jerked up, light flashing off his spectacles. "Yes," continued Rheinhardt, reading his friend's mind. "Of the same type used to kill Madam Borek—and the two fräuleins, Draczynski and Glomb. Now, take a look at the final photograph."

Liebermann did as he was instructed. "A padlock?"

"Professor Mathias noticed some abnormalities: some bruising, a swollen Adam's apple. His attention was drawn to Vanek's throat."

"And he found this?"

"Yes. It had been pushed down Vanek's esophagus and had to be pulled out with forceps."

"That wasn't mentioned in the *Neue Freie Presse* article."

"No, the censor finds such details . . . distasteful. The lock is manufactured by a company called Sicherheit. They have a large factory in Landstrasse. Unfortunately, they supply half the empire—so we have no idea where this particular lock was purchased."

Liebermann slumped down in his chair, his chin finding support on his clenched fist. "Was anything else concealed in the body? The key, perhaps?"

"No."

"Mathias searched?"

"Yes." Rheinhardt's shoulders shivered as a memory of the mortuary cold returned to tickle his upper vertebrae.

"The concealment of a closed padlock in the throat," said Liebermann, "suggests that the perpetrator wanted to emphasize that the victim had been silenced. Now, if Herr Vanek had been a celebrated orator, then such a gesture would make sense. But clearly he was nothing of the sort."

The young doctor stared into the flames of the fire. His right eyebrow lifted, suggesting that his train of thought had continued beyond the point where he had stopped speaking.

"I have something else to show you," said Rheinhardt. "Take a look at this." Liebermann turned. It was a pamphlet, of a type usually produced by small political presses. The paper was coarse and the print left dark smudges on Liebermann's fingers.

Gothic lettering proclaimed: *On the secret of the Runes—a preliminary communication by Guido von List.*

Beneath this announcement were two concentric circles. The inner ring enclosed a crooked cross, and the gap between the inner and outer rings was filled with primitive angular characters. They looked as if they had been scratched into the bark of a tree with a fork.

"The swastika," said Liebermann.

"I beg your pardon?"

"That's what it's called—the crooked cross. It's an Indo-European symbol representing goodness and health. Professor Freud looked it up for me in a volume of Sanskrit." Liebermann waved the pamphlet. "Where did you get this?"

"It was left at a table in a beer cellar. Haussmann found it."

"Where?"

"Mariahilf—it's near where he lives."

Liebermann flicked a few pages and began reading: "*The runes were* more than letters are today, more even than mere syllables or word signs—that is, they were holy signs or magical characters. They were, in a certain way of thinking, something similar to the spirit sigils of later times, which played a conspicuous role in the notorious hellish conjuration of Dr. Johann Faust . . ." Liebermann's upper lip curled. "It's nonsense, Oskar. Gibberish."

"Not quite. It purports to be a treatise on the origins of the German language. The author, Guido List—"

"*Von* List," Liebermann said, correcting Rheinhardt and tapping the author's poorly defined ink-splotched name.

Rheinhardt shook his head. "He is a writer who, to our knowledge, has only ever been known as Guido List. It must be a typographic error."

"Or he has decided to ennoble himself!"

"Well, now you say that—it wouldn't surprise me. He's obviously a rather grandiose fellow. Although much of the pamphlet is concerned with the mystical significance of runes, he chooses to end his exegesis with a peculiar and rather disturbing polemic. He condemns and vilifies a number of institutions and groups: the Catholic Church, enemy nomads—by which I think he means Jews— the internationals (I'm not sure who he means there), and the Freemasons. He is particularly scornful about the Masons."

"What is it about these groups that he objects to?"

"I really don't know, Max. None of it is very coherent. . . . He was originally a journalist. His articles appeared in the *Neue Deutsche Alpenzeitung* and the *Deutsche Zeitung*. But now he's most famous for being the author of a historical novel called *Carnuntum*—have you heard of it?"

"No."

"Very popular a few years back. It was about a Germanic tribe who won a victory over the Romans in AD 375."

The clock struck ten and the two friends waited until the last chime had faded before continuing their conversation.

"You think there's a connection, then?" asked Liebermann. "Between this writer and the Spittelberg murders?"

"When Haussmann showed me the crooked cross—I beg your pardon, what did you say it was called?"

"The swastika."

"When Haussmann showed me the swastika, I imagined that there must be. But now, if the symbol is a Sanskrit character, as you say it is, then I'm not so sure. Perhaps we should be looking for an Indian gentleman."

"Does List mention the swastika in this pamphlet?"

"Yes, he does. But he refers to it as the *fyrfos*, the hooked cross, or the eighteenth rune."

Liebermann offered his friend another cigar.

"Thank you," said Rheinhardt. He passed the corona under his nose and nodded with approval.

"Where was List on the day of the Spittelberg atrocity?"

"When we interviewed him, he said that he was at home—with his wife."

"Do you believe him?"

Rheinhardt cut his cigar. "It's irrelevant—he didn't do it."

"Why do you say that?"

"He's blind, Max—and has been for several months. He had some cataracts surgically removed and he is still wearing the bandages. If there *is* a connection between List and the murders, then it must be indirect."

Rheinhardt lit his cigar and produced two perfect rings of smoke.

"So where does all this lead us?" asked Liebermann, sounding mildly irritated. "The women in the Spittelberg brothel—with the exception of the girl Ludka—and Evzen Vanek were all killed with a sabre. The Spittelberg murders and the Ruprechtskirche murder are also linked by oddities: a Sanskrit character signifying goodness and health—and a padlock that was used, perhaps, to signify that the victim will no longer speak. Neither seem to be very meaningful." Liebermann viewed the flames through his cognac. His glass appeared to be filled with a magically lucent elixir. "It occurred to me," he continued, "that the swastika, being a symbol representing health, might have some medical significance. I was reminded of your observations concerning the Whitechapel murders."

"Indeed, the London Ripper may well have been a doctor. But if *our* perpetrator had wanted to let us know that he was a medical man, why daub an obscure Sanskrit character on the wall?"

"To give us a problem to solve—to show us that he is more knowledgeable than we are."

"Why would he do that?"

"Arrogance?"

Rheinhardt sighed.

"I agree," continued Liebermann. "None of this is terribly coherent; still, the unusual choice of murder weapon is promising. A sabre is large and difficult to conceal."

"Unless you already happen to be wearing one as part of your uniform."

"But why would a military man who hated women then choose an impoverished male Czech stallholder as his next victim? And what are we to make of this?" Liebermann lifted the pamphlet and waved it in the air. "Is the fiend a student of the early Germanic alphabet—and if so, what in God's name are we supposed to make of that?"

Liebermann sipped his cognac and turned to looked at Rheinhardt. The policeman shrugged, and the young doctor, normally full of ideas and interpretations, was worryingly silent.

36

Lieutenant Ruprecht Hefner, his seconds, Renz and Trapp, and the regimental doctor all stepped down from the carriage. One of the horses snorted violently, expelling two jets of steam from its quivering nostrils. Another carriage had preceded them and was already parked on the verge. It was finished in black lacquer, and would scarcely have been out of place beneath the dome of the Hofburg Palace.

"Lemberg," said Trapp.

The observation did not merit a response from his companions.

Above the eastern horizon of the Vienna Woods a strip of pellucid sky had begun to brighten. Within the pale band a pink halo of luminescence surrounded an unusually radiant point of light. The doctor paused, considered the nature of the object, and concluded that this lovely sentinel was in fact the planet Venus.

"Come, Herr Doctor," Renz called back. "Now is not the time for stargazing."

The doctor, somewhat embarrassed, nodded and hurried along. He touched his cap as he passed the other carriage, and the driver, perched on his high box, returned the greeting by raising his whip in a silent salute.

Hefner had taken the lead and was searching among some gorse bushes by the roadside. He waved, clutching in his hand something he had found. It was a tattered red handkerchief. The others followed. They descended a steep track that was slippery with scree and ice.

Their path took them through woods and for a few minutes they could see nothing but a corridor of black spruces and an arch of sky above their heads. Hefner crushed a cone beneath his boot. It broke with a pleasing crunch.

Eventually the track led them to the floor of a narrow valley. A nearby brook had been reduced to a trickle but its noise was surprisingly loud.

Halfway across the "field of honor" stood the *unparteiische*. He wore a tall silk stovepipe hat and a dark frock coat. Tucked under his right arm was a mahogany case. Beyond the *unparteiische*, standing next to a solitary beech tree, was Hefner's opponent, Lemberg.

Hefner and the regimental doctor held back, while Renz and Trapp continued walking. Lemberg's seconds, when they saw the two Uhlans approaching, also came forward. The four men struggled toward one another, their feet dragging in the snow. They converged in front of the man in the stovepipe hat, where they halted and bowed. After exchanging some preliminary remarks, they turned to address the *unparteiische*, who opened the mahogany case and offered them a view of its contents. Renz and his opposite number (who Hefner assumed must be Glöckner) each removed a pistol and examined it closely, testing its aim and mechanism. Then they swapped guns and repeated the inspection. The loading of each weapon was undertaken jointly. When both seconds were satisfied, the pistols were returned to the *unparteiische*.

Meanwhile Trapp and Riehl, Lemberg's other second, had made their way onto the "field" and, from a starting position that required both men to stand back-to-back, were now measuring out an agreed distance in precise synchronized steps. Trapp's voice could be heard counting out paces: "Five, six, seven . . ." Both men were carrying something bulky in their arms.

"How are you feeling?" asked the regimental doctor.

"Couldn't be better," Hefner replied. "Steady as a rock." To prove it, the lieutenant thrust out his hands. They were still—more like carved marble than flesh and bone. "To tell the truth, Herr Doctor—I'm anxious to get this morning's business out of the way so that I can have breakfast. There's a splendid roadhouse in the village we passed on the way up. The Postschänke—do you know it?"

"No."

"Their cabbage soup is beyond compare. And the bread that they serve is like . . ." He paused, and waited for his brain to supply an appropriate superlative. "Ambrosia. Yes, ambrosia. Are you hungry, Herr Doctor?"

"I can't say that I am."

"Shame."

Trapp and Riehl had stopped, and it was now easier to see what they had been carrying: wooden stakes. Each man placed his stake upright against the ground and pressed down on the blunt end, ensuring that the sharp end sank deep into the snow. These markers were set approximately fifteen paces apart. Trapp and Riehl then measured a farther distance either side of the stakes, which was marked at both ends with brightly colored handkerchiefs held in place by rocks.

Renz made his way back to Hefner, breaking into a trot as he came nearer. "Fine pistols," he called out. "German. A little heavy, perhaps, but very well made."

"Excellent," said Hefner.

Trapp followed close behind. "The light is acceptable. No shadows. No wind—and, apart from the beech tree, there's nothing else to distract you. Are you ready?"

"Yes."

"Let's go, then—and good luck."

"Yes, good luck, Hefner," Renz added.

The doctor—who was obliged to be impartial—inhaled deeply.

He wasn't altogether sure what he felt concerning Hefner's fate. He admired him, certainly; but whether he *liked* him or not was another matter.

Renz and Trapp led Hefner and the regimental doctor across the valley floor. Their progress was mirrored by Lemberg and his two seconds. Both groups came to a halt in front of the *unparteiische*, who turned out to be a very distinguished-looking gentleman with a well-waxed mustache.

Hefner caught Lemberg's eye. The industrialist's son was angry—but his anger was not so fierce that it could conceal fear. Hefner fancied himself a good judge of character, and he was reassured by what he saw: a telling glint of animal terror.

Yes, thought Hefner, *the Jew has weak nerves. He'll make a poor decision under pressure. . . .*

The *unparteiische* requested that the opponents empty their pockets, the contents of which were given to their seconds for safekeeping. Dishonorable duelists had been known to secrete watches, wallets, coins, and keys about their person in order to protect them from the low-velocity but nonetheless lethal bullets. When the searches were complete, the *unparteiische* turned to Lemberg.

"You are the offended party?" The young man nodded. "Then, in accordance with the code, it is for you to confirm before the assembled witnesses here gathered the terms of engagement. First blood or death?"

"Death," said Lemberg. His voice caught on the heavy syllable.

Herr Riehl—who was the older of Lemberg's two seconds—winced.

"Freddi," he growled, "I beg you to reconsider. It's not too—"

"Enough!" said Lemberg sharply, attempting to recover some of his ebbing dignity.

"This is madness," muttered Riehl under his breath, appealing to the regimental doctor, an expression of desperation in his wide eyes. But it was not the doctor's place to interfere.

The *unparteiische* opened the mahogany case and showed the interior to both parties. Inside, nestling in a deep bed of green fabric, were the specially modified dueling pistols. The octagonal barrels were fashioned from Damascus steel and had been darkened to stop reflection. All metal appurtenances had been left unengraved for the same reason. Sights—fore and back—had been removed. The guns were stripped down and entirely functional, reduced to their essential parts for a singular and fatal purpose.

The *unparteiische* tilted the case toward Lemberg.

"Sir?"

Lemberg removed the nearest pistol.

The box was then offered to Hefner, who removed the remaining weapon. He checked its weight in a loose grip and was unable to suppress a smile. It was perfect.

"Gentlemen? Are you ready?" The *unparteiische* looked from Hefner to Lemberg. "Please take your places."

Lemberg slipped off his coat and let it fall to the ground. It was a maneuver designed to give him a small advantage. The white of his shirt would make him less visible against the snowy landscape. Hefner—who was duty-bound to wear his Uhlan uniform at all times—was not at liberty to do the same. Even so, he could do one or two things to mitigate his vulnerability. Discreetly, he lifted the lapels of his greatcoat to cover the stars on his collar.

The two duelists were led by their seconds to their respective positions, the places that had been marked with the brightly colored handkerchiefs. Then, with great solemnity, the seconds retraced their footsteps, returning in due course to the *unparteiische*.

The regimental doctor sighed and opened his bag. He took out a scalpel and a bottle of carbolic.

"Herr Doctor," said the *unparteiische*. "I respectfully request that you put your instruments away. We do not wish to demoralize the parties."

The doctor protested, "An unnecessary delay can sometimes be the difference between a man living and dying."

"May I remind you, Herr Doctor," said the *unparteiische* sternly, "that in the present contest matters of life and death are secondary to those of honor and propriety. I must insist: put your instruments away."

It was not the first time that the doctor had encountered such pedantry. With some reluctance, he replaced the scalpel and bottle in his bag.

A curious stillness descended on the valley. The two opponents stared at each other across a white no-man's-land, featureless except for the vertical wooden stakes. The forty paces that separated the men might have been a vampire's graveyard. Above the snowcapped hills, the light of the morning star was fading.

The man in the stovepipe hat called out, "Forward!"

His baritone bounced off the steep valley walls like the voice of Jehovah.

The opponents began walking toward each other.

Hefner held his pistol up, pointing the muzzle at the clouds and compressing his crooked arm against his chest. In the unlikely event of Lemberg's aim being true, the lieutenant's forearm would protect his heart and the pistol would shield his nose. He turned his torso slightly to the left—thus reducing the amount of his body's surface area exposed to Lemberg.

They drew closer, taking long, stately strides.

The rules of the barrier duel were simple. Both parties could—at any point—stop, aim, and fire. The advantage of shooting first was the preemptive demise of one's opponent. However, if the shot missed, the premature action would incur a significant penalty: the presumptive party was required to stand still and await an answer. The opponent was given a full minute to reach the nearest barrier, from where he could make his leisurely riposte. Thus, the disadvantage of firing second was compensated for by the advantage of firing at an immobile target at shorter range. Hefner was a great advocate of the barrier duel. He found its mathematics deeply satisfying.

The opponents drew closer.

Thirty-five paces, thirty paces, twenty-five paces . . .

Lemberg stopped and raised his pistol.

Hefner had been expecting this.

The Jew has no nerve.

The Uhlan did not break his measured step. He checked that his arm was still in the correct position and tightened his abdominal muscles. A concave stomach would be less easy to hit.

He looked directly at Lemberg.

The muzzle of Lemberg's pistol was not true.

If he fires now, he'll miss.

There was a loud report. Hefner heard snow falling from the branches of the pines behind him. The air became acrid with the reek of saltpeter and sulfur. He felt no pain, and he was still walking.

Missed!

Lemberg lowered his pistol and awaited his fate.

Hefner showed no elation. He did not quicken his pace. His heartbeat was sounding a regular tattoo in his chest. When he reached the nearest stake, he stopped, took aim, and considered his target. Lemberg was shaking. The tremor was clearly visible.

Hefner squeezed the trigger.

A loud crack—more snow falling. A dull thud, and a rustle like rice on paper.

Lemberg swayed. His pistol fell from his hand and his knees

buckled beneath him. Before he had hit the ground, the regimental doctor was running toward him.

There was only one thought occupying Hefner's mind: breakfast at the Postschänke. The doctor would not be unduly delayed. Of that, Hefner was quite certain.

IT WAS LATE AFTERNOON and the hospital was uncharacteristically quiet. Even the most distressed patients, whose mournful cries could usually be heard reverberating down the corridors, had fallen silent. Perhaps it was the cold. The hospital heating system had been unable to withstand the Siberian temperature, which had advanced through the walls and was now taking possession of every ward. Many of the patients were still in bed, shivering under starched sheets.

Herr Beiber's bulging stomach rose and fell beneath the loose hospital gown. He was a short, stocky man who possessed a mutinous mustache and beard of a startling orange-yellow hue. From Liebermann's vantage, he could see that the poor fellow was going bald. A lightly freckled tonsure had been exposed on his crown. He looked like a mendicant friar. In fact, Herr Beiber worked for a firm of accountants whose offices were close to the Graben.

"She is such a fine woman." His voice was rich and mellow. Declamatory, like an actor's. "Her skin is like china, and her eyes burn with an ardent fire." He stretched his legs on the divan and wiggled his toes, the extremities of which had turned blue with cold. "Are you familiar with Plato's *Symposium*, Herr Doctor?"

"Not really."

"It is one of the earliest works on love. According to Greek legend, human beings were once double-headed creatures with four legs and four arms; however, we humans were then a proud race, and Zeus resolved that we should be humbled. To this end, he devised a punishment. He cut each body in half—producing two creatures where there had formerly been only one. Thereafter, each incomplete being yearned to be reunited with its other half. It is a legacy that affects us to this day. We are not properly born into this world. We are unfinished."

"And you believe this Platonic doctrine?"

"It is not a question of belief, Herr Doctor. It is something I know to be true."

"But surely it is just a metaphor . . . a fable."

"No, Herr Doctor. It is something that I have experienced, something that I have lived."

The line of Herr Beiber's mouth curved gently to form a saintly introspective smile. His fingers interlocked on the crest of his stomach, and he sighed with pleasure.

"But how?" asked Liebermann.

"When we discover our counterpart, the power of mutual attraction is irresistible—it is an overwhelming and undeniable truth. I could as much doubt the Platonic doctrine as I could doubt the existence of this divan." He rapped the wooden side panel to emphasize his point. "For that reason, I am happy to go through this . . . this *procedure*. You seem a pleasant enough chap, and I have no reason to doubt your sincerity. I am content to lie here, Herr Doctor, and answer your questions in good faith, because I know that whatever obstacles are placed in our path, she and I will be together one day. It would be easier for you to stop the sun from crossing the heavens than to prevent our ultimate union."

Liebermann opened Herr Beiber's file and made a simple note.

Monomania. Platonic myth—paranoia erotica?

"But how can you say that this power of attraction is mutual?" Liebermann persisted. "The lady in question has never corresponded with you, spoken to you, or given you the slightest indication that she even knows of your existence."

Herr Beiber began to chuckle quietly to himself as if he were party to a private joke. "That is what *you* think, Herr Doctor!" Herr Beiber tapped the side of his nose with a chubby index finger.

"I am mistaken?" asked Liebermann.

"Herr Doctor, it was not I who noticed *her* first—it was she who noticed *me*."

Liebermann decided to humor the clerk. "Can you remember the first time she noticed you?"

"Yes. It was a Sunday afternoon last summer. I had been to the zoo and was walking to the streetcar stop, just beyond the Schönbrunn Palace. It was a glorious day, a little too hot for my liking, and I paused just outside the main gates to catch my breath. I turned to look at the palace, which was bright yellow in the sunshine. I squinted against the glare, and something . . . something drew my attention to the fourth floor. There are five windows below the balustrades of a roof balcony. I saw something moving behind the middle window . . . and I knew that it was her."

"You could see her from that distance?"

Herr Beiber smiled benignly, as if Liebermann had asked an innocent but stupid question.

"It was her," he said again, with quiet confidence.

"What did she want?" asked Liebermann.

"Initially, just to capture my interest—to reveal herself."

"And what did you do?"

"I acknowledged her signal with a gesture—"

"What kind of gesture?" Liebermann interrupted.

The clerk rocked his head from side to side. "That, Herr Doctor, is something I cannot disclose."

"Very well," said Liebermann. "What happened then?"

"I caught my streetcar and went home. As you can imagine, I was quite restless. I kept going over in my mind what had happened, and found it almost impossible to sleep. But the more I thought about it, the more it became clear to me that the communication had had greater meaning . . . and the more I contemplated this meaning, the more I found myself possessed by a giddy excitement. Was it possible? I wondered. Was it really possible that such an exalted personage should have feelings for an ordinary chap like me? A humble accountancy clerk in the employ of Hubel & Wiesel. It seemed absurd, ridiculous, but I could not deny the great swell of emotion in my breast. The bright fire of recognition was burning in my soul. . . . She had found me, and I was powerless to resist."

Herr Beiber's face flushed a little as he recollected his night of transfiguration.

"I returned to the palace at various times over the following week. I spent long hours, waiting—often in darkness. But I knew that she would sense my presence and would come to the window, eventually. She was, I am sure, as overwhelmed and frightened, yes, *frightened*, by the experience as myself. . . . She needed to see me there, beyond the gate, steadfast and true. She needed to be reassured, comforted, and fully persuaded that what we were both enduring was absolutely real. Be that as it may, the certainty of our fate was inescapable. The communications became clearer and more numerous. She was desperately unhappy, and I resolved to rescue her."

"Which was when you had your altercation with the palace guards?"

"Indeed. It is regrettable that I failed in my attempt—but I am no way dissuaded from this course of action. She cannot—poor lady— escape the clutches of her royal keepers, and I am obliged to persevere."

Although Liebermann had found the deluded clerk's story mildly amusing, he could not help himself from feeling a sharp pang of pity. It was sad that this otherwise ordinary gentleman had suffered some convulsion in his psyche, a disturbance that made him believe wholeheartedly in a romance that had supposedly begun in the mythic glades of ancient Greece.

Closing his eyes, the little man added, "I will do whatever is necessary." For the first time, Herr Beiber's tone sounded somewhat sinister.

Liebermann leaned back in his chair and picked a hair off his trousers. It was a wiry, auburn strand. He had no idea who it had originally belonged to.

"Herr Beiber," he began. "You said that her communications became clearer and more numerous. . . . How else has she communicated with you?"

The clerk plunged a hand down the front of his gown and pulled out a postcard. He said nothing but simply held his hand out, allowing Liebermann to take the card.

It was a family portrait. A balding gentleman wearing spectacles sat to the right with a young girl on his lap. He was wearing a military-style uniform with braided fastenings and a high collar. Next to him sat a striking woman with a long, elegant face. Her hair was pinned up and she too dandled an infant. Other children, somewhat older, stood on either side of their parents.

Liebermann recognized the striking woman immediately. It was the emperor's daughter, the Archduchess Marie-Valerie, who was the subject of Beiber's fantasy.

"I don't understand," said Liebermann.

"Look at the table," said Beiber.

In the foreground of the picture was a small wooden structure. It was unobtrusive—a prop, no doubt, carefully positioned to satisfy the compositional requirements of the royal photographer. A closed book had been placed on the surface, its embossed spine facing the viewer.

"Can you see it?" asked Beiber.

"I can see the table—and a book."

"Exactly," said Beiber. "She put it there."

"And what does it mean?" asked Liebermann.

"Surely you do not need to ask such a question, Herr Doctor."

Liebermann tilted the postcard to get more light.

"I'm sorry, Herr Beiber, but I really can't—"

"The book, Herr Doctor. Can't you see what it is?"

The postcard lacked sufficient definition to make the title readable.

"Forgive me, Herr Beiber, but my eyesight is rather poor," said Liebermann politely. "Perhaps you can enlighten me?"

"Plato's *Symposium*!" exclaimed Beiber, clapping his hands together.

Liebermann sighed, and underlined *paranoia erotica*.

38

It was early morning. A few flakes of snow floated down from the monotonous sky, frosting the square with a fine white powder.

Andreas Olbricht paused in front of the Academy of Fine Arts and tilted his head back to take in the impressive neo-Renaissance façade. A wide staircase led to three sets of double doors, and on either side of the stairs, on large blocks of gray stone, stood two centaurs. The one on the left had his hand raised, as if commanding the onlooker to stop. The entrance was made yet more imposing by six Doric columns on top of which stood a line of male and female classical figures. Above these were several floors of round arched windows, between which were interposed individual niches housing yet more deities. To Olbricht these were not indifferent gods but gods who stood in judgment. This building was a fortress, jealously protected by its troop of sacred guardians.

Many years ago Olbricht had applied to study at the academy. He had passed the entrance exam, but his portfolio had been rejected. The professors had considered his work "unoriginal."

You will see. The words sounded in Olbricht's head like a Russian bell.

An exhibition of his oil paintings had been arranged in a gallery near the Opera House. It had been made possible with the aid of a generous donation from his patron, the baroness, but Von Triebenbach had also been kind enough to make a small contribution to the costs.

Soon they would be having the posters printed.

Olbricht—Our Heroes and Legends.

Black and white lithograph—the figure of Wotan, spear held aloft.

The artist proudly inflated his chest and ascended the stairs. As he entered the vestibule, the porter nodded a greeting. He recognized Olbricht, who was well known for his early-morning visits to the study collection. If Olbricht arrived any later, he would have to mingle with the students—all of whom he found insufferable. Their very existence annoyed him.

Unoriginal.

The word fell into his consciousness like a drop of acid. He could feel it eating into him, converting his very substance into smoke and air. This always happened in the academy. But he could never resist these visits because the collection included a particular painting that he found utterly fascinating. He needed to see it—to peer into its depths—and examine its myriad dramas in minute detail. It was a painting that merited continual examination because it always yielded something new.

Olbricht walked down the barrel-vaulted corridor. Although the windows were high, they admitted only a feeble, exhausted light. He ascended a grand staircase, allowing his hand to strum the thick stone balustrades. His gloomy journey ended outside the study collection, where an emaciated custodian, whose face was half-concealed by the abundant windings of a scarf, sat shivering by a small stove. Like the porter, the man nodded in recognition and Olbricht pressed a coin into his hand as he passed.

There were many works in the study collection: Murillo's *Boys Dicing*, Rubens's *The Three Graces*, and Rembrandt's *Young Dutchwoman*. But Olbricht was blind to them all, except one: *The Last Judgment*, a triptych by Hieronymus Bosch.

Olbricht approached the three panels, not with excitement,

pleasure, or veneration, but rather with intense curiosity, expectation, and a strange combination of darker emotions such as prurience, horror, and disgust.

Bosch's triptych depicted three fantastic landscapes: *Paradise*, *The Last Judgment*, and *Hell*. The central panel, from which the triptych took its name, was the largest and most intricate piece. The upper quarter was occupied by a clear blue firmament, at the center of which sat a regal red-gowned ruler of the universe. Exiguous angels with diaphanous wings floated at the highest altitudes of heaven, blowing into long trumpets, heralding the end of time. Below the celestial canopy was a blasted landscape of burned-out buildings and apocalyptic fire—a terrible place of shadows, over which antlike humans crawled in almost total darkness. The rest of *The Last Judgment* was crowded with naked men and women, all being subjected to varieties of torment and torture. Their bodies were bent, stretched, skewered, and lacerated, subjected to the most horrible depredations by a host of demons. Enormous contraptions dominated the scene—diabolical machines whose sole function seemed to be the infliction of unimaginable pain. A bare, unadorned building housed the carcasses of destroyed humanity, their barely visible forms hanging on hooks like those of animals in an abattoir. It was a scene of extermination conducted on an industrial scale, like a nightmare vision of the great factories on the fringes of the city, whose chimneys endlessly belched clouds of black smoke.

The more Olbricht looked, the more he saw. Little details: a woman, her vulnerability exposed, about to be ravished by a monster; another, mounted by an enormous beetle; so many people, crammed into beer kegs, hung on trees, prepared on spits for roasting—each private agony represented with indifferent precision.

Herr Bolle had been pleased with Olbricht's *Rheingold* and had requested that the artist consider accepting another commission for a companion piece, *Götterdämmerung*. Thus, he would possess both the very beginning and the very end of Wagner's epic cycle. Herr Bolle found such symmetries deeply satisfying. Olbricht had accepted the commission, but was not sure how he would represent the twilight of the gods. Now, looking at Bosch's *The Last Judgment*, he had an inkling of how it might be achieved.

Fire spreading across the sky, flames invading the halls of Valhalla, tiny gods—rendered with a miniaturist's fine brushstrokes—engulfed by a mighty holocaust—

"Excuse me, sir."

The speaker's German was slightly accented.

Olbricht turned around sharply.

It was a young student, no more than twenty years of age, preparing to make a copy. A slim, faunlike fellow, wearing a short black cape and cap.

"If I could just . . . If you wouldn't mind." The student bobbed his head to indicate that Olbricht was obstructing his view.

"What?" said Olbricht, irritated. "Am I not allowed to stand here?"

The student made an appeasing gesture with his hands. "I must prepare a sketch for this morning's class. Professor Münchmeyer . . ."

Olbricht felt a wave of anger rush through his body. "To hell with you," he said, and stormed out of the gallery.

39

Liebermann placed Franz Liszt's *Consolations* on the music stand. It was almost eleven o'clock, and he would have time to play only one of these miniatures before he was legally obliged to stop playing. Yet he could hear the low growl of a cello emanating from somewhere else in the building—possibly the apartment below—so a few extra minutes would not offend at least one of his neighbors.

Liebermann turned the pages of the score until he found the third piece, a *lento placido*—the most popular and pleasing of the set. His fingers found the familiar notes and he enjoyed the feel of the piano keys surrendering to his touch. Depressing and releasing the pedals carefully, to give the music depth without muddying its harmonic subtleties, Liebermann allowed the pure, meditative melody to soar above the shimmering accompaniment. It was supposed to be a work celebrating the virtues and rewards of solitude, but it drew its sustenance more from the romantic wellhead of Chopin than from the ascetic aspirations of its actual composer.

As the music progressed, Liebermann found himself thinking of his patient, Herr Beiber. His love for the Archduchess Marie-Valerie was so intense, so deep, so profound, but it was merely a delusion. Cases of monomaniacal love had been described for centuries.

What makes one man mad, and another a great romantic?
What is the difference between real love and insanity?

If the Archduchess Marie-Valerie were to reciprocate, then Herr Beiber would no longer be a lunatic, but a very lucky man.

The music seemed to recede as his thoughts became more involved.

Professor Freud is of the opinion that all forms of romantic love are—at least to some extent—delusional.

If so, then how can love be trusted?

A mistake in the left hand alerted Liebermann to how far his mind had wandered from the music. He tutted to himself and refocused his attention on the score. But his playing had become soulless, and he executed the final bars without feeling. Dissatisfied with his mechanical rendition, he did not allow the final notes to linger and closed the piano lid abruptly.

Liebermann retired to the smoking room, where he examined the bookcase. He found Freud's *The Interpretation of Dreams* and sat down in one of the leather armchairs. He began reading the section titled: "The Dream Is a Fulfillment of a Wish." Professor Freud wrote beautifully: "*When, after passing through a narrow defile, we suddenly emerge upon a piece of high ground, where the path divides and the finest prospects open up on every side, we may pause for a moment and consider in which direction we shall first turn our steps.*" No other professor at the university would compose such daring prose—turning the experience of reading into an imaginary Alpine journey. Liebermann read on, seduced by the author's insistent, persuasive voice. He continued reading for some time until his eyelids became heavy and the continuity of Freud's thesis was lost among intermittent brief noddings-off. The room flickered in and out of existence, as if Liebermann's consciousness were a flame, illuminating the world in fits and starts before its inevitable sputtering extinction. In due course his mind lost its tenuous purchase on conscious awareness, and fatigue dragged him down into darkness. . . .

Miss Lydgate sits in the laboratory of the Schottenring police station; but it is also the Grand Hotel in Baden. She is looking through a microscope. She makes a note and removes the glass slide, but when she offers it to him, he discovers that she has something else in her hand. It is an oversize fig. The fruit is round, purple, and the skin has a powdery bloom. It has been cut, from top to bottom, and the red pulp glistens within. He scoops the fleshy interior out with his finger, and lifts it to his mouth—at which point there is a tremendous crash of thunder, and he is overwhelmed by intense fear.

Liebermann opened his eyes.

Tachycardia.

His heart was beating, fast and furious in his ears.

There was someone pounding at his front door.

He glanced at his watch. It was quarter to one in the morning.

Liebermann stood and limped to the door, his limbs resisting their rude awakening.

In the hall he called out, "Just a moment. I'm coming."

When he opened the door, he discovered Haussmann standing outside.

The two men looked at each other for a moment, and Liebermann, immediately grasping the significance of the other man's presence, said, "Another one—already?"

"Yes, Herr Doctor. I am sorry to disturb you at this late hour, but Inspector Rheinhardt respectfully requests your assistance."

The carriage rattled to a halt outside a large bow-fronted villa in Wieden. Two other carriages were already parked nearby. Liebermann surmised that one of them had only recently arrived—the horse's flanks were still steaming. Stepping out of the vehicle, Liebermann raised the collar of his astrakhan coat against a bitter wind. Black clouds raced across the face of a brilliant moon.

Liebermann followed Haussmann to the front door of the villa. The assistant detective gripped the large black knocker, which had been cast in the unusual shape of a scarab beetle, and tapped out a rhythm that reminded Liebermann of Beethoven's Fifth Symphony. *Dit-dit-dit Dah*. They stamped the snow off their shoes and were admitted by a uniformed police constable.

"This way, Herr Doctor," said Haussmann.

Liebermann felt odd. It was as though he were gliding down the hallway, his buoyancy assisted by the thickness of a deep oriental carpet. When they reached an open door, Haussmann turned to look at his companion. The assistant detective's expression was pained, as though he wished to spare Liebermann the coming trial but was powerless to grant the necessary reprieve.

They crossed the threshold, entering a generously proportioned reception room. It reminded Liebermann of Professor Freud's study. The walls were decorated with pictures of Egyptian monuments—pyramids, Sphinxes, and obelisks—and the mantelpiece was crowded with figurines: the familiar parade of animals, falcon-headed deities, and hierophants.

Rheinhardt was standing behind the police photographer, who was making a minor adjustment to the height of his tripod. When the operation was completed, the photographer disappeared beneath a dark cloth and signaled to his assistant. The boy lit a strip of magnesium ribbon and a violent incandescence illuminated the object of their attention.

In the center of the room was a massive circular table. Spread-eagled across its surface was the body of a man, whose skin was the color of a *brauner* coffee. Liebermann had seen pictures of black men in books, and had even seen one or two real black men on the Prater. This man, however, looked rather different. He had long curly hair and his features were sharper, his lips and nose being not so full and wide. His head was thrown back, exposing a deep cut that had opened the trachea and severed both carotid arteries and jugular veins. In the magnesium glare the gaping wound looked as bright and moist as the flesh of a watermelon. His arms were outstretched, hanging lifelessly over the edge of the table. He was wearing a loose, collarless cotton shirt (that might once have been white but that now was drenched in blood) and a small embroidered vest. His trousers were loose, like pantaloons, and were made of cotton.

Where his legs met, the material had been torn away, and a ragged, pulpy cavity occupied the place where his manhood should have been. In a dark pool of blackening blood on the floor, an assembly of fleshy parts revealed the magnitude of the perpetrator's malevolence and perversity.

Rheinhardt walked over to welcome his friend, but when they shook hands, all that he could utter was, "I'm sorry." He rested a hand on Liebermann's shoulder and guided him into the hallway, calling back as he did so, "Haussmann—the floor plan, if you will."

The two men retired to an adjacent room, smaller than the first though more comfortably furnished. They sat down on a large, low sofa.

"The same monster—undoubtedly," said Rheinhardt. "There are no obvious oddities like the Sanskrit symbol, but he may have tampered with the body again—which will, of course, be for Professor Mathias to discover. But we did find this outside." Liebermann was still so overwhelmed by the crime scene that he had not noticed that his friend was holding a large paper bag. Rheinhardt tilted it toward Liebermann. Inside was a bundle of green and yellow material. "It's a gentleman's scarf. Notice, there are no bloodstains. It was either dropped by someone else entirely, or the perpetrator must have changed his clothes before leaving."

"Who is the victim?" asked Liebermann.

"We don't know—that's why I needed you here."

"Oskar, I'm a psychiatrist. I can't commune with the dead!"

"You won't have to—well, not exactly. The murder was reported by a businessman from Trieste—Signore Borsari. He arrived on the late train just after eleven. As he was passing this building, the front door was flung open and he was confronted with the sight of an elderly gentleman in an evening suit, who pleaded with him for help. When the Italian saw the body, he was understandably fearful and made a swift exit. As luck would have it, he bumped into a constable from the local police station and the crime was registered at the security office by twenty past eleven. We have been able to establish—from papers found on the premises—that the old gentleman who hailed Borsari was Professor Moritz Hayek, an archaeologist of some repute. But we don't have a clue who that unfortunate next door is."

"Where is Professor Hayek now?"

"In a bedroom upstairs."

"Then why don't you ask him?"

"I have."

"And . . ."

"He doesn't reply."

"What, he refuses to speak?"

"No, Max. He *can't* speak."

40

PROFESSOR HAYEK'S BEDROOM WAS a shadowy cavern, the air of which was tainted with a pungent, musky fragrance. Like all olfactory sensations it provoked and teased memory. Liebermann had certainly smelled it before, but it was a few seconds before he remembered where—a rather sordid club in Leopoldstadt that he had once frequented as a medical student. The source of the smell was hashish.

On a bedside cabinet a single candle burned with a steady yellow flame. It illuminated the figure of a man in full evening dress, seated on the mattress. Professor Hayek had distinctive features. His skin was brown and leathery, with deep vertical creases scoring his cheeks, but his beard and mustache were short, neatly trimmed, and pure white. The professor's hair was white too, but it was also comically horripilated. There were frequent convulsive tic-like movements of his face and the muscles of his neck. His eyes were open, green like emeralds, and staring blankly into his lap, where his fingers coiled around one another with the slow sinewy movements of a nest of serpents.

Liebermann pulled up a chair and sat down directly in front of the aged archaeologist.

"Professor Hayek?"

There was no response.

"Can you hear me?"

Liebermann passed his hands in front of the professor's eyes. Hayek did not blink.

"What's wrong with him, Max?"

Rheinhardt was standing patiently by the door.

"Severe trauma can sometimes produce a dissociative hypnoid state—a narrowing of consciousness. He has also developed a tic affecting the right sternocleidomastoid."

"I beg your pardon?"

"He's in shock, Oskar."

"Indeed . . . But can you do anything to help him?"

The young doctor passed his hands in front of the patient's eyes again.

"I don't know—but I'm perfectly willing to try."

With that, Liebermann stood up and eased the professor's coat and jacket from his shoulders. Then he unbuttoned the professor's vest. With great care, he loosened the old man's necktie and removed the stiff collar. Taking the candle from the bedside cabinet, he returned to his seat in front of the professor and swung the flame from side to side over the old man's lap. The solitary miniature beacon flared with each oscillation.

"Watch the flame, Professor," said Liebermann. "Watch it carefully. Concentrate on the light. See how it dances. See how it burns. How beautiful it is—see how the flame conceals patterns. The more closely you attend, the more obvious they become."

Liebermann continued talking in this manner, gently but insistently, and as he did so the professor's head began to dip and swing with a distinct pendular motion. The young doctor lifted the candle, and the professor's head began to rise so that he could follow it with his stare. Rheinhardt was reminded of an Indian snake charmer coaxing a cobra out of a basket.

"Observe the flame," continued Liebermann. "Its light is now very strong, and your eyes are tired. Your eyelids are becoming heavier . . . heavier and heavier . . . and soon you will fall into a deep, comfortable sleep. A special sleep, in which you will still be able to hear my voice and answer my questions."

The professor's eyelids began to flicker.

"It is almost impossible to keep your eyes open. On the count of three you will close your eyes, on the count of three you will sleep. One . . . two . . ." Liebermann threw a quick triumphant glance at Rheinhardt. "Three."

The professor's eyelids fell.

"Can you hear me, Professor Hayek?"

"Yes," came the reply. A dry, parched voice.

"I must ask you some questions. And you must reply with absolute honesty. Do you understand?"

"Yes."

Liebermann leaned back in his chair. "Where have you been this evening, Professor?"

"I went to the opera."

"On your own?"

"Yes."

"Was it a pleasant evening?"

"Delightful."

"And what did you do after the performance?"

"I had coffee at the Imperial—as is my custom—before returning home."

A muscle on the professor's neck stood out and he grimaced.

"No harm can come to you now," said Liebermann encouragingly.

"I knocked on the door," the professor continued. "Expecting Ra'ad to answer."

"Ra'ad?"

"My servant."

"The black man?"

"Yes. I took out my key and entered the house. The door of the reception room was open. I called out, 'Ra'ad, where are you, my boy?' But there was no reply. There was a strange smell in the air. . . . I knew that something was wrong. I stepped into the reception room and saw . . ." Again the professor's face and neck went into a rigid spasm.

"No harm can come to you, Professor," Liebermann said emphatically.

"Ra'ad . . . My beautiful boy . . . dead. Murdered." The register of the professor's grating voice changed, becoming more animated. "His lustrous hair, his smooth soft skin . . . How could anyone perform such an act of wickedness on such a perfect, noble creature?"

Rheinhardt shifted from one foot to the other, somewhat embarrassed by the professor's eulogy.

"What did you do? When you saw Ra'ad's body?"

"I was overcome with terror . . . panic. . . . I ran into the street and pleaded with a gentleman for help. He came into the house, saw poor Ra'ad, and ran out. . . . And then . . . And then . . ."

"Yes, Professor?"

"Nothing. Nothing but darkness."

"Where does Ra'ad come from, Professor?"

"He is a Nubian. He has been my servant—and my companion—for some five years. I found him in Kerma when I was supervising an excavation. The great cemetery . . . a complex of tunnels and tumuli full of remarkable treasures. Ra'ad was one of our guides."

The tic returned and a tensed network of facial muscles appeared. The old man looked as if he were in pain.

Liebermann leaned forward and placed the palm of his hand on Hayek's cheek.

"The muscles are becoming loose . . . looser, looser. Feel the heat on the side of your face—a gently penetrating heat, like that of the sun. It warms and soothes—the tension melts away. There is no tension in your face, no tension in your neck. . . ." When Liebermann removed his hand, the thick raised cords of muscle had vanished. "It is time for you to rest, Professor."

The young doctor bent down and removed the professor's shoes. He then lifted Hayek's legs onto the bed, rotating the professor's body in the process. He then touched the man's forehead and commanded, "Lie back."

The old man's head went down slowly, landing comfortably on a pillow.

"You must sleep now," said Liebermann. "A deep restorative sleep—it will be peaceful—calm—tranquil—and undisturbed. When you wake, you will remember all that has happened to you this evening—but these memories will not overwhelm, frighten, or confuse you. Now sleep. . . . Sleep, Professor."

The professor's breathing became shallow and stertorous. Liebermann signed to Rheinhardt that they should leave.

Outside, on the landing, Rheinhardt offered Liebermann a cigar.

"He should be all right," said Liebermann. "I was only using the simple *suggestion method* employed by Charcot and Janet, but it can be effective if the dissociative process is interrupted early. Make sure that one of your men is here in the morning, to assist him when he wakes."

"Of course," said Rheinhardt, striking a Vesta. As the match flared, both men became aware of a massive sarcophagus propped up against the wall. "Well, Max," continued Rheinhardt, lighting Liebermann's cigar. "A madam, three prostitutes, a Czech poultry seller, and a Nubian servant. How are they connected?"

"I don't know," said Liebermann. "It is incomprehensible."

Rheinhardt lit his own cigar and blew a cloud of smoke toward the sarcophagus. "There must be some link, some relation. Is it possible for a mind to rebel so violently against reason?"

"The fact that two of the prostitutes—it might have been three if he had had the opportunity—and the man downstairs were sexually mutilated must be of some significance. But then why did the perpetrator fail to inflict the same kind of injury on the Czech?"

"Perhaps he was interrupted again."

"He had sufficient time to conceal that padlock. If he'd really wanted to castrate the Czech, he could have done so."

"None of the victims have so far been natives of Vienna."

"That is true, Oskar. But if xenophobia was the perpetrator's guiding principle, he could have killed any number of foreigners more conveniently—and at less risk of discovery—by operating in the purlieus of the city: Favoriten, Landstrasse, Simmering. And why would a xenophobe choose to sexually mutilate his victims? Cutting their throats would have been quite sufficient for his purposes. I agree, Oskar, that there must be a scheme—a design behind his actions, some kind of logic, however obscure. But I am at a loss as to what that might be."

41

ASCHENBRANDT HAD BEEN COMPOSING at the piano all day. He had been working on *Carnuntum*—more specifically, on an orchestral interlude that was provisionally titled *The Eve of War*. It was programmatic—like the overture—and evoked the approach of a great storm with timpani rolls and angry bursts of double bass and cello. He wondered whether the score needed the additional depth of a Wagner tuba—but was undecided.

The interlude was a dark, brooding piece that had required careful attention to detail. The triumphal theme that appeared at the end of the overture and signified the Quadi's victory was reprised, note values extended, and in the relative minor key. At first there was just a stygian plainchant in the bassoons, but then it was transposed several octaves higher and rendered with exquisite tenderness by a *solo cor anglais.* The interlude ended with a trumpet call that represented the sound of a cock crowing. Dawn was breaking—a Homeric "rosy-fingered" dawn. In the next scene the leader of the Quadi would rally his troops and sing an aria that would swell the chest of any good, honest German.

> The day has arrived,
> Our day of destiny.
> Let us be victorious
> Or die a hero's death.

> "In days to come
> Around the hearthstone
> Children will beg to hear the tale
> Of brave ancestors who dared to challenge
> The might of Rome.

> "Blood and thunder,
> Blood and thunder.
> Salvation and victory.
> Fields incarnadine.
> Wotan—let this sacred day be ours."

Aschenbrandt was exhausted. He left the piano and collapsed on an armchair, closing his eyes. Yet he could not rest. The themes of his opera kept on returning—like reminiscences. Rising, he removed his cello from its case, scraped the bow over a cube of rosin, and placed Bach's first *Cello Suite* on the music stand. Aschenbrandt was not an accomplished cellist but he was proficient enough to render a tolerable performance of some of the Bach suites. Although his pitch was sometimes suspect, he could easily produce a big, expressive sound.

He began the *G Major Prelude*.

His head cleared immediately. It was like standing in a shaft of sunlight.

Bach had created music without melody.

Out of texture, structure, and flowing rhythm the listener was carried through cycles of tension and resolution. But when Aschenbrandt allowed the last note to die, the silence was not complete. The leader of the Quadi was singing the last verse of his aria—a resonant bass:

Blood and Thunder, Blood and Thunder.

It was a good melody.

If he didn't commit it to paper now, he might forget—and it would be lost forever. Reluctantly, Aschenbrandt laid the cello aside, went to the piano, and began to write the melody down: D, G, B-flat, A. Dotted crotchet, quaver, crotchet, minim.

His muse was heartless, but he had a duty to obey her.

Whatever was demanded, he *must* find the strength.

42

"I WOULD LIKE TO SEE Inspector Rheinhardt," said Amelia Lydgate.

"Is he expecting you?" asked the duty officer.

Amelia handed him the letter. It read:

Dear Miss Lydgate,

Because of the intemperate weather our technical staff at the Schottenring laboratory have been laid low with various forms of winter infirmity. It was subsequently suggested by our mutual friend Herr Doctor Liebermann that you might be invited—once again—to assist us with our work. I understand that your academic commitments are considerable, and I therefore respect your proper right to refuse us. However, if, dear lady, you are disposed to make us the gift of yet one more hour of your valuable time, the Viennese security office will be most grateful.

With kindest regards,
Sincerely,
Detective Inspector Oskar Rheinhardt

The officer smiled at Amelia and escorted her to the laboratory, where she found Rheinhardt and Liebermann waiting.

The two men bowed as she entered.

"Inspector Rheinhardt, Doctor Liebermann."

She looked at each man in turn as she said their names: her

detached delivery made the greeting sound more like an act of identification.

"Miss Lydgate," said Rheinhardt, "thank you so much for coming."

"It is my pleasure, Inspector," said the Englishwoman. Then, obviating any opportunities for small talk, she added, "How can I assist?"

"Indeed!" said Rheinhardt, as if some unreasonable third party had been attempting to stop them. "On Friday evening there was a murder in the fourth district. A gentleman of African origin, in the employ of an archaeologist of some renown—Professor Hayek. Outside the house we found this scarf." The inspector picked up a paper bag, removed the seal, and showed Miss Lydgate the contents. "It is one of a batch sold at a gentlemen's outfitters situated just behind the Opera House. The shop assistants have been unable to help us with our inquiries. Many scarves have been purchased since the cold spell began and they simply cannot remember anything useful concerning specific customers. Now, it may be that this item of clothing was lost by someone who had nothing at all to do with the murder. However, if it did belong to the villain, then a microscopic analysis might yield some clues to his identity."

"You have established that it does not belong to the professor."

"We have indeed." Then, changing the tone of his voice, Rheinhardt added, "The only member of our technical staff to have been spared a debilitating cold seems to be your old acquaintance in the cage over there." Rheinhardt gestured toward the brown rabbit, whose twitching nose was pressed between the bars. Rheinhardt had expected the Englishwoman to show some small sign of pleasure but she merely glanced at the animal, nodded curtly (as if to suggest that things were in order), and returned her attention to Rheinhardt.

The inspector felt somewhat foolish, coughed into his hand, and continued, "We at the security office have benefited from your forensic skills in the past. Would you be prepared to undertake a microscopic examination of our evidence and write a short report?"

Without hesitation the Englishwoman responded, "With pleasure, Inspector."

She turned to hang her hat on the stand and began to shrug off her coat. Liebermann stepped forward to assist.

"Thank you, Doctor Liebermann."

Leaning closer, Liebermann said in a somewhat confidential tone, "Are you well, Miss Lydgate?"

"Very well, thank you."

Their hands touched as her arm came out of the sleeve.

"I beg your pardon," said Liebermann. But she didn't seem to have noticed and threw him a fleeting, puzzled look. Before he could respond, she was walking toward the very large microscope that occupied one of the benches. She examined the equipment at her disposal and then turned toward Rheinhardt.

"Inspector," she said, addressing him. "Would you be so kind as to seal the bag?" He did as he was told. "Now shake the bag and beat the sides."

Rheinhardt gave the bag a vigorous shake, his jowls wobbling with the effort. He then struck the side of the bag several times with his open palm.

"No," said Amelia. "That is not sufficient. I would like you to continue beating the bag for some time—and with greater violence."

Rheinhardt raised his eyebrows. "How much violence, exactly?"

"Considerable violence."

"As you wish," said Rheinhardt. He drew his big hand back and repeatedly slapped the bag. The noise was loud and precluded conversation. While Rheinhardt was thus occupied, Amelia washed her hands and began to lay out several rows of glass slides. She found a bottle marked *gum arabic* and spread the contents lightly on each glass oblong.

After a significant amount of time had passed, Rheinhardt's brow began to bead with sweat. He stopped to catch his breath and during the pause Liebermann stepped forward.

"Oskar, I am perfectly happy to relieve you if—"

"That won't be necessary, Doctor Liebermann," interrupted Miss Lydgate. "I am confident that a good quantity of dust has been dislodged from the fibers."

Amelia took the bag from Rheinhardt, removed the seal, and carefully lifted the scarf, shaking it a little before she extracted it completely. She then tipped the bag over her slides and gently tapped its base. Nothing appeared to fall out. Discarding the bag, Amelia selected another bottle and a pipette, sniffed the bottle's contents, and placed a small droplet on each slide. When this operation was completed, she opened a box of square cover slips and carefully placed one on each of her specimens.

Amelia lifted the first slide, inserted it into the microscope's stage, and leaned over the eyepiece. She then changed the objective lenses. She worked silently and swiftly, examining each slide at different levels of magnification. Some of the slides she placed to the right, others to the left. When she had finished, she raised her head from the microscope and faced Liebermann and Rheinhardt.

"Very interesting," she said. A vertical crease had appeared on her forehead.

"Miss Lydgate?" asked Rheinhardt tentatively.

"The scarf held mostly paper fibers," she said.

"From Inspector Rheinhardt's bag?" asked Liebermann.

"Well, yes, Doctor Liebermann; however, the slides show

numerous *types* of fiber—indicating different methods of production, and different ages."

"Which suggests?" Liebermann prompted.

Amelia raised a finger to her bottom lip and appeared to be lost in thought.

"Miss Lydgate," Rheinhardt tried again.

"Oh yes . . . forgive me." The Englishwoman roused from her reverie. "There were also traces of cloth, tiny crystals of a substance that I suspect is glue, and minute particles of leather. Some of the latter were very old indeed."

"I see," said Rheinhardt. "Most, erm, puzzling."

He twisted one tip of his mustache.

"Not *that* puzzling, Inspector!"

"I don't understand," Rheinhardt said. "Are you saying, Miss Lydgate, that these particular substances are significant?"

"If the scarf belonged to the murderer—then yes."

"In what way?" said Rheinhardt, feigning nonchalance.

"They reveal his profession."

"They do?"

"Yes. He is the proprietor of an antiquarian bookshop—or he is a librarian."

43

THERE WERE SEVEN OF them in the carriage.

Liebermann, Jacob Weiss, and his wife, Esther, were on one side; Clara, Konrad, Bettina, and Rachel on the other.

The carriage's interior was sumptuously appointed: ornate moldings, deep carpet, pleated-satin headrests, two carved mirrors, fawn trimmings (with matching silk lace), French door handles, and— most unusually—an electric bell to capture the driver's attention. The exterior was even more impressive: olive-green panels, thick rubber tires, wide fenders, and two massive silver-plated headlamps.

"This is such a beautiful carriage," said Clara, stroking the shiny green leather. "Now, wasn't it the right thing to do—wasn't I right, Father? We couldn't have arrived in our old trap, we just couldn't have."

Jacob Weiss looked over his spectacles at his daughter.

"Yes, my dear," he said indulgently. "You *were* right. And this *is* a splendid carriage. An electric bell! Who would have thought it? I am sorely tempted to press it again."

"No," said Esther. "You've already troubled the driver twice for no good reason—a third time will be inexcusable."

Jacob Weiss shrugged, and patted his wife's hand.

"Will the emperor be there?" asked Rachel.

"No," said Clara.

"You don't know. He might be," said Weiss.

Clara ignored her father and continued to instruct her younger sister. "There will, however, be many other important people: politicians, diplomats, the Rothschilds, the Wittgensteins—"

"The Lembergs," added Bettina.

"I don't think so, not this evening," said Clara.

"Why?" Bettina asked.

"Haven't you heard?" Clara said. "They say that young Lemberg was killed in a shooting accident last week. But everyone knows that it was really a duel."

"How terrible," said Bettina.

"I don't know what's wrong with young men these days," said Jacob. "What possesses them? Such a waste, such a pointless waste."

"Anyway," continued Clara, "there will be many important people at the opera—which is why we must look our very best." Then, turning toward Liebermann, she added, "Oh, I almost forgot—I saw Frau Trenker yesterday, and she is still suffering from very bad headaches. Her doctor said she should wrap her head in a cold wet towel for an hour a day, but it isn't doing very much. I said I would ask you for some advice."

"Tell her to take aspirin," said Liebermann.

"Aspirin?" repeated Jacob Weiss. "It works?"

"Yes," said Liebermann.

The carriage began to slow down, and joined a short line just outside the Opera House. Eventually, the vehicle passed through the archway under the grand balcony and came to a halt. The driver knocked the handle of his whip, discreetly, on his box.

"Well, we're here!" said Jacob.

An attendant approached the carriage, pulled down the folding step, and opened the door. One by one the Weiss family emerged, enjoying the attention of a small crowd of well-dressed onlookers.

Liebermann paused beneath a tree of gaslights. He had been to the

Opera House many times before, but he had never noticed—before that moment—that the lamp's feet were cast in the form of four winged Sphinxes.

For some inexplicable reason he was transfixed.

Secrets, secrets, secrets . . .

"Come on, Max," said Clara. "What are you staring at?"

"Oh, it's nothing."

He took her arm and they entered the building.

After visiting the cloakroom and purchasing their programs, the Weiss family assembled at the foot of the grand marble staircase. Liebermann looked up into the vastness—the wide-open dizzying expanse above his head. It was so immense: the chandeliers and wall lights seemed like whole worlds, suns, planets, softly glowing in the void. Massive round arches surrounded the central space and, through these, other arches could be glimpsed. On tall square pillars stood seven statues representing personifications of architecture, sculpture, poetry, dance, art, music, and drama. They were like custodial gods, marshaling the glowing worlds through the infinite. And beyond the guardians, columns, and balustrades was an artificial sky of transverse vaulting, enlivened by the colors of shadowy frescoes—white, blue, and vermilion.

Clara was leaning toward Rachel and whispering something behind a fan.

"What is it?" Liebermann asked.

Her stare darted to the left, where a portly man was standing with two women wearing thick fur stoles.

"Hammerstein," she whispered.

"Who?"

Clara's eyes rolled upward. "The cigar manufacturer. They say he's as rich as an archduke."

Liebermann was not a great lover of the opera. He did not like the fact that most people—including Clara—attended not for the music but to participate in a social event. Also, the music itself was usually not to his taste. He found it too rich, too excessive, too melodramatic. He much preferred the simplicity of lieder, the intimacy of a string quartet, or the abstract purity of a symphonic work. Even so, he was eager to hear *The Magic Flute* again. The reviews had been exceptionally positive. Even the critic Theodor Helm—in the traditionally anti-Semitic *Deutsche Zeitung*—had praised Director Mahler's new production. The director had reduced the size of the orchestra and encouraged them to play in the style of a chamber group. Liebermann was convinced that he would find this treatment of the work particularly rewarding.

The family ascended the grand staircase.

Clara drew Liebermann closer to her. For the first time all evening, their gaze met in privacy. Liebermann found the moment troubling. She was so very pretty. Whenever he saw her face turned up toward his, he wanted to smother it with kisses. But was this enough? Was the sweetness of her breath and the softness of her pale cheeks sufficient to sustain a union supposed to last forever?

"Are you happy, Max?"

It was an innocent question but it resonated so deeply with concerns and doubts that he could barely acknowledge—let alone face up to—that his collar tightened and the words he tried to speak came out sounding half-strangled.

"I haven't seen *The Magic Flute* in years," he uttered costively, trying to smile. "I'm sure it will be a delightful evening."

Now he understood why he had been transfixed by the quartet of Sphinxes. He too was the keeper of a terrible secret. The engagement ring on Clara's finger weighed heavily on his conscience—as if each diamond was a millstone hanging around his neck.

Jacob Weiss led the group to their box, where two bottles of champagne awaited them in a bucket of ice. Champagne flutes were arranged on a small folding table, next to a tray of white chocolate truffles. While Konrad poured the champagne and Rachel offered around the chocolates, Liebermann gazed out into the auditorium.

A massive chandelier, like a girdle of stars, hung from the center of a fabulously decorated ceiling. Below the emperor's box—a cave of tantalizing shadow—was an area reserved for individuals who had lined up for cheap tickets. This "standing enclosure" was divided by a bronze pole. One half was reserved for civilians, the other half for soldiers. These two divisions had started to fill with roughly equal numbers of men.

The orchestra, mostly string players and a few woodwind, had begun to appear in the pit.

Rachel arrived with the tray of truffles and circled it under Liebermann's nose—as if to waft the enticing fragrances. The sound of a clarinet, doodling in the low registers, produced a pleasant, liquid accompaniment.

The young doctor smiled.

"Have you spotted anyone famous?" asked Rachel.

"To be honest, I wasn't looking." He took a chocolate and bit it in half.

"Yes, you were—you were trying to see if there was anyone in the emperor's box."

Esther overheard the challenge and cried out, "Rachel! Don't be impolite!"

The girl's cheeks burned.

Liebermann glanced at Esther, and waved his hand as if to say *It was nothing*. He then returned his attention to Rachel. "In fact, I was looking at the standing area." Rachel's blush subsided. "You see? Where the soldiers are gathered?"

Rachel peered over the edge of the box.

"Where do the women stand?" she asked.

"They don't—women aren't allowed in there."

"Why not?" she persisted.

"I'm not sure," said Liebermann, electing to give an uncomplicated answer. "Perhaps their dresses take up too much room."

He popped the remains of the chocolate into his mouth and took his seat. Clara passed him a champagne flute, and settled next to him. She produced a pair of opera glasses and began to systematically scan the five rows of boxes on the opposite side of the auditorium. Occasionally she would whisper a society name. "Baroness von Ehrenstein . . . Hofrat Nicolai." Then, more animatedly, "Countess Staray!"

Strings—the tinkling of a glockenspiel—the hollow, soft thunder of the kettledrum.

Although Liebermann found this incessant naming mildly irritating, he could not deny that the presence of so many luminaries was certainly contributing to the atmosphere. The volume of conversation grew steadily louder, until eventually he could no longer hear what Clara was saying.

The musicians were tuning up. Liebermann took his spectacles out of his top pocket and curled the wire arms around his ears—he wanted to examine the scene more closely. The stalls were now full—a veritable crowd had gathered in the standing area—and clusters of white oval faces hovered like ghosts above the rim of every balcony. The lights began to dim. There was movement in the pit, and suddenly Director Mahler's wiry frame materialized on the podium. The audience applauded and some of the officers at the back rattled their sabres. Liebermann felt a sense of relief. He was eager to lose himself in the evening's music.

Mahler turned, raised both hands above his shoulders, and thrust his baton at the orchestra. The sound that emerged from the pit had a wonderful organic quality: a divine progression of chords, each swelling and opening up, as if the music were actually blooming like a flower. This sublime unfolding was followed by passages of extraordinary delicacy. The scoring was pellucid, suffused with a quality of exquisite airy lightness.

The curtain rose to reveal a desert landscape of wild rocks and isolated trees. Huge mountains loomed on either side of a round temple.

Clara clutched Liebermann's hand. The audience gasped. A giant serpent was emerging from the backstage shadows. It was huge, like a Chinese dragon. The musical accompaniment became agitated and stormy as the creature reared up above a tiny human figure.

"Help me," sang Prince Tamino. "Or I am lost."

"There is no escape from this serpent."

The beast circled the desperate prince.

"Closer and closer it comes."

"Someone help me."

Clara squeezed Liebermann's hand.

It seemed that the prince was about to meet his end. He swooned and fell to the ground. Above him the snake's massive head swung from side to side. Its great jaws opened, revealing terrifying long fangs. At the point when all seemed lost, the gates of the temple opened and three veiled ladies appeared.

"Die, monster," they cried, "by our power."

They raised their arms and called down from the heavens a magical nemesis.

The beast lashed its tail, writhed, squirmed, and snapped its jaws. Then, rearing up one last time, the serpent seemed to cry out before collapsing in a twisted heap.

"Victory," sang the mysterious trio of women. The music became triumphal. "The heroic deed is done."

They approached the unconscious prince and praised his beauty. Then, after expressing regret, they took their leave, in order to report to their mistress—the Queen of the Night.

The next scene was comic.

The prince awoke and, somewhat confused, concealed himself behind a rock. Then a man in a plumed costume appeared, carrying some pipes and empty cages. He was attempting to catch birds, singing a jolly song as he set about his business. At the end of the song the prince made himself known to the bird catcher, who mischievously allowed the prince to think that it was *he* who had slain the monstrous serpent with his bare hands.

The three ladies returned and identified the bird catcher as Papageno. It was apparently Papageno's custom to offer the ladies birds in exchange for wine and cake. On this occasion, however, the three ladies did not honor their tradition. Instead of wine they gave him plain water, and instead of cake they gave him a stone. And to prevent Papageno from lying again, they sealed his mouth with a golden padlock. . . .

Liebermann loosened his hand from Clara's grip and leaned over the edge of the box.

The drama continued to unfold and new characters appeared: the Queen of the Night, who explained to Tamino that her daughter Pamina had been abducted by the evil Sarastro. Three boys—or genii—who entered the drama in a flying chariot, to guide Tamino on his quest. Slaves, Princess Pamina herself, and finally the lascivious Moor, Monostatos.

Liebermann became increasingly agitated.

There were *definite* parallels.

He could hardly believe what he was seeing. It seemed too extraordinary, too strange.

Clara tutted as he fidgeted in his seat.

When Monostatos the Moor appeared, Liebermann's agitation turned into excitement.

The experience was like vertigo. The box felt insecure, as though it might tip and deposit him and all of the Weiss family into the stalls below. His heart felt engorged and banged violently against his ribs as if seeking to escape its bony confinement.

He leaned toward Clara. Her soft hair tickled his lips.

"I have to go," he said.

She turned and drew back, her expression confused and disbelieving.

"What?"

Surprise had amplified her voice. Herr Weiss craned his head to see what was going on.

Liebermann drew her closer again and whispered into her ear.

"It's important. I have to go—I'll explain . . . I'll explain tomorrow."

Clara grabbed his arm, stopping him from getting up.

"What are you talking about? You can't just go." Her voice was conspicuously loud.

Liebermann removed her hand from his arm and stood up.

"I'm sorry."

The entire Weiss family was looking at him. He took a deep breath, opened the door, and left.

44

THE THREE REPRESENTATIVES OF Primal Fire had come bearing gifts, all of which had been placed at the great man's feet. Collectively the group resembled a strange Epiphany in which the adoring Magi were obeisant not to a divine child but to a wizened prophet. Guido List had responded to the party's votive offerings with an extempore disquisition on the Aryan origins of classical civilization. But while still discoursing on Roman architecture, he was interrupted by his wife.

Frau List was a striking woman: youthful, attractive—and an actress of some renown. As Anna Wittek, she had read the part of the Wala in List's *The Wala's Awakening*. Von Triebenbach remembered the celebrated performance seven years earlier, sponsored by the German League. The statuesque Wittek had declaimed List's poetry into the balmy night, and Von Triebenbach recalled the squareness of her shoulders, the swell of her bosom . . .

Anna pinched the lint that circled her husband's head and tugged at it to see if the dressing had become slack. It gave a little.

"I will have to tighten the strip," she said softly.

"Very well, my dear," said List. Then, addressing his guests, he said, "Excuse me, gentlemen. This will only take a moment."

The actress manipulated some hidden pins and the bandage became taut. Satisfied with her handiwork, she lowered herself onto a stool and straightened the tartan blanket that covered her husband's legs.

"My angel," whispered List, taking her fingers and pressing them into the gorse of his beard. He moved his head so that he appeared to be looking directly at his guests. Von Triebenbach was standing behind Aschenbrandt and Olbricht, who were seated next to each other and facing their host.

"I don't know what I would do without her," List added with tenderness.

"You are a very fortunate man," said Von Triebenbach, modulating his voice to disguise a trace of envy that threatened to squeeze the bonhomie from his avuncular baritone.

"Indeed," said List, allowing Anna's hand to fall into his lap. "Very fortunate."

He did not relinquish his grip.

Seeking to preempt an embarrassing eulogy, Anna turned to the young composer and said, "Herr Aschenbrandt, I understand that you are writing an opera based on my husband's *Carnuntum*?"

"Yes . . ." Aschenbrandt replied, unsure of whether he was expected to elaborate before List had completed his disquisition.

"It will be a fine work," said Von Triebenbach, patting Aschenbrandt's back.

"With the exception of *The Wala's Awakening*," said Anna, "to which I have a particular sentimental attachment, I would very probably count *Carnuntum* as my favorite among my husband's works."

"It is a masterpiece," agreed Aschenbrandt. "The greatest novel in the German language—and I am truly honored to have received the author's benison." Then, raising his voice, Aschenbrandt added, "Thank you, sir. I will not disappoint you."

"On the evidence of your overture," said List, "I know that my favored child is in capable hands. I have every confidence in your gift."

"Thank you, sir," said Aschenbrandt again. "You are too kind."

Olbricht reminded the baron of his presence by shifting in his seat. Von Triebenbach had promised Sophie von Rautenberg at the Wagner Association soirée that he would introduce the artist to Guido List.

"Herr Olbricht," said Von Triebenbach, "is to have an exhibition in December featuring several oil paintings inspired by your work."

"Is that so?" said List.

"Yes," said Olbricht. "I am particularly proud of a canvas based on *Pipara*."

"*The Germanic Woman in the Purple of the Caesars*," said Anna, completing the novel's full title.

"She is depicted on a balcony, surveying a mighty Roman army under her command," said Olbricht.

"Perhaps," said List, "when these wretched bandages are removed, my eyesight will be restored and I will have the opportunity to admire your . . . interpretation."

"That would give me the greatest pleasure."

List did not make any further inquiries about Olbricht's exhibition. Instead, he addressed Aschenbrandt again.

"Perhaps, Herr Aschenbrandt, you would like to attend one of our musical evenings. My dear Anna would love to hear the *Carnuntum* overture, I am sure."

"But of course . . . and I have recently completed an orchestral interlude, *The Eve of War*, that I could arrange for piano. It employs the triumphal theme that appears at the end of the overture, but with values extended. It is a dark tenebrous piece, full of atmosphere . . . and it is followed by an aria, an exquisite battle hymn, *Blood and Thunder*, sung by the leader of the Quadi. With your permission, I could invite a tenor—a friend of mine, one Herr Hunger. Then you could hear the interlude and aria together."

List and his wife agreed that this would be an excellent idea. A further attempt by Von Triebenbach to reintroduce the topic of Olbricht's exhibition failed abysmally. He consoled himself with the thought that at least he could tell the alluring Von Rautenberg widow that he had kept his word.

In due course the subject of Aschenbrandt's opera was exhausted, and the young composer tactfully invited List to finish the disquisition on the Aryan origins of classical civilization that he had started earlier, but had not—so far—had the opportunity to conclude.

List obliged, describing how the Aryans were forced to leave their boreal cities during the Ice Age, and how, by mixing with the inferior peoples of the south, they had seeded the civilizations of Greece and Rome. This led him, by an oblique argument, to an affirmation of the nationalist Pan-German agenda and a vitriolic condemnation of their enemies. After he had denounced the Church and the monarchy, he directed his diatribe at a third and no less reprehensible institution.

"We must not underestimate the Freemasons. They are a growing threat. They have played no small part in influencing world events in the past, and they will seek to do so again—with devastating consequences. We have grown complacent. Politicians have short memories. They may have forgotten about the Masonic uprising of 1766—but I, on the other hand, have not!"

"With respect," said Von Triebenbach tentatively, "I am ashamed to admit that I too cannot recollect this . . . important historical event."

"Seventeen sixty-six!" said List, thumping his free hand on the arm of his chair. "An uprising, planned to begin in Prague and intended to spread across the whole of Europe. The brotherhood would have seized power in every significant state. Fortunately, the secret police knew of their scheme and arrested the principal conspirators. But I tell you . . ." List touched his temple and shook his head. His expression became pained, fearful, as though his shadowy world were being visited by horrible visions.

"My love . . ." Anna reached forward and stroked a furrow from his troubled brow.

"I tell you," List continued. "It could happen again. I have heard that the Masons are fomenting dissent in Bohemia and Hungary . . . and no one is doing anything to stop them. Our politicians are feeble. Weak. Dullards! Unaware of the imminent danger."

The room fell silent.

"We are in dire need of a hero," said Von Triebenbach solemnly. "A youngblood—a new Siegfried."

His hand found Aschenbrandt's shoulder and rested on it briefly.

It was a small gesture, but it did not escape Anna's notice. She smiled at the baron, then at the young composer.

Part Three

Salieri

45

LIEBERMANN RUSHED OUT OF the Opera House and marched briskly to the rear of the building. To his left was the eastern extremity of the Hofburg Palace, the bastion of which was surmounted by an equestrian statue of Archduke Albrecht. In spite of the archduke's overbearing presence, the plaza in front of him was dominated by another figure: a white marble likeness of Mozart examining an open score on an ornate music stand. He was dressed in a long cape that tumbled artfully off his left shoulder, a short jacket, frilly cuffs, and tight breeches. Putti danced and cavorted around a substantial pedestal, which was decorated with discarded manuscripts, laurel wreaths, and a somewhat chaotic jumble of instruments. Next to this arresting monument was Liebermann's destination, the eponymous Café Mozart.

Once inside he was immediately blinded as his glasses steamed up. He removed them impatiently and approached one of the waiters.

"Good evening—could I use the telephone, please?"

The waiter bowed and escorted him to a private kiosk. Being somewhat preoccupied, Liebermann tipped the waiter an excessive amount. The waiter smiled obsequiously and opened the door with the florid flourish of a courtier. Once inside, Liebermann called Rheinhardt.

"Oskar—it's Max. I need to see you immediately." His words were animated with a breathless urgency. "I know how he's doing it. I know how he's choosing his victims."

The line crackled. Liebermann heard the sound of Rheinhardt's two daughters laughing in the background.

"Where are you?"

"Café Mozart."

"Wait there. I'll be with you shortly."

Liebermann replaced the receiver in its cradle and stepped out of the kiosk. Nearby, two rakish gentlemen in striped jackets were entertaining a loud lady friend. A dark green magnum bottle of champagne suggested that she had been plied with an injudicious, if not positively reckless, quantity of alcohol. Peering through thick, undulating curtains of cigar smoke, Liebermann tried to locate an empty table. None seemed to be available; however, he was soon rescued by the waiter, who—perhaps anticipating further tokens of gratitude—guided the young doctor to a vacant window seat.

Liebermann ordered a *schwarzer*.

"And something to eat, sir?" The waiter offered him the menu. Liebermann gestured to indicate that he did not need to read it.

"Mozart torte," he said decisively.

"An excellent choice, sir," said the waiter, smiling and stepping backward, his head lowered between hunched shoulders.

The inebriated woman threw her head back and produced a shrill, abrasive laugh. Her hair had begun to unravel and loose dark strands tumbled wildly past her shoulders. The two rakes exchanged eager glances, their eyes alight with concupiscent interest. A group of portly burghers at an adjacent table shook their heads and scowled disapprovingly.

Liebermann's attention was recaptured by the waiter, who had returned with his coffee and cake. The Mozart torte was a colorful checkered arrangement of chocolate and pistachio sponge, on top of which was a marzipan coin bearing the profile of the great composer. Liebermann took a mouthful, found it a little too sweet, and decided that the time might pass just as quickly with a cigar.

Some twenty minutes later Rheinhardt appeared at the door. He did not take his coat off and came directly to Liebermann's table.

"Well, Max," said Rheinhardt. "This is most unexpected."

Liebermann rose and they shook hands firmly.

"Please, sit."

Before they had settled, the waiter seemed to materialize out of a vortex of cigar smoke.

"Another *schwarzer*," said Liebermann. "And a *türkische* for my friend."

"Strong—with extra sugar," Rheinhardt added.

The waiter retreated into the yellow-brown fug.

"It's extraordinary," Liebermann began. "He must be unique . . . peerless in the annals of abnormal psychology. We are dealing with a most remarkable individual. A mind of singular peculiarity."

"Max," said Rheinhardt, halting his friend with an expression that demanded moderation. "Slowly, please. And from the beginning."

Liebermann nodded. "I am quite feverish with excitement."

"And I do not doubt that you have good reason to be; however . . ."

"Yes, of course. Slowly, and from the beginning." Liebermann sat back in his chair and loosened his necktie. "This evening I went to the opera."

"It must have been uncommonly short."

"I left early."

"Was it that bad?"

"Not at all—Director Mahler's *Magic Flute*."

"Then why—"

"Do you know it?"

"*The Magic Flute?* Not very well . . . I haven't seen it in years."

"Nor have I."

"Well?"

"The characters, Oskar—can you remember the characters?"

"There's a prince—Tamino . . . and a princess, Pamina. The Queen of the Night, who has that glorious aria—the famous one in which the melody hops about on the very highest notes."

"Yes, the Queen of the Night! Now think, Oskar! Does *that* name—the Queen of the Night—not sound to you like a certain colloquialism?"

Rheinhardt twisted the right tip of his mustache between his thumb and forefinger. "Lady of the night?"

"Or, as the French would say, *fille de nuit*. Meaning what?"

"A prostitute, of course!"

"The Queen of the Night has three attendants—or serving women . . ."

The inspector's eyes widened until he began to resemble an exophthalmic patient whom Liebermann had examined earlier the same day.

"Good heavens," Rheinhardt gasped. "Madam Borek and the three Galician girls."

"Exactly! And then there is Papageno, the bird catcher. Who is punished for lying. Can you remember the punishment, Oskar?"

"Dear God! His mouth is sealed with a padlock!"

"Now think of the Wieden murder. The black man."

"Why, he *must* correspond to the Moor."

"Monostatos."

Suddenly Rheinhardt's expression changed. It vacillated on some nameless cusp before collapsing into unequivocal despondency.

"Oh, no, no, no." The inspector groaned as if in physical pain.

Liebermann was puzzled at his friend's unexpected response. "Oskar?"

Rheinhardt placed his head in his hands.

"What a fool I've been. What an absolute fool!"

Liebermann felt rather deflated by his friend's response. "It wasn't *that* obvious, Oskar. The recognition of these correspondences did require *some* imagination."

"Forgive me, Max. I did not mean to belittle your achievement. But it really should have been obvious . . . to *me!*"

"Why? You are a policeman. Not a Mozart scholar."

The waiter arrived with the coffees. The inspector lifted his head, tasted his *türkische*, and dropped two pieces of crystallized sugar into the cup. His melancholy sagging eyes looked close to tears.

"It begins with a snake, doesn't it?"

"I beg your pardon?" said Liebermann, somewhat confused.

"*The Magic Flute*: it begins with the slaying of a snake."

"Yes."

"Well, so did this series of murders."

Liebermann slid the remains of his Mozart torte across the table toward the dejected inspector. On numerous occasions he had witnessed Rheinhardt's spirits rallying after a few mouthfuls of pastry. Almost unconsciously, Rheinhardt plunged the fork through the invitingly pliant sponge.

"Before the Spittelberg atrocity," said Rheinhardt, "a giant anaconda was killed at the zoo."

"Hildegard."

"That's right—did you read about it?"

"Yes. I recall that the animal was supposed to be a favorite of the emperor's."

"Indeed. I investigated the incident myself. It was a highly irregular crime, but in the light of subsequent events, it paled into insignificance. The Spittelberg murders occurred the following day . . . and I simply forgot about the emperor's prize snake. Even the life of the most exalted royal animal should not be valued above the life of a human being—however wretched—and with that thought in mind I transferred all my attention from one case to the other. But now, of course, I can see the error of my ways. How stupid of me!"

Rheinhardt mechanically deposited a corner of Mozart torte into his mouth. He chewed, swallowed, and continued: "The anaconda was cleanly sliced into three sections with a large weapon—most probably a sabre. The perpetrator entered the snake-pit and made his exit without leaving a single mark in the soil. Madam Borek and two of her girls were also killed with a sabre . . . and even though the brothel had been flooded with blood, the perpetrator escaped without leaving a single footprint on the floorboards. It was clearly the same man."

Rheinhardt examined the remnants of sponge on his plate. "Mozart torte? Is this your idea of a joke, Max?"

"It seemed appropriate but I discovered that I wasn't very hungry."

Rheinhardt took another mouthful and for the first time exhibited his usual appreciative response.

"Very good—are you sure that you don't want some?" Liebermann shook his head. The inspector sampled a pistachio square and continued speaking. "Now that you have discovered his method, Max, what does this tell us about him? Is he a devotee of Mozart, do you think? A fanatical student of his operas?"

"Oskar, no one who appreciates Mozart could possibly commit such atrocities." The young doctor straightened his back. "Mozart is an entirely civilizing influence."

"Yet the perpetrator is certainly very familiar with Mozart."

"Yes, but I find it difficult to believe that an individual truly fond of Mozart's singspiel could divine within its plot and characters a program for murder. Indeed, I suspect that the very opposite is true.

The perpetrator is no friend of Mozart and very probably despises *The Magic Flute.*"

Rheinhardt scraped some chocolate curlicues from the outer circle of his plate. "Yet I can't think of a less offensive opera."

"It is, without doubt, a work of incomparable charm. But in the perpetrator's mind *The Magic Flute* has become shadowed by the darkest of emotions: hate, fear, envy." Liebermann pressed his hands together. "It would not surprise me to discover that something very bad happened to him in early childhood—perhaps while listening to Mozart's music."

"But would such an experience—however unpleasant—have predetermined that this unfortunate child should in due course become a monster?"

"No, not at all. Professor Freud insists that psychopathology arises when the mental apparatus draws power from a primal source, or origin. I would suppose that *The Magic Flute* acquired terrible significance during the perpetrator's infancy; however, it has since become a means of organizing and directing his *current* violent impulses. To understand *them* we would have to have knowledge of his history—and the contents of his unconscious."

A waiter passed the table and discreetly removed Rheinhardt's empty plate.

"There's a legend, isn't there?" said Rheinhardt. "Connected with an Italian composer accused of murdering Mozart. What was his name?"

"Salieri," Liebermann replied. "Although some say that Mozart was murdered by his Masonic brothers for revealing their secrets in *The Magic Flute.*"

"A suitable sobriquet for our perpetrator—don't you think? Salieri?"

"Salieri." Liebermann savored the exotic combination of vowels and consonants. "Yes, very apposite."

"Salieri it is, then!" said Rheinhardt.

As if in response, the inebriated woman clapped her hands together and squealed with pleasure. One of her companions had handed her a small box. She opened it up and removed a piece of cheap jewelry.

"There are two further questions that must be raised concerning *The Magic Flute*," said Liebermann. "First, can we learn anything more of Salieri's objectives by making a study of the opera? And second, to what extent does the opera cast new light on evidence already in our possession?"

Rheinhardt tugged at his lower lip.

"I am no expert on Mozart operas, but *The Magic Flute* must surely be counted the least coherent."

"That is because nothing in *The Magic Flute* is what it appears to be. It is full of arcane Masonic symbols." Liebermann suddenly remembered that he was still carrying the Court Opera program. He pulled it out of his pocket and flicked through the pages until he found some biographical notes on the composer. "Here we are . . . Mozart . . . initiated into the degree of apprentice in the *Loge zur Wohltätigkeit* on 14 December 1784 . . . and in 1785 initiated into the degree of fellow and that of master one month later . . . libretto by Schikaneder—who has been described as a Lodge brother. . . ." Liebermann flicked over the page. "Baron Ignaz von Born . . . Grand Secretary of the Vienna *Loge zur wahren Eintracht* . . . The outline of the opera was discussed at the bedside of Born, a master of Masonic symbolism and an authority venerated by all Viennese Masons."

"Does it say anything about what these symbols are supposed to represent?"

"No. For that you will probably have to consult a Freemason."

"I very much doubt whether *they* will agree to help."

"Why do you say that?"

"Relations between the security office and the Freemasons are not good." Liebermann tilted his head questioningly. "Oh, it's all very complicated." Rheinhardt fussed with his napkin.

"Go on."

"The Freemasons have not been allowed to perform their rituals in Austria for more than thirty years. The law permits them to meet under the aegis of friendly societies—but nothing more."

"Freemasonry is illegal?"

"Well, not exactly. Many years ago it was decided that something should be done about the proliferation of subversive societies. People were more worried about dissent in those days, which is understandable: the revolution of 1848 was still a recent memory. So the Law on Associations was passed. This established state control of all associations."

"What does that mean?"

"Very simply, if you wish to form a society—philosophical, artistic, political, or otherwise—you must apply for a license that is granted at the discretion of a specially appointed commissioner. Now, the outcome of this process was—for the Freemasons—quite unsatisfactory. It is not illegal to be a Freemason. Nor is it illegal for Freemasons to meet. However, it *is* illegal for Freemasons to gather for the purpose of conducting a 'secret' ritual. So the security office has been obliged to monitor the Freemasons quite closely, which has been the cause of considerable bad feeling. If we are to discover more about the symbolism of *The Magic Flute*, then I suspect this will be best achieved by long hours spent poring over books in a library. Fortunately, I have Haussmann at my disposal."

"I wonder whether . . ." Liebermann's voice trailed off as his brow furrowed with concentration.

"You wonder what?"

Liebermann looked at Rheinhardt. "I wonder if the swastika features in their arcana."

"Very possibly. I believe that the Masons make use of many ancient emblems. Alchemical signs, the all-seeing eye, the sevenfold flame . . ." Rheinhardt stopped listing enigmatic symbols. "Max?"

The young doctor had already detected the expression of deep concern on the inspector's face.

"Yes, Oskar. Salieri has murdered the Queen of the Night, her three ladies, Papageno, and Monostatos. But the cast of *The Magic Flute* contains so many more characters: Tamino, Pamina, Sarastro."

"And children! Isn't there some sort of chorus—composed of three boys?"

"Yes," said Liebermann, turning the page of the program and staring ruefully at the long list of singers. "If he means to eliminate all of them, his work has hardly begun."

46

IT WAS LATE IN THE afternoon. The gas lamps had been lit, and most of the exhibition halls in the Natural History Museum were deserted.

Earlier in the day Liebermann had written a note to Clara and her family, apologizing for his rude and precipitate departure the previous evening. He had requested their forgiveness and promised a full explanation. In truth, however, he was still unsure what he was going to say.

Clara had sent a prompt reply to the hospital, coolly informing her fiancé that the Weiss family would be expecting him for dinner at half past seven. The communication did not end with her customary list of gushing endearments. Liebermann folded the note into quarters, slipped it into his top pocket, and spent the rest of the afternoon concentrating on his patients: Fräulein Allers, who suffered from hysterical abdominal pains; Herr Fogel, who wept bitterly for no apparent reason; Frau Huhle, who could not stop washing her hands; and finally Herr Beiber, the monomaniac who had fallen in love with the Archduchess Marie-Valerie. As soon as Liebermann had finished his case notes, he remembered Clara's letter and felt a certain heaviness around his heart. This physical sensation was accompanied by a general sense of despondency.

On leaving the hospital, Liebermann decided that he might benefit from a brief sojourn in the Natural History Museum. Even if it failed to improve his mood, it would at least give him an opportunity to collect his thoughts.

Liebermann climbed up the great staircase and wandered unhurriedly through the main galleries. He peered into the glass cabinets and examined the exhibits: brightly colored birds; a rangy fox; a pride of lions; tarantulas, bigger than a man's hand; magisterial tigers and butterflies with crêpe-paper wings of turquoise and yellow; a massive crab given as a gift by the emperor of Japan to Emperor Franz Josef; the fossilized remains of great lizards; the freestanding skeleton of a whale; and, finally, a prehistoric man and woman, huddled together in the dusty bed of their burial pit.

Here was an enduring marriage.

Liebermann tried to imagine his bones and Clara's, intermingled forever beneath the soil. But he could not do so. The proscenium of his imagination remained stubbornly dark.

A custodian was closing the large wooden door ahead. Behind it, a life-size lacquered papier-mâché model of a stegosaur fell into shadow.

Liebermann turned, and retraced his steps.

The gas lamps in the Geological Hall had been dimmed, but the gemstones and geodes still played with the meager light. The effect was quite magical. As Liebermann strolled down the central aisle, he was accompanied by waves of coruscation. Rocks flared and glinted as though an invisible retainer were scattering stardust in his path.

Ensconced in a window seat on the far side of the gallery was a woman. Her flaming hair and straight back instantly announced her identity: it was Miss Lydgate. The Englishwoman's nose was buried between the covers of a book. With a quick, mercurial movement she turned the page. She seemed to be devouring the text at an alarming speed.

Liebermann approached, allowing his footsteps to sound more loudly. As he drew closer, her concentration broke and she looked up from the volume.

"Doctor Liebermann—what a pleasant surprise." The words were spoken softly, dreamily, as if she were waking from a deep sleep. She was about to stand, but Liebermann gestured for her to remain seated.

"Miss Lydgate." Liebermann bowed.

The gas lamps hissed and the unusual stillness was disturbed only by the distant groan of creaking hinges and the soft jangling of keys. The galleries were being closed off one by one.

"I came to see the meteorites," said Amelia.

"Indeed," said Liebermann, not altogether sure how to continue the conversation after such an unusual declaration. Fortunately, Amelia rescued them both from a potentially embarrassing hiatus with a polite inquiry. "How is Inspector Rheinhardt?"

"Very well."

"And the investigation?"

"Progressing." Liebermann felt disinclined to provide a more comprehensive answer. He did not want to spoil this unexpected rendezvous with talk of Salieri, blood, and mutilated corpses. "What are you reading?" he asked, willing their talk toward a more pleasant topic of conversation.

The familiar vertical crease appeared on her forehead and deepened.

"An indulgence. I would be better served by a textbook of anatomy; however, today I received some parcels from London, one of which contained this work of fiction." She held up the slim publication. "A gift from my father."

Liebermann translated the title and was somewhat puzzled. *An indulgence?* He did not think that a story about a timepiece sounded so terribly indulgent.

"*The Time Machine*," he read out loud in English, "by H. G. Wells."

"Yes, my father is a great admirer of the author, who—unlike his peers—is unusually conversant with scientific ideas."

"It is a story about a clock?"

"No, the term *time machine* refers to something far more interesting. It is a device that can actually travel through time—which is itself ingeniously represented as a fourth dimension, supplementing the more familiar Euclidian measures of length, breadth, and thickness."

Miss Lydgate handed the volume to Liebermann, who inspected the spine. The novel was published by a company called Heinemann. Liebermann wondered why Mr. Wells was published by a German firm.

"The narrator travels to the distant future," Amelia continued, "where he discovers that humanity has degenerated into two separate species. The Morlocks, an apelike race who live below the surface of the Earth, and the Eloi, a helpless, feeble folk with childlike qualities. Although *The Time Machine* is only a . . . ." The vertical crease on Amelia's forehead deepened as she searched for a precise term. "A *scientific romance*, I cannot help but feel that it was Mr. Wells's intention to provoke more than just excitement in his readers. Indeed, I am of the opinion that this story is also meant to serve as a kind of prophecy—or warning."

Once again, Liebermann found himself entranced by this remarkable woman: her pedantic speech, her steady gaze, the power of her intellect.

"Warning?" he repeated her last word, hoping this modest prompt would provoke a lengthy exposition.

"In our modern world," Amelia began, "there is an increasing rift arising between the rich and the poor. Moreover, there is a tendency for those who are born into the laboring classes to live—and work—underground. In London, for example, it is customary for household servants such as maids, cooks, and launderers to spend the greater part of their existence in basements and cellars. Indeed, it is not uncommon for serving people to use the terms *upstairs* and *downstairs* as appellations to distinguish the *gentlefolk* from their own kind. There are many more dramatic examples of the same phenomenon. Think of coal miners, whose terrible fate it is to descend into the very bowels of the earth. Think of train drivers, many of whom must now work underground— some never see the light of day. In fact, think of any great modern city: London, Vienna, New York. All are now built on a subterranean honeycomb of boiler rooms, tunnels, and workstations."

The Englishwoman's eyes brightened.

"Mr. Wells seems to be suggesting that if the trend continues, the human race will eventually divide along the fault lines of social stratification. There will be fewer and fewer opportunities for intermarriage, resulting in subspeciation. We are destined to become Morlocks and Eloi."

Liebermann handed the book back to her.

"It is an extremely interesting hypothesis, Miss Lydgate. However . . ." He smiled kindly, not wishing to extinguish her enthusiasm with harsh criticism. "I find it somewhat implausible. Humanity has made its home in the snowy wastes of the Arctic, the sere deserts of Arabia, and the jungles of darkest Africa. Yet the basic human form has remained constant."

"With respect," said Amelia, clutching the book to her breast. "I would beg to differ. The human form is very pliable. Does the Eskimo look like the Bedouin? The Bantu exactly like his Nordic cousin?"

"No—but, to my knowledge, this has not resulted in any biological prohibition on procreation between races. In spite of our propensity to explore and inhabit different environments—which has inevitably resulted in some superficial variegated adaptations—we remain a single humanity."

"But eventually, Doctor Liebermann, if such differences were to be exaggerated over millennia—over periods of time of the order required to turn, let us say, a carboniferous forest into coal—then surely—"

A custodian appeared at one end of the gallery. He clicked his heels and announced in an officious, haughty tone, "The museum is about to close."

Amelia stood up and a faint smile flickered across her face.

"I would very much like to continue this conversation, Doctor Liebermann, but I am afraid that I must now collect my coat and hat from the cloakroom."

Liebermann glanced at his wristwatch. He knew that what he was about to say was improper—and that if Miss Lydgate answered him in the affirmative, then he would almost certainly arrive late for dinner at the Weiss household. Even so, he heard himself saying, in a disembodied, airy voice, "But we *can* continue this conversation if you wish. There is a coffeehouse on Museumstrasse . . ." His invitation trailed off.

Miss Lydgate looked at him with her arresting, metallic eyes.

The hiss of the gas lamps seemed to become louder in the ensuing pause, filling the lacuna with a disconcertingly violent rush of sound. The custodian coughed impatiently.

"That is a delightful idea," Amelia replied. "Tell me—where do you stand with respect to the writings of Jean-Baptiste Pierre Antoine de Monet?"

47

"Inspector Rheinhardt?"

"Herr Arnoldt."

"Would you like to come in?"

Rheinhardt peered over the zookeeper's shoulder but could see very little of the dim interior beyond. There were clumps of dense foliage: large, spatulate, dripping leaves and hairy hanging creepers. The air that escaped through the half-open door was warm and fetid.

"Not really," said Rheinhardt, each syllable extended by equivocation.

"Why not? It's perfectly safe. Giselle has the sweetest temperament, I can assure you."

Rheinhardt was not convinced that the zookeeper's assurances could be trusted. Even so, he crossed the threshold and allowed his shoes to sink into a carpet of springy moss. Herr Arnoldt turned abruptly and tramped down a gentle slope. "Please, Inspector," he called out. "I would be grateful if you would close the door behind you. Firmly."

Rheinhardt did so, but could not stop himself from asking—albeit silently—*Why?*

He hurried after Herr Arnoldt, who had vanished behind a matted curtain of trailing vines. Rheinhardt followed him through and discovered the zookeeper standing with his legs apart and his hands on his hips, staring across a still expanse of dark green water. The virid glassy surface was surrounded by lush swamp vegetation. On the opposite bank was a massive reptile with a broad, flat snout. Its scaly skin was brown and black, although the area surrounding its jaw and the visible parts of its neck and belly were creamy white.

"Giselle," said Herr Arnoldt.

"A crocodile?"

"No," said Herr Arnoldt. "She's an American alligator. *Mississippiensis.*"

"Ah," said Rheinhardt. "And you are sure she's not . . . dangerous?"

"Quite sure."

Suddenly, two olive-green eyes appeared silently just above the surface of the water.

"My God, what's that?" cried Rheinhardt.

"Oh, that's only Richard," said Herr Arnoldt.

"Richard . . ."

"Yes."

"You never said anything about Richard." Herr Arnoldt remained ominously silent. "Is *he* dangerous?"

"Not if we keep our distance."

"Herr Arnoldt, I had no intention of getting any closer."

The zookeeper turned toward Rheinhardt and let his hands fall loosely by his sides.

"I just thought . . . I just thought you might enjoy seeing them like this. Few people are afforded such a privilege. They are magnificent creatures."

There was something in the keeper's tone of voice that made Rheinhardt feel he had been mean-spirited. Herr Arnoldt's invitation had been well intended—an eccentric but essentially friendly gesture.

"Yes," said Rheinhardt. "You are quite right. They *are* magnificent creatures. Thank you . . . Most kind."

The zookeeper nodded, realizing that some subtle misunderstanding had now been resolved. "So," he said, clapping his hands and rubbing them together eagerly. "Have you caught him?"

"No," Rheinhardt replied. "Unfortunately not." The zookeeper pushed out his lower lip. "However, we are making good progress. Not as much as I would have liked at this stage, but progress nevertheless. I wondered if you would help us again? I have a question pertaining to the statement you gave at the Schottenring station."

Herr Arnoldt nodded.

"After your memory returned," continued Rheinhardt, "you were able to remember the approach of the assailant, who marched down the corridor, whistling a . . . *jolly* tune?"

"Yes, that's right," said Herr Arnoldt. "I told your assistant everything. I'm afraid there isn't any more to tell."

"Indeed. But I understand that you were able to reproduce the melody for my assistant—Haussmann. Could you possibly do so again, for me?"

There was a gentle rippling sound. The previously submerged alligator broke through the pool's surface, revealing its full size.

"God in heaven—it's huge!"

"Just over thirteen feet," said Herr Arnoldt, calmly. "Among male *Mississippiensis*, Richard is not exceptionally large."

The animal's jaws opened. It appeared to be yawning.

"So many teeth . . . ," said Rheinhardt, feigning a light conversational tone, while suppressing a very strong urge to run.

"Yes, about seventy or eighty. And each one is as sharp as a razor."

"Have you ever been bitten?"

The zookeeper laughed. "No, Inspector. Few people get bitten by *Mississippiensis* and live to tell the tale."

"Just as well, then," said Rheinhardt. "Now, where was I?"

"The melody—you said you wanted me to sing the melody again."

"If you can still remember it—yes."

The zookeeper cleared his throat, and began to sing:

"Pa, pa, pom, pom, ta-ta-ta-ta, pom, pom, pom . . ." The first few phrases were distinctive and the pitches accurate. Thereafter the melody became loose and improvisatory, eventually degenerating into a piece of pure invention. "That's about it," Herr Arnoldt added. "I'm not sure about the last bit—but the beginning is correct."

Rheinhardt opened a large cloth-bound volume that he was holding under his arm. Herr Arnoldt noticed that the pages were covered in musical notation. When Rheinhardt had found the right page, he took a deep breath and began to sing from the score:

> "Der Vogelfänger bin ich ja—"
> I'm the merry bird catcher,
> A familiar sight to young and old.

Rheinhardt's deliciously resonant baritone filled the enclosure. It rolled out across the water and bounced back from the high ceiling. He had never performed in such a strange arena and to such a strange audience. Indeed, so peculiar was his situation that for a fleeting moment he entertained the possibility that he was, in fact, still lying in his bed and the events of the morning were occurring in a dream.

Giselle and Richard did not respond, but the zookeeper's expression was utterly transformed.

"Yes, that's it," he cried. "That's it!"

Rheinhardt continued singing:

> I know how to set a trap
> And whistle like a bird . . .

The melody was playful, charming, and composed in the style of a popular song.

"What is it?" asked Herr Arnoldt.

Rheinhardt gently closed the score. "It's from *The Magic Flute*."

The sound of displaced water disturbed them. Richard had begun to move forward. He seemed to be traveling quite fast. His snout was producing a high bow wave.

"I think . . . ," said Herr Arnoldt, looking a little concerned. "I think it's time to go."

48

OLBRICHT STARED ACROSS THE paint-spattered floorboards and caught sight of himself in the full-length mirror. He relaxed his legs and turned his wrists inward, assuming an attitude reminiscent of that of Michelangelo's *David*. Then he raised his right hand and imagined his fingers closing around a laurel wreath. He felt a curious thrill, as though his fanciful conceit had been translated into authentic communion with the *weltseele*—the world soul. He closed his eyes, hoping to prolong the moment, but the strange feeling dissipated, leaving him with only a dull headache.

The artist turned and surveyed the paintings he had prepared for his coming exhibition.

Alberich and the three Rhine maidens; a blind skald in a timbered hall; Siegfried, slaying the dragon . . .

He circled the studio, admiring his accomplishments, but stopped in front of the canvas of *Pipara*—the heroine of List's eponymous novel. Square shoulders; yellow braided hair; a strong, almost masculine face. She was standing on a raised stone balcony, looking out over a sea of heavily armored Roman legionaries.

Olbricht took a step closer.

He could remember feeling extremely pleased with his *Pipara* when the painting was completed; however, having put it aside for a while, he was now somewhat dissatisfied with her appearance. Olbricht picked up his palette and a fine-haired brush, and began reworking the empress's features.

There was something about the bridge of her nose that was not quite right. The height of her cheekbones, too low—the shape of her chin, too broad. Olbricht's movements became more fluid. Something of his communion with the world soul had stayed with him. He felt inspired, guided by a spirit hand toward the realization of an elusive ideal.

Finally, he took a step back.

The empress now bore an uncanny resemblance to Frau Anna, the wife of Guido List. She was so very beautiful, Frau Anna. Such a perfect example of Aryan womanhood.

If only he had seen her in the *Wala* . . .

If only he had been there—on that celebrated occasion, sponsored by the German League.

If only . . .

Something inside him crumpled, like an eggshell trodden underfoot.

Olbricht reached out and traced the curve of the empress's bosom with a trembling finger.

List was not an attractive man, and he was considerably older than the beautiful Anna. Yet she had married him. Her love had been won by the power of his intellect—the nobility of his spirit—the ferocity of his genius.

"I too am a great artist." Olbricht had unconsciously said the words out loud.

His thoughts returned to the exhibition.

She would be impressed. Of that he was certain. She, and women like her. It was inconceivable that she was the only one—the only one who could recognize a hero. The only one who might want a pure, unsullied union—a union of souls.

Olbricht withdrew his shaking hand from the painting.

"I can make this better . . . better still," he muttered. "Much, much better."

He lifted his palette and inspected the brighter colors.

It must be a bolder work, a more challenging work, a work that reflected not only Pipara's inner strength—but his own.

49

THEY WERE SEATED BESIDE one of the Belvedere Sphinxes. A great wedge of snow had collected between the statue's stone wings, and her expression suggested wounded pride. Beyond the sunken hedge gardens and frozen fountains, the lower palace was shrouded in a nacreous winter mist.

Clara's mood was congruent with the landscape: frigid and unforgiving. They had barely spoken since leaving the Weisses' house.

"Your father was very understanding," said Liebermann, softly.

"He had to be civil," said Clara. "He accepted your apology because he doesn't want to cause any arguments. Especially now."

"Is he angry with me, then?

"Max, I am angry with you."

Liebermann sighed, and looked down at his shoes. "It was important, Clara. Extremely important."

"I'm sure it was. . . . But so was going to the opera with my family. You ruined the evening. For all of us."

Liebermann raised his hands in the air, as if beseeching the Sphinx to support him. "*The Magic Flute* is the key. I had to let Inspector Rheinhardt know immediately."

"Did you? It couldn't have waited for an hour or two?"

"No. I have seen what this madman does. People's lives are at risk."

"Has he struck again, then, this madman of yours?"

"No, he hasn't. But—"

Clara cut in, "Then it could have waited!" She managed to contain her anger for a few moments before it boiled over again.

"And why were you late for dinner yesterday?"

"I had a fencing lesson."

The lie came all too easily.

"I thought your lessons were in the morning?"

"Signore Barbasetti was indisposed last week." Liebermann spoke in an even voice, all the time staring into the Sphinx's face. Her expression seemed to change from wounded pride to disapproval. "We had rescheduled the lesson for yesterday evening. Unfortunately, I got rather overinvolved . . . and forgot the time."

Clara shook her head. "And what does that tell us about your . . . your attitude?"

Liebermann was somewhat taken aback by this curious question. "I'm sorry?"

He turned to face Clara, whose dark eyes now seemed unusually penetrating.

"I remember," she began slowly, as if the act of remembering were hard. "I remember you once said that *everything* means something— everything we do, however small: slips of the tongue, minor accidents, not being able to find things. . . . So what does forgetting our dinner engagement mean?"

Liebermann felt as if the earth had shifted. He had underestimated her. She was more than just pretty, amusing Clara—a young woman from the right kind of family, with the right kind of background, his fiancée, a future wife. She had depths, some of which neither he— nor anybody, perhaps—would ever know, and a basic, inalienable right to be happy on her own terms. She had many faults, but at least she was honest, which was more than he could say of himself at that moment.

"Well?" Clara insisted.

Liebermann knew what he must do—and the mere thought of it brought him close to the edge of an inner precipice. Darkness and despair were aching to swallow him.

50

HERR BEIBER SHOWED NO signs of anxiety or discomfort. He seemed perfectly content to be lying on a hospital divan, following the young doctor's injunction to say—without censorship—anything that might come into his head. Indeed, it seemed to Liebermann that the accountant was enjoying himself.

"I can remember, one morning—about a month or so ago, just before the snow started falling—I was standing outside the Schönbrunn Palace." Beiber raised his hand and let it fall onto his stomach, making a loud slapping sound. "It was very early. The mist had only just lifted, and I knew—I just knew—that she was still asleep. I imagined her, slumbering in a gilded four-poster bed, her sweet nose pressed into soft, downy pillows. Now, at that moment I saw this fellow making his way toward me—a musician, carrying a cello on his back. And it struck me, all at once, that it would be a truly wonderful gesture to arrange a little concert—so that she might wake to the strains of some beautiful love song. There's a famous, oft-quoted line, by an English author: *If music be the food of love, play on* . . ."

"Shakespeare," said Liebermann.

"Is it?

"Yes. *Twelfth Night.*"

"Perhaps I saw it at the Court Theater. To be honest, I can't remember. Anyway, I thought it a most agreeable sentiment, so I raised my hand and the cellist halted. I asked him if he would be kind enough to play a love song, for the Archduchess Marie-Valerie. He was an odd fellow . . . something about him . . . Oh, it doesn't matter. He went to move off and I begged him to wait a moment. 'I'll make it worth your while,' I said. 'Naturally.' He didn't respond. 'What shall it be?' I asked. 'Two krone?' I thought it a generous offer—but the fellow didn't budge. 'All right,' I said, 'let's call it three kronen.' Still—no response. 'Four, five, ten?' Still nothing. So, more out of curiosity than anything else, I offered him twenty, then fifty, and finally, one hundred krone. And do you know what? He still didn't accept. Instead, he said: 'The Archduchess won't be able to hear.' I disagreed. 'My good man'—I said—'it's a very still, quiet morning. The cello has a full, deep voice—of course she will be able to hear.' He shook his head. 'I can assure you,' he said, 'she won't. This is the summer palace—there's no one home.' And then he walked off. It wasn't empty, of course. The fool was totally wrong. She was in the palace— I knew it!"

A note of petulance had crept into his final exclamation. But he sighed, pulled at his vibrant orange-yellow beard, and continued, speaking more calmly now.

"Such a shame . . . If he had been more of a game fellow, it would have been a glorious way for her to wake. Those sweet eyelids, still heavy with sleep, fluttering open. Her head turning, to hear better the sweet melody . . . she would have known that it was me, of course."

He closed his eyes and blissfully contemplated the imaginary royal chamber.

"Herr Beiber," said Liebermann. "If you were . . . united, with the Archduchess Marie-Valerie, how do you think you would spend your time together? What would you do?"

"That is an interesting question, Herr Doctor," said the accountant, "and one to which I have devoted much consideration. You will forgive me, however, if I correct your language slightly. It is somewhat misleading. The question is not *if*—but *when*. When the Archduchess Marie-Valerie and I are united, how shall we choose to spend our time together?"

"Very well," said Liebermann.

"We shall take walks. We shall go to concerts. We shall read poetry. We shall hold hands. I shall spend whole days gazing into her soft, compassionate eyes. I shall comb her hair. We shall talk—endlessly—about our miraculous love, and we shall tell and retell the story of our coming together."

Herr Beiber licked his lips and continued to enumerate.

"I shall fill her pen with ink when she wishes to write letters. I shall open doors for her when she wishes to pass from one room to the next. I shall give her roses . . ."

Herr Beiber went on in this vein for some time; the life that he envisaged for himself as the Archduchess's consort was curiously sterile. It was nothing more than a series of frozen tableaux: tiny gestures of affection and tired romantic motifs.

Liebermann coughed in order to interrupt the mundane litany.

"Herr Beiber." He paused and looked down at the freckled bald patch. "I am sorry, but . . . What of erotic feelings?"

"What of them?"

"You have not mentioned them."

"Why should I? I am in love with the Archduchess. Have I not made myself clear?"

Liebermann tapped his index finger on the side of his temple.

"Herr Beiber," said Liebermann, "have you ever experienced sexual relations with a woman?"

The great romantic looked somewhat flustered.

"I . . . erm . . . There has never been anyone . . . special to me. No."

"Does the idea of sexual congress frighten you?"

Beiber laughed. "Good heavens, no, Doctor. What a ludicrous idea!"

Liebermann was familiar with the work of the French neurologist Guillaume Duchenne, particularly his *The Mechanism of Human Facial Expression*. Although Beiber's mouth had curved upward, the orbicularis oculi muscles around his eyes had not contracted. The smile was—without doubt—false.

51

A LARGE MAP OF Vienna hung on the wall behind Rheinhardt's desk. The heart of the city was clearly demarcated by the Ringstrasse— really a horseshoe, the ends of which connected with the Danube Canal. Farther north was the wide diagonal of the mighty Danube itself. To the east were the open grassy spaces of the Prater, and to the west the foothills of the famous Vienna Woods. In the bottom left corner of the map was a complex grid that represented the paths and gardens of the Schönbrunn Palace. A tack with a broad silver head had been planted within the boundary of the imperial zoo. There were three more: one just outside the eastern curve of the Ringstrasse, one in the town center, and one in Wieden—close to a delta of black railway lines that terminated under the word *Südbahnhof*.

Rheinhardt connected the tacks with four strokes of an imaginary pen. The exercise produced a mental impression of something that looked vaguely like a kite. The inspector wondered if—in the unfortunate event of more pin-tacks being added—a more significant pattern might possibly emerge. Salieri clearly had a weakness for programs and symbols. He could autograph the entire city by striking in carefully chosen locations.

The inspector's thoughts were disturbed by the sound of Haussmann turning the pages of his notebook.

"We've been keeping a close eye on the List residence for three weeks now," said the assistant detective.

Rheinhardt raised and lowered himself on his toes, unaware that he was doing so. "Indeed."

"And, in spite of his infirmity," continued Haussmann, "or perhaps because of it, he has been receiving many visitors. His eye doctor, of course; the Englishman, Chamberlain; Counselor Schmidt; a student called Hertz; the actor, Bernhard—I've never heard of him but I understand that he's supposed to be quite famous."

"Yes, yes, Haussmann," said Rheinhardt, trying to hide his growing impatience. "But if I'm not mistaken you told me this last week."

Haussmann turned another page. "Quite right, sir. Please accept my apologies. In addition to the aforesaid gentlemen, Herr List has also received . . . Viktor Gräsz, a publisher; August Haddorf—another actor, and a well-known patron of the arts called Gustav von Triebenbach."

Rheinhardt trained his melancholy baggy-eyed gaze on his assistant. Trying hard not to sound impatient, he said, "Haussmann, do you actually have something interesting to report?"

The assistant detective reddened slightly. "Yes, sir—although it may only be interesting in my estimation, you understand."

"I am happy to proceed on that basis."

The younger man blinked, unsure how to interpret the inspector's arch expression. "All these people," he continued warily, "are affiliated with associations and societies. For example, the Richard Wagner Association, the German League, the Alemania Dueling Fraternity, and the Aryan Actors' guild."

"Well, given the nature of Herr List's writings it does not surprise me that he mixes with individuals who share his Pan-German sympathies."

"Yes, sir. But Baron von Triebenbach . . ."

"What about him?"

"He is the president of a small group who call themselves the Eddic Literary Association."

"The *Edda*, Haussmann," said Rheinhardt, suddenly striking a pedagogical attitude, "are the two collections of early Icelandic literature that together constitute the principal source of all Norse legends."

"Yes, sir. However, it wasn't the name of the society that struck me as interesting, but rather where they meet."

"Which is where?"

"At Baron von Triebenbach's apartment, on Mozartgasse."

Rheinhardt swallowed. "What did you say?"

"Mozartgasse, sir. I thought that . . ." The younger man shrugged. "What with all this talk of *The Magic Flute* . . . there might be some . . . connection?" Haussmann touched the map and ran his finger down the length of the Naschmarkt. He stopped at a minor road adjoining a square. "Mozartgasse. It's in Mariahilf—I know it quite well."

Rheinhardt rested a gentle hand on Haussmann's shoulder. "That is interesting, Haussmann—very interesting."

"Shall I obtain a list of members?"

"Haussmann," said Rheinhardt, leaning closer, "I am bound to disclose that for some time now I have harbored the suspicion that you are, in fact, a psychic. I swear, the security office's loss would be vaudeville's gain."

The assistant detective risked a fragile smile.

"Well done, Haussmann!" bellowed Rheinhardt. "Commendable detection!"

52

THE SHELVES OF THE library were now full. The packing cases had been cleared away and the librarian, ever industrious, was working on a more advanced cross-referencing system. All that could be heard was the scratching of his nib on pieces of card, like the movements of a mouse behind a skirting board.

The venerable stepped over the threshold and the librarian looked up.

"Please," said the venerable. "Do carry on—I did not mean to disturb you."

The librarian nodded and returned to his task.

In the corner a new and very handsome porcelain stove had been fitted. Leather reading chairs had been placed beneath gas lamps. All in all, the ambience was most welcoming.

The venerable walked across the rectangular space and examined the colorful embossed spines.

Humanitas: Transactions, Societas Rosicruciana, The Order of the Secret Monitor.

Below these was a shelf of much larger volumes. They were extremely old and were concerned with ceremonials of all kinds.

The Kabbalistic Master Ritual, The Egyptian Rite, Anointing and Purification.

Then there were the works on philosophy and alchemy.

"Has he agreed?"

It was the librarian.

The venerable turned and smiled. "Yes, brother."

"He will be initiated here?"

"Yes. He will stay for a few nights with our friends in Pressburg—and then he comes to Vienna."

The coenobitic librarian put his pen down on the desktop. The venerable noticed that the man was breathing heavily.

"Are you well?"

"Yes, of course," said the librarian, his face flushing slightly. "Very well. I am simply excited by the prospect . . ."

The venerable walked over to the desk and laid a hand on the librarian's shoulder. "It is wonderful news. But now we have much work to do: such an auspicious occasion must be celebrated with a unique rite. I have some small modifications in mind. . . . Tell me, brother, where can I find the rituals of the Grand Lodge of the Sun?"

53

MAXIMILANPLATZ WAS A CONVENIENT place for them to meet, being equidistant from the Schottenring police station and the General Hospital. Liebermann was sitting on a bench, watching Rheinhardt— who was in the process of buying a large bag of roasted pumpkin seeds from a street vendor. The coals in the vendor's brazier glowed brightly and the air was filled with a sweet smell—like caramelized sugar. Beyond the pumpkin-seed stall stood the gray stone edifice of the Votivkirche, its twin Gothic spires thrusting up energetically into the clear blue sky.

The small park in which Liebermann sat was surrounded by a wide road around which a merry-go-round of red and white streetcars circulated, seemingly in perpetual motion. This fine spectacle was accompanied by the ringing of bells.

Rheinhardt returned, carrying a paper bag that had become mottled with oil. Liebermann extended his cupped hands and the inspector obligingly filled them with a pile of hot green seeds. They emitted a smoky fragrance that combined the scent of burning wood with honey and spices. Liebermann's stomach tightened and grumbled.

"I've been to see Herr Arnoldt," said Rheinhardt.

"Who?"

"Hildegard's keeper—at the zoo." Liebermann nodded, and tipped some of the seeds into his mouth. "It was Salieri," Rheinhardt added, bluntly.

"You're sure?"

"Herr Arnoldt paid us a visit about three weeks ago, claiming to have recovered his memory—you will recall that the poor fellow had lost consciousness after being struck on the head. It appears that the man who knocked him out had been whistling a tune. Unfortunately, it was young Haussmann who took Herr Arnoldt's statement."

"I had formed the impression that you thought quite highly of Haussmann?"

"Oh, I do. He's very competent. It was just unfortunate on this occasion because, unbeknownst to me, Haussmann is tone-deaf. As a result I couldn't get him to reproduce Herr Arnoldt's melody." Rheinhardt sampled some pumpkin seeds, and nodded approvingly. "What with the Spittelberg, Ruprechtskirche, and Wieden murders, establishing the musical tastes of Herr Arnoldt's assailant was not my uppermost priority and I decided to let the matter rest. However, after our meeting in Café Mozart, I realized that I had—once again, perhaps—overlooked an important detail. The following afternoon I journeyed out to Schönbrunn. Herr Arnoldt was most helpful and sang me what he was able to remember of his assailant's ditty. Herr Arnoldt doesn't have a terribly strong voice, but the melody he produced sounded very much like this." Without pause, Rheinhardt began to softly sing: "*Der Vogelfänger bin ich ja . . .*"

" 'The Bird Catcher's Song!' " exclaimed Liebermann.

"Indeed. Thus, we can now be quite certain that it was Salieri who disposed of Hildegard!"

A little boy dressed in a hussar's uniform, with a buckled-on sabre and a pistol in his belt, marched by. He saluted Rheinhardt, who adopted a deadly serious expression and returned the gesture. The diminutive hussar was followed by a pretty nursemaid who was carrying a much smaller child in the crook of her elbow—she smiled at the two gentlemen as she passed. Liebermann felt an unwelcome tug of carnal attraction.

"We know that, in all probability, Salieri will kill again," continued Rheinhardt. "And we know that his next victim will also correspond with a character in Mozart's singspiel. But which one, Max? If we knew that, then we might have some chance—albeit small—of preventing yet another atrocity."

Liebermann shook his head. "Salieri might contrive to organize his program of murder according to any number of principles," said Liebermann. "But he is certainly not following any of the obvious ones: for example, the disposal of characters according to the order in which they appear in the opera, or the elimination of minor roles before major ones. This suggests two possibilities. One, Salieri is conducting his campaign according to a scheme that is simply too eccentric for us to comprehend. It exists—yet we cannot see it. Or, two, there is no scheme other than that of which we are already aware. That is to say, Salieri's choice of victim is guided by the dramatis persona of *The Magic Flute*, but there are no further consistencies to discover. If so, we have absolutely no way of predicting where he will strike next. Salieri will be operating opportunistically. When he encounters an individual who—in his mind—represents Tamino, Sarastro, the Speaker of the Temple, or any of the other remaining characters in the cast, his murderous instincts will be aroused and he will begin to plot their slaughter." On this grim note, Liebermann raised his hand and poured the remaining pumpkin seeds into his open mouth. Then, after some vigorous chewing, he added, "Now, Oskar . . . you really must tell me."

"Tell you what?"

"About the significant breakthrough. That is the purpose of our meeting here today. Is it not? I am expected back at the hospital within the hour, and would therefore urge you to divulge this important information without further delay."

"Ha!" said Rheinhardt. "You've done it again! How on earth did you know that?"

"We are meeting on Sunday to practice Dvořák's *Gypsy Songs*. It is our custom to discuss cases after our musical activities have been brought to a satisfactory conclusion. You obviously couldn't wait until then. Clearly, you mean to tell me something important."

Rheinhardt chuckled and shook the paper bag. "More pumpkin seeds, Herr Doctor?"

"No, thank you."

"You're quite right. There has been a significant discovery." Rheinhardt leaned closer to his friend. "Since finding Guido List's pamphlet, young Haussmann has been keeping a close eye on the great man's apartment. List and his wife—an actress called Anna Wittek—have received numerous guests. All of them share List's obsession with Germanic folk traditions and culture. One of them—Baron Gustav von Triebenbach, a well-known patron of the arts—is president of an organization called the Eddic Literary Association." Rheinhardt removed a pamphlet from his coat pocket and handed it to his friend. "This is an example of their work. It is very similar in content to List's *preliminary communication*. We find references to the skaldic tradition, Norse legends, the religions of the Aryo-Germanic peoples . . . and again, just as with List, a conclusion in which various groups and institutions are denounced."

"The enemy nomads?"

"I'm afraid so—as well as the Jesuits, the Freemasons, Slavs, supporters of women's suffrage, Secessionists, and anarchists."

"What's this?"

Liebermann pointed to the symbol on the front page. It looked like three sticks arranged in the form of a lopsided arch.

"Ur—a letter of the runic alphabet. It is referred to in List's pamphlet."

"Does it have any special meaning?"

"It is supposed to represent the primordial—primal light or primal fire. List suggests that it has healing powers and that doctors should employ it as a kind of charm." Unable to contain his disgust, Liebermann made a loud plosive sound. He brushed a stray pumpkin seed from his coat. "But what's really interesting about all this," Rheinhardt continued, "is where the Eddic Literary Association meets. . . ."

He paused, theatrically delaying the moment of revelation.

"Mozartgasse," said Liebermann—a flat, preemptive interjection.

Rheinhardt's lower jaw dropped open like a mechanical toy. "Sometimes, Max, you can be so *very* irritating."

"Was I right?"

"Yes."

"Given our previous conversation, it couldn't really be anywhere else."

Rheinhardt shook his head, a little peeved at the ruination of his dramatic coup, and continued doggedly, "The Eddic Literary Association was approved by the commissioner of associations some eight years ago. By law, all societies are obliged to provide the commissioner's office with a list of members. The Eddic Literary Association has forty-three full members and ten associates."

The inspector produced a sheet of paper on which two columns of names—one short, one long—had been neatly copied out. Two names in the long column had been underlined: *Hefner* and *Aschenbrandt*. Below the second name, Liebermann's attention was captured by another name with which he was very familiar.

"Professor Erich Foch."

"Do you know him?"

"I know *of* him—he lectures at the university. Professor Foch is a surgeon and a very disagreeable individual. In fact, he recently tried to expel Miss Lydgate from one of his classes. He believes that women are inferior to men and therefore should not be allowed to study medicine."

"We have always thought that Salieri might be a doctor. And all these runes and symbols . . ." Rheinhardt gestured toward the pamphlet. "They *do* seem to be associated with the craft of healing."

"It seems inconceivable, though," said Liebermann, "that a man in Professor Foch's position should be capable of such appalling inhumanity. Having strong views on the education of women is one thing—but murder? Brutal, mindless murder?"

"May I remind you again of the London Ripper—he too was supposed to be a surgeon."

"But it was never proved, Oskar. Was it?"

The inspector shrugged.

Liebermann returned his attention to the list of society members.

"Lieutenant Ruprecht Hefner?"

"An Uhlan with the eighteenth. I've already interviewed him—I did so a few days after the Spittelberg murders. His name was found on a promissory note in Madam Borek's brothel. He had an alibi— provided by his batman—which of course means nothing. It is extremely interesting that we should encounter his name again."

"What was he like?"

"Young, handsome, and insufferably arrogant. Even though he professed to have developed a certain fondness for the Galician girl, Ludka, he was completely unmoved by her terrible fate. He struck me as a man who was deficient in natural feelings."

Rheinhardt's modest reference to psychological abnormality was enough to arouse the young doctor's interest. Liebermann sat up and turned to face his friend.

"What else do you know about him?"

"We made further inquiries and learned that Lieutenant Hefner has a reputation for being something of a ladies' man and that his romantic involvements usually end in scandal. He is also rumored to be an inveterate duelist."

"So, we have an arrogant, narcissistic man, who is motivated by the pursuit of sensual pleasure. He does not develop sincere attachments, he exploits women, and he is content to risk his life repeatedly on the field of honor. He subscribes to a supremacist doctrine, which identifies certain institutions and groups as 'enemies.' Moreover, he is a soldier and can carry a sabre with him at all times without arousing the slightest suspicion. Do you think, perhaps, that I should interview Lieutenant Hefner?"

"No."

Liebermann raised his eyebrows. "No?"

"Sadly," said Rheinhardt, "the army are not very cooperative. They seem to consider any investigation conducted by an outsider as an outrage—a personal affront to the emperor. It was difficult enough for me, a detective inspector, to secure an audience with His Majesty's precious Uhlans, so the chances of you, a humble hospital doctor, being granted the same privilege are vanishingly small. Besides, there's someone else I want you to interview."

Liebermann glanced down at his list. "Hermann Aschenbrandt?"

"Indeed. Herr Aschenbrandt is a musician—a composer, in fact. He has had a number of chamber works performed, most of which have been very well-received."

"Did he write *The Invincible* quintet?"

"Yes, that's one of his works."

"I saw it performed at the Tonkünstlerverein."

"And?"

Liebermann revolved his hand in the air. "It went on rather.

Creeping chromaticism that slid around to no great purpose. The string writing was very accomplished—technically perfect, in fact. But it was all rather soulless and unoriginal—tepid Wagner."

"Well, he's writing an opera now—*Carnuntum*."

"Based on List's book?"

"Indeed."

"I assume that you have identified Aschenbrandt as a suspect on account of his being a musician. Thus we might reasonably assume that he is conversant with the operas of Mozart."

Rheinhardt smiled. "Herr Aschenbrandt knows the operas of Mozart very well, particularly *The Magic Flute*, of which he has a very definite opinion. So much so that he was minded to write a letter to the *Zeitung* lambasting Director Mahler for championing such an inane, nonsensical work."

"He doesn't like Mozart?" exclaimed Liebermann—as if to hold such an opinion merited public execution.

"He doesn't merely *dislike* Mozart," said Rheinhardt. "He *hates* him!"

54

"MY NAME IS DOCTOR MAX Liebermann. I have been issued with a special commission by the security office to conduct an interview with Herr Aschenbrandt."

The sound of a piano could be heard: turgid rumblings in the lower octaves followed by descending chromatic thirds.

"Do you have an appointment?" asked the maid.

"No."

"Herr Aschenbrandt does not like to be disturbed."

"Indeed," said Liebermann. "But this is a police matter."

The maid knocked timidly on a single-paneled door at the end of the hallway—but the grumbling piano continued. After a second, louder knock, the music stopped and a muffled "Enter" could be heard. The maid turned the handle and went in. As the door opened, the pianist shouted, "What is it now, Elga?"

A few moments later the maid reappeared. "I am sorry, Herr Doctor." She glanced down in embarrassment. "But Herr Aschenbrandt would like to see your documents."

"Of course," Liebermann said, removing the papers from his breast pocket and handing them to the maid.

Elga returned with the documents and he was admitted into the composer's study.

Herr Aschenbrandt turned in a perfunctory manner. He did not move from his piano stool, and gestured that Liebermann might take a seat if he wished. Liebermann chose a threadbare armchair.

The room was not large and felt distinctly cluttered, occupied for the most part by an immense Blüthner concert grand. Score sheets, showing abandoned drafts of various musical ideas, were strewn across the floor. On a long shelf, sagging under the weight of many literary and philosophical works, was a plaster bust of Richard Wagner. The décor was rather dowdy, and the curtains, because they were half-drawn, reduced the natural light, creating an impression of must and gloom. A cello case stood against the far wall, its long neck terminating next to a pen-and-ink sketch of a Gothic castle executed in the manner of Caspar David Friedrich.

"Forgive me for being impertinent, Herr Doctor," said Aschenbrandt. "But I am currently writing a rather demanding development section. Therefore, I humbly request that this interrogation be brought to a satisfactory conclusion as soon as possible."

Liebermann smiled. "It is hardly an interrogation, Herr Aschenbrandt. I merely wish to ask you a few questions on behalf of the security office. If you can help, I will be most grateful."

"Then let us proceed, Herr Doctor."

For a young man he seemed surprisingly self-assured.

"What are you composing?" asked Liebermann. "It sounded like a dramatic piece from the hallway."

"An opera, yes."

"Your first?"

"Apart from some juvenile music dramas—yes."

Liebermann spotted List's novel next to the music stand.

"It is based on *Carnuntum*?"

"Indeed."

"I have often wondered what it is that makes a composer

choose a particular text. Because music is such an elevated art form, I would suppose that—in some small part, at least—you must resent burdening your inventions with words?"

Aschenbrandt's pale blue eyes seemed to emit a strange phosphorescent glow.

"Naturally," he replied. "I am indeed of the opinion that music is the highest art form. Yet if a text expresses some noble sentiment, the task of marrying a melody to an appropriate verse can be deeply satisfying. As Wagner so clearly demonstrated"—he glanced briefly at the bust on the shelf—"the whole can be greater than the sum of its parts."

"And has List provided you with such a text?"

"I believe so."

Liebermann sat back in his chair and rested his loosely clenched fist against his cheek. His index finger uncurled so that its extremity touched his temple.

"I must confess, I am not familiar with List's writings."

"*Carnuntum* is a masterpiece," said Aschenbrandt. "An inspiration: the tale of a beleaguered, courageous people overcoming a mighty foe. It is a work of great clarity—and insight—although . . ." He craned forward, and seemed to be inspecting his visitor more closely. "Not to everyone's taste. There are some, inevitably, who cannot appreciate its depth."

Aschenbrandt's nostrils flared: a subtle but nevertheless discernible expansion and contraction. It left Liebermann with the disconcerting impression that he had just been "sniffed out." His finger gently tapped against his temple.

"I recently attended a performance of your quintet at the Tonkünstlerverein."

"Did you?" The composer recoiled a little.

"Yes—*The Invincible*. Why did you call it that?"

Aschenbrandt's expression hovered somewhere between surprise and contempt.

"Because of the prophecy, Herr Doctor."

"The prophecy?"

"As you are not conversant with *Carnuntum*, I daresay"— Aschenbrandt's upper lip curled—"that you cannot be expected to know of List's more scholarly works."

"*The Invincible* is the title of a book?"

"*The Invincible: Basics of a German Weltanschauung*. It was published a few years ago."

"And the prophecy, Herr Aschenbrandt?"

"*Der Unbesiegbare*—The Invincible—the strong one from above."

Liebermann raised his eyebrows, tacitly requesting further elaboration.

Aschenbrandt sighed. "Herr Doctor, I wish to continue with my work. What is the purpose of your visit?"

Liebermann chose to ignore the composer's question and persisted with his own. "The prophecy, Herr Aschenbrandt? I didn't realize your quintet was programmatic." Liebermann leaned forward, affecting surprise and great interest. Aschenbrandt—perhaps weakened by flattery—found it difficult to resist responding.

"It is not programmatic in the sense of following a narrative. It merely seeks to embody the spirit of the prophecy."

"Which is?"

"That the German people will be tested, and finally redeemed, by a great leader—the Invincible. The prophecy goes back to Eddic times."

"You said *strong one from above*: do you believe that Guido List is a kind of . . . Messiah?"

"No, of course not!" Aschenbrandt spat out the words, but then fell into a strange state of abstraction. "However," he added in a distant voice, "List may be preparing the way . . ."

The composer's right hand drifted to the keyboard and found three ethereal chords. It was as though his thinking had been accompanied by imagined harmonies and he had been overcome by a need to hear them.

Liebermann coughed to regain his attention.

"Herr Aschenbrandt . . . you wrote a rather scathing attack on Director Mahler for championing Mozart."

The musician looked up, his blue eyes gleaming. "These are serious times, Herr Doctor. The Opera House should be performing more substantial works."

"Is not *Don Giovanni* a substantial work?"

"No, Herr Doctor—it is a burlesque."

"Really?"

"*Così Fan Tutte* is a shallow comedy. And as for *The Magic Flute* . . ." Aschenbrandt shook his head, allowing a curtain of platinum hair to fall across his eyes. "It is so whimsical, so incoherent, so utterly lacking in merit—I can hardly believe that Director Mahler is still in his post."

"Herr Aschenbrandt, when did you first hear *The Magic Flute*?"

"I beg your pardon?"

"Was it when you were a child?"

Aschenbrandt removed the curtain of hair by tossing his head. There was something equine and precious about the mannerism.

"Yes, I suppose it was."

"When, exactly?"

"I must have been about eleven or twelve. My father took me—we saw it in Salzburg."

"Did you enjoy good relations with your father?"

"I'm sorry?"

"Did you get on?"

"Well enough . . ."

"And did you enjoy it—this particular performance of *The Magic Flute*?"

"Well, as it happens I did. But that is my point. . . . It is an entertainment for children. It is not acceptable to use the world's greatest opera house—with the exception of Bayreuth, of course—as a children's theater. The Viennese public deserve better than a string of popular songs and nursery rhymes."

"I am no expert, of course, but it is my impression that Mozart's undeniable lightness—the incomparable transparency of his scoring—can mislead. Mozart addresses lofty themes, but he does so with an extraordinary deftness. There are subtleties in Mozart that might escape the attention of those whose senses have been blunted by listening to more bombastic music."

Aschenbrandt leaned forward.

"Herr Doctor . . ." He could barely believe what he had just heard. "Herr Doctor, am I to understand . . . Are you suggesting that the music dramas of Richard Wagner are—"

"Perhaps the fault is mine," said Liebermann, interrupting. "But I have always found Wagner's music rather crude. Overblown. And it has never spoken to me personally, as it were."

Aschenbrandt's pale skin colored a little. "Well, with respect, Herr Doctor—that is hardly surprising."

"Oh?"

"You are a Jew." Aschenbrandt turned to the keyboard. "Wagner did not write his music for your kind. And how can you suggest that Wagner's music is unsubtle, when he wrote this . . ." His fingers found the plaintive opening of the Prelude to Act One of *Tristan and Isolde*. The lonely melody rose and fell, supported by harmonies that refused to resolve, tormented by uncertainties and a sense of anxious anticipation. "I must be candid, Herr Doctor," Aschenbrandt continued. "I do not believe your race can appreciate German music. You have your own culture."

"Yes, Jews do have a separate musical tradition," said Liebermann, sitting up. "But we are perfectly capable of appreciating German music. The opening bars of *Tristan* are exquisite, I agree. So much so that I found your rendition somewhat disappointing. You neglected to play the D sharp in the interrupted cadence...." Aschenbrandt looked startled and glanced down at his fingers. "It is absolutely necessary to include the D sharp to achieve the effect that Wagner intended." With that, the young doctor smiled and stood up. "Thank you for your time, Herr Aschenbrandt, and good day."

The composer appeared confused. "But you said you had come on behalf of the security office. A police matter?"

"I did."

"Then what about the interrogation?"

"It is over, Herr Aschenbrandt—and you have been most helpful."

55

LIEBERMANN SWALLOWED HIS SLIVOVITZ and stared through the empty glass at his friend.

"Where was I?" asked Kanner.

"You were telling me about Sabina."

"Ah yes . . . Sabina."

Kanner lifted the bottle from the table but his grip was weak and it slid through his fingers. A small quantity of plum brandy spouted from the top, producing a circle of yellow spots on the white tablecloth.

They were sitting in one of several private dining rooms situated behind a restaurant in Leopoldstadt. It had no windows, and contained only four pieces of furniture: a small table, two chairs, and a green sofa. The latter was a standard feature (private dining rooms being more commonly reserved by married men for clandestine meetings with barmaids, shopgirls, and dressmakers).

The food, although not imaginative, had been very wholesome: sliced-pancake soup, boiled beef with vegetables, followed by *germknödel*—yeast dumplings served hot with melted butter, sugar, and ground poppy seed.

Liebermann rotated the empty glass, and his inebriated friend fragmented. Kanner's bright red cravat and embroidered vest shattered into shards of kaleidoscopic color. A swift reverse movement—and Kanner was reconstituted. As Liebermann repeated this procedure, he was troubled by a doubt concerning the psychological report he had written for Rheinhardt. Had he mentioned that Aschenbrandt had first seen *The Magic Flute* in Salzburg? The question hovered in his mind for a few moments but soon lost its urgency, eventually sinking to some inaccessible depth.

"Have another slivovitz!" Kanner cried, decanting an eccentric quantity of plum brandy into Liebermann's glass. He loosened his cravat and scratched the stubble on his cheek. In the flickering gaslight, Kanner appeared disreputably handsome. "It's always the way," he groaned. "You fall in love, you become intimate ... for a short while you are in paradise . . . but then things start going wrong. I thought I really loved Sabina—and I was sure she felt the same way about me."

"Did you quarrel?"

"No."

"Then what happened?"

"I don't know."

They had both smoked far too much; however, the asphyxiating atmosphere in the windowless room failed to discourage Kanner from lighting the last of his Egyptian cigarettes.

"I was walking her home, one night last week," Kanner continued, "and we stopped to admire a pretty little square. I'd never come across it before: a little church, a water fountain, and a string of arc lights. . . . It was very peaceful. There was a bench, and we decided to sit down for a while. Sabina was quite tired. We had been to the theater. I turned to kiss her ... and she drew away."

"Had that happened before?"

"No—although . . ." He paused to reconsider. "Although, if I am honest, there were times when I suspected that she was—shall we say— less *comfortable* with intimacy than before. Of course, I asked her 'What's the matter?' And she looked at me with those beautiful dark eyes and said, 'Something's changed—hasn't it?' My instinct was to say 'No, no—nothing's changed, my sweet.' But I knew that she was right. Something *had* changed. I'd known it for some time. It's difficult to say when it started. A month ago, perhaps, maybe even longer: a slow cooling of affection, a growing discomfort with shared silences. . . . Yes, I knew it, of course, but didn't have the courage to say anything. I didn't want to hurt her. Fortunately, she—of the two of us—was the stronger."

The room seemed to Liebermann to pitch like a boat. Kanner drew on his cigarette and continued, "One cannot live a lie, Max. One cannot *pretend* to be in love."

Liebermann felt an intense pressure in his chest—as though his lungs had become inflated, and their expansion was placing a profound strain on his rib cage.

"Stefan, I can't do it. I can't go through with it."

The words came out involuntarily in a garbled rush, but once he'd said them, Liebermann experienced an enormous relief. The pressure in his chest subsided and he was left slightly breathless and feeling light-headed.

"I beg your pardon? What did you say?" Kanner asked.

"I can't go through with it, Stefan—my marriage to Clara. You're absolutely right. One cannot live a lie. It would be wrong. Clara will be heartbroken, but it will be better for her if she marries a man who truly loves her."

Kanner sat very still, blinking. "What? You . . . I thought . . . I thought . . ." Connecting words to make sentences was simply too demanding for him.

"It's just as you describe," Liebermann continued. "*Something* has changed. I didn't mean to stop loving her—it just happened."

Kanner sat back in his chair and rang the service bell. Almost immediately, the door opened and a waiter appeared.

"More slivovitz," Kanner called out, his speech slurring slightly.

The waiter waved his hand to clear away some of the smoke.

"Are you sure, sir?" he asked in slow, sinewy German. Liebermann thought he sounded Transylvanian.

"Yes, quite sure," Kanner replied. The waiter bowed and stepped backward out of the room, smiling contemptuously at the two young men. "Well, Max," continued Kanner, pouring the last few drops of alcohol into his glass. "I don't know what to say."

A long silence ensued.

"For the last three weeks," said Liebermann softly, "I've been treating Herr Beiber."

Kanner's brow furrowed as he set his mind to the task of producing a sensible reply. "The monomaniac obsessed with the Archduchess Marie-Valerie?"

"Indeed," said Liebermann. "I know that he is unwell, but during our sessions it has become plain to me that in his madness he comes much closer to the general conception of true love than I ever have. In a peculiar way, I envy him. I have desired Clara, enjoyed her company, and been excited at the prospect of consummation—but I have never . . ." His words trailed off.

"What?"

"I have never felt that . . . that I could not live without her, that we are soul mates, that we were destined to meet and that we have been drawn together by a higher power."

"Maxim, what *are* you talking about? You don't believe in any of those things: the soul, destiny, a higher power."

Liebermann shook his head. "It's difficult to explain . . . but talking to Herr Beiber has underscored the deficiencies of our relationship. I have never loved Clara improvidently, wildly—and that is how it *should* be." He paused for a moment, and repeated his last words, more to himself than to his companion. "That is how it should be."

The door opened and the waiter entered. He placed the bottle on the table, and made a preternaturally discreet exit.

Kanner filled their glasses again.

"Max, forgive me for being so blunt, but as your friend . . ." Liebermann gestured that he should continue. "Is there someone else?"

"No!" Liebermann's denial was far too strong and even in Kanner's inebriated state his suspicion was aroused. Something of his clinical sensitivity had survived the evening's excesses and he scrutinized his companion more closely.

"These things happen, Max." Kanner's tone was forgiving. "If there is someone else . . ."

Miss Lydgate, sitting in the window seat of the Natural History Museum. Her flaming hair in the darkness. Rocks and gems surrounding her—sparkling, like stars in the firmament.

"No," Liebermann said again. "There is no one else."

He snatched up his glass and gulped down his plum brandy. It was rough and astringent—almost caustic.

"What are you going to do?" Kanner asked.

"What *can* I do? I have no choice. I will have to end our engagement."

"Max, you need to think about this."

"I *have* thought about it, Stefan. I've thought about it day and night. In fact, I've thought of little else since the spring."

"Then why didn't you say anything before?"

"The opportunity never seemed to present itself. I almost said something to you when we dined last at the Bristol."

"But that was months ago."

"Yes, I know."

Kanner bit his lower lip. "And I thought *I* had problems."

They talked into the early hours until the conversation became desultory and incoherent. At some point Liebermann must have fallen into a fitful sleep, for he woke with a start—and discovered that the chair opposite was empty. He turned his head and saw Kanner lying on the sofa. He was evidently not asleep, for he was singing quietly to himself.

"O heiliges Band der Freundschaft treuer Brüder . . ."
Oh holy Bond of Friendship of true Brothers . . .

Kanner possessed an untrained tenor voice, yet the melody possessed an unmistakable sweetness and clarity.

"Stefan?"

Kanner opened one eye. "Ah, Max!" It was as though he had not been expecting to see his friend seated at the table.

"Is that Mozart?"

Kanner smiled and shrugged his shoulders. "What?"

"That song. Is it Mozart?"

"I . . . er . . . I have no idea."

"It sounded like Mozart."

"Well, perhaps it is."

"Where did you hear it?"

Kanner seemed inexplicably embarrassed. "I don't know . . . must have picked it up from somewhere. I really don't know." He raised himself up from the sofa and winced. "Oh, my head. What time is it?"

"Three o'clock."

"I have a clinic in five hours."

"No, you don't—it's Sunday morning."

"You know, Max, I had a most curious dream. I dreamt that you said . . . you said that you were going to break off your engagement with Clara."

Liebermann threw some coins onto the table. "Come on, Stefan. Get up. We have outstayed our welcome."

56

RHEINHARDT STARED INTO THE mirror. In the reflected distance stood a short man wearing a soft cap and a paint-spattered smock.

"And how, Herr Olbricht, does one become a member of the Eddic Literary Association?"

"You are invited."

"By whom?"

"The president, Baron von Triebenbach. Any member can nominate interested parties; however, it is the president who has the final say. It is he who extends the invitation."

Rheinhardt turned. "And who nominated you, Herr Olbricht?"

"I am proud to say that it was none other than the president himself."

The artist was unable to suppress a self-satisfied smile. Two rows of stunted uneven teeth made a brief appearance. Rheinhardt approached a large unfinished canvas that was leaning up against the wall. It showed a man with long yellow hair, plunging a sword into the neck of a dragon. Red-black blood spurted out between broken metallic scales.

"Siegfried?" asked Rheinhardt.

"Of course."

The inspector twisted the points of his mustache and tested their sharpness with the soft pad of his forefinger.

"How did you and the baron become acquainted?" asked Rheinhardt.

"Through the kind intercession of my patron, Baroness Sophie von

Rautenberg. She was of the opinion that I would be inspired by the poetry and stories of the *Edda*."

"And were you?"

"Most certainly. Immersion in the Eddic tradition has completely revitalized my art."

"Did you study at the academy, Herr Olbricht?"

Olbricht's face tightened. Rheinhardt noticed that the lines around his mouth were particularly marked.

"No, I didn't. They . . ." He seemed flustered for a moment and his eyes searched the room nervously. "I am self-taught." Then, somewhat defensively, he added, "There has always been a demand for my work."

"Do you have a dealer?"

"Yes. Ulrich Löb; however, his gallery is quite small and he's only interested in architectural drawings—St. Stephen's, the Hofburg, the town hall, that sort of thing. Almost all my substantial works have been commissioned by my patron's circle of friends."

"You are most fortunate, Herr Olbricht. There must be very few artists in Vienna who have the support of such a devoted champion."

"That is very probably true. Nonetheless . . ." Olbricht paused. "There are also few artists in Vienna to whom their patrons owe such a debt of gratitude." Rheinhardt inspected the artist's face more closely. It was distinctly batrachian. His nose seemed unfinished, and his eyes were set too far apart.

"Oh?"

With what appeared to be genuine reluctance, Olbricht muttered, "When I was a young man, I . . . saved Von Rautenberg's life."

"Did you really?" said Rheinhardt, nodding to encourage further disclosure. But the artist did not respond. Instead, he wiped some brushes on his smock and dropped them into a bottle of turpentine. "You are too modest, Herr Olbricht. Other men would seize such an opportunity for self-aggrandizement."

"It was many years ago."

"How many?"

"Twenty or so."

"And what were the circumstances?"

The artist chewed his lower lip thoughtfully. "Bosnia-Herzegovina—the campaign of 1878. In those days I was a foot-rag Indian."

"I beg your pardon?"

"An infantryman. Von Rautenberg was our commanding officer."

"And how did you come to save his life?"

"There had been some skirmishes with small groups of insurgents. Not very well organized. Even so, it was necessary to undertake daily patrols. It was early evening and we were in woodland going down to a river." Olbricht indicated the gentle gradient in the air with a movement of his hand. "The baron insisted that he should lead the party. A more junior officer could have done the job—but that was what Von Rautenberg was like: never one to shirk responsibility—a military man of the old school. If only we had more men like Von Rautenberg today, this empire of ours would be a power to be reckoned with." Olbricht crossed his arms with unusual vehemence. "I noticed some movement among the trees and acted—more from nerves, or instinct perhaps, than intention. I can't honestly say I was being courageous. Still, I was very young—eighteen or thereabouts. I can remember pushing the baron down, the sound of gunfire and losing consciousness. When I awoke, I was being attended by the doctor. A bullet had grazed my head." Olbricht raised his hand and stroked his right temple to show the bullet's trajectory. "It went straight into a silver birch—just where the baron had been standing. I thought I'd be in a military hospital for a few days and then back with my regiment. But it wasn't to be. . . . I suffered from dizziness, nausea, and headaches—terrible, blinding headaches." He winced at the recollection. "Sometimes my vision blurred. It was impossible to continue. In due course I was discharged on medical grounds."

"You returned to Vienna?"

"Yes. While convalescing, I had formed the habit of sketching—pen-and-ink drawings of men in the infirmary. The doctors said I had a talent."

Rheinhardt returned his attention to the unfinished canvas of Siegfried slaying the dragon. A subtle change in his expression indicated that he found the image quite pleasing.

"It needs much more work, of course," said the artist.

"Yes," said Rheinhardt, nodding his head and pulling at his chin. "Even so, an arresting image."

"There is something about Siegfried's posture that is not quite right," said Olbricht. "It does not suggest sufficient strength and power . . . the way his left knee is buckling. I thought that this detail would make the figure seem more animated, but I fear that it has only succeeded in making him appear weak."

"No, not at all," said Rheinhardt. "Fafner is a terrible adversary. One would expect even the greatest hero to falter during such an encounter."

Olbricht was flattered by the inspector's evident pleasure. "I will be including this work in my next exhibition, Inspector. If you wish to come, you would be most welcome. It opens next week." Olbricht walked over to a battered chest, his feet sounding a hollow knock on the bare floorboards. He lifted the lid and removed a small poster, which he handed to Rheinhardt.

The image was simple: an ancient Germanic god, most probably Wotan, holding his spear aloft. Heavy Gothic script set large announced the title of the exhibition: *Olbricht—Our Heroes and Legends*. "It will be at the Hildebrandt Gallery on Kärntner Strasse," the artist added.

"Thank you," said Rheinhardt. "May I bring a friend?"

"Of course."

Rheinhardt folded the poster and slid it gently into his breast pocket.

"I cannot help but notice, Herr Olbricht, that you are very fond of operatic subjects."

"The baroness has many friends in the Richard Wagner Association."

"Are you ever asked to paint scenes from operas other than those by Wagner?"

"Some: *Der Freischütz* and *Euryanthe*. And earlier this year a concert violinist wanted a scene from *Fidelio* as a present for his wife."

"Have you ever been asked to depict any scenes from Mozart?" asked Rheinhardt.

"No," Olbricht replied. The syllable dropped into a pool of silence. Their stares locked together but Olbricht's blank expression showed no sign that he understood why Rheinhardt had asked him that particular question. Gradually his features softened. "No," he said again, with a minute shake of the head. "No one has ever asked. Although I doubt that I would enjoy such a commission. I am convinced that German opera is most successful when it addresses romantic or epic themes."

Rheinhardt had been ready to observe some small sign: a flinch, a blink, a pause—restless, fidgeting fingers. The kind of sign that his friend, young Doctor Liebermann, was in the habit of identifying as significant. But there was nothing unusual about Olbricht apart from his amphibian-like features.

Reverting to more traditional methods of investigation, with which he felt more comfortable, Rheinhardt patted his coat pocket and withdrew a small notebook and a stub of pencil.

"I wonder, Herr Olbricht," he began. "Can you remember what you were doing on the morning of Monday the sixth of October?"

57

PROFESSOR FOCH EXCHANGED HIS frock coat for a quilted black smoking jacket.

His supper had been frugal—nothing more than a small portion of goulash. He had decided to forgo the pleasure of Frau Haushofer's impressive but very sweet *salzburger nockerln* with cassis sauce because he had been suffering from borborygmus of late and had come to the conclusion that he must be eating too much.

Frau Haushofer was a conscientious woman, and when the *nockerln* was returned to the kitchen, she immediately left her station by the stove and went up to the dining room to ask if everything had been to the professor's satisfaction. Foch was not disposed to provide her with an explanation. After all, she was only a member of his household staff. Rising from the table, he stated frostily that she had given him no cause for complaint. Foch instructed his butler that he was not to be disturbed for the rest of the evening—except in the event of a medical emergency—and then, quitting the dining room, he beat a hasty retreat to his study.

Foch closed the study door, clasped his hands behind his back, and began to pace. As he did so, he occasionally muttered to himself. In spite of his earlier abstinence, these vocalizations were accompanied by a grumbling commentary emanating from his intestines.

After much toing and froing the agitated professor came to a halt in front of a small line drawing. It depicted "The Wounded Man"—a form of instructive surgical illustration that had become popular from medieval times onward.

Foch rocked backward and forward on the balls of his feet. As he did so, the floorboards emitted a querulous squeak.

The figure in the drawing looked like a fugitive from hell: a soul condemned to the most appalling mortifications of the flesh. Naked except for a genital pouch, he stood with one knee bent and one hand turned toward the onlooker. His body was little more than a pincushion: every part of his anatomy had been ripped, torn, punctured, or lacerated by a weapon drawn from a vast and unusually comprehensive armory. A short sword jutted out from his forehead, a knife from his cheek, and a massive hammer hung from a deep gash in his upper arm. The trapezius muscle had been sliced through by a sabre.

Foch scrutinized the wounds, and considered the excruciating pain that such injuries might cause.

In imitation of Christ, the Wounded Man's side had been pierced by a spear, and numerous arrowheads were embedded in his knotted thighs. Foch took a step closer. The hand that had been turned toward the onlooker was, in fact, hanging loosely from the arm, connected only by a thin threadlike tendon. The wrist had been slit, exposing a circle that represented the truncated main artery. Curiously, the Wounded Man's expression was ambiguous. There was something about his raised eyebrow and crooked mouth that suggested amusement—even pleasure.

The walls of Professor Foch's study were lined with books; not just ordinary books of the sort one might discover in the personal library of any university professor. Among the usual technical works, histories, biographies—and classics such as *The Iliad, The Edda, The Nibelungenlied,* Goethe, and Shakespeare—were several tomes of considerable age and value. Foch had been an enthusiastic collector since his student days, and through a combination of shrewdness, perspicacity, and luck he had acquired many antiquarian volumes, mostly of scientific and medical writings.

In a glass case below the line drawing of the Wounded Man was Foch's most valued possession: a thick book, opened to display an engraved frontispiece. It was an original edition of *De curtorum chirurgia per insitionem* ("On the Surgery of the Mutilated" by Grafting) by the sixteenth-century Italian, Gaspare Tagliacozzi. Within its dry, disintegrating pages, Tagliacozzi had described an inventive procedure for the reconstruction of human noses: this particular operation had acquired considerable contemporary relevance in Vienna, where syphilis had become rife and every sixth house was occupied by a doctor whose brass plate proclaimed him a "Specialist for Skin and Venereal Diseases." Syphilis often damaged the nose, and because one of Foch's specialties was nasal surgery, acquisition of a biblical scroll could not have afforded him more satisfaction than did his ownership of *De curtorum chirurgia*.

Contemplation of this treasure had the immediate effect of calming Foch's agitation. The professor lifted the lid of the display case, inhaled the book's musty perfume, and smiled. It was as sweet as a flower. Then, closing the lid, he turned and walked over to his desk. An electric lamp made an oblong inset of red leather glow with incarnadine fury.

It must be done. . . . Carpe diem, carpe diem.

Taking his seat, he pressed his fingers together and allowed them to bounce on his puckered lips.

Enough is enough.

Foch had been wondering what to do for some time. Since receiving the letter of reprimand from the dean, a reservoir of bile had been collecting in his stomach. It was this, most probably, that accounted for the professor's digestive problems. But he was not a very insightful man. He did not look inward often, fearful, perhaps, of what he might discover.

Earlier that year he had attended one of Professor Freud's Saturday lectures on the subject of psychoanalysis. But he had found the content insufferable: all that talk of repressed sexual urges and phallic symbols—it was obscene. He had registered his objection by storming out, making as much noise as possible. The idea of lying on a couch and telling one's innermost secrets to a smug, self-satisfied Jew who was preoccupied with filth filled him with horror. Even so, Freud's insistence that early experiences have a profound impact on later development had lodged uncomfortably in his memory. Foch was dimly aware of the distant events that had shaped him: his impassive mother, the precocious girl who lived next door, the icy fingers of the Czech nursemaid sliding beneath the eiderdown.

It must be done. . . . Carpe diem, carpe diem.

Enough is enough.

He would write an open letter to the *Zeitung*, explaining his predicament. In due course, common sense would prevail, public opinion would rally in his support, and the dean—obsequious lickspittle hypocrite that he was—would be obliged to resign. This plan of action had been slowly solidifying as it curdled in the gentle but persistent heat of his own ruminative malice.

In preparation for his assault, Foch had laid out some paper, a gold fountain pen, and several volumes and periodicals. He would begin his argument by making an appeal to the sensible gentlemen of Vienna, calling upon the highest scientific authority for support. He reached for his first edition of Darwin's *The Descent of Man, and Selection in Relation* to Sex. Removing a silk bookmark, he opened the volume and began to translate the stately English prose:

> The chief distinction in the intellectual powers of the two sexes is shewn by man's attaining to a higher eminence in whatever he takes up, than can women—whether requiring deep thought, reason or imagination, or merely the use of the senses and hands . . . Man has ultimately become superior to woman.

Foch grunted, and opened an old copy of an English medical journal called *The Lancet*. It was more than a decade old but he had saved it, knowing that a particular passage would one day prove very useful.

> The female is undoubtedly from a developmental point of view an animal in which the evolutionary process has been arrested or, more accurately speaking, diverted from the general to the particular, for special reproductive purposes, before the culminating point could be reached . . .

The professor picked up his pen and began writing.

> We live in troubled times. The commonsense values that have prevailed for centuries are now under attack, and nowhere is this folly more evident than in matters concerning the Women's Question. It is my belief that the admission of female medical students into the medical faculty of the University of Vienna is a mistake, and a matter in need of urgent review . . .

After justifying his position with reference to Darwin and various evolutionary theorists, Foch proceeded to give an account of several experimental studies conducted by Doctor Heydemann that showed that women were inferior in the senses of smell, taste, sight, and hearing. He then cited the work of many celebrated neurologists who had found a relationship between brain size and intelligence. It was quite absurd to expect the much smaller female brain to function as well as its larger male counterpart. Women were simply physically incapable of becoming good doctors.

There are those who maintain that such intellectual differences as exist between men and women can be accounted for because of social inequalities. That is to say, women generally—in this and past ages—have received little in the way of education. But there is considerably less truth to this argument than is generally supposed. In the Periclean era in ancient Greece, women such as Aspasia were highly cultured, and counted themselves as disciples of the great philosophers. Sappho, Hypatia, and many others prove the existence of a class of women to whom the religions of antiquity had given a position of unqualified honor. Yet in those times, and in all subsequent times, the education of women has failed to have an impact on their eminence in the grand scheme of human endeavor. Their gender has not produced one great artist, author, musician, inventor, or scientist. As the traditional German proverb has long informed us: Long skirts, short senses.

Foch sat back in his chair, pleased with his invective.

58

The landlord's daughter had come out from behind the counter and was standing proudly, almost defiantly, in the middle of the floor. For the regular patrons of Café Haynau this was a time-honored ritual. The audience, mostly military men from the barracks, began to clap and stamp their feet. The dense fog of cigar and cigarette smoke responded to the sudden movement, revolving into marbled, ghostly pillars. Mathilde pushed forward her plentiful cleavage, acquiring in the act an unexpected statuesque grandeur. Unfortunately, her posturing provoked a coarse remark from a young ensign, and her fragile dignity disintegrated when she lashed out and cuffed his ear. The ensign's companions roared with laughter and encouraged Mathilde to strike him again. She declined the invitation and instead recovered her poise, appealing for silence by repeatedly pressing her palms down toward the floor. The high-spirited banter died down.

"This song," she announced, "is called *The White City of Rijeka*. I learned it off a Croatian soldier—"

"And what did he learn off you?" shouted the ensign.

There was more laughter, and Mathilde raised a minatory finger. She signaled to the old accordion player, who squeezed the bellows of his instrument. A few wheezy chords of unsteady pitch escaped. Mathilde chose an arbitrary note and launched into the song.

"Rika je bili grad mej dvima gorama"
Rijeka is a white city between two mountains
"Onaj ograjena hladnima vodama . . ."
Surrounded by cold fountains . . .
"Tan ta-na-na-na, ni-na ne-na"

She did not have a good voice, yet what she lacked in technique she compensated for with an abundance of dramatic gestures and expressions. Swishing her skirt, she rapped her clogs against the floorboards and mimed looking into the distance to see the mist-shrouded white city nestling in the gap between two imaginary peaks. In fact, she was also looking to see if she had attracted the attention of Lieutenant Hefner. She hadn't. The handsome Uhlan was glumly and determinedly contemplating a half-empty bottle of vodka. Disappointed, Mathilde made coquettish eyes at the regimental doctor, who—having drunk more than his usual two glasses of slivovitz—tapped his lap. This surprising invitation caused something of a stir among the members of the eighteenth, who had become accustomed to viewing the good doctor as a model of propriety and restraint.

Hefner was oblivious to this *coup de foudre*. He was totally self-absorbed, preoccupied. It had been an extraordinary day.

Early that morning, he had had to endure another interview with the ludicrous Inspector Rheinhardt. This interview had been even more irritating than the first. The old fool had droned on and on about the recent spate of murders, beginning with the slaughter of Madam Borek and the three girls. Then there had been other victims: a Czech stallholder, a black man.

All of them were killed with a sabre.

At regular intervals the policeman had paused and allowed the silence to condense. He had played with his mustache and eyed Hefner closely. It soon became plain that the inspector was no longer merely asking Hefner to assist him with his inquiries. He was communicating something much more serious. Hefner was a suspect.

What did the buffoon expect him to do? Break down and confess?

None of the inspector's tactics had been particularly successful. His habit of letting implications hang in the air was largely ineffective. The lieutenant was quite comfortable with unresolved silences. What really disquieted Hefner was the inspector's knowledge of his private affairs: his links with Von Triebenbach, the Richard Wagner Association, and the Eddic Literary Association (although, thankfully, the inspector seemed to have no idea that the latter was merely an expedient for the better concealment of Primal Fire). The inspector even seemed to know what operas he had seen. He had been impertinent enough to ask if Hefner had enjoyed Director Mahler's production of *The Magic Flute*.

> "Tan ta-na-na-na, ni-na ne-na
> Tan ta-na-na-na, ni-na ne-na"

Ludka: he remembered her compliant flesh, the way she obediently knelt to receive him in her mouth, the way she would guide his hand to her cheek and look up at him with knowing eyes, understanding his pleasure. He remembered the satisfying report of his palm as it made violent contact with her young face, accompanied by the explosion of heat in his loins.

Stupid little slut. . . . It was bound to happen some day.

Hefner forced himself to look at the chanteuse, who was now swinging her hips in front of the inebriated doctor and reaching out to toy with his curly black hair. She winked, gay syllables tripping off her tongue in a cascade of suggestive nonsense.

"Tan ta-na-na-na, ni-na ne-na"

The interview with Rheinhardt had not been unduly long, and Hefner had treated the policeman with all the contempt he deserved. But the lieutenant had still been unable to get away in time for the morning drill, and Kabok had reprimanded him severely. Hefner had tried to explain the situation but the old martinet had given him what-for, his verbal lashing finally degenerating into a series of half-muttered execrations that made immoderate and audible use of words such as "whoring," "syphilis," and "shit for brains." Hefner knew better than to respond. The humiliation was intolerable.

That evening he had gone to the opera, but had been unable to enjoy the performance. He had become obsessed with the notion that he was being followed, and that a particular sharp-featured young man was one of Rheinhardt's spies. He was on the brink of challenging the fellow when he thought better of it. What was the point? Besides, he knew that he would be able to lose the scoundrel in the crowd as it spilled out onto the Ringstrasse.

As Hefner left the Opera House, he was confident that he had achieved his objective. The youth was nowhere to be seen in the cloakroom and did not appear to be waiting in the foyer. But the uhlan had only got as far as Schillerplatz when, to his astonishment, he became painfully conscious of footsteps following close behind him. He turned around abruptly, expecting to see the sharp-featured young man, but was taken aback by the sight of a curious-looking gentleman in a fur coat and pongee suit. He was carrying a cane, the top of which was shaped in the likeness of a jaguar, and a monocle hung from his vest on a length of black ribbon. The gentleman's face was broad, and he sported an oriental drooping mustache and a small goatee beard. His eyes could barely be seen below the wide brim of his hat.

"Do I know you, sir?" asked Hefner.

The stranger took a few leisurely steps forward and smiled. A frigid smile that seemed more like a grimace.

"No." His breath condensed in the frozen air. "But I believe that *you* are familiar—very familiar—with my sister."

His accent was Hungarian.

"Your sister?"

"The countess? You remember the countess?"

Hefner shook his head.

The stranger then produced a string of colorful and quite shocking insults, each one delivered with an almost gleeful relish. Occasionally he would slip back into his native tongue—presumably because he could not find a German word sufficiently plosive to express the desired degree of opprobrium that his insult required. He spat out harsh consonants and flattened vowels. From this cataract of curses and maledictions the nature of the gentleman's accusation gradually became clear. Hefner had misled his kind, good-hearted sister, taken advantage of her, and in doing so had ruined her good reputation.

The eighteenth had been stationed in Hungary that summer at a godforsaken outpost on the banks of the Tisza. There had been absolutely nothing to do there, and Hefner had been forced to relieve his boredom with a few inconsequential assignations: a milkmaid, a doctor's wife . . . and yes, there *had* been a countess, a countess whose family had fallen upon hard times. What was her name?

That was it—Záborszky.

Countess Borbala Záborszky.

Hefner was in no mood for a confrontation of this kind. It had all been such a long time ago—he could hardly remember the woman.

"Look, my friend," Hefner said, somewhat dismissively. "I think you have the wrong man."

The stranger shook his head. "No. There has been no mistake."

Languidly—almost lazily—he pulled at the fingers of his glove, stretching the material covering each digit in turn. Eventually the thin, adhesive material snapped off, contracting in the process. The stranger then raised the glove up, with its pathetic cluster of drooping, shriveled udders, and said, "Consider yourself slapped."

A small group of well-dressed men had gathered close by. They too had probably been to the opera. The stranger's raised glove was enough to signal what was happening.

In matters of honor there were three categories of slur. The simple slight, the direct insult, and the blow or slap. The first two might be resolved without bloodshed—but not the third.

Hefner executed a brief bow, then he and Záborszky exchanged the names of their seconds. The uhlan made his way back to the Café Haynau, where he found Renz and Trapp at their usual table. They were immediately dispatched to the Café Museum, instructed to liaise with the stranger's seconds: Doctor Jóska Dekany and Herr Otto Braun.

"Tan ta-na-na-na, ni-na ne-na"

Mathilde rotated her hips provocatively in front of the doctor's face. The men sitting at adjacent tables began to clap and yell.

> *"Lipje su Bakarke po drva hodeći*
> *Nego Rikinjice v kamarah sideći"*
> The girls from Bakar collecting wood for the fire
> Are more beautiful than the girls from Rijeka
> Sitting in solemn attire . . .

The door of the café swung open, and Renz and Trapp appeared. The smoke eddied around their feet and a few stray snowflakes followed them in.

"Well?" asked Hefner.

The two men slumped down and removed their caps. Snow had collected on their shoulders.

"Yes, all done," Trapp replied.

"Where is it to be?"

"In a private room above Kryschinski's whorehouse."

"*What?*" Hefner looked from Trapp to Renz, as if Trapp had declared himself a lunatic and could no longer be trusted.

"They insisted on an American duel," said Renz.

"An American duel!" cried Hefner. "And you *agreed?*"

"When we left, you said *anything*—it was *all the same* to you."

"God in heaven, I can't believe it!" said Hefner shaking his head. "An American duel . . ."

Trapp and Renz exchanged worried glances.

"Renz is right," said Trapp. "You *did* say *anything*. It's what you *always* say."

"But an American duel . . ."

A loud cheer went up, and the three men turned to see the busty chanteuse straddling the lap of the regimental doctor.

"*Tan ta-na-na-na, ni-na ne-na*"

"Well," said Hefner, "at least this time we won't be needing his services."

59

"FASTER!"

The driver cracked his whip and yelled another imprecation at the horses. Inside, the portly inspector felt like a mariner caught in some dreadful storm, his little vessel being tossed from one wave to the next. Rheinhardt tried to peer out of the window but could see very little. Covered shop fronts and yellow gaslights flashed past. He gave up and closed his eyes. The vestigial tatters of an interrupted dream were still flapping around, incomprehensibly, in his mind.

A great ballroom, viewed from above.

Couples rotating in triple time beneath a glorious chandelier, each pair like cogwheels in a great machine, endlessly turning. And then a sentence, spoken by a pleasant, pensive, world-weary voice: "No one escapes The Eternity Waltz, my friend. As you will see, it goes on forever."

The Eternity Waltz? What would Max make of that?

A pothole in the road made Rheinhardt's buttocks part company with the seat. He landed with a dull thump, which returned him, somewhat rudely, to the present. The carriage shook and Rheinhardt's forehead bumped against the glass. He cursed loudly.

Only twenty minutes earlier he had been fast asleep in a warm, comfortable bed. A tactile memory teased his peripheral nerves: his wife's soft, accommodating body, the reassuring feel of her breasts beneath the cotton of her nightdress. Something of her scent still lingered in his nostrils, as homely as freshly baked bread and as sweet as honeysuckle.

The telephone had rung out with unusual harshness. The rotating couples in his dream had spun into oblivion and he had sat bolt upright, staring into the shadows, his heart pounding as loudly and insistently as the kettledrum in a Brahms symphony. A sense of horror had overwhelmed him long before his critical faculties had engaged sufficiently to invest the impatient bell with meaning. Eventually, though, the horror connected with a name: Salieri.

The carriage slowed and came to a halt. Immediately, Rheinhardt opened the door and stepped down. The horses snorted violently and rapped the cobbles with their restive hooves. Flecks of foam had appeared on their steaming haunches. The driver leaped off his box and pressed some crystallized sugar between the lips of the nearest animal.

"Fast enough for you?"

"Yes," said the inspector, bluntly.

"Another murder, is it?"

"I'm afraid so."

"And here of all places."

Rheinhardt looked across the deserted Neuer Markt, which was dominated by the Donner fountain. Nude figures, each of which represented a tributary of the Danube, lounged and stretched on its rim. The edifice was covered in a salty rime that sparkled like mica. The sky above was cloudless, and the stars looked as if they had been strewn across the firmament by a careless angel. The effect was one of negligent perfection.

One of the horses rocked its head from side to side, its bridle producing a silvery carillon.

"Nothing's sacred, eh?" added the driver.

Rheinhardt turned and looked upward. The Kapuzinerkirche was not an attractive building—it resembled a child's drawing of a house, with its steep triangular roof and few distinguishing features. An arched niche in the gable contained a figure carrying a crucifix, and below this was a simple arrangement of three windows and a porch. The lack of ornament suggested grim austerity—mortification and self-denial. Adjoining the church was a square-shaped annex, the entrance to which was a large half-open door. It led to the Habsburg crypt. A solitary constable stood outside, stamping his feet and rubbing his hands together.

Rheinhardt approached the young man and introduced himself.

The constable could barely respond. His teeth were chattering and a water droplet hung precariously from the end of his pointed, murine nose.

"You should stand inside," said Rheinhardt with concern.

"But I've been given orders, sir."

"No one will be wandering in off the street at this time. Come, now. If there are any questions, tell your seniors I insisted."

"Thank you, sir," said the constable. "You are most kind."

The young man entered the building and guided Rheinhardt to a steep staircase. A faint light came from below.

Rheinhardt began his descent, pressing against the reassuring presence of the wall with his fingertips. His eyes had not properly adjusted to the darkness and his step was cautious. The air became redolent with a distinctive waxy perfume, and he could hear a faint, eerie susurration.

The light grew stronger, and when he reached the foot of the stairs, he discovered another constable standing next to a tall candelabra.

"Inspector Rheinhardt?"

"Yes."

"Constable Stroop, sir."

"Good man."

"It . . . he . . . the body, sir." He gestured into the shadowy distance. "Down there." The constable's eyes shone, emphasizing his youth but also suggesting fear.

Rheinhardt nodded, and carefully lifted a candle from its clawed sconce. He proceeded to walk into the cold, whispering darkness. The sound of his boots echoed on the stone flags. He moved between two rows of hexagonal bronze caskets, vainly attempting to protect the wick of his candle with a cupped hand. The nervous flame flickered and flared, fitfully illuminating the casket decorations: grinning death's heads, floral wreaths, and ghostly coils of ivy. Rheinhardt's attention was suddenly captured by an arresting cast of a human skull, incongruously adorned with a veil and crown. The inspector glanced at the superscription and registered the name of a long-dead Habsburg monarch. He was reminded of something he had once heard concerning the royal burial rite. Traditionally, the faces of the Habsburg emperors were stoved in so that they would not appear vainglorious before the Almighty. They were also equipped with a bell and bellpull with which to sound an alarm should they find themselves buried alive. Rheinhardt imagined the interior of the casket: fragments of smashed bone beneath a dusty periwig—a skeletal hand reaching for the bellpull handle. He was surprised by an involuntary shudder. Raising his candle to press back the darkness, he continued his journey.

Rheinhardt's breath preceded him, clouding the frozen air. Through the billowy haze he detected two winking lights that grew brighter as he drew closer. The inchoate sibilance increased in volume, resolving itself into the regularities of language—one that Rheinhardt recognized.

"Requiem aeternam dona eis, Domine . . ."

Forms began to appear—penumbral outlines that might be human figures—and there was not one voice but several, each chanting a different prayer.

"Da, quaesumus Dominus, ut in hora mortis nostrae . . ."

At first, it seemed to Rheinhardt that he was approaching a scene that could not be real. Three hooded figures knelt between seated females in flowing gowns. Above them, apparently floating in the air, he could discern a couple—facing each other and separated by a ghostly cherub.

"Pater noster, qui es in caelis, sanctificetur nomen tuum . . ."

A little closer, and the mystery was revealed. Three Capuchin monks were kneeling in front of a monumental casket. The other figures were life-size bronzes—the two women leaning out from an ornate prow with the couple and cherub perched on its lid. The weak candlelight did not illuminate much beyond the casket, but Rheinhardt suspected that the canopy of darkness concealed a dome or cupola. In front of the three Capuchins was a supine body.

Rheinhardt's pace quickened.

One of the monks looked up, made the sign of the cross, and stood to greet the inspector. As he approached, he rolled back his hood. His hair had receded, but as if to compensate he had grown a large snowy beard and mustache.

Rheinhardt bowed. "I am Inspector Rheinhardt—from the security office."

"God bless you, my son. Thank you for coming so swiftly. My name is Brother Ignaz."

Even though the light was poor, Rheinhardt could see that the Capuchin's eyes looked raw and bloodshot. He had clearly been crying.

"I am so sorry . . ." Rheinhardt's sentence trailed off. His instinct was to console, but he wondered whether he could really offer the holy man anything that the man's spiritual convictions had not already provided. "Have any of my colleagues arrived yet?"

"No, my son—only the two constables."

"Father, I am obliged to examine the body. And very soon there will be others here . . . my assistant, the photographer."

Brother Ignaz nodded. "Of course."

He shuffled over to the other monks, who had not broken their intense, hushed chanting, and whispered something that Rheinhardt could not hear. The two monks made the sign of the cross, rose, and, taking one of the candles, silently retreated into the shadows. Brother Ignaz beckoned to Rheinhardt.

"Have you touched the body?"

"Why, yes—does that matter?"

Rheinhardt sighed. "No—it doesn't matter."

The dead monk's limbs had been arranged so that his feet were together and his arms crossed on his chest. Rheinhardt crouched down and brought the candle closer to the corpse's face. It was wrinkled, bearded, and the eyes were closed. The flagstones on the left side of the body were covered in blood.

Rheinhardt tugged at the loose sleeves of the man's robe and uncrossed the arms. He then traced a slow circle with the flame and observed—consistent with his expectations—that the coarse brown fabric had been slashed with a sharp blade. Between the precise straight edges of the material the man's blood had coagulated.

"Who is he?"

"Brother Francis."

"What happened?"

"We had come to the church to pray. He had excused himself and said that he was going down to the crypt. He had been asked to recite a special prayer at the tomb of the Empress Maria Theresa, by a . . ." Brother Ignaz hesitated, before adding, sotto voce, "By a royal personage. It was getting late and I decided to come down to the crypt myself.

Francis has been unwell—I was concerned for his health. As I came down the aisle, I saw something on the floor. At first, I thought he had simply collapsed. I ran and . . ." The monk shook his head.

"What is it?"

"I think—I can't be sure . . ."

"What?"

"I think I heard someone—somebody running up the stairs. Francis was lying facedown . . . and there was so much blood. I rolled him over and tried to revive him—but, of course, there was nothing I could do. In due course I returned to the church, where I found two young brothers—Casimir and Ivo. I dispatched the younger, Ivo, to the Schottenring police station. Casimir and I returned to Francis, in order to pray." The old Capuchin shook his head. "We have been visited by an unspeakable evil. Who would do such a thing? On sacred soil, in this most holy place. It is an abomination!"

Rheinhardt lowered the candle again and inspected Francis's wizened features.

The dead man's eyelids trembled for a moment, and then—quite suddenly—flicked open. A gout of black blood oozed from his mouth as his chest convulsed.

Rheinhardt gasped, drew back, and allowed his candle to drop to the floor.

"Blessed Jesus," cried Brother Ignaz. "He is still alive. It is a miracle."

Suppressing an instinctive wave of horror and fear, Rheinhardt placed a hand on the old man's blood-soaked chest. There was a slight, barely perceptible movement.

"He is alive."

"A miracle, Inspector. *Benedictus Dominus Deus.* A miracle."

Brother Francis wheezed and his lips quivered. He seemed to be attempting speech.

"Brother Francis—my name is Inspector Oskar Rheinhardt. I am from the Viennese security office. Can you hear me?"

He grabbed the monk's cold, papery hand.

"Can you hear me, Brother Francis?"

There was no response. But the monk's lips continued to quiver—and his whistling respiration acquired a marked rhythmic quality.

"Who did this to you? Who attacked you?"

Rheinhardt pressed his ear against the monk's thin blue lips.

A liquid rattle increased in volume, followed by a whisper—an inflected expulsion of air that suggested a syllable or two with form and meaning.

"Brother Francis?"

A final crepitating sigh . . .

Rheinhardt pulled back, just in time to see the old man's eyes closing.

He knew that this time Brother Francis really was dead—as dead as the Habsburg emperors and empresses in their caskets of bronze. Yet he dutifully removed the hand mirror from his inside pocket and held it beneath the old monk's nose. There was no condensation. Rheinhardt looked up at Brother Ignaz and shook his head.

"Did he say anything?"

"Yes, he did."

"What, my son? What did he say?"

Rheinhardt's face shadowed with uncertainty.

"I asked him who did this." Rheinhardt was speaking more to himself than his companion. "And he replied—well—at least, I believe I heard him reply—'a cellist.' "

"I beg your pardon?"

"A cellist," Rheinhardt repeated.

From the entrance came the sound of footsteps and voices. The others had arrived.

60

Jacob Weiss stood and welcomed Liebermann into his office.

"Max, what an unexpected surprise—please, come in. This is Herr Pfeffer, my accountant." He gestured toward a plump man in a gray suit who leaped to his feet with freakish agility. "Emmanuel, this is Max. Clara's Max."

"Herr Doctor Liebermann," chirped the accountant. "I have heard so much about you. It is a great pleasure to meet you." He executed a low, almost comic bow.

"Perhaps we could finish this business some other time?" asked Jacob.

"Of course, of course," Herr Pfeffer replied, scooping up a pile of densely annotated papers in both hands. Liebermann held the door open to facilitate his exit. Pausing momentarily on the threshold, Herr Pfeffer caught Liebermann's gaze and whispered, "Oh, and congratulations."

This innocent felicitation could not have been more inopportune. Liebermann felt as though a dagger had been plunged into his chest. He returned a tepid smile and closed the door, silencing the heavy metallic clatter of a typewriter.

"Come now, do take a seat," said Jacob, proffering a wooden chair. "How are you? Busy as usual, I suppose." He sat down behind his desk, linked his fingers, and leaned forward. Behind the oval windows of his spectacles Jacob's eyes sparkled. Liebermann squirmed in the heat of the man's benevolent scrutiny.

"Herr Weiss . . ." Liebermann had rehearsed the speech he had intended to deliver for days. Even as he had climbed the stairs leading to Herr Weiss's office, the words he had chosen felt trustworthy, solid, dependable. But now they had become fluid and vaporous, impossible to discipline.

"Max—what is it?" For the first time, Jacob's bluff bonhomie faltered.

"Herr Weiss . . . I have come here today to discuss a delicate matter."

The older man's expression suddenly lightened. "Ah yes, I see. The loan is it? You need a little something earlier than expected?" Herr Weiss anticipated an interruption. "Please, you owe me no explanation. I am delighted that you have decided to accept my offer."

The encounter was becoming intolerable.

"Herr Weiss." The name sounded like an entreaty.

"We want you to stay in medicine," Jacob continued. "It's your calling. And it won't be *that* long, surely, before you become a . . . what do you call it? A *privatdozent*?" Jacob waited to be corrected but Liebermann remained silent. "And then your circumstances will be very different. The Viennese love a specialist."

"Herr Weiss, I do not require financial assistance."

Jacob drew back slightly, puzzled.

"Oh . . ."

Liebermann looked directly into Jacob's eyes. He could think of no way to soften the blow. Indeed, to preface his news with qualifications and apologies seemed unconscionable. It would prolong the ordeal. He was not only thinking of himself but of Jacob too. Liebermann took a deep breath and said, with remarkable evenness of tone:

"Herr Weiss, I cannot marry Clara."

In spite of the importance of this declaration it seemed to have little effect on Jacob, whose expression remained simply perplexed.

"I beg your pardon?"

"I cannot marry your daughter."

"What do you mean?" Jacob's head tilted to one side. "I don't understand."

Liebermann looked away and registered some of the items in the room: a pen in its stand, a rubber stamp, a calendar hanging on the wall.

"My feelings for Clara have changed."

Jacob floundered, struggling to make sense of the young man's curious confession. "Changed? What do you mean, 'changed'?"

"I am fond of her—very fond of her. But I am not sure that I love her."

"Max . . ."

"I do not expect you to forgive me. I am guilty of a terrible misjudgment: a terrible misjudgment that will cause you, your family, and, most regrettably of all, Clara much pain. My behavior is unpardonable." Fragments of the rehearsed speech began to insinuate themselves into his sentences. "At the time of our engagement I believed that my feelings for Clara were sincere. However, over the last few months I have come to doubt the authenticity of my affection. I am aware that I can never make amends for my inexcusable folly, and no apology—however heartfelt—will compensate for the disappointment and sadness I shall have caused."

The ensuing silence opened up like a chasm—a rift that carried the two men farther and farther apart. Jacob pushed a clenched fist against his mouth and rearranged a few objects on his desk with a series of abrupt and ultimately purposeless movements. When the brief flurry of activity abated, he broke the silence with a harsh accusation.

"Have you become involved with another woman? Is that it?"

A suspicious pause delayed Liebermann's denial.

"No, Herr Weiss, there is no one else. I have always been faithful to Clara."

Weiss shook his head, attempting to assume—somewhat unsuccessfully—a conciliatory tone.

"Max . . . all men doubt. I remember when—"

Liebermann cut in: "Herr Weiss, I promise you that I have given this matter the deepest and most thorough consideration." He knew that this interruption might sound peremptory but he was anxious to spare Jacob from further disappointment. Any attempt that Herr Weiss might make to persuade him to reconsider would inevitably raise false hopes and end in frustration.

"Have you told your father of your decision?"

"No."

"Your mother?"

"No."

"They will be very upset."

"I know."

Jacob paused, and tapped his index fingers together.

"Max, if you were wrong about your feelings before, how do you know you're right about them now?" Jacob sighed—a long, protracted exhalation. "Perhaps you have been working too hard? Perhaps you have made yourself unwell? Get away for a short period—go for a walking holiday. Southern Italy. What do you think? I'll pay . . ."

"I am sorry, Herr Weiss." Liebermann shook his head.

Life had no spiritual purpose for Liebermann. His values were pragmatic, his philosophical outlook informed by simple medical virtues: helping others, the unquestionable good of alleviating pain. Now that he found himself to be the cause of suffering, something trembled at the core of his being. Something essential began to crack and splinter. He was suddenly overcome by a powerful need to exonerate himself.

"Herr Weiss . . . I have proved myself to be utterly undeserving of your respect and kindness. But please permit me to express a single hope pertaining to our future relations. When your anger—which is both inevitable and justified—subsides, I earnestly desire that you will appreciate that I have tried my very hardest to act in good faith. To marry Clara without truly loving her would be tantamount to betrayal. Even I—now a deplorable wretch in your eyes—cannot bring myself to deceive such a sweet-natured creature."

Jacob allowed his head to drop into his hands. "Dear God . . . poor Clara."

"I will arrange to meet her this afternoon."

Jacob's body jerked upright. "What?"

"I will arrange to meet her this afternoon. I must explain—"

"Are you *insane*?" Jacob interrupted. "You will *not* see Clara this afternoon, Max. I forbid you!"

"But I must. It is my responsibility—a responsibility that I do not intend to shirk. I will not compound dishonor with cowardice."

Herr Weiss's lips twisted to form an ugly smile. The acidity of what followed was not unexpected. "You have already shown yourself to be a coward, Max. In my day, a man honored his commitments—whatever the cost!"

61

"Where is Doctor Liebermann?"

Rheinhardt looked at the Englishwoman and shrugged. "I have been trying to contact the good doctor since this morning—without success. I can only assume that he is indisposed."

Miss Lydgate nodded curtly. "Am I to understand that you wish me to make another microscopic analysis?"

"Indeed. There has been another murder—a Capuchin monk, can you believe, whose body was discovered last night in the crypt of the Kapuzinerkirche. We collected various samples of dust from the floor, and I was wondering whether you could make a comparison with the slides that you prepared earlier this month."

Rheinhardt gestured toward a wooden box. It had a label gummed to the lid on which was written:

Ra'ad. 7 November 1902. Samples from scarf.

Prepared by Miss Lydgate 10 November 1902—Schottenring Laboratory.

"As you are already familiar with the materials," Rheinhardt continued, "I thought that you would be best qualified to undertake the task. . . ." The pitch of his sentence rose like a question.

"I am sure your technical staff are capable of making such a comparison. But because I am both present and flattered by your request, let us proceed. Where are the new samples?"

Rheinhardt produced a stack of isinglass envelopes.

"Each of these contains samples of dust taken from various locations in the crypt."

Amelia took the first envelope and observed an inky script in the top right-hand corner.

"*Emperor Franz Stephan and Empress Maria Theresa?*"

"Ah yes. That refers to the occupants of the casket closest to where the sample was taken from."

"I see."

"As it happens, that is also the most important sample. The Capuchin's body was discovered next to that very casket—so we know that the murderer stood close by. I would be most grateful if you would give that particular sample your most thorough attention."

"Herr Inspector, I will give *all* of them my most thorough attention—without exception."

There was something almost defiant about the Englishwoman's tone: the coolness of her delivery, and the preternatural intensity of her expression.

"Thank you," said Rheinhardt, a little worried that he might have offended her.

"Inspector, why don't you return to your office? This exercise will take some time and your presence here serves no purpose. You will, I suspect, have many other things of importance to attend to."

"Oh, but you cannot be left here alone."

"Why ever not?"

"It would be discourteous."

"Inspector, it is my preference."

"Are you sure?"

"Quite sure, Inspector."

Amelia turned toward the microscope. Rheinhardt thanked her again but she did not hear him. Her mind was entirely absorbed by the task in hand. Rheinhardt tiptoed to the door and departed like a shadow. Peering through the corridor window, he could see Miss Lydgate organizing the laboratory equipment with ruthless efficiency. She was, Rheinhardt thought, a very peculiar woman. But he was delighted to have made her acquaintance.

62

THE LIBRARIAN ENTERED THE small room that had been designated for use as the chamber of reflection. Its walls were covered in roughcast plaster, giving it the appearance of a hermit's cave. An iron table and a wooden stool were the only pieces of furniture. He lit the single candle on the table, which projected its feeble light on a crude mural, painted white upon a black background. It depicted a cockerel and the word *vitriol*—an acronym of an ancient command to self-knowledge: *visita interiora terrae, rectificando invenies occultam lapidem* (visit the center of the earth, and by rectification you shall find the hidden stone). Resting against the table was a large rusting scythe.

Opening his sack, the librarian carefully removed several objects. The first of these was a human skull and several long bones. He arranged them carefully on the table, and next to them placed a lump of dry bread, an hourglass, and two metal dishes. From his pocket he removed two vials, the contents of which he emptied onto the dishes, creating two powdery mounds of white and yellow. The first substance was salt and the second sulfur. He made a mental note that he must return with a glass of water.

Before leaving, he paused and turned the hourglass. He watched the grains of sand pouring into the lower chamber. In just over two weeks, *he* would be there—sitting at this very table, writing his philosophical will. The librarian reached out and gripped the scythe. Anyone approaching him from behind might well have mistaken him for the Grim Reaper.

63

Herr Beiber was lying on the divan, describing a dream he had experienced in his childhood.

"It's strange, but I can remember it quite clearly."

"How old were you at the time?" asked Liebermann.

"Very young."

"*How* young?"

"Ooh . . . about four or five, perhaps. I was still sleeping on a cot in my parents' bedroom."

After his traumatic interview with Herr Weiss, Liebermann had immersed himself in his work at the hospital. It had been a therapeutic exercise from which the doctor had benefited more than his patients. Four walls, a supine body, speech, and meaningful silences: this was Liebermann's world. An intimate, protected space—a still center. There was something extraordinarily soothing about the therapeutic situation, its emollient familiarity: the careful listening, which if sustained resulted in a complete loss of self-awareness. The gas lamp flickered and the day receded.

"Four or five? That is quite old—to be sleeping in one's parents' bedroom, I mean."

"Yes. I could be wrong," said Herr Beiber. "Maybe I was younger. On the other hand, I was a very sickly child. I suffered from terrible fevers. My mother told me that once or twice she and my father thought I was going to die. I suspect that they were worried about my health—they didn't let me sleep on my own until much later."

Herr Beiber tapped a finger on his stomach.

"And the dream?"

"Oh yes, the dream. I dreamed that it was the dead of night. The curtains had not been drawn and there was a full moon—so the room was well lit. I could see my mother and father's bed, my mother's dresser, and the wash table with its jug and bowl. Everything was silvery-white. What I remember most vividly, though, was the wardrobe. I never liked that wardrobe. It was a large plain box. It reminded me of a casket. I'd seen caskets on the backs of hearses, and in my childish mind I am sure that I had made some form of association. It was my fancy, I suppose, to imagine that the wardrobe concealed something macabre." Herr Beiber smiled and tilted his head back. "Ahh, I seem to have inadvertently accepted your psychoanalytic ideas, Herr Doctor—was that not an *interpretation*?"

Liebermann shook his head. "Please continue. Your dream is of considerable interest to me."

"Is that so? Well, I suppose dreams *are* a fascinating phenomenon. . . . I hadn't given them very much thought before coming here." Beiber's voice became eager. "I hope that when the Archduchess and I are united we shall spend many happy hours sharing each other's dreams. I have often wondered what fantastical dramas must unravel behind those beautiful eyes when they are closed by sleep."

"Herr Beiber," said Liebermann. "Your dream?"

"Oh yes—where was I?"

"The wardrobe. It reminded you of a casket."

"Indeed. Well, there I was, staring at this tall, plain box, which I had childishly imagined was the repository of all manner of horrors, when what should happen next? The realization of my worst fear. The doors began to creak open, and as they did, I became conscious of a heavy-breathing sound—a kind of hungry panting. Slowly, slowly, the doors opened—seemingly of their own accord—to reveal an impenetrable darkness, impervious to moonlight. I could see nothing inside. No coats, jackets, or hatboxes—no possessions—none of the expected items that had come to represent the day-to-day presence of my mother and father. I was transfixed and, needless to say, consumed by terror. I wondered what manner of creature might make that horrible panting sound, and whether it would attempt to escape its lair. Two red eyes appeared. They glinted in the moonlight. Then another pair appeared above them. . . . I wanted to scream, but I was struck dumb. Not so much as a squeak escaped from my lips. Then something extraordinary happened. A great shaggy black creature jumped out of the wardrobe. It was a massive, salivating thing—as a wolf might be depicted in a children's picture book. Then out jumped its companion—a beast of the same lupine breed and almost equal in size. The two of them were staring at me, their tongues hanging from their slack open jaws. And all of the time that horrible, horrible panting . . . They began to advance. They were coming toward me." Herr Beiber's voice was now strained. The mocking, superior tone had completely vanished. "Their great paws on the floorboards, the scratching of their claws, long tails wagging, merciless feral eyes . . ." Herr Beiber's chest rose and fell with increasing speed and his breathing grew ragged. "They were going to eat me up. I imagined those sharp teeth sinking into my flesh, ripping, tearing, shaking. . . . I screamed and screamed. And suddenly I found that I really *was* screaming! I was sitting up on my cot—wide awake—clutching my eiderdown with both hands."

Herr Beiber gripped his hospital gown as the haptic memory made his fingers spasm. He remained silent for a few moments.

"And what happened then?"

"My mother came to my assistance. She petted and kissed me—

told me that it had all been a bad dream and that I had nothing to fear. But I did not believe her. And . . . and . . ."

"Yes, go on."

"I was right to disbelieve her. This will no doubt sound odd to you, Herr Doctor—but you have asked me to be candid. On subsequent nights I listened very carefully, and I swear that I could hear that horrible breathing emanating from the wardrobe."

"Perhaps you were asleep again—and it was another dream."

"No, Herr Doctor, I was awake. Wide awake—as awake as you or I right now."

"What was it, do you think?"

"You will concede—I hope—that there are many things in this world for which we have no ready explanation."

The young doctor did not reply.

64

LIEBERMANN ARRIVED HOME LATE to find his serving man hovering anxiously in the hallway.

"Ernst, what is it?"

"Your mother is here."

"My mother?"

"Yes."

"Where is she?"

"In the music room."

Ernst took Liebermann's astrakhan coat.

"When did she arrive?"

"At eight-thirty, sir."

Liebermann glanced at his wristwatch. It was ten-fifteen.

"She's been here all evening! Thank you so much for waiting."

"It was my pleasure, sir."

Liebermann took a deep breath and entered the music room, where his mother was seated on the sofa. For a moment she did not react. She looked small, hunched, and worried. Then, with remarkable alacrity, she was standing and looking vaguely combative.

"Maxim!"

"Mother . . ."

Liebermann walked over to her and hesitated before kissing her. She pulled a curious face (which somehow managed to combine condescension with compassion and resignation) and offered him her powdery cheek.

"I suppose you've heard," said Liebermann.

"Yes, I've heard. And when did you intend to tell us, exactly?"

"Tomorrow. I'm sorry. I had to get back to the hospital."

"The hospital, the hospital, always the hospital. You know, sometimes I think your father's right. You would have been better off managing one of the factories. Sit down, Max."

He did as he was told and his mother sat back down on the sofa beside him.

"I'm sorry, Mother—really I am." Rebecca Liebermann shrugged, made an ambiguous gesture with her hand, and picked a speck of fluff from her son's trousers. "How did you hear?"

"Jacob spoke to your father."

"Ah . . ."

"He's furious. When I left Concordiaplatz, he was threatening to disown you."

Liebermann swallowed. "Did Herr Weiss mention Clara?"

"Yes."

"How is she?"

"They're sending her away with her Aunt Trudi for a while."

"Where?"

"I don't know—just away."

"I wanted to see her, but Herr Weiss forbade it."

"Can you blame him?"

Liebermann shook his head. "All I wanted was to behave honorably—that's all." Liebermann fingered a loose button on his jacket. "Months ago, you asked me whether she was really *the one*—whether I really loved her. I thought I did, but I was wrong. I don't love Clara—well, at least, not like I should. I didn't know that *then*, but I know it *now*. And if we had gone ahead with the marriage, it would have been a *bad* marriage. A marriage based on a lie. What possible good could have come of that? I wasn't only thinking of myself—I was thinking of Clara too."

Rebecca stopped her son from worrying the button on his jacket. "Leave it alone—it'll come off," She took his hand in hers and squeezed his long, elegant fingers. "I had my suspicions."

"You did?"

"Mother's intuition. I know you think I'm a silly old fool when I say such things, but it exists, whether you like it or not."

Liebermann looked into his mother's eyes. They were glinting, but there were no tears.

"What shall I do about Father?"

"Stay away from him—for a while. He's writing you a letter. Ignore it—he's upset, that's all. You know what he's like. And if you do respond, remember that he's your father. I'll do what I can."

Rebecca tucked a stray strand of her son's hair behind his ear—one of her tics that Liebermann found most irritating (but which he was now content to forgive)—and stood up abruptly.

"I've got to go," said Rebecca. "It's late. Your father didn't want me to come in the first place."

"But we've hardly spoken—and you've been waiting here all evening."

"It doesn't matter. . . . I've seen you. That's enough."

"Enough for what?"

"All that education, and sometimes you still don't understand anything." On her way to the door she paused by the Bösendorfer. "I never get to hear you play these days. I used to love listening to you play."

65

STEFAN KANNER AND PROFESSOR Pallenberg were standing in an attic room of the General Hospital. A rope, one end of which disappeared into an elaborate winching device, had been thrown over a central support beam. The exposed mechanism of the winch consisted of several large wooden cogs, a central drum, and a low crank handle. The other end of the rope formed a noose that had been pulled tightly around the feet of a middle-aged man who was now suspended upside down approximately five feet from the floor. He was wearing a restraining jacket of brown canvas. The flesh on his face had been redistributed by gravity, creating a unique expression that married the inscrutability of a Japanese Buddha with the comedic painted lineaments of a clown, and his hair hung straight down. The scene was lit by a thin pasty light that seeped apologetically through a narrow window.

"Well?" said Professor Pallenberg.

"I must confess that I am not familiar with this particular"—Kanner hesitated, bit his lower lip, and finally forced out the word—"treatment."

"No," said Pallenberg. "It is largely unknown to students of your generation."

The patient rotated clockwise, slowing by degrees to a perfect standstill. After a moment of stillness, the rope began to unwind and the hanging man turned in the opposite direction. The restraining jacket gave him the appearance of a giant pupa.

"As you know," Pallenberg went on, "Herr Auger has not responded to conservative treatments—particularly morphia and veronal—and I thought it time to try a different approach . . . something that I remembered from my student days in Paris."

"Suspension is a French treatment?"

"Indeed. I am one of a select company of Viennese doctors who had the pleasure of studying under Charcot at the Salpêtrière. Do you know Professor Freud?"

"Not personally."

"He was another. A great man, Charcot. The Napoléon of the neuroses."

"I have read some of Professor Freud's translations. But I have never come across this specific"—he found himself hesitating again—"therapy."

"Well, that isn't surprising. Charcot's pioneering work using hypnosis as a treatment for *la grande hystérie* has somewhat eclipsed his other contributions. In my estimation, iron-filing ingestion and suspension in harness are two original interventions that have been sadly neglected."

"Might I ask," said Kanner tentatively, "how suspension works?"

"Well," Pallenberg replied, "Charcot proposed certain theories that—to be frank—are not compelling. But I always suspected that his work in this domain merited further consideration. I remember the case of an engineer who suffered from delusions of persecution and who benefited greatly from suspension. Then there was a sailor who believed that one of his legs had been amputated while he slept somewhere off the coast of Portugal. . . . I have long since wondered whether certain forms of delusion—among which we must include the Cotard—are caused by an abnormality of circulation. Perhaps Charcot achieved these successes because suspension had some subtle effect on the course of arterial blood flow in the brain. It is my earnest hope that Herr Auger will be the beneficiary of such a process."

"Could a similar effect not be achieved by encouraging Herr Auger to lie in bed with his feet raised on some pillows?"

Professor Pallenberg shook his head. "No, I doubt that very much."

Kanner, accepting his role as the junior party in the exchange, stood corrected.

Professor Pallenberg approached his inverted patient. A dull creaking sound accompanied the periodic clockwise and anticlockwise rotations.

"Herr Auger," said Pallenberg, addressing the reverse-horripilated head. "How are you feeling?"

"I do not exist," came the gentle, resigned reply.

"That is self-evidently not true, Herr Auger," Pallenberg responded somewhat tetchily. "Now, would you be so kind as to tell me how you feel?"

"I am not here."

Kanner was relieved to hear Herr Auger's usual response. If the poor man did not believe in his own existence, then it seemed unlikely that he could be suffering very much.

Pallenberg shrugged and caught Kanner's eye. "One cannot expect very much progress at this very early stage. I would be most grateful, Doctor Kanner, if you could ensure that Herr Auger receives fifteen to twenty minutes of suspension daily. The winch is simple to operate but you will obviously need some assistance from the porters."

"Very good, sir."

Pallenberg nodded curtly. "Good afternoon, Herr Doctor."

Recognizing that he had been dismissed, Kanner bowed, and left the room. He descended the stairs in an oddly detached state, somewhat overwhelmed by his encounter with Professor Pallenberg and the unfortunate Herr Auger.

By the time Kanner had reached his office, his mind was occupied by other matters. Before entering the room he looked down the corridor both ways and then quickly slipped inside. He went immediately to his desk, unlocked the bottom drawer, and took out a heavily embroidered sash and apron. The apron bore the image of a temple between two columns that were marked J and B respectively. Kanner quickly stuffed the items into his doctor's bag and closed the hasp. Then, sighing with relief, he looked at his watch.

66

LIEBERMANN AND RHEINHARDT WERE attempting Guglielmo's aria from the first act of *Così Fan Tutte*. Rheinhardt's Italian was less than perfect.

> *"Guardate . . . taccate . . ."*
> Look . . . touch . . .

He struggled with the liquid vowels.

> *"Il tutto osservate . . ."*
> Observe everything . . .

They had not conferred greatly on the selection of songs, yet their musical evening contained an unusual number of piano and voice arrangements taken from the operas of Mozart. It was a fact that made Liebermann feel distinctly uncomfortable. Unconsciously, they were looking for clues.

> *"Il tutto osservate . . ."*
> Observe everything . . .

Their music-making had always been sacred: they had always resisted discussing other matters, however urgent, until the final chords of the final song had faded into silence. But now Salieri seemed to have violated their tradition. He had insinuated himself into the music room—between the very notes of Mozart's divine melodies. He stood in the shadow of the Bösendorfer: an unwelcome, ghostly presence.

After performing the Mozart pieces, they returned to more familiar territory—lieder by Brahms. The luscious, romantic harmonies seemed to repel the spectral visitor (at least temporarily) to some distant outer region. But when the recital was done—ending with *Wir wandelten*—Liebermann still felt uneasy. For it was not only the thought of Salieri that was causing him discomfort. There was also the matter of his pending confession. He had resolved to inform Rheinhardt of his decision to terminate his engagement to Clara, and he was not sure how his friend would receive such news.

The two men retired to the smoking room and took their respective places in front of the fire. They lit cigars, sipped brandy, and permitted themselves a few moments of quiet repose. When the room had become hazy with smoke, the young doctor spoke.

"Forgive me, Oskar. I owe you an apology."

The inspector turned. "Oh?"

"It was remiss of me not to respond to your note last week."

"I had assumed that you were ill."

"No, I was not ill. And you are due more than the dashed-off reply that I sent on Monday."

Rheinhardt detected that his friend was unusually tense. His restless fingers betrayed an inner state of agitation.

"What is it, Max?"

Liebermann hesitated. Then, bracing himself, he threw back his head and swallowed a medicinal quantity of brandy. "Last week," he said deliberately, "I had to make a decision regarding a personal issue, which left me feeling utterly dejected. Indeed, my spirits were so low that I could barely summon the energy to attend my patients." Liebermann studied the refracted rainbows in the finely cut glass. "The decision I made was one that I believe will not meet with your approval." He looked anxiously at his friend. Rheinhardt dismissed the remark with a hand gesture and signaled that Liebermann should continue. "You will recall that I once expressed some doubt as to whether I should proceed with my engagement to Clara Weiss."

"Indeed. We spoke at some length on the subject."

"Well, Oskar. In spite of your wise counsel, I have found it impossible to dispel the feelings of apprehension surrounding the prospect of our union. I arranged an interview with Clara's father and explained that I could not—in good faith—marry his daughter. Needless to say, he was horrified and forbade me to see Clara. I understand she has since been removed from Vienna, and I suspect that she has been taken to a sanitorium." Liebermann drew on his cigar and expelled a great cloud of smoke. "So, you see, Oskar, I have achieved much since we last met. I have thoroughly embarrassed my parents, caused incalculable pain to a woman whom I had previously professed to love, and declined membership of a family who have hitherto shown me only kindness and the deepest affection. I wouldn't blame you for thinking badly of me."

A log on the fire suddenly blazed up and a fierce shower of sparks erupted onto the hearth. The inspector squeezed his lower lip and appeared to descend into a meditative state. After a considerable length of time had elapsed, Rheinhardt stirred. He cleared his throat, hummed, and finally spoke.

"First of all, Max, I hope that you will accept my most sincere commiserations. I had no idea that you were so very racked with doubts, and if I had, perhaps my advice to you would have been different. Second, I have every confidence in your character. I cannot claim to have any special knowledge of the human mind—I am no psychiatrist—but I am a fair judge of men, and I understand you well enough to appreciate that your intentions were honorable. You did not want to enter upon a sham marriage—that much is clear. To do so would have been bad for you, and even worse for Clara. Finally, I have always found you to be a man of singular courage. In my small estimation—for what it is worth—this act is perhaps the bravest I have ever known you to perform. The right course of action is rarely the easiest, and to have proceeded with an insincere marriage, for the sake of maintaining appearances, would have been morally reprehensible. As a man whose calling . . . no, whose very reason for existence is to alleviate human suffering, the events of last week must have cost you dearly. I am so very sorry. Be that as it may, I suspect that this trial need not prick your conscience forever. Given time, they will *all* come to realize the propriety of your decision—your family, the Weisses, and, most important, your dear Clara."

Liebermann turned slowly, and looked at his friend's world-weary face: the sagging pouches of skin beneath his eyes, the heavy jowls, and the incongruously jaunty pointed mustache. And as he did so, he felt a wave of affection that brought him close to tears. *What a great and generous soul this man possessed,* he thought.

"Oskar, I don't know what to say. You are too kind. I do not deserve such—"

"Nonsense, nonsense," cried the inspector.

"No—I really don't deserve—"

"Enough!" Rheinhardt raised his hand. "The quality of your character is not in question. You have nothing to thank me for." Then, unexpectedly, he stood up to leave. "As you know, there were many things that I wished to discuss with you this evening concerning Salieri . . . but let us instead postpone. I do not wish to burden you with the concerns of the security office at this difficult time. We shall meet again in due course—when your spirits have rallied."

"But, Oskar," Liebermann protested, "my spirits have already rallied. Your kind words have acted as a restorative. Moreover, I can think of no better remedy than to make myself useful to the security office. Now, please, do sit down!"

Rehinhardt's eyes narrowed. "Are you sure?"

"Yes."

The inspector smiled. "Excellent."

Rheinhardt opened his bag and produced a stack of photographs. Then, returning to his seat, he handed them to Liebermann.

The young doctor looked at the first image: a dark, grainy impression of a hooded figure lying on a stone floor.

"Another Salieri killing?"

"I'm afraid so."

"When did he strike?"

"Thursday."

"Has the murder been reported?"

"In the *Zeitung*, the *Freie Presse*, and that dreadful new rag, the *Illustrierte Kronen-Zeitung*."

Liebermann began working through the pile of prints. Each image showed the body from a different perspective. Close-up, long view, looking down from above.

"His name is Brother Francis," Rheinhardt continued. "A Capuchin monk. His body was discovered by one of his confrères, Brother Ignaz, in the crypt of the Kapuzinerkirche. In Salieri's scheme, his corresponding character in *The Magic Flute* must be one of the many priests."

"Or the Speaker of the Temple, perhaps—who is a kind of high priest."

"Indeed. Professor Mathias ascribed the cause of death to loss of blood, resulting from a sabre wound."

"The *same* sabre?"

"*That*, he couldn't say." Rheinhardt shifted in his chair and leaned closer to Liebermann. "When I descended into the crypt, several monks had stationed themselves by the body and were reciting offices for the dead. Naturally, I assumed that Brother Francis was no longer with us. But I was very wrong."

"He was still alive!"

"Yes. The poor fellow had certainly arrived at death's door, but he was yet to step over the threshold. He managed a few desperate gasps, and seemed to regain consciousness. I immediately asked him who had performed the dastardly deed. His reply was . . . intriguing. He said, 'A *cellist.*' Then he passed away."

Liebermann examined a close-up photograph of the dead monk's face. A hooked nose projected out from between two sunken eyes.

"Extraordinary," said Liebermann, working down to the last of the shots. It showed the royal tomb, emerging out of the darkness like a galleon crewed by ghosts. "The crypt was not desecrated with symbols?"

"No."

"Professor Mathias did not discover any objects concealed in the Capuchin's corpse?"

"No."

"And no mutilations?" Liebermann tapped the pile of photographs.

"Salieri was disturbed by the arrival of Brother Ignaz. I imagine that he did not have time."

"Which would also explain why he did not deliver an efficient sabre blow."

"Indeed, he must have been distracted at the key moment."

" 'A *cellist.*' " Liebermann rotated his glass. The rainbows broke and re-formed. "What are we to make of that? Salieri couldn't have been sitting in the crypt, playing a Bach sonata. So, did Brother Francis recognize him? Is he an artist of some renown? A virtuoso? Or perhaps some rank-and-file orchestral player who participated in a recent religious concert?"

"All are possible." Rheinhardt smiled grimly. "And are we to suppose that in styling the murderer 'Salieri' our choice of name was more apposite than we could possibly have imagined?"

"I believe that the real Salieri studied the harpsichord and violin rather than the cello. Whatever, the evidence gathered so far certainly suggests that *our* quarry is a musician."

"Aschenbrandt?"

"He is the only musician to be counted among your suspects—and he is also a cellist. I saw the instrument leaning against the wall when I visited his apartment."

"Yes. Aschenbrandt—could he be the killer? I read your report with great interest. But I found it rather . . . perplexing."

"Oh? Why?"

"You draw several conclusions, Max—but were they really merited by that interview? I take it that your transcript is faithful and nothing more was said?"

"That is correct."

"Perhaps my memory is at fault, but was it not the case that you talked to him about a single topic only? That is to say, music."

"What did you expect me to do? Raise the subject of murder?"

"Well . . . under the circumstances . . ."

"Oskar, what is the point of such questions? People lie, misdirect, and make up alibis that are subsequently confirmed by confederates. I am interested only in the truths that people reveal about themselves inadvertently: a raised eyebrow, a hesitation, a slip of the tongue—subtle reactions. These are far more valuable. They are authentic communications, emanating from the unconscious. Had I mentioned murder, it would almost certainly have put Aschenbrandt on his guard."

Liebermann lit another cigar.

"Aschenbrandt," he continued, "is definitely a disturbed young man. An anti-Semite who entertains semi-delusional beliefs about a Teutonic Messiah whose destiny it is to save the German-speaking peoples. It is possible that he has surrendered himself to this potent mythos, and it has now taken hold of his mind like a possessing demon. He may even see himself as 'the Invincible' of his string quintet— whose mission it is to rid Vienna of enemy nomads, Slavs, Negroes, and even, perhaps, representatives of the old order—a corrupt Catholic Church. But as to whether he is Salieri . . . Well, I have my doubts. When we were discussing *The Magic Flute*, Aschenbrandt seemed unperturbed. *The Magic Flute* is Salieri's organizing principle—the channel through which he expresses all his hate and violence. If Aschenbrandt is Salieri, there should have been more signs. He was angry, of course—angry about being interrupted, angry that I called Wagner's music bombastic—and he found my delight in Mozart extremely irritating. But at no time did discussion of *The Magic Flute* produce a discernible change in his demeanor. He seemed quite comfortable debating a subject that should have stirred up the most powerful emotions; emotions that he should have struggled to conceal."

"That's all very well, Max," said Rheinhardt." But I am still minded to launch a full investigation into Aschenbrandt's musical activities. If we discover that he has participated in any chamber concerts in the Kapuzinerkirche, or any other church for that matter . . ."

"Of course," said Liebermann, "I offer you only an opinion—and Salieri might be such an exceptional creature that his mental processes might not even obey the laws of psychoanalysis." He knocked the ash from his cigar. "Now, tell me, what of the other suspects?"

"I went to see the artist, Olbricht. What a peculiar fellow."

"Why do you say that?"

"Something about his expression."

"I do hope you are not going to invoke Lombroso again. Once and for all, Oskar, there is no relationship between a man's appearance and his nature."

"Yes, you're quite right. Curiously enough, Olbricht is something of a war hero. He saved his commanding officer's life in the Bosnia-Herzegovina campaign of 1878. And—for a military man—he was rather reticent about the whole affair. He invited me to the opening of his next exhibition. It's at the Hildebrandt Gallery—on Kärntner Strasse. Other members of the Eddic Literary Association are bound to be there. Would you be interested in coming along?"

"Very much so."

"Excellent."

"And what of Lieutenant Hefner?"

Rheinhardt's features contracted into a small circle of disgust. "Haussmann spent some time in Café Haynau, a sordid little place much frequented by military men. It is also a hotbed of gossip. Hefner is rumored to have killed more than a dozen men in duels—probably an exaggeration, but if it proves true, it wouldn't surprise me. His name was recently linked with that of Lemberg, the industrialist's son. The young man is supposed to have died after sustaining a fatal wound in a *shooting accident*."

Liebermann sank lower down in his chair. "It seems that killing is Hefner's sport."

"And they say he is a stranger to fear. Always keeps his nerve—always the second to shoot in a barrier duel."

"Cold, calculating . . . and arrogant?"

"Insufferably."

"There is a professor in Berlin who has described a certain pathological 'type,' characterized by blunting of the emotions, self-obsession, and lack of conscience. He attributes this syndrome to a disease process affecting the frontal lobes of the brain."

Both men stared into the flames. The gas lamps hummed harmoniously on a major third.

"The thing is," said Rheinhardt, not wishing to be drawn into a technical discussion on an arcane branch of medicine, "neither Hefner, nor Aschenbrandt, nor Olbricht, nor any member of the Eddic Literary Association—to my knowledge—is a librarian, or a seller of antiquarian books."

"I beg your pardon?" said Liebermann. Rheinhardt suspected that his friend was still occupied with thoughts of frontal lobes.

"While you were"—Rheinhardt smiled—"absent, I took the liberty of calling upon Miss Lydgate again to analyze samples of dust found close to the Capuchin's body."

"Oh?" Liebermann sat up.

"She occupied the Schottenring laboratory for almost two whole days."

"And what did she conclude?"

"She concluded that the dust from the crypt contained particles of leather, glue, and cloth that were identical to those found in her previous analysis—although they were present in much smaller quantities. She even went so far as to say that one kind of leather—of reddish hue—appeared in both samples, and very likely came from the same book." Rheinhardt poured himself another brandy. "We have interviewed most of the city's librarians and antiquarian book dealers. None of them could possibly be Salieri. Moreover, her evidence is inconsistent with the rest of the investigation: none of our suspects are librarians. I hesitate to say this, because I am very fond of this remarkable lady, but could it be that Miss Lydgate is simply mistaken?"

"No, Oskar," said Liebermann solemnly. "I think there is very little chance of that."

"In which case," said the inspector, taking a sip of brandy, "we are still utterly lost."

67

THE EXHIBITION WAS WELL attended, providing Liebermann and Rheinhardt with a degree of anonymity. Somewhere behind the milling crowd a string quartet was playing a gentle ländler.

Occasionally Rheinhardt leaned closer to his friend and pointed out a particular individual.

"That fellow there—the distinguished-looking gent—that's Von Triebenbach. And the woman he's talking to is Baroness von Rautenberg—Olbricht's patron."

They stood in front of a full-length portrait of Wagner's Brunhilde.

Rheinhardt nodded toward the entrance. "Plump fellow with the ruddy complexion—Counselor Hannisch. He's talking to—"

"Professor Foch," Liebermann interrupted.

"Of course, you know him."

The counselor and the professor made an odd couple. Foch wore his usual funereal garb, and Hannisch was dressed in a green suit with a bright blue cravat.

"I know *of* him," Liebermann said, correcting Rheinhardt.

Liebermann resumed his scrutiny of the Valkyrie. She wore the horned headdress of a Viking, thick furs, and her spear was tipped with a daub of red paint. Rheinhardt's head swiveled around.

"No Aschenbrandt."

The general hubbub rose in volume, swelling with the sound of jovial greetings and cries of satisfaction. Close by, the crowd parted, affording Liebermann and Rheinhardt a glimpse of a short man whose hand was being squeezed by a colonel of the infantry.

."The artist," whispered Rheinhardt.

Olbricht was delayed for a few moments before continuing his tour of the room. Seeing Rheinhardt, he smiled, revealing his stunted teeth.

"Ah, Inspector, I am so glad you came."

Rheinhardt gestured toward his companion. "My friend, Dr. Max Liebermann."

Olbricht acknowledged the younger man's presence but did not bow.

At that moment a very attractive young woman, her hair fashioned in dangling coils of gold, broke through a drab wall of suited figures.

"You will excuse me," said Olbricht.

"Of course," said Rheinhardt.

"Herr Olbricht," cried the young woman. "There you are! I promised my father I would find you—he wishes to introduce you to Hofrat Eggebrecht."

"Of course, Fräulein Bolle—I am yours to command."

They linked arms and vanished behind two chattering dowagers whose bony fingers sparkled with diamonds.

The young doctor looked a little perplexed.

"What is it, Max?"

Liebermann lowered his voice. "His face . . ."

"What?"

"There is *something* about it . . ."

"Ha! Didn't I say so! And wasn't it you who scolded me! What was it you said? You went on about Lombroso again!"

Liebermann grimaced. "Please accept my apology."

"I do so with . . . with munificence."

They moved along the wall, stopping to look at each painting.

The dwarf Alberich and the three Rhine maidens; a mage standing in a pentacle decorated with runic symbols; a blind skald weaving his spell by the hearth in a timbered hall.

"Do you like them?" asked Rheinhardt, surprised that his friend was examining the images so closely. He knew that Liebermann's artistic preferences were modern and could not understand why he was spending so much time in front of each canvas.

"Definitely not."

"Then please can we move along. We will never finish the exhibition at this rate!"

Liebermann sighed and followed his friend.

The next canvas was a large battle scene crammed with tiny figures. It reminded Liebermann of the work of Hieronymus Bosch— particularly *The Last Judgment*, which was permanently exhibited in the art school. But when he drew closer to the canvas, it was apparent that Olbricht did not possess Bosch's technique, nor any of his humor. Liebermann fished his spectacles out from the top pocket of his jacket and pressed his nose up close to the painting.

"What on earth are you doing, Max?"

"Looking at the detail."

A rather large burgher said "Excuse me, sir" in a gruff voice, indicating that Liebermann was in his way. He was wearing an artificial white carnation in his buttonhole, signaling his membership of the Christian Social party. The young doctor apologized and took a step back. The burgher narrowed his eyes at Liebermann and said something to his wife. Neither the young doctor nor his companion needed to hear the words to comprehend the nature of the slur. Rheinhardt was about to challenge the burgher but Liebermann raised his hand. They moved away quietly.

"Disgraceful," said Rheinhardt. "You really should have let me—"

"Oskar," Liebermann cut in. "It happens all the time. Come now, let us continue with the exhibition."

The next canvas showed a woman with flaxen hair looking out at an infinitely receding Roman army. It was titled *Pipara: The Germanic Woman in the Purple of the Caesars.* Liebermann read an accompanying note: *Adapted freely from the two-volume novel by Guido von List, recounting the legendary rise of a German slave to the position of empress in the late third century.*

"What a fine woman," said Rheinhardt, innocently.

The young doctor did not reply. He studied the painting for some time, and motioned that he was ready to move on. Then—strangely—at the last moment he found himself unable to proceed. His feet seemed fixed to the floor. It was as though the painting were exerting a strange influence, producing immobility.

Liebermann's mind was suddenly invaded by a haunting image: the shopgirl he had met on the streetcar—her carmine glove, receding into the gloom.

Rheinhardt, who had already taken a few steps away, paused and looked back at his friend. "Max?"

"This painting . . ." Liebermann whispered.

The string quartet struck up the introductory bars of a Strauss waltz. Liebermann recognized it immediately: *Vienna Blood.* Suddenly the spell was broken and he was walking toward his friend, an enigmatic smile raising the corners of his mouth.

68

THE ROOM CONTAINED NO furniture except for a small card table that had been placed in the center. From downstairs the muffled sound of carousing rose through the bare floorboards. An inebriated chorus of male voices seemed to be exploring the limits of musical coherence over an out-of-tune piano. The instrument rang out its discords, and occasionally a shriek of delight betrayed the presence of several indecorous females.

A single gas flame sputtered, tainting the air with pungent fumes. Above the lamp's stanchion and cracked glass bowl a black smear of sooty ejecta broke the continuity of a floral motif on the yellowing wallpaper.

Gathered around the table were seven men: Lieutenant Ruprecht Hefner, his seconds, Renz and Trapp, Count Zoltan Záborszky, his seconds, Braun and Dekany, and the *unparteiische*—a pale-faced emaciated man with blue lips and transparent fingers.

Thirteen slivers of wood had been laid out on the table's green baize, arranged in a semicircle like the struts of an open fan. Twelve were identical. The thirteenth, however, was distinguished by a daub of red paint. The *unparteiische* pushed it into position, attempting to create a perfectly symmetrical arrangement.

"You may inspect the lots," said the *unparteiische* in a voice that was surprisingly stentorian for such a cadaverous man.

Renz picked up one of the wooden slivers and rotated it in his hand. Being more accustomed—in his capacity as a second—to testing the weight and quality of pistols, he was not sure what more he could do. He shrugged, somewhat puzzled, and tossed the sliver back onto the baize.

"I am satisfied," he said.

"Herr Braun?" said the *unparteiische*.

The younger of the count's seconds stepped forward. He was a gaunt fellow, whose prominent jawline and dark eyes suggested a certain rugged charm. However, the inherent nobility of his lineaments had evidently been ruined by a dissolute life. His thick hair was greasy and his chin scabrous, while the stubble on his cheek was speckled with silver bristles.

Braun touched each of the slivers, working his way systematically through the half-dial arrangement. Hefner noticed that the cuffs of his jacket were frayed, and that the man's hand was disfigured by a thin white weal—it looked like a dueling scar. The wretch toyed with the red slip for a few moments and then said, "I am satisfied." This utterance was accompanied by an exhalation of breath that smelled strongly of alcohol.

The *unparteiische* handed Braun a velvet drawstring bag. The young man stretched it open and offered the exposed interior to Renz.

"Lieutenant?" The *unparteiische* prompted.

"Yes, of course," said Renz, suddenly comprehending his role. The officer scooped the slivers together and dropped them into the open mouth of the bag. Braun pulled the string tight and began shaking the bag. The wooden slivers clattered inside. From the room below came a sudden burst of raucous laughter.

Braun continued shaking the bag.

Clatter, clatter, clatter . . .

He seemed to be taking his relatively minor task far too seriously. The *unparteiische*, unable to contain himself any longer, glared at the over-earnest second. The baleful look from his luminous eyes had the desired effect, and the young man handed the bag back with a muttered apology.

The *unparteiische* addressed Hefner and the count. "Gentlemen, are you ready?" Both nodded. "Good. Let us begin."

The duelists positioned themselves at either side of the *unparteiische*, who loosened the string of the bag. Then, holding it out in front of him, he tilted it toward Záborszky.

The count tucked his cane under his left arm and stroked his drooping oriental mustache. The expression on his broad, almost Mongolian features was difficult to interpret. It had a curious, almost alien intensity. He crossed himself slowly, allowing a limp forefinger to touch his forehead, chest, and shoulders—his hand moving over his body in extravagant arcs. An emerald ring glittered, then disappeared into the black velvet bag. Before withdrawing his hand, the count locked stares with each of the three Uhlans. He withdrew the lot. Holding it up, he turned the sliver around, demonstrating that it was unmarked.

Disgusted with the count's excesses, Hefner plunged his hand into the bag and removed another unmarked lot. He held it up for a few moments, then threw it angrily onto the table.

The count was not persuaded by Hefner's example to change his ways. Again, he executed a lymphatic sign of the cross before tugging at the black ribbon attached to his vest. He retrieved the dangling monocle and pressed it into the orbit of his left eye.

"Insufferable," whispered Trapp.

When the count was ready to proceed—determinedly in his own time—he explored the contents of the black bag for what seemed like an eternity before withdrawing another blank sliver.

The *unparteiische*—whose neutrality was being sorely tested— offered the bag to Hefner. But before the soldier could respond, Braun called out, "Stop!"

. He stepped forward and peered at the bag. The three Uhlans shifted impatiently, their collective movement producing a jangling of spurs.

"Would the gentleman explain," said the cadaverous umpire, "why he has seen fit to interrupt us?"

Braun pointed at the bag. "I thought I could see a hole."

"Where?"

Braun took the bag from the *unparteiische*, lifted it above his head, and turned it around.

"No—I'm sorry. I was mistaken."

He handed the bag back to the *unparteiische*.

Renz and Trapp groaned.

Braun faced them indignantly. "Sirs—I will not be party to an improper contest. When our business here is concluded, my conscience dictates that I must leave this building secure in the knowledge that it was fate alone that harmonized the discord. As you well know, it is our solemn duty—mine *and* yours—to intervene if there is even the slightest possibility that the code of honor is being violated!"

Before the Uhlans could respond, the *unparteiische* raised his hand.

"Thank you, Herr Braun. You have been most vigilant. I take it you are now satisfied that the duel can continue?"

"I am," said Braun, still glaring at the restive Uhlans.

The *unparteiische* offered Hefner the bag for the second time.

Without hesitation, Hefner plunged his hand into the bag and pulled out his lot. He glanced at it in the sheltered bowl of his cupped fingers. The Uhlan's face showed no sign of emotion. Turning the sliver of wood around, he exposed the fatal red daub.

Renz and Trapp gasped.

The *unparteiische* looked directly at Hefner. "The duel is concluded. Count Záborszky has won. You know what this means. . . . I trust that you will respect the code and fulfill your obligation within the next week."

69

THE LONG, DESCENDING STREET was almost empty, and as Liebermann drew closer to the Danube Canal, a dense frozen fog seemed to be building up. It curled around his legs with feline curiosity. The ninth district, a bastion of respectable middle-class values, was strangely transformed, as if an old dowager had exchanged her wardrobe for that of a Circassian dancer. In her new garb of twisting diaphanous veils, she seemed suddenly equipped to deliver illicit pleasures. And perhaps—on this particular evening—she would. . . .

Professor Freud had invited Liebermann to become a member of his Wednesday-evening psychological society long before its inaugural meeting. But so far a combination of factors—Clara, hospital work, Salieri—had stopped Liebermann from attending. Subsequently the society had been convening in his absence for more than a month. When the first opportunity to attend finally presented itself, Liebermann dispatched a note to the professor expressing his earnest hope that the invitation was still standing. Freud's response was friendly and included a request that—if at all possible—Liebermann should bring with him some case material for discussion. So it was that Liebermann came to be clutching in his hand a manuscript provisionally titled *Herr B: Notes on a case of paranoia erotica*.

It occurred to Liebermann that Sigmund Freud's Psychological Society was, in many ways, similar to the numerous secret societies that congregated in Vienna. Once again, a charismatic leader had gathered a small group of followers around him—a cabal who would spread the tenets of his doctrine and challenge the settled order of things. There was something about this city—*his* city—that attracted intrigue, conspiracy, and sedition. Visionaries and prophets found it irresistible.

Liebermann suddenly remembered the lampposts outside the Opera House, the feet of which were cast in the form of four winged Sphinxes. Then he recalled the Sphinxes in the Kunsthistorisches Museum, the Sphinxes in the Belvedere gardens, and the Sphinxes on Professor Freud's desk. The city was full of Sphinxes. . . .

Secrets, secrets, secrets.

Conscious of a mounting and almost childish excitement, Liebermann quickened his step.

The large doors of Bergasse 19 were open. He crossed the threshold and walked down the long cobbled entryway, his footsteps echoing in the enclosed space. At the other end of the passage were panels of black glass, which ordinarily would have afforded the prospect of a pretty little courtyard and a chestnut tree. But this evening they reflected back the semi-transparent image of a young doctor wearing a long astrakhan coat.

Liebermann turned right, ascended a small curved staircase, and walked past a single spherical gas lamp that was mounted on a floridly ornate iron banister. It was surrounded by a foggy halo, and the muted light barely illuminated a black lacquered door at the center of which was a simple nameplate: PROF. DR. FREUD.

Liebermann rang the bell and was admitted by a maid who took his coat. He was ushered into Freud's waiting room, the decor of which conveyed an impression of shadowy opulence: red drapes and dark wood; a cabinet displaying a small collection of statuettes; and, on a pedestal, a large plaster copy of Michelangelo's *Dying Slave*. The walls were covered with pictures that reflected Freud's preoccupation with antiquities: Roman ruins, some eighteenth-century prints of classical scenes, and, inevitably, a Sphinx, brooding in front of a pyramid. Around an oblong table sat Freud and three others.

"Ah, there you are," cried the professor, rising energetically. "I am delighted you could make it! And, if I am not mistaken, I observe that you have brought us some case material. *Paranoia erotica*, you say? Well, that will be a rare delight."

Freud introduced his three companions, using only their surnames: Stekel, Reitler, and Kahane. Liebermann recognized the first two from Freud's Saturday lectures at the university. The third man was not familiar, but it transpired that he was the director of the Institute for Physical Therapeutic Methods. As they made polite conversation, Liebermann was surprised to discover that in spite of Kahane's professed interest in psychoanalysis, he was still treating (or, more accurately, tormenting) his patients with electrotherapy.

A few minutes later Freud's final guest arrived. He was a man in his early thirties: a stocky individual whose facial features contracted disdainfully around a large nose. He wore round glasses, sported a small mustache, and his prominent chin was divided by a deep vertical cleft. Liebermann knew him to be Alfred Adler, a doctor to whom he had been introduced by a mutual friend the previous year. Liebermann had once been asked to accompany Adler at a party, and had been truly amazed by the power and sweetness of the singing voice that had issued from his crooked mouth. It was as if—by divine intercession— the man's deficiencies of appearance had been compensated for by an extraordinary musical gift.

Eventually, all the company were seated and Freud passed around a large box of cigars. As an incentive to partake, each place at the table was furnished with an attractive jade ashtray. No one refused, and as matches flared and dimmed, the room became filled with clouds of billowing smoke.

The professor indicated that he was ready to begin. He announced that there would be two presentations: the first delivered by Dr. Stekel and the second by Dr. Liebermann (whom he also welcomed to the society). Proceedings would then be suspended for fifteen minutes before they resumed with a group discussion.

Stekel, a good-natured general practitioner, gave a lively description of a twenty-two-year-old female patient suffering from hysterical hyperalgesia—a disorder characterized by excessive physical sensitivity. It was not, however, a remarkable case study, and Liebermann found his attention wandering. He was feeling somewhat apprehensive and had begun—almost unconsciously—to rehearse his talk.

Herr B.

Thirty-eight-year-old accountancy clerk.

Employed by a reputable firm with offices in the city center.

No previous history of psychiatric illness . . .

When Stekel brought his presentation to a close, there was some restrained applause and a grumbled vote of thanks. Freud then turned his gaze on Liebermann. The old man's eyes were dark brown and peculiarly lustrous.

"Herr Doctor?"

"Thank you, Herr Professor."

Liebermann put on his spectacles and straightened his papers. "Gentlemen," he began, "this evening I shall be describing the case of Herr B.—a thirty-eight-year-old accountancy clerk who was admitted onto a psychiatric ward at the General Hospital in early November. The circumstances surrounding his admission were somewhat dramatic. It seems that Herr B. had attempted to force his way into the Schönbrunn Palace in order to rescue Archduchess Marie-

Valerie—who, he claimed, was being held there against her will. The police were called after an unfortunate incident involving the palace guard . . ."

As Liebermann became more confident, he spoke more freely and consulted his papers less. His audience appeared to be extremely interested, most notably the professor, whose attentive figure had become hazy behind an increasingly murky accumulation of cigar smoke.

When Liebermann began to describe Herr Beiber's dream, Freud's eyes widened, and he adopted a melodramatic pose. Like a hammy actor at the Court Theater, he pressed his right hand against his temple. Liebermann paused, expecting to be interrupted, but the old man remained silent. Adler too had raised a hand but only to obscure Freud's view of his mouth, which had twisted into a mocking smile.

Liebermann was relieved when he reached the conclusion of his presentation. The task had proved more demanding than he had anticipated, and the close scrutiny of Freud's inner circle had been unnerving. He was acutely aware that any minor slip of the tongue would be subject to psychoanalytic interpretation. In such company, all mistakes—however minor—would be revealing. Fortunately, his delivery had been steady and he had not even allowed himself to be distracted by Adler's irreverence.

When the applause had died down, the professor thanked Liebermann for a fascinating presentation and rang for the maid. She appeared carrying a large tray of coffee and cakes. Once the plates, napkins, and forks had been laid out, the atmosphere in the room immediately changed. The group relaxed and even engaged in some lighthearted banter. Stekel told an amusing story that hinged on a confusion of identities, and the professor was quick to respond with a joke of his own.

"Prague. Moscovitz the tailor is praying in the Old New Synagogue. Suddenly, there is a flash of light—the walls shake and a horrible figure with horns and a tail appears. The air smells of sulfur. . . ." The professor drew on his cigar and paused for effect. "Moscovitz looks up, but continues with his prayers. The terrible figure shakes his fist and the ark tumbles to the ground. But Moscovitz is indifferent, and continues praying. 'Hey, you,' the terrifying figure shouts. 'Are you not frightened?' Moscovitz shrugs and shakes his head. Enraged, the terrifying figure lashes his tail—bricks fall. 'Little Jew,' says the terrifying figure, 'do you know who I am?' 'Yes,' Moscovitz replies, 'I know exactly who you are—I've been married to your sister for the last thirty years!' "

As the gentle ripples of laughter subsided, the company stood up and stretched their legs. They milled aaround the table and in due course Liebermann found himself standing next to Freud, who was enjoying his second slice of *guglhupf.* The sponge was thick and moist, and exuded a sharp lemony fragrance. Before Freud could regale him with another one of his jokes—of which he seemed to have an inexhaustible supply—Liebermann seized the moment to ask a question that had occupied his mind for several days.

"Professor," he said tentatively, "I was wondering whether I could trouble you for an opinion . . . on a theoretical matter."

Freud fixed him with his penetrating stare. "Have you tasted this cake?"

"Yes, I have."

"Good, isn't it?"

"Extremely."

"I have a particular weakness for *guglhupf.*" Freud harpooned a bright yellow segment of sponge with the tines of his fork. "But you were saying . . . a theoretical matter?"

"Yes," said Liebermann. "Do you think that the principles of dream interpretation can be applied to works of art?"

The segment of sponge did not reach Freud's mouth. Its journey came to an abrupt halt somewhere in the vicinity of his collarbone.

"That is a very interesting question." The professor paused, swallowed, and placed his plate down on the edge of the table. He had suddenly lost interest in his *guglhupf*.

"In dreams," the young doctor continued, "the contents of the unconscious—traumatic memories, desires, and so forth—are transformed. They appear in a disguised form. And, of course, by employing your techniques it is possible to establish their true meaning. Might we not consider a painting or sculpture as a kind of . . . creative dream?"

"Have you heard of Lermolieff—the Russian art connoisseur?" asked the professor.

"No."

"Lermolieff was a pen name—he was really an Italian physician called Morelli. He caused a furor in the art galleries of Europe by questioning the authorship of many famous pictures after he had devised a method for establishing authenticity." The professor pulled at his neatly trimmed beard. "Lermolieff insisted that attention should be diverted from the general impression of a picture, laying stress instead on the significance of minor details: like the drawing of fingernails, of the lobe of an ear, of halos and such unconsidered trifles that the negligent copyist is bound to overlook, but that every genuine artist executes in his own very distinctive style. Now, it seems to me that Lermolieff's method of inquiry is closely related to the technique of psychoanalysis. The psychoanalyst is accustomed to divining secrets from unnoticed features—from the rubbish heap, as it were, of our observations." The professor reached for a cigar, lit it, and cleared his throat. "I can see no reason why the principles of our discipline cannot be applied to the interpretation of art. One might look for evidence of unconscious material that has—so to speak—broken through. . . . Anomalies, perhaps? Distortions and symbolization . . . Indeed, a painting might be likened to a window through which an analyst might steal glimpses of the artist's unconscious mind."

It was the answer that Liebermann had been hoping for.

The table clock chimed.

"Good heavens," said Freud. "How time flies."

The maid was called again, and when she had finished clearing the table, the company returned to their seats in order to discuss the case presentations. This final part of the evening was largely dedicated to a collective analysis of Herr Beiber's dream. Freud insisted that Liebermann should reiterate the main points, occasionally stopping him to ask seemingly obscure questions. "Are you sure Herr B. was five years old?" "How big were the wolves, exactly?" "Did one of the wolves have a tail?" And so on.

When Liebermann had finished describing the dream again, Freud invited those present to comment.

"It reminds me of a fairy story," Stekel began. "Something from the Brothers Grimm, like *Little Red Riding Hood*. I believe that the appearance of wolves in children's stories is inextricably bound with the fear of being devoured."

"It might be that the wolves—issuing from a cavernous space—are a substitution for a more fundamental fear—that of the *vagina dentate*," added Reitler.

"Thus," Adler cut in, "Herr B., fearing the loss of his manhood, has eschewed sexual experience altogether."

"And," said Stekel, raising his finger, "has subsequently become obsessed with Archduchess Marie-Valerie—with whom he can never form a relationship."

"Obviating the conjugal requirement of consummation," concluded Freud.

Liebermann was astonished at the speed of debate. How ideas sparked across the table.

When the initial flurry had exhausted itself, Freud continued to speculate:

"Gentlemen, there can be no question that Herr B.'s *paranoia erotica* is a defense—an unhappy compromise between the need to find love and the fear of sexual congress. However, it is my belief that the wolf dream does not represent a primal, mythic fear but an early memory of a very real traumatic event. Herr B. was a sick child who was taken into his parents' bedroom. It was his misfortune to wake one night whereupon he witnessed his parents engaging in coitus *a tergo*—hence the transfiguration of his mother and father into beasts. The panting, however, survived the dream work, breaking through without distortion. Herr B. had violated the most significant taboo of all human societies. What child—indeed, what adult—can contemplate the circumstances of his own conception in the absence of guilt and anxiety? Herr B. expected to be punished for his transgression. A punishment appropriated from the traditional folk tale—that of being eaten alive!"

Remarkably, Freud reached for another cigar. In the ensuing silence he finally faded behind a roiling nimbus. Only a rasping cough reminded those present that he was still there.

70

ANDREAS OLBRICHT HAD SPENT the evening in several coffeehouses, examining his reviews. He did not return to his apartment. Instead, he walked across the city to his studio, where he lit a single candle and poured himself a large glass of vodka.

Various words and sentences kept bobbing up in his mind—breaking the surface tension of consciousness, splashing vitriol. It felt as though the interior of his head were sizzling, as though it were being eaten away by corrosive droplets of malice.

An artist bereft of talent.

A poor technician.

Crude, unimaginative, and without merit.

Lacking in originality.

How could they say such things? Through the fog of his own condensed breath, he could just make out an unfinished canvas. He had hoped to include it in his exhibition, but he had run out of time. It showed Loge—the god of fire and cunning: an impish silhouette against a holocaust of leaping flames. The air smelled of turpentine and linseed oil.

Deficient brushwork.

A poor colorist.

Tired themes.

Olbricht drained his glass.

There had been one good review. It had appeared in a small Pan-

German publication. The writer had praised Olbricht's noble aspirations: his vision, his sensibility, his weltanschauung. But what good was that? He needed the support of the *Zeitung, Die Zeit, Die Fackel*, the *Neues Wiener Tagblatt*, the *Neue Freie Presse*. He needed so much more.

Suddenly, desolation was replaced by anger. Rage electrified his body and for a moment all he could see was a sheet of brilliant white light. He threw his glass and watched as it shattered against the opposite wall. Curiously, he found himself transported across the room. He was standing by the image of Loge, penknife in hand. The blade glinted as it descended—ripping, tearing, rending. He did not stop. He slashed wildly, breathlessly, until nothing of his work was left but tattered ribbons.

Olbricht allowed himself to slump against the wall. Exhausted, he closed his eyes and whispered into the darkness, "The Last Judgment."

71

AT FIRST, LIEBERMANN HAD been uncertain about the legitimacy of the professor's interpretation. Freud's growing tendency to postulate a sexual origin for all forms of psychopathology had not gone unnoticed. Indeed, Liebermann had once overheard a visiting professor describing Freud as suffering from an incipient sexual monomania. Still, the more Liebermann considered Freud's interpretation, the more he found it easier to entertain. Did it require such a leap of imagination to connect a disturbance in the faculty of love with a repressed sexual trauma?

"Do you think dreams have meaning, Herr Beiber?"

"I'm sure they do. Particularly when they are associated with strong feelings."

"Like your wolf dream."

"Yes, I suppose so."

"In which case, what do you think your wolf dream means?"

"I don't know. But, as I have already suggested, it may have been influenced by a supernatural presence."

"You say that because you heard the breathing, the *panting* on other occasions?"

"Yes."

Liebermann leaned forward and scrutinized his supine patient.

"What if this dream was a memory?"

Herr Beiber frowned.

"There are mechanisms in the mind," Liebermann continued,

"that function to keep distressing memories out of awareness. Subsequently, these memories are pushed down, or repressed. But they do not thereby become inactive—they are merely dormant. When we sleep, the repressive mechanism weakens and they can rise up again. It is supposed that there is a censor in the mind that struggles to distort these memories in order to make them less distressing so that sleep may continue. Sometimes the censor works, sometimes it is partially successful, and sometimes it fails. The fact that you were awakened by your dream suggests that it represents a particularly traumatic memory. The kind of memory that would overwhelm the mind of a young child."

Liebermann paused, allowing Herr Beiber to consider his account. He could see that his patient was thinking. The clerk's bushy ginger-yellow eyebrows were still knotted together.

"Go on," said Herr Beiber.

"You were a sickly child. Consequently, you slept in your parents' bedroom beyond infancy. It is possible that you saw things . . ."

With great care and sensitivity, Liebermann presented Freud's interpretation of the wolf dream to his patient. When he had finished, a long silence prevailed. Herr Beiber's index finger tapped the gelatinous mass of his stomach, producing a continuous ripple of flesh beneath the cotton gown.

"A memory, you say . . . a traumatic memory." Herr Beiber spoke the words softly.

"To a child, much of the behavior of adults must appear strange and disconcerting . . . but what *you* witnessed must have been terrifying. Nevertheless, you have made the transition to adulthood yourself now—you have nothing to fear anymore."

Beiber's finger stopped tapping.

"If you were to form a relationship," Liebermann continued, "with a woman—an *ordinary* woman: a typist in your office, a shopgirl, a seamstress, who knows?—but a woman whom you might one day realistically marry, then I suspect that your feelings for Archduchesss Marie-Valerie would soon diminish."

Herr Beiber bit his lip.

"The process of psychoanalysis is one of reclamation," Liebermann continued. "Once we have insight, we can recover the life that we have lost. What was previously jealously guarded by the unconscious mind becomes conscious—the irrational is superseded by the rational. Should you choose, one day, to enter the conjugal bedroom, remember that you will do so as a man—not as a confused, frightened child."

For the first time since the beginning of Herr Beiber's analysis, the accountancy clerk was subdued. There were no chirpy retorts or flights of fancy. No florid proclamations of undying, transcendent love. It was as though Liebermann had planted a seed that had already begun to take root. He was reminded of the common sight of a sapling emerging from a cracked paving stone. It was remarkable how something so fragile, so delicate, could eventually pry heavy slabs apart. Yet this was exactly how psychoanalysis worked: the small seed of insight growing, developing, acquiring strength, and, in due course, shattering the rigid carapace of psychopathology.

Outside, a church bell struck the hour.

"Herr Beiber." Their time together had expired, but Liebermann could not let his patient leave before asking him one more question. "In a previous session, you mentioned an incident involving a cellist. You tried to get him to play an aubade outside the Schönbrunn Palace. Do you remember?"

"Yes. What of it?" Beiber's response was rather tetchy, as if he resented having his thoughts disturbed.

"You said," continued Liebermann, "that he was an odd fellow. You said that there was . . . *something about him.*"

"Did I?"

"Yes. What did you mean?"

Herr Beiber was still distracted. "A traumatic memory," he whispered.

"Herr Beiber?" Liebermann raised his voice. "The cellist. You said he was odd—there was *something about him*. What did you mean?"

The accountancy clerk disengaged from his thoughts and his brow relaxed. "His face, I suppose."

"What about it?"

"Well . . . This may seem uncharitable, and I recognize that I am far from perfect myself, but this poor chap—why, he looked like a frog!"

At that precise moment someone rapped on the door.

"Come in," Liebermann called out.

Kanner's head appeared around the door frame. "Max?"

Liebermann rose and went over to his friend. "What is it?"

Kanner lowered his voice. "A young man from the security office has just arrived—by the name of Haussmann? He says it's a matter of some urgency. Something about having found *Salieri*? One of your Italian patients, perhaps?"

72

IN THE CENTER OF the room was a small circular table—around which three chairs were arranged. One of them was occupied by Lieutenant Ruprecht Hefner. His legs were wide apart and his head was thrown back. His right hand looked as though it had been thrust into his mouth. On closer inspection it was possible to detect the dull metallic barrel of a small pistol, as well as burn marks and blisters. A large pool of blood had collected behind the chair, its still surface broken by lumpy gray nuggets of brain tissue. Remarkably, Hefner's uniform was in pristine condition: the blue was unstained and the brass buttons were as bright as marigolds.

Liebermann stepped closer and squatted down. A ragged hole had been blasted through the back of Hefner's skull, out of which droplets of fluid were still falling at irregular intervals.

"He was discovered earlier this morning by his batman," said Rheinhardt. "He lost an American duel."

"How do you know that?"

Rheinhardt offered Liebermann a sheet of paper. "His suicide note."

Liebermann took the paper and began to read:

I, Lieutenant Ruprecht Georg Hefner, being of sound mind, depart from this life a man of honor . . .

Liebermann scanned the introductory paragraphs.

My sabre I leave to Lieutenant Trapp and my pistols to Lieutenant Renz . . .

My horse Geronimo I leave to the regimental doctor—who has been of considerable assistance on many occasions. . . .

Further on, there were references to some outstanding gambling debts that Hefner regretted he would not be able to pay.

Rheinhardt pointed to a passage lower down on the page. "Look at this."

Liebermann continued reading:

It is all over. The sun is setting on our people and there are too few good men willing to speak out. A lone voice here, a lone voice there: but it is not enough. The cowards in the parliament building and the town hall do nothing. Our glorious city has become infested. I did what I could. But Vienna cannot be saved. . . .

A malicious diatribe followed, denouncing the enemies of the German people: the Jews, the Slavs, the Catholic Church—the southern races.

"There you are!" exclaimed Rheinhardt. "It must be him. It's as good as a confession!"

Liebermann turned the paper over. Nothing was written on the other side.

"We know that he frequented Madam Borek's brothel," Rheinhardt continued, excitement widening his eyes. "He was a member of the Eddic Literary Association and a member of the Richard Wagner Association. He carried a sabre and wished to save Vienna from all those peoples and institutions despised by Guido List. It must be him. He *must* be Salieri!"

"No, Oskar," said Liebermann. "I'm afraid you're mistaken."

Rheinhardt snatched Hefner's note from Liebermann's hand and read out aloud, "*Our glorious city has become infested. I did what I could.*"

The sentence hung in the air between them.

"He means dueling, Oskar—that is all. He obviously took great pleasure in provoking those whom he counted as enemies: Jews, Czechs, Hungarians . . . people like Freddi Lemberg."

Rheinhardt sighed, suddenly deflated. "But the evidence, Max. . . . Madam Borek's, the sabre."

"Salieri would not have been able to resist mentioning *The Magic Flute*."

"He is a member of the Richard Wagner Association."

"And then there are Miss Lydgate's findings."

"She must have made a mistake."

"As I have said before, I very much doubt it."

Rheinhardt suddenly turned on his friend. He could not keep the irritation from his voice. "Max, how can you be so sure!"

Liebermann smiled and clapped his hands on Rheinhardt's shoulders.

"I can be sure, Oskar, because tonight you and I will be paying Salieri a house call."

73

COUNT ZÁBORSZKY LOOKED ACROSS the low Turkish table at Otto Braun. He sucked the mouthpiece of his hookah and blew out a cloud of pungent smoke. The candle flickered in the draft created by his opiated exhalation.

"So," he said. "The fool is dead?"

"Yes," Braun replied. "It was reported in the late edition of the papers."

The count's lips parted, and he showed his sharp teeth. Braun took it to be a smile.

"You Germans . . ."

Braun tutted. "He was Austrian. Born in Vienna."

The count dismissed Braun's remark with a sneer and a languid gesture.

". . . with your ridiculous code of honor."

The sound of a squeaking mattress came from above. A repeated, querulous rhythm. The count's eyes flashed toward the ceiling. "Have you tried the new girl yet? The Galician?"

"No."

"You should."

"I don't have any money." Braun spoke these words deliberately.

The count slid his hand into his pocket, took out a small leather purse, and tossed it onto the table. The younger man picked it up, weighed it in his hand, and put it into his pocket.

The squeaking stopped.

"How did you do it?" asked the count.

"It's easy. . . . I used to do something very similar in my magic show at the Blue Danube Theatre. A little routine built around a wager in which I always won. A quick swap—it was nothing."

"Yes. But how?"

Braun shook his head. "That would be telling." Then, assuming a mock-dignified pose, he added, "No honorable magician would break the code."

The count sucked gently on his hookah and allowed himself a gravelly dry laugh. "Very good, Braun. Very good."

A door opened and closed upstairs. The sound of footsteps on the landing, and boots making unsteady progress down the stairs. A cavalryman appeared out of the darkness.

"Good evening," said the count. "I wonder whether you would care to join us for a game of cards."

The Uhlan's cap was perched at an acute angle. "I am duty bound to warn you—I have a formidable reputation."

"I'm sure you do," said the count. "Please . . ." He gestured toward the seat next to Braun. The magician produced a deck of cards, which he dropped next to the candle. "What shall it be?" he asked, throwing a wicked glance in the count's direction.

Part Four

Underworld

74

THE COBBLED STREET ROSE up, leading to a short, elevated cul-de-sac. It was a dark place, illuminated by a solitary gas lamp, and somewhat desolate. All the squat two-story buildings had been converted for commercial use, and their occupants had long since concluded their business for the day. Large wooden signs identified the premises of a wheelwright, a blacksmith, and a carpenter. The cul-de-sac was overlooked by the fenestrated eminence of a tall apartment block. Lights shone from a few of the higher windows, suggesting that not all of the residents were asleep.

Earlier that evening the warm, dry föhn wind had descended from the mountains, melting all the snow and ice in a matter of hours. The air was filled with the sound of trickling and dripping as rivulets of running water sought out drains. This freakish meteorological phenomenon could raise the temperature by more than twenty degrees Réaumur.

Liebermann opened his coat and loosened his necktie. "It's associated with insanity, you know."

"What? The föhn?" Rheinhardt responded.

"Yes. Ask any hospital psychiatrist. The patients get restless and there are always more admissions."

"How does it have its effect?"

"We have absolutely no idea." The young doctor sighed. "It's not a good omen."

"I thought you didn't believe in omens."

"Salieri is disturbed enough as it is—without the föhn making his mental state worse. Did you bring your revolver?"

"Of course," said Rheinhardt.

They were concealed in a deep doorway. Rheinhardt leaned out and looked up at a row of blank, black windows.

"Still nothing. . . . He's not in." Rheinhardt puffed out his cheeks. "You do realize, Max, that if you're wrong about this—and if we get caught—then I will be severely reprimanded by Commissioner Brügel." The young doctor gazed out across the damp cobbles. "And to be frank," Rheinhardt continued, "you haven't been very forthcoming about your method of deduction."

"I will provide you with a full explanation in due course."

Rheinhardt twisted the points of his mustache. "He isn't a librarian."

"I know."

"You and Miss Lydgate can't *both* be right."

Liebermann shrugged.

The inspector tutted but did not press his friend. He was prepared to give him the benefit of the doubt, being familiar with the young doctor's habit of appearing at his most enigmatic when his deductions were correct. *Be that as it may*, Rheinhardt reflected, *his mannerisms can be most irritating.*

"It may be possible to enter and leave the property without damaging anything," said Rheinhardt. "In which case, no one need ever know we've been there. On the other hand, if we discover anything incriminating, I shall have to wait here in order to make an arrest. You must not feel obliged to stay. Indeed, it would be better, perhaps, if you went to get help."

"And leave you to face the monster alone? That is out of the question."

Rheinhardt smiled. "You wait here. Call out if you see him coming." He then crossed the street and began inspecting a plain wooden door. Liebermann could see that his friend was busying himself with the lock, which rather surprised him. To his knowledge, the inspector had no special understanding of lock mechanisms. But after a few minutes Rheinhardt beckoned, scooping the air in wide arcs with his hand. Liebermann crept out from his hiding place and hurried across. As he arrived, Rheinhardt turned the door handle and pushed it open.

"How did you do that?" asked Liebermann, thoroughly impressed.

Rheinhardt held up a bunch of curious-looking rods with spindly protrusions.

"Skeleton keys," said Rheinhardt. "They don't always work—but this time we were lucky."

He produced an object that Liebermann had never seen before: a short cylinder, not unlike a telescope, encircled by several silver hoops.

"What on earth is that?"

"A flashlight."

"A what?"

"It's from America. Watch. I slide this bridge switch . . ." Rheinhardt pushed a raised metal bar forward with his thumb and a pulse of light illuminated the hallway. It lasted for a few moments before fading.

"Remarkable," exclaimed Liebermann. "A portable electric lightbulb!"

"Indeed," said Rheinhardt. "It'll revolutionize police work: the incendiary risk associated with conducting nighttime investigations is now a thing of the past!"

They closed the door behind them and ascended steep stairs that led to a small landing. To one side was a small, sparsely furnished room containing a camp bed, stove, wardrobe, and bookcase.

"In here," said Rheinhardt.

They entered the room and began a systematic search, starting with the wardrobe. It contained nothing exceptional and smelled strongly of mothballs. Under the bed they found a half-full chamber pot. The bookcase was filled with predictable titles: *Carnuntum, Deutschmythologische Landschaftsbilder, Der Unbesiegbare, Pipara,* and other volumes by Guido List. There were also works by the Englishman, Houston Stewart Chamberlain: a biography of Richard Wagner and his famous history, *Die Grundlagen des neunzehnten Jahrhunderts.*

Their investigation was slow, its pace dependent on the brief periodic illumination of the flashlight. After a time, though, both men fell into the rhythm dictated by the device's limitations. It became almost hypnotic.

Flash—fade—darkness. Flash—fade—darkness.

Move—stop, move—stop.

Liebermann glanced anxiously through the open door. "Come on," he said. "There's nothing in here. We must hurry."

"Well, there's not much in there, either," Rheinhardt answered, directing a burst of luminescence across the landing.

"Oh, there will be—I can assure you."

Rheinhardt recognized a new note of confidence in Liebermann's voice.

"You've seen something, haven't you?"

"Later, Oskar," Liebermann hissed.

Rheinhardt silently endured another wave of irritation.

The two men cautiously entered the studio.

It was much the same as Rheinhardt remembered: a battered chest, a small table, wooden frames, and a full-length mirror against the wall. The only significant difference was the absence of paintings.

Liebermann walked ahead, his shoes making a hollow noise against the floorboards. The sound suddenly changed as something began to crunch underfoot.

"Oskar . . ."

Rheinhardt lowered the flashlight to reveal a mass of glittering fragments. Liebermann crouched down. Reaching out, he touched one of the bright points of light.

"Glass."

As Liebermann stood up, he accidentally kicked something hard. It rolled across the floor, making a curiously loud rumble, which for a brief moment rose to a higher pitch.

Flash—fade—darkness. Flash—fade—darkness.

The sound had been made by an empty bottle that had come to rest against one of the legs of an easel. Liebermann picked it up and read the label. "Vodka," he muttered. His attention was then drawn to what was left of the painting. Red strips of canvas hung in tatters from the frame.

"It's been cut to pieces," he whispered.

"Why would he do that?"

"Because of his reviews. Did you read any of them?"

"Yes, a few. They were all terrible. Rather unfair, I thought—he's not *that* bad."

"He got drunk to deaden his pain, threw a glass against the wall in a rage, and then, overcome with despair, destroyed his latest work. I wonder what it was."

Rheinhardt opened the battered chest and directed the flashlight's beam inside.

Flash—fade—darkness. Flash—fade—darkness.

Some dirty smocks, a plaster-cast torso, and a few exhibition posters.

"Well, we won't get a conviction on the basis of what's in here."

Rheinhardt lowered the lid of the chest and stopped working the bar of his flashlight. The room dissolved into dark nothingness. Outside, the gentle music of trickling water could still be heard—and in the distance the clop of hooves and the jangling of a carriage horse's harness.

The inspector sighed. "You were certain that we would find evidence." The young doctor was silent. "Well," Rheinhardt continued, at last unable to disguise his irritation, "where is it?"

"Did you notice the sound that the bottle made as it rolled across the floor?" The change in pitch?"

"No."

"We analysts always listen very carefully. You'll find what you're looking for over there somewhere."

Rheinhardt slid the bridging switch forward, illuminating his companion. The young doctor's arm was outstretched, his index finger pointing at the floor space between the table and chest.

"Under the boards?" said Rheinhardt.

"Yes," came the blunt reply.

The inspector got down on all fours and began to crawl along a single floorboard. He held the flashlight very close to the ground.

"What on earth are you doing, Oskar?"

It occurred to Rheinhardt that he might use this opportunity to give the young doctor a taste of his own enigmatic medicine so he remained silent.

"Oskar?" Liebermann persisted. "What are you doing?"

When Rheinhardt was satisfied that he had made his point—and that the young doctor had registered the purpose of his unusual taciturnity—he deigned to answer.

"It would take too much time to raise all the boards," he began, "so I'm looking for signs of recent disturbance. When a floor is first constructed, the nails holding the planks to the crossbeams are driven in as far as possible—it is impossible to get them out without damaging the surrounding wood. If there are no such signs, then it is pointless proceeding."

Rheinhardt crawled backward and forward across the floor, his knees protesting with percussive *cracks* and *snaps*. Eventually he cried out, "Aha! Here we are—damage! Come over here, Max, take a look." Liebermann went over to his friend and observed splintering and bruising of the wood around some of the nail heads. "And this board here," Rheinhardt continued, rocking a plank from side to side, "is quite loose."

"I suppose this means that you will have to come back to conduct an official search in the morning?"

"Not at all."

"But we don't have the means to take up these boards."

"Oh yes, we do."

Rheinhardt sat back on his haunches and produced a pair of pliers from a pocket of his baggy coat.

"Good God, Oskar, what else are you carrying in there?"

"In addition to my revolver and skeleton keys, I have a notebook, a pencil, a penknife, another smaller pair of pliers, tweezers, a magnifying glass, handcuffs, and some gusseted envelopes. One must always be prepared, Max. Here—you take the flashlight."

Rheinhardt then set about extracting nails. He did so with the systematic, grim determination of a skilled dentist.

Squeeze, twist, pull. Squeeze, twist, pull.

When he had completed drawing the nails from the first plank, he used his penknife to lift it from the underlying crossbeam. Liebermann directed a burst of light into the hole. "I think there's something there," he gasped.

Rheinhardt lay flat on his stomach and thrust his arm into the opening. As he felt around, the expression on his face changed from determined concentration to a curious mixture of surprise and triumph.

"God in heaven!" he cried. "It feels like . . . I can hardly believe it . . . a cello case!" His tactile exploration became more frantic. "Yes, yes—a cello case!"

Rheinhardt withdrew his arm and grabbed his pliers. "Come, let us continue."

The inspector returned to his task with renewed gusto, wresting each nail free with a single powerful wrench. Beads of perspiration began to appear on his forehead. Soon the second plank had been removed, and the flashlight revealed a telling curve of scuffed leather. Its undulating form clearly followed the waist and belly of the instrument inside.

As Rheinhardt began work on the third plank, he found that the pulsing beam had wandered away from the nail head.

"Max!" said Rheinhardt. "More to the right!"

But the young doctor did not respond. Instead, he raised the flashlight and aimed it at the doorway. Time seemed to dilate. He slid the bar forward, but its progress was strangely delayed. Light oozed out like viscid liquid. It rolled across the room with the sluggish momentum of spilled honey.

Flash—fade—darkness.

The figure of the artist lingered in his memory like the patterns that appear after staring at the sun. What he saw had the quality of a theatrical illusion. A stocky man with widely spaced eyes, dressed casually. Olbricht did not appear frightened. Indeed, he seemed to be quite calm.

When Liebermann delivered the next pulse of light, the doorway was empty and the air was vibrating with the sound of Olbricht's running footsteps.

75

LIEBERMANN LEAPED TO HIS feet and ran for the door. From the landing he directed the flashlight's beam down the stairs and saw Olbricht veer to the right. Without pausing to consider the wisdom of his actions, Liebermann threw himself into the darkness, using the wall as his guide. His descent was unsteady, and on the final step he stumbled. He was able to regain his balance as he burst through the open door.

Liebermann stopped and peered into the shadowy depths of the cul-de-sac. The single gas lamp sputtered. Could he see something moving? No more than a shimmer—a certain hint of instability in the fabric of the night?

He continued his pursuit, running across the damp cobbles. As he penetrated the pitchy shadows, he became aware that he was approaching a high wall, a daunting structure that linked the last houses in the cul-de-sac and effectively closed the street off. There was no sign of Olbricht, yet it was obvious that the artist, however agile, could not have scaled the precipitous wall. Liebermann leaned forward, rested his hands on his thighs, and attempted to catch his breath. As he did so he became conscious of Rheinhardt's approach.

The inspector ran right up to the wall, stopped, and looked around in all directions.

"Where is he?" Rheinhardt placed his palms against the brickwork and pressed, as though expecting to find a secret egress. "How on earth did he escape?"

"I don't know."

"Are you sure he came this way?"

"I couldn't see *very* clearly, but yes."

Rheinhardt took a step backward. "Perhaps he went into one of the other houses?"

"No—he was heading in this direction."

"But he can't have just vanished!"

Rheinhardt turned on his heels. He looked distraught, desperate. His breathing was labored. In an uncharacteristic display of frustration he discharged a fusillade of curses and slapped his hand against a round advertisement pillar. It resonated like a gong—a deep thrumming made complex with internal beats. But as the reverberations faded, the pillar began to emit another sound, a metallic creaking. The two men stood aghast as a steel door slowly swung open on rusting hinges.

The inspector's response was surprisingly quick. In an instant his revolver was in his hand. He approached the door cautiously and gestured to Liebermann that he would need light. The young doctor followed. They made brief eye contact before Liebermann squeezed the bridging switch.

Flash—fade—darkness.

The light revealed a shabby corroded interior—but no Olbricht.

Liebermann stepped into the metal column and found that he was standing at the top of a spiral staircase that sank deep into the ground.

"He must have gone down there," Liebermann whispered. "Where do you think it leads?"

"The sewers."

"It's so dark. . . . How could he find his way?"

"I very much doubt that he discovered this by chance. He must be familiar with it."

Liebermann began his descent. Rheinhardt followed close behind, his pistol arm stretched out over the young doctor's shoulder. As they circled downward, the flashlight illuminated a thick canopy of cobwebs: not the usual network of gossamer threads but great rolls of densely matted spiders' silk. It felt like being in a tent; however, secreted in the pleats and folds of this white-yellow fabric were hundreds of brown multilegged creatures—fat arachnid bodies, bloated with eggs, trembling in the miasma that rose from the depths. Liebermann shuddered as something dropped from above, hitting the iron handrail with an inordinately loud impact. As they continued their descent, the infested canopy gradually dropped lower until it was necessary for the two men to bow their heads and hunch their shoulders.

When they reached the bottom of the spiral staircase, the cobwebs suddenly vanished. But Liebermann, suffering from the illusion that his skin was crawling with spiders, felt compelled to beat at his clothes with his hands with considerable force.

Rheinhardt raised a finger to his lips. "Shhh."

They were in a narrow corridor with an arched ceiling. The inspector tilted his head to one side. Almost at the limits of audibility, there was a faint sound, more a disturbance in the air than something that could be heard. Yet its regularity suggested a resolute step, receding into the distance.

"Come," said Rheinhardt. "We can still catch him."

It was impossible to determine the length of the corridor. The flashlight pushed the darkness back only by a few yards. They found themselves walking for some time. Deprived of any distinctive features whereby they could judge distance, it seemed to them that they were making no progress but simply treading the same strip of gravelly ground. As they proceeded, Liebermann thought that the walls appeared to be drawing closer together. He sensed the oppressive weight of the saturated clay above his head. The atmosphere was cold, dank, and claustrophobic. He felt a rush of anxiety rising from the center of his being. It swept away his powers of reason, and his mind became occupied by a fear of being trapped beneath the earth—buried alive.

Oblivion, the taste of soil in his mouth, suffocation.

Liebermann forced himself to continue, willing first one leaden leg to move forward, then the other, until the corridor mercifully disgorged him into a wide tunnel. He leaned back against a wall and sighed with relief.

"Are you all right?" Rheinhardt asked.

"Yes," Liebermann replied. "It's nothing—a little nausea, that's all."

The flashlight's illumination was reflected back by a slow-moving black canal. Its greasy, sluggish flow prompted Liebermann to recall the rivers of the underworld: Acheron, the river of woe; Cocytus, the river of lamentation; Styx, the river of hate. He hoped that he had not been visited by a predictive vision of his own death, that he would not soon see a ferryman's lamp approaching or hear the gentle lapping of a bow wave.

"Which way shall we go?" Liebermann asked, dismissing the dreadful image from his mind.

Rheinhardt shrugged.

"He's right-handed?" Liebermann asked.

"Yes—according to Professor Mathias's autopsy report."

"In which case, all things being equal, right-handed people tend to favor turning to the right. Well, at least that is what I once read in a textbook of neurophysiology."

"Then let us hope that its author was correct."

Liebermann stood up straight and turned to the right, following a path that ran parallel with the subterranean canal. The stench of ordure became more intense—a malodorous reek that made every intake of breath a trial, and each shallow gasp a triumph of reflex over revulsion.

Their progress acquired an unwelcome accompaniment: the skittering of claws and a restless commentary of chirrups and squeals. Something large and sleek ran from a fading pulse of light and plopped into the water.

"Was that a rat?"

"I fear so."

"But it was enormous."

Concentric ripples identified the point where the creature had taken its plunge.

Rheinhardt touched Liebermann's shoulder and gave him a gentle push.

Only a short distance ahead, the flashlight's beam revealed a large iron door. Rheinhardt raised a finger to his lips. Liebermann positioned himself so that when the door was pulled open he would be able to direct the flashlight at whatever awaited them on the other side. Rheinhardt stood close by, his revolver raised. The inspector signaled, and Liebermann wrenched the door open. It emitted a torturous, metallic scream.

Flash—fade—darkness.

The light caught the distinctive reflective surface of the human eye. But it was returned not from a single pair belonging to Olbricht but from many pairs, all of them wide open, the whites glinting with fear.

"God in heaven," breathed Rheinhardt.

They found themselves looking into a square stone-walled

chamber. A motley collection of adults and young children were lying on the ground. Their clothes were little more than rags, and the acrid air smelled strongly of ammonia. Some of the children were not wearing shoes, and their pathetic little faces were striped with sooty smears. One of them began to cry.

Rheinhardt lowered his revolver.

A woman with long matted hair crawled forward, grabbed Rheinhardt's free hand, and kissed it. She was mumbling in a language that he could not understand. The relieved tone of her utterances suggested that she was thanking him, or God, for being merciful. Embarrassed, Rheinhardt took a few steps backward.

"Have any of you heard someone passing by . . . a few minutes ago, perhaps?"

None of the emaciated faces registered comprehension. They all looked blank: an old man with a long grizzled beard, a child with black hair, a youth wearing a flat cap. . . . There were more than a dozen in all, huddled together, trying to conserve their warmth. The old man coughed into his sleeve.

"Do any of you speak German?" Rheinhardt continued.

Nothing.

"*Magyar . . . čeština?*"

A woman at the back of the chamber called out—a string of harsh, abrasive syllables.

"Where on earth are they from?" asked Liebermann.

"I haven't a clue," Rheinhardt replied. "Come—we should keep going." The inspector turned to leave but suddenly stopped. It was an abrupt movement, as though his coat had caught on something, jerking him backward. He searched his pockets and pulled out a handful of loose change. He offered it to the woman at his feet, who, instead of appearing grateful, glanced fearfully at her associates.

"Take it," said Rheinhardt. "Please. I want nothing in return."

He allowed the silver coins to fall into the folds of her tattered dress, and made a swift departure.

"Who are they?" Liebermann asked.

"Unlicensed immigrants," Rheinhardt replied. "They come down here in the winter to keep warm and avoid deportation. It's said that there are thousands of them."

"Thousands?"

"Yes, tens of thousands. The sewers are immense, with as many thoroughfares, byways, and rivers as the city on the surface. It is a city beneath the city. Another Vienna that few, thankfully, ever see."

"This place is hell," said Liebermann, shaking his head. "Hell."

"Indeed," said Rheinhardt.

"I never realized . . . I never realized that under our glorious concert halls, palaces, and ballrooms . . ."

"I know—it is truly scandalous."

The two men resumed their pursuit, walking side by side in pensive silence. Liebermann found himself remembering his encounter with Miss Lydgate in the Natural History Museum and her description of the scientific romance that she had been reading. The author, H. G. Wells, had speculated about a future division of the human race, the poor being driven underground—and the eventual splitting of humanity into two different species. Liebermann had thought the idea absurd, yet now, having witnessed human beings living in such deplorable conditions, he was forced to reconsider his position.

"What's that?" Rheinhardt's question interrupted Liebermann's vatic ruminations. "Listen! It sounds like a waterfall."

As they progressed, the splashing and roiling sounds of water grew louder.

They arrived at a low archway adjoining their path, through which they could see stone stairs descending to a lower level.

Liebermann worked the flashlight's bridging switch.

Flash—fade—darkness.

The stairs were steep and the walls were damp to the touch. As the two men descended, the crashing and swoosh of churning water increased in volume and Liebermann became aware of a curious phenomenon. The walls were gleaming. He had become so used to the unrelenting night of the underworld that he had failed to recognize the cause: a weak light, emanating from below.

They entered a large chamber that was lit by electric bulbs suspended on cables. A large pipe, big enough for a man to walk through, projected out from one of the walls. It was a conduit for a steady stream of brown glutinous liquid that tumbled into a fast-flowing river. The river itself entered through an arch on one side of the chamber and exited through an identical opening on the opposite side.

Liebermann peered into the rushing torrent and observed slicks of oily effluent, lumps of excrement, and suds of yellow foam. He gagged on the vile spindrift that moistened the air.

Halfway up the wall on the other side of the noxious river was an elevated iron walkway. Looking down at them from it was Olbricht.

Rheinhardt immediately raised his revolver and shouted over the turbulent waters.

"Do not move, Herr Olbricht, or I shall shoot. Stay exactly where you are."

The artist's expression was calm and his posture relaxed. From his lofty vantage point he seemed to be studying them with an air of detached inquisitiveness, like an emperor observing his subjects with imperial disdain.

"He could be armed, Oskar," said Liebermann.

"Herr Olbricht," Rheinhardt shouted again. "Raise your hands slowly and place them on your head."

The artist did as he was told. But as soon as he had completed this action the chamber filled with the sound of raucous laughter. Two sewerage workers, holding lamps, suddenly appeared behind Rheinhardt and Liebermann.

"What's goin' on 'ere, then?"

Rheinhardt was distracted only for an instant. But it was enough for Olbricht. He recognized the opportunity—and bolted. Rheinhardt pulled the revolver's trigger, but it was too late. Olbricht had escaped through an entrance at the end of the walkway.

Rheinhardt turned on the sewerage workers, who drew back, fearful of the gunman.

"I am Inspector Oskar Rheinhardt of the Viennese security office. Where does that walkway lead?" He pointed his smoking revolver upward.

"Upper tunnels," replied the larger of the two men.

"Do they rise to the surface?"

"Yeah, they do."

"Where do they come out?"

"Postgasse, Fleischmarkt, Parkring . . . lots of places." He spoke in a rough dialect that Rheinhardt could hardly follow.

"How long would it take us to get up there?" Rheinhardt waved his revolver at the elevated walkway.

"Up there?" The worker raised his chin and jutted out his lower lip. "About half an hour?" He looked at his smaller colleague, who nodded but didn't speak.

"You are sure?"

The worker consulted his colleague again, who nodded vigorously. Rheinhardt turned his tired, world-weary eyes toward his friend.

"Well, Max," he said, sighing, "For the time being, I think, we must concede defeat."

76

DAWN WAS BREAKING AS Liebermann and Rheinhardt arrived back at the artist's studio. A thin light seeped through the windows, illuminating the disordered scene: the smashed glass, the shredded canvas, and, most noticeably, the hole in the floor. Outside, the sound of voices and hammering suggested that some of the businesses in the cul-de-sac were already opening.

Rheinhardt set to work again with his pliers and lifted another two planks, which permitted the removal of the cello case. It was old and battered, its brown leather scuffed and its hasps tarnished. Indeed, it looked so battered and worn that Liebermann suspected it must once have been owned by a professional concert performer.

They picked the case up and placed it on Olbricht's table. The two men glanced at each other, acknowledging the suspense of the moment. Then Rheinhardt tested the hasps.

"Not locked," he whispered.

They clicked open, and he raised the lid.

The interior, lined with moth-eaten crushed velvet, was crammed full of old clothes. Rheinhardt began removing some of the items: a paint-stained smock, a grubby shirt, a light and heavily creased summer jacket.

Both men gasped.

Removal of the jacket had revealed an ornate sword hilt underneath it.

Liebermann reached into the case and, grasping the hilt, drew out a fine military sabre. The curved edge glinted as he turned it in the morning light.

"Salieri's weapon, I believe," said the young doctor.

Rheinhardt continued to remove articles of clothing from the case. When it was almost empty, he made a second discovery: a notebook bound in red cloth.

"Ah, yes," said Liebermann knowingly.

Rheinhardt flicked through the pages. It was densely illustrated with pen-and-ink drawings. These were similar in nature to Olbricht's other works—warriors, maidens, and mythical beasts. In addition, there were quotes, copied out in bold Gothic script. Rheinhardt ran his finger along the page. "*What is good? All that heightens the feeling of power in man, the will to power, power itself. What is bad? All that is born of weakness. What is happiness? The feeling that power is growing, that resistance is overcome.*" A number of crude arcane sigils occupied the margin.

"What a dreadful sentiment," said Liebermann.

"I wonder where it comes from?" Rheinhardt turned another page and his eyes widened.

Liebermann shifted position to get a better view.

The page was crammed with detail: curling vines, forest animals, the columns of a temple. At the top was a snake, its body divided into three parts. Below were listed all the characters of *The Magic Flute*: Tamino, Papageno, the Queen of the Night, the Speaker . . . Blotches of ink were splattered everywhere as though the artist had worked at speed, digging the nib of his pen into the paper.

"Look," said Liebermann, "he has inscribed something beside some of the names." He took out his spectacles and leaned forward to examine the minute writing.

"The Queen of the Night . . . the number seven . . . a runic symbol of some kind . . ."

"Thorr, I believe." Rheinhardt pointed at what looked like an angular letter P.

". . . and the numbers one, five, two, and eight."

The inspector's finger dropped to another character. "Papageno—the bird catcher . . . the number twenty-seven, Thorr—and again one, five, two, and eight."

"The final number sequence is constant—it is only the first number that changes."

"But he uses another runic symbol after Monostatos and the Speaker of the Temple . . . and a third after Prince Tamino, and Sarastro. I can't remember what the first is called, but the second is featured in List's pamphlet: Ur—primal fire."

"Oskar—I think these are dates. When did the Spittelberg murders take place?"

"The seventh of October."

"And the Czech?"

"The twenty-seventh."

"So here we have it: the seventh, and the twenty-seventh—he has simply substituted Thorr for October."

"Why, yes! The professor's servant was murdered on the seventh of November—the rune changes to represent a different month! But why substitute 1528 for 1902?"

"I remember my father once told me that Minister Schönerer has devised his own calendar. His Pan-German followers count their years not after the birth of Christ but after the battle of Noreia—believed to have been the first Teutonic victory over Rome."

"When was that?"

"I don't know—some time before the birth of Christ."

"Well, Olbricht can't be using the Schönerian calendar—years would have to be added to 1902, not subtracted from it."

"In which case, Olbricht has used a much later date. If we subtract

1528 from 1902, we get . . ." Liebermann paused to do the calculation. "A difference of 374 years."

"Carnuntum!" Rheinhardt cried. "He has calculated his dates from the battle of Carnuntum! AD 374! Just what one would expect from a devotee of Guido List!"

Liebermann did not share Rheinhardt's happiness at breaking the code. Instead he remained silent, his expression deeply troubled.

"What is it?" asked Rheinhardt, concerned.

"If you are correct, then it would seem that Olbricht killed Papagena two weeks ago—a murder of which we know nothing—and intends to commit a double murder in a few days' time: Prince Tamino, and Sarastro." Liebermann tossed the sword back into the cello case and closed the lid. "Oskar, it has been an extraordinary night—and if I am unable to find a coffeehouse in the next half hour, I swear I shall expire."

77

RHEINHARDT HAD ORDERED TWO pieces of poppy seed strudel, a *türkische* coffee, and a *schwarzer* for his friend. A waiter with thinning hair, a walrus mustache, and the grumpy manner of a privy counselor delivered their order promptly but with little ceremony.

While Liebermann gazed out of the window, Rheinhardt made light work of his breakfast. When Liebermann finally turned his head, he saw the inspector shamelessly staring at his own untouched pastry with intense interest. The older man's expression was difficult to describe, as it somehow managed to embody in equal measure yearning, whimsy, regret, and avarice.

Liebermann pushed his strudel across the table.

"Eat it."

"Are you sure?"

"Yes, I'll have a croissant later."

Rheinhardt smiled and a certain tension in his attitude was relieved. He attacked his second breakfast with remarkable energy, creating an explosion of powdered sugar and papery caramel flakes as his fork plunged through the soft, yielding confection.

Raising his fork and waving it in a mock-minatory manner, he exclaimed, "Now! I want to know exactly how you discovered that it was Olbricht! No enigmatic statements, cryptic looks, or evasion! You will appreciate, I hope, that the rest of my morning will be spent writing a report for Commissioner Brügel." Rheinhardt swallowed his strudel. "So, if you would be so kind, Herr Doctor, I am eager to be enlightened."

This was a conversational juncture that the two men had reached on several previous occasions, and Rheinhardt was not surprised to see his young friend assume an air of casual, languid disinterest. He picked some lint off his trousers, raised his coffee cup, inhaled the aroma, and in due course, with evident reluctance, confessed. "It was the pictures. The pictures we saw at his exhibition."

"What about them?"

"You will recall that Professor Freud is of the opinion that dreams can be interpreted. I simply applied Professor Freud's technique of dream interpretation to Olbricht's paintings."

"I would be grateful if you would be more specific, Max."

"Olbricht is preoccupied by blood, in two senses. First, he is preoccupied by the blood that he sees when he wields his sabre. I am reminded of a case reported by Krafft-Ebing in *Psychopathia Sexualis*: a tinsmith who made a prostitute sit undressed on the edge of her bed while he stabbed her with a long knife, three times in the chest and abdomen. Krafft-Ebing reports that the tinsmith sustained an erection throughout. I suspect that Olbricht may derive some erotic pleasure from the sight of blood. I also believe that I was correct in an earlier conjecture. Olbricht is impotent. His use of a sabre has phallic connotations. When he wields his sabre, he is powerful, potent . . . irresistible. The weapon compensates for his deficiencies as a man."

Rheinhardt coughed uncomfortably. "I'm not sure I can put *that* in my report. But you were saying, he is preoccupied by blood in *two* senses."

"Yes, he is also preoccupied with blood in the sense of stock, race, and heredity—an obsession that I presume has arisen through his familiarity with the writings of List and his ilk."

"So what has this got to do with his paintings?"

"Oskar's canvases are full of blood. He cannot stop himself from enlivening his heroic scenes with daubs and splashes of red paint. Moreover he favors a curiously sanguinary palette: coral, russet, cerise, scarlet, carmine, crimson, rust. . . . It is like a compulsion. And the most extraordinary example of this . . . this obsession, was the painting titled *Pipara: The Germanic Woman in the Purple of the Caesars*. Do you remember it?"

"Yes, I do."

"Did you notice anything odd about it?"

Rheinhardt thought for a few moments. "No, I can't say that I did."

"Her cape was *red*, Oskar . . . red! She is supposed to be dressed in the *purple* of the Caesars! Professor Freud has frequently observed that verbal blunders—slips of the tongue—can be very revealing. Olbricht's *Pipara* is the artistic equivalent. A slip of the eye!'

"Mmm . . . how very interesting." Rheinhardt placed his fork on the plate and took out his notebook. "Go on."

"Dreams conceal wishes—often forbidden wishes. Olbricht's repressed, forbidden wish was to paint with blood—or, at least, with the blood of those he counted as dangerous or threatening. This terrible desire was partially satisfied by his frequent use of red paint . . . that is, until Spittelberg. There the repressed wish surfaced and the psychic energy was discharged when he desecrated the wall in Madam Borek's brothel. Olbricht's paintings also dramatize another form of wish-fulfillment. They depict various visions of a Teutonic heaven: skalds, beautiful maidens, and conquering knights. The skyline is broken by the turrets and spires of great Gothic castles. It is a world that any visitor to Bayreuth would recognize. A world without Slavs, Jews, and Negroes. A world liberated from the Catholic Church. A world in which the old gods have been restored to their former glory."

"Extraordinary."

Rheinhardt quickly flicked over a page of his notebook.

"Do you remember Olbricht's depiction of a vast barbarian horde?"

"Yes—a great sea of minute faces."

"If you had studied them more closely, you would have noticed that each one was a miniature essay in xenophobic prejudice. The horde was comprised of crude caricatures of Jews, Slavs, and the southern races: the enemies who must be defeated in order to protect and preserve the purity of the ancient German bloodlines."

The morose waiter returned and placed a bill under the sugar bowl.

"With respect," said Rheinhardt, "we would like more coffee. The same again, please."

The waiter grumbled something under his breath, cleared the dirty cups away, and shuffled off.

Liebermann continued, "Another of Olbricht's works that captured my attention was his *Rheingold*—showing the Nibelung dwarf, Alberich, and the three Rhine maidens. Alberich is almost always depicted as an ugly, misshapen figure, but in Olbricht's rendering Alberich looks more like a romantic hero. Now, Herr Olbricht is not, by any estimation, an attractive man, not with his peculiar eyes and wrinkles, and he may have identified himself with the dwarf. I am inclined to believe that, like Alberich, Herr Olbricht would have experienced teasing by women. Women whom he would subsequently perceive as beautiful, heartless, cruel, and, most significant—unattainable. . . . This identification may have been strengthened by the possession of a similar name: Olbricht, Alberich." Liebermann paused to allow Rheinhardt to appreciate the shared resonances. "So, when we look at Olbricht's representation of Alberich, we are in fact looking at a self-portrait, how he really sees himself: handsome, brave, powerful. Not unlike List's *Unbesiegbare*— The Invincible, the strong one from above."

"Ah, I see. That is what you saw on Olbricht's shelf when we were searching his bedroom: List's book."

"Indeed: *The Invincible: Basics of a German Weltanschauung.*"

Rheinhardt stopped taking notes in order to consume another mouthful of strudel.

"I am most impressed," said Rheinhardt. "But your reasoning is rather complex, and I am not altogether confident that Commissioner Brügel will be satisfied with such an explanation."

"In which case," said Liebermann, "you will be pleased to hear that a psychoanalytic interpretation of Olbricht's paintings was not the only factor that influenced my thinking."

"Oh?"

"For the past month I have been treating a patient called Herr Beiber. He suffers from *paranoia erotica.*"

"Which is?"

"A delusion of love. He believes that he and Archduchess Marie-Valerie are—by some spiritual edict—amorously connected. Moreover, he believes that his feelings for her are reciprocated and that she communicates her affection through certain signs. These can be virtually anything but at one time they took the form of curtain movements behind the windows of the Schönbrunn Palace. Early one morning Herr Beiber had stationed himself outside the royal residence when he observed a man approaching carrying a cello. Herr Beiber offered the man a very considerable sum of money if he would play an aubade for the archduchess. The man refused, and he did so not because Herr Beiber's offer was unpersuasive but because there was no cello in his case, merely a sabre, which he had just employed to dispatch the emperor's favorite snake in the Tiergarten."

"But how can you be sure it was Olbricht?"

"Herr Beiber commented on the peculiarity of the cellist's face. He described him as looking like a frog!"

"Astonishing!" Rheinhardt began to scribble in his notebook.

"Vienna is full of musicians. The sight of a man carrying a cello case is never conspicuous—at any hour of the day. It was an ideal contrivance for carrying and concealing a sabre. Further, Olbricht could carry laundered clothes in the case and exchange them for blood-spattered garments after performing his acts of carnage. I imagine this is what he did after the Spittelberg and Wieden atrocities."

The morose waiter returned, deposited their coffees on the table, scowled, and departed. Rheinhardt, indifferent to the man's bad manners, finished scribbling and scored a thick line under his final sentence.

"Excellent! The commissioner should have no trouble accepting that as an explanation. I am afraid, however, that I must dispense with your clever psychological deductions concerning Olbricht's art—and with all that phallic business, of course. You will understand, I hope, that when dealing with a man like Brügel "pragmatism" is the watchword."

"As you wish," said Liebermann. "Although if it is permissible . . . One day I might wish to include my observations in an academic work—a forensic case study, perhaps."

"If we apprehend Olbricht, you can do whatever pleases you, Max. Which brings us to the matter of his notebook. It would seem that Olbricht killed Papagena on the first of December. If I am not mistaken, in *The Magic Flute* she first appears as an old woman, and is then transformed, becoming young and pretty. The slaughter of any woman—young or old—would hardly go unnoticed. Perhaps these notes of his are not entirely reliable?"

"I cannot agree."

"Then where is the body?"

Rheinhardt dropped some sugar into his *türkische*.

"The sewers. Olbricht was clearly familiar with that dreadful underworld. Finding a suitable victim down there would have been easy—and who would have cared about her demise?"

"Indeed," said Rheinhardt, nodding his head gravely. "Bodies recovered from the sewers are simply carted off to the cemetery of the unnamed. I will notify the relevant authorities." Rheinhardt stirred his *türkische* and sucked pensively on his lower lip. "Whatever the ultimate fate of Papagena—poor unfortunate soul—we must now turn our attention to Tamino and Sarastro." Rheinhardt sipped his coffee. "Olbricht knows that we have found him out. Of course, a sane man would abandon his schemes and attempt to escape."

"But he is not a sane man."

"You think he will proceed with his plan?"

"I am certain of it. The ruined painting, the empty vodka bottle, and the smashed glass—he despaired after reading his reviews. He was forced to accept that he will never be recognized as a great artist. But the narcissism that drives the creative impulse cannot be extinguished so easily. It can be diverted and its aim displaced. Olbricht has always blurred the boundary between art and slaughter. Think of the attention he gives to the composition of his death scenes: Hildegard, Madam Borek's brothel, the servant in Wieden. . . . He may still achieve immortality by elevating ideological murder to the level of a fine art."

Liebermann gazed out of the window. On the other side of the road, two Bosnian soldiers were passing by, dressed in distinctive regimental uniform: collarless tunics, knickerbockers, ankle boots, backpacks, and tasseled fezzes. Bosnians were not a common sight around the city, yet they were frequently seen on sentry duty outside the Hofburg Palace. Their presence in such a conspicuous location was clearly intentional—old Franz Josef, sending a message to his subjects: *Even the Muslim mountain people are valued members of our great Austro-Hungarian family.*

"If Tamino is a prince," said Liebermann softly, "then it is just possible that . . ." He trailed off, shaking his head. "No. It is too dreadful to contemplate."

"The royal family?" cried Rheinhardt.

"If Olbricht assassinated a Habsburg, that would certainly ensure his immortality. Which of us will ever forget the name of Luigi Lucheni?"

"We must inform the palace immediately."

Liebermann raised his hand, gently counseling restraint.

"It is only one of several possibilities, Oskar. . . . Olbricht might interpret the title *prince* idiosyncratically. Evzen Vanek was not a bird catcher, and Ra'ad was not a Moor. His victims are merely approximations of Schikaneder's characters."

The lineaments of anxiety faded somewhat from Rheinhardt's face—but they did not vanish entirely.

"And what of Sarastro?

"A sage, a philosopher-king." Liebermann's fingers played on the edge of the table as he recollected the aria: *In diesen heil'gen Hallen*—In these sacred halls. "The head of a secret order," he continued.

"Well," said Rheinhardt, "given that *The Magic Flute* is a Masonic opera, could it be that Sarastro is the head of a Masonic lodge?"

"It is certainly a possibility—but which one?"

"Well, strictly speaking there are no Masonic lodges in Vienna. As you know, they are not permitted to perform their rituals. But they meet as friends—under the banner of a charitable organization called Humanitas."

Rheinhardt wrote down a few more lines in his notebook. He then looked up, a puzzled expression furrowing his brow. "Olbricht intends to murder Tamino and Sarastro on the same day. Why would he do that?"

"Perhaps Tamino and Sarastro are going to be in the same place. Like the Queen of the Night and her three ladies."

"It seems unlikely that a member of the royal family will be attending a meeting of Humanitas."

Liebermann sniffed, suddenly aware of an unpleasant odor. He lifted his coat sleeve and held it beneath his twitching nose. It was redolent of mephitic subterranean vapors. He understood now why the waiter had given them such a graceless reception.

78

HERR BEIBER AWOKE FROM a particularly vivid dream.

The races: a humid day in early summer, damp air blowing across a field from the invisible Danube. Hurdles and ditches surrounded by a bright white fence, and in the distance woods, luxuriant with heavy foliage. Jockeys on their mounts—gray, dapple gray, bay, chestnut, piebald—shiny bright silk shirts puffed up by the wind—sashes of red, blue, and gold. The crowd, dark and swarming around the track: counts, bankers, cavalry officers, students, salesmen, clerks—and elegant ladies with parasols, the breeze rippling their long muslin skirts.

The evocation of the Freudenau had been so vivid that something of the summer air—hay, meadowsweet, manure, and every kind of exotic perfume—still lingered in his nostrils, masking the insistent and ubiquitous monotony of hospital carbolic.

Herr Beiber had had similar dreams before, and in all of them his companion had been Archduchess Marie-Valerie. They were usually seated together, in the royal enclosure, where they sipped champagne and laughed at the horses' names: Kiss Me Quick, Lord Byron, Fräulein Minnie. This dream, however, was different.

He had not been dressed in his sombre work clothes. Instead, he had been wearing a wide-brimmed straw hat, pale flannel trousers, and a red-striped jacket. A pair of binoculars hung from his neck and in his hand he carried a stylish ebony cane. He hardly recognized himself.

And more peculiar still, his companion was not Archduchess Marie-Valerie but Frau Friedmann—a typist who occupied one of the three desks in his small office.

He closed his eyes and tried to recover the dream world.

The horses assembled at the gate—nostrils flaring, flanks glossy and shimmering in the sunshine.

Which is yours?

The black-brown stallion.

Their arms were linked and Frau Friedmann's body was pressed against his. As he remembered the sensation, he felt an unfamiliar stirring in his loins.

The red flag lowered and the stallion broke away, taking the lead at once. It surged forward—ten, fifteen, twenty lengths.

If Apollo wins, I'll take you out to dinner at Leidinger's. And afterward, we'll get orchestra seats at the Weidner Theater. Front row.

Herr Beiber opened his eyes and stared at the ceiling.

Frau Friedmann.

He had hardly noticed her at work. She was simply part of the office furniture. But now that he thought about her, it occurred to him that she was a pleasant enough woman. A plump red-cheeked widow, who had a sweet, kindly smile. And—yes—he could recall that she had once complimented him on his choice of neckties.

Because of her ample figure, Frau Friedmann's dresses were always rather tight. When she sat, the stretched material revealed little ridges of folded flesh.

Again, the unfamiliar stirring.

He would be seeing Doctor Liebermann later that morning. He would tell him all about the dream. It was the sort of thing that the young doctor would be interested in.

Herr Beiber sat up.

He felt strangely altered. In fact, he was feeling rather well. Perhaps all this talking to Doctor Liebermann was doing him some good after all.

Frau Friedmann.

"Now, why didn't I notice her before?" he whispered into the crisp bedsheets.

79

On Herr Lösch's desk was a small ornament made of silver and gold: compasses, opened over the arc of a circle inscribed with strange letters. It was the only item in the room that suggested the significance of their whereabouts. As for Herr Lösch himself, he reminded Rheinhardt of nothing more subversive than a bank manager or tutor. It was difficult to believe that he was the most senior Freemason in Vienna: Venerable Lösch—Grand Master of Humanitas.

"I am most grateful for your consideration, Inspector," said Lösch, "and I can assure you that I will take the utmost care."

The cadence suggested that the audience had come to an end.

Rheinhardt wondered whether his explanation had been adequate.

"He is an extremely dangerous man," said Rheinhardt. "And quite mad."

"Indeed," said Herr Lösch, stroking his white Vandyke beard. His gaze flicked away to register the time on the table clock.

"I would be happy," Rheinhardt persisted, "to provide you with police protection on the twelfth."

Herr Lösch smiled and said, "Thank you. But that won't be necessary."

The smile faded and the pulse on his temple suggested that he was becoming annoyed by Rheinhardt's continued presence.

The inspector sighed.

"Herr Lösch, the palace is treating this matter very seriously. My superior was received by the court high commissioner this morning."

"And that is how it should be. Now, if you will excuse me, Inspector, I have some business to attend to."

Herr Lösch rang for his servant and the double doors opened.

Rheinhardt rose from his chair.

"Ah, Hugo," said Lösch. "Would you be so kind as to accompany Inspector Rheinhardt to the door?" The servant bowed. "Good day, Inspector."

"Good day, Herr Lösch. Should you change your mind with respect to my offer, I can be contacted at the Schottenring station."

"Of course. Thank you again."

When Rheinhardt had left the room, Herr Lösch removed some notepaper and a pen from his desk. In a hurried hand he began to write: *The security office may be on to us. I suspect that they have heard something about the twelfth. I think they will try to follow me. Must go into hiding. Elysium is the only safe place now. Let others know.* He scratched a symbol in lieu of a signature, folded the paper, and slid it into a plain envelope.

80

THE FIRST COURSE OF cabbage and raisin soup had been very filling, but not sufficiently so to deter Stefan Kanner from insisting that the waiter should bring large helpings of Wiener schnitzel, Brussels sprouts, baked breaded tomatoes, and *innviertler speckknödel* (diced bacon mixed with chopped parsley, wrapped in dough and cooked in salted water). He also ordered two bottles of a rough local wine that since his student days had always been jovially referred to by young medical men as atropine.

"The guilt is intolerable," said Liebermann. "I can hardly bear to think about it."

"It had to be done," said Kanner, spearing a bacon dumpling. "You did the right thing. Clara will get over it—and it'll be for the best. Now, stop punishing yourself and have some more atropine." Liebermann mechanically did as he was told, gulping down the astringent liquid. "Of course, what you really need right now," Kanner continued, "is the company of a sweet girl with whom you have an understanding. My own melancholy mood has much improved thanks to such an arrangement."

Kanner popped the dumpling into his mouth.

"I beg your pardon?" said Liebermann.

"Her name is Theresa," said Kanner. "She's the cashier at a little coffeehouse in Mariahilf. I go there sometimes to play billiards in the afternoon—and cards at night. I suspect that she is having some sort of liaison with the pay waiter—a roué who looks more elegant than most of his customers. One afternoon I happened to meet Theresa just as she was leaving. We conveyed to each other what was on our minds, achieved a perfect understanding, and drove in a closed fiacre to a secluded spot on the Prater, where we spent a very merry evening. She is extraordinarily pretty—eyes like saucers—although she's in the habit of humming an old operetta song more times than I consider strictly necessary: *Love requires endless study, who loves but once is a fuddy-duddy. . . .*" Kanner paused and shrugged. "And—as is the way with such things—thoughts of my dear Sabina soon faded."

"Mmm," said Liebermann.

"You don't approve?"

"It's not a question of approval, Stefan. One's treatments should meet the specific needs of the patient. And I fear, Herr Doctor, that in my particular case at least, such a cure will only exacerbate the illness. My guilt will not be relieved by taking a turn around the Prater with a cash girl."

"Then what is your solution?" asked Kanner, looking a little miffed at Liebermann's gentle rebuff.

"Industry." Liebermann was aware that he was sounding pompous even as the word escaped from his lips.

"Maxim, you sound like my father!"

Liebermann made an appeasing gesture with his hands and smiled.

"I'm sorry, Stefan. What I meant to say was—I have, of late, found my police work with Inspector Rheinhardt very . . ." He paused to find the correct word. "Diverting. I really must tell you about it. There have been some quite extraordinary developments."

Liebermann proceeded to give Kanner an account of his recent adventures: the discovery of the cello case and the pursuit of Olbricht through the sewers—the sabre, and the contents of Olbricht's notebook. Kanner listened carefully.

"And there is to be another murder—a double murder?" said Kanner. "On the twelfth? But that is tomorrow."

"Almost certainly," said Liebermann.

The atmosphere in the room had become muted. Kanner seemed unusually meditative and subdued.

"And you are of the opinion that . . ." Kanner took a box of Egyptian cigarettes out of his jacket pocket. "That this Olbricht character will try to murder an aristocrat and the chief Freemason of Vienna—on the same day?"

"I cannot be certain. But it is a reasonable hypothesis."

Kanner took out a cigarette and tamped it on the side of the box.

"Inspector Rheinhardt spoke to the head Freemason yesterday afternoon," Liebermann added. "But I understand that he didn't seem to take the threat very seriously. Rheinhardt suspected that the gentleman believed his warning was some kind of security office deception: relations between the police and the Freemasons are not good. Inspector Rheinhardt considered it prudent to have the gentleman followed but to his great consternation found that by yesterday evening he had completely vanished."

Kanner lit his cigarette and blew a perfect smoke ring that rose up and hovered above his head, creating the illusion of a disintegrating halo.

"And you're quite sure it *isn't* a police trick?"

Liebermann's expression conveyed his incredulity. "Of course it isn't a trick!"

Kanner pulled at his chin and grimaced. "In which case, I have a confession to make."

Liebermann inspected his friend closely. Kanner's blue eyes were startlingly bright. "You do?"

"Yes. I am a Freemason: and tomorrow, on the twelfth of December, Prince Ambrus Nádasdy of Hungary will be initiated as an entered apprentice at a secret temple known as Elysium. The ceremony will be presided over by the head of our fraternity, Venerable Grand Master Lösch—the gentleman who has so successfully evaded your friend Rheinhardt."

Liebermann stared at Kanner, dumbfounded. "Then we know where Olbricht's going to strike!"

"Max." Kanner's expression was grave. "What I have just told you must not be revealed to anyone."

"But the police . . . I have to."

"It would be utterly pointless. No member of the craft in Vienna would ever disclose the location of Elysium. We are acting illegally."

"But Stefan, Prince Nádasdy and Herr Lösch could be killed!"

"Perhaps, with your assistance, we will be able to prevent such a catastrophe. Now swear! Swear to me that you will say nothing of this to the police."

Liebermann swallowed. "I will not betray your trust, Stefan. I swear."

"Good. Now, where is that waiter? We must settle our account at once and leave."

"Leave? Where are we going?"

"Elysium!"

81

PROFESSOR FOCH TOOK THE volume from the shelf and examined the spine: *The Relationship Between the Nose and the Female Sexual Organs* by Wilhelm Fliess. It was utter nonsense—everything that one might expect from an associate of Freud. The only sensible thing in the entire book was the finding that labor pains could be ameliorated by the application of cocaine to the nose. But as for the rest . . . mystical nonsense and gobbledygook! There were indeed certain similarities between nasal and genital mucosae, but the edifice that Fliess had constructed on such flimsy foundations was far too ambitious—too expansive, too grandiose. It would soon be consigned to the midden heap of otorhinolaryngology—and rightly so.

Professor Foch's mood suddenly darkened.

Fliess was based in Berlin.

This did not bode well.

Were his ideas accepted there?

Fliess had proposed that the nasal membranes and bones were of etiological significance with respect to a range of medical conditions: migraine headaches; pains in the abdomen, arms, and legs; angina pectoris; asthma; indigestion—and disturbances of sexuality. The last condition, of course, was of considerable interest to that reprobate Freud. Indeed, he had defended Fliess's opus when it had been criticized by members of the faculty. But then again, what was one to expect? That was how they worked, these Jews. They stuck together . . . polluting the discipline with their sexual preoccupations, filth, and nonsense.

Professor Foch tossed the book into his packing case, where it landed on three huge yellow Kaposi atlases on syphilis and diseases of the skin.

Berlin.

That it should come to this.

Damn them all.

He had been summoned to the dean's office on Thursday afternoon—for an informal, friendly discussion on a professional matter.

Your article in the Zeitung . . . The obsequious lickspittle hypocrite had shifted in his chair as if he were sitting on a hot plate. *You have made it very difficult for us. Very difficult indeed.* . . . He had wrung his hands, sighed, and equivocated. But in the end he had arrived at the nub. *Your intention was to reach a wide audience and, my dear fellow, you certainly succeeded. It was read by one of His Majesty's advisers.* . . . The word *displeasure* was repeated with some frequency thereafter.

He had not been dismissed—as such. But rather, he had been permitted an opportunity to make a discreet exit.

A friend of mine, Lehmann—perhaps you've heard of him? Wrote a fine paper on the vestibular system a few years back. The dean had smiled unctuously. *Well, as luck would have it, he's looking to fill a post at the General Hospital—a specialist in nasal surgery, no less. Of course, I would be more than happy to provide you with a glowing reference.*

There had been little point in protesting. If it were true—and the signal of disapproval had been issued from the Hofburg itself—then his career in Vienna was over. Even his most trusted colleagues would begin to avoid him. Their gazes would not meet his. Invitations would be declined. There would be whispering in the corridors. He had seen it happen to others.

Damn them all.

He looked up at his print of *The Wounded Man*. He found the image curiously uplifting. The black mood lifted a little.

Berlin.

It might not be so bad. Things in Vienna had gone too far—and his shabby treatment by the faculty of medicine was just another symptom of its decline into a quagmire of decadence and depravity. It would take not one but a hundred—no, a thousand—Primal Fires to purify this doomed city. Perhaps in Berlin they would appreciate a man like him—a man with good honest *German* values.

82

LIEBERMANN TOOK HIS SEAT in the cab, from where he could hear the muffled voice of his friend talking to the driver. The vehicle was a rickety affair, with worn seats and sconces holding stubs of candles. Liebermann lit a match and held it to the nearest wick.

When Kanner entered, he drew the curtains, making sure that every part of the window was properly covered.

"Where are we going?" Liebermann asked.

"I am afraid I cannot say. The location of Elysium is a closely guarded secret."

The cab began to move.

"But why are we going there now? The initiation is tomorrow."

"It is where our venerable has gone into hiding."

After they had been traveling for some time, Kanner lifted the curtain and peeped out.

"Maxim, I am sorry. But I must blindfold you."

"What!"

"We shall be arriving at our destination soon—and it is strictly forbidden for non-Masons to know the whereabouts of Elysium. If you do not comply, we cannot proceed. I am obliged to do this."

Liebermann rolled his eyes. "Very well."

Kanner produced a dark handkerchief from his coat pocket and tied it around his friend's head.

"I'm sorry," Kanner muttered.

"Yes," said Liebermann, unable to disguise his irritation.

The cab drew to a halt. Kanner leaped out and spoke to the driver, who responded with a cry of satisfaction and profuse thanks. He had been encouraged to exercise discretion with a very large gratuity.

"Here . . . let me help you."

Kanner guided Liebermann out of the cab.

The driver cracked his whip and the cab rattled off.

Liebermann listened carefully. A slight echo suggested a wide street but the ensuing silence indicated that they were a long way from the town center. He guessed that they were probably in the suburbs— and the cool, fresh air informed him that they had gained altitude. Perhaps they had traveled west?

"Come on," said Kanner.

Liebermann heard the sound of an iron gate opening and then the crunch of gravel underfoot.

"Be careful, Maxim. There are some steps just here—three of them: quite deep and high."

Liebermann imagined the façade of a smart villa. Perhaps they had driven out to Penzing or Hietzing?

Kanner knocked on the door.

Rat-a-tat-tat. Rat-a-tat-tat. Rat-a-tat-tat.

The precise repeated rhythm suggested a code.

When the door opened, Liebermann heard a gasp.

"I must see the venerable at once," said Kanner. "It is a matter of the utmost importance."

They were admitted and were escorted down what Liebermann assumed was a long hallway smelling of polished wood and lavender. This led to a flight of carpeted stairs, which Liebermann supposed would deposit them in the basement. However, when they arrived, there was a rolling sound—like that of the castors beneath a university bookcase. They then negotiated a more precipitous descent around a tight spiral stairwell. When Liebermann reached out to touch the wall, he felt cold, slightly damp stone. The air smelled of earth. Once again, for the second time in as many days, Liebermann found himself in the underworld.

Elysium.

Yes, the name was beginning to make sense.

Behind the venerable was a large painted wooden panel. It appeared to show a pelican with outstretched wings, feeding three young with its own entrails. It stood below a crucifix decorated with a single red rose.

Liebermann had just come to the end of his story, and a heavy silence prevailed. His attention returned to the panel—which had fascinated him from the moment Kanner had removed his makeshift blindfold.

The venerable let his forefingers meet to form a steeple.

"Very interesting." He then looked at Kanner and nodded approvingly. "Thank you, brother. You acted wisely." Kanner inclined his head in grateful acknowledgment. "Herr Doctor Liebermann," continued the venerable, "you have been considerably more lucid than Inspector Rheinhardt. But in evaluating the risk—to ourselves and to our guests—we must be mindful of the facts. If the fiend is a devotee of Guido List, then he is certainly no friend of Freemasonry—and his debasement of Brother Mozart's blessed creation is further proof." The venerable paused again, tapped his fingers together, and added: "It *is* possible, we must suppose, that I am to be his Sarastro, and Prince Nádasdy his Tamino. But you cannot be certain, Herr Doctor."

"No," said Liebermann. "But I think it very likely."

The venerable stroked his snowy Vandyke beard. "How on earth could he have learned of our intentions?"

"Perhaps one of your number has been indiscreet?"

The venerable shook his head. "I doubt that very much. Tomorrow's initiation ceremony is the most important date in our calendar for more than a hundred years. Moreover, there is not a single member of our lodge who does not recognize the political sensitivity of the occasion. Prince Nádasdy still claims to be the rightful ruler of Transylvania. His father's estates were confiscated after the revolution.... When we meet tomorrow, we are not only defying the police but the Hofburg. Indiscretion would cost us dearly. None of us are keen to spend the rest of our lives locked up in the Landesgericht."

"Then it may be that Olbricht has intercepted some document?"

"Impossible," said the venerable. "Sensitive information has always been encrypted."

"He may have broken your code."

"Our Masonic cryptograms are inviolable. He would have to be a genius." The venerable leaned back in his chair. "All of which raises— in my mind—some significant doubts." He squeezed his protruding lower lip and frowned. "With respect to the accuracy of your . . . *theory*."

"Herr Lösch," said Liebermann, "I very much hope that you do not intend to proceed with tomorrow's ceremony."

The venerable sighed and turned a ring on his finger.

"Herr Doctor Liebermann, I am indebted to you. But, in truth, I do not accept that we are in as much danger as you imagine. How would this Olbricht enter the temple? It is situated four stories beneath the earth! And although there will be many in attendance, we are all known to one another. We are as brothers. An intruder would be highly conspicuous."

"Olbricht has an extraordinary knowledge of the sewers. There may be some entry point with which he is familiar."

The venerable shook his head.

"I was party to the design of Elysium. There is no such thing. And even if there were, we would simply guard it, or seal it up! Herr Doctor, this Olbricht is only mortal. Yet you speak of him as if he were some supernatural being. He may be capable of monstrous acts—but he cannot walk through walls or become invisible." The venerable's features hardened, reflecting a sudden resolve. "The inaugural meeting will take place as planned. And Prince Nádasdy will become an entered apprentice of the craft."

Liebermann examined the venerable's face. The armature of rigid muscle around his jaw relaxed, and his resolute expression was replaced by a somewhat self-satisfied smile.

For some reason that Liebermann could not identify, Herr Lösch seemed curiously unwilling to heed his warning. Liebermann felt frustrated—close to anger. He suppressed the urge to reach across the table and shake the old fool. What was wrong with him? Wasn't he troubled by the possibility of his own imminent demise—or, for that matter, the death of his Hungarian guest?

Liebermann found himself staring in mute incomprehension at the old man's enigmatic smile, and his mind was suddenly occupied by the image of a Sphinx. Once again he was reminded of the vast number of these mythical beasts that inhabited Vienna: crouching among sarcophagi in the museum, adorning the feet of lampposts, lining the paths of the Belvedere Gardens, squatting on Professor Freud's desk . . . All at once, he realized the nature of his error. He had entirely misjudged his appeal. The Masons were a secret society. His emphasis should not have been on the physical threat of death, but on the psychological threat of exposure!

"Herr Lösch," said Liebermann calmly, "I am most impressed by your courage and resolve. However, I beg you to consider: what if I am correct? Suspend your disbelief for a moment and contemplate what might happen if some terrible harm *does* befall Prince Nádasdy? There will be a full murder inquiry. Eventually, the police will find Elysium and all your activities will be revealed. Within days this place will be swarming with reporters from the *Kronen-Zeitung*, the *Tagblatt*, and the *Freie Presse*."

A flicker of anxiety unsettled the venerable's calm features. His shoulders tensed.

"Yes . . . yes." He gave a soft, purring hum of rumination. "That would be most unfortunate."

"Everything that you hold dear will be sensationalized—subjected to unsympathetic public scrutiny. Such a scandal would probably herald the end of Freemasonry in Vienna. Surely, Herr Lösch, you do not wish such a thing to happen during the span of your protectorate?"

The venerable raised his hands. The pitch of his voice communicated something close to desperation.

"But what do you suggest? What can I do?"

"Abandon the ritual."

The venerable's expression snapped back to a mask of stubborn intransigence. "Never."

"Then let me attend."

"I beg your pardon?" said the venerable, tilting his head and leaning forward a little as if he were hard of hearing.

"Let me attend your ceremony," said Liebermann softly. "If Olbricht does appear, I may be of some assistance: at least I will be able to recognize him. And if you are right, and he does not appear, then I give you my word that your secrets will be safe with me."

The venerable assumed an expression that Liebermann associated with the ingestion of a particularly bitter pill.

"But that is impossible, Herr Doctor. You are not a Mason!"

Kanner, who had been sitting quietly throughout the exchange, coughed to attract the venerable's attention. "Master Lösch?"

The venerable turned his head.

"The fundamental tenet of the Royal Art," said Kanner, "is that all men are brothers and must be judged according to their good works. I am proud to call Doctor Liebermann my friend and honored to count him among my most esteemed colleagues. I trust him implicitly. Tomorrow's ceremony will be exceptional in so many ways. . . . I beg you to give Herr Doctor Liebermann's request the most serious consideration."

The venerable sighed and allowed his fingers to come together again.

"To allow a man who has links with the security office into Elysium is one thing. But to permit him to attend a ritual is altogether different. Herr Doctor Liebermann is evidently of good character and we have much to lose if his speculations prove to be correct. Moreover, it is incumbent upon me to take whatever measures are necessary to ensure the survival of the lodge. . . . Brother Kanner, I promise that I shall give Doctor Liebermann's request the careful thought that it deserves."

83

It was a glorious morning. Clara was seated on the terrace, next to the stone balustrade, from where she could enjoy the most spectacular alpine views. The sunlight was dazzling. So much so that she had to lower the brim of her hat to examine the snow-covered slopes. She took a deep breath—and felt quite dizzy: the air possessed the invigorating vitality of champagne.

Clara had already taken a bath in the hot springs and was feeling quite virtuous. However, she had decided to abandon the lettuce and buttermilk diet prescribed by Doctor Blaukopf, which seemed to be doing her no good at all. Besides, she was singularly unimpressed by Doctor Blaukopf. How could she respect a man who failed to notice the stains on his necktie and hunched his shoulders? Like all medical men, she reflected, his priorities were entirely wrong.

When the waiter arrived, she realized that the fresh air had sharpened her appetite, and so she ordered cinnamon coffee, freshly baked *Kaisersemmel* rolls, plum preserve, honey, eggs—and a little fruit.

While she was waiting for her breakfast to arrive, Clara observed the marchioness stepping through the open veranda doors. She was wearing a long black dress buttoned up to the top of her neck and had a fur pelt wrapped around her shoulders. Clara recognized the pelt from the previous evening. One of its extremities was decorated with a diminutive feral face with needle-sharp yellow teeth and black glass eyes. Clara marveled at how young the marchioness looked—a quite extraordinary phenomenon, considering that Aunt Trudi had established that the woman must be at least thirty-two.

The marchioness glided past.

"*Buon giorno,*" she said softly, managing the strange accomplishment of being both polite and indifferent at the same time.

Clara bowed, then wondered whether she had committed a social indiscretion. Had she bowed properly? Had she bowed too low? Should she have bowed at all? Perhaps she should have merely returned the greeting. She would consult Aunt Trudi later.

The waiter arrived with a tray piled with breakfast things. Clara broke the *Kaisersemmel* in half. The warm bread steamed in the cold air and emitted a fragrance like ambrosia. She smeared one of the pieces with creamy yellow butter and heaped on a generous mound of preserves that seemed to glisten from within like amethyst. When she bit through the crust, an explosion of sweet pleasure rippled through her body. This was not a delight that she was prepared to forgo again, irrespective of medical opinion.

As she contemplated the nearest summit, memories of the previous evening surfaced in her mind. She had been playing cards in the games room with Aunt Trudi and they had been joined by a young cavalry officer called Lieutenant Schreker. She had found his conversation most entertaining. He was witty, amusing. He had attended countless balls and seemed to know hordes of important society people. And how romantic that he should be convalescing after receiving an almost fatal sabre wound in Transylvania. His regiment had suppressed a revolt organized by some renegade Hungarian aristocrats. It all sounded so very exciting.

How different he was from other men she had met. How different he was from Max, who was always talking about the hospital—patients and illness. Psychoanalysis!

While they had been playing a round of taroc, her feet had accidentally come into contact with Lieutenant Schreker's boots. She had blushed and looked down at her hand, but before doing so she had caught a glimpse of Schreker's expression. He had been smiling. It was a wicked smile, but at the same time, she had to admit, he looked devilishly handsome. Clara conjured in her mind an image of the dashing Uhlan. How smart he looked in his uniform—the star on his collar, his polished spurs, and those blue breeches that clung tightly to his long rider's legs. . . . Even though she was alone, Clara blushed again.

A few more early risers had wandered out onto the terrace. Frau Gast and her daughter Constance; the wretched little banker who had taken an unwelcome interest in Aunt Trudi; Herr Bos, who suffered from a rare respiratory disorder and constantly coughed into his handkerchief; and the eccentric English professor (who attempted German with great enthusiasm but was at all times utterly incomprehensible).

Clara found herself gazing at the open veranda door and wishing that Lieutenant Schreker would be the next person to step out. And that was exactly what happened. Her heart was suddenly beating faster—and unaccountably she found herself a little breathless.

The handsome officer stood tall and straight-backed, enjoying the spectacular view. Turning to find a seat, he spotted Clara instantly, smiled, and marched across the terrace.

"Good morning, gnädige fräulein."

"Good morning, Lieutenant Schreker. I trust you slept well?"

"Very well, and what a beautiful morning it is."

"Yes—very beautiful."

The sun had burnished the officer's blond hair.

"May I join you for breakfast?" Clara glanced at the open doors. The officer read her thoughts and, wary of impropriety, added, "I presume your splendid aunt will be along shortly."

Clara raised her eyebrows, parted her lips, and—assuming her most flirtatious expression—replied, "I hope not."

84

Rheinhardt sat in his office at the Schottenring station. There was nothing more to be done. The palace had been informed and a number of plainclothes officers were keeping the Masonic charity Humanitas under surveillance. He would soon join them.

The inspector absentmindedly opened his desk and discovered a bottle of slivovitz and a bag of marzipan mice. He had purchased the mice some time ago as a treat for his daughters but had forgotten to take them home. Unable to resist, he took one of the mice from the bag and was about to put it into his mouth when he noticed the creature's expression. It was a little masterpiece of the confectioner's art, capturing exactly the murine equivalent of resignation. Rheinhardt assumed this was intentional. Thus, children could bite their heads off with equanimity, knowing that each mouse had already accepted its fate.

Rheinhardt wished he could do the same.

There is nothing more to be done.

Suddenly he was gripped by a superstitious sentiment that his fate and that of the mouse had become connected: if he ate the mouse, he would be colluding with the forces of destiny. He did not like the idea that things were preordained and the feeling of impotence that came with it. He dropped the mouse back into the bag and hoped that the animal's reprieve would be translated into corresponding good fortune for him.

Aware of the irrationality of his behavior, Rheinhardt imagined the censorious gaze of his friend Liebermann. The young doctor could not abide superstition, and the inspector felt quietly ashamed of his desperate act.

Earlier, he had tried calling Liebermann on the telephone. He had spoken to Ernst, the doctor's serving man, who had not been informed of his master's whereabouts. Rheinhardt had then tried the hospital, where he learned that Doctor Liebermann was not expected until the following day. Finally, he had asked Haussmann to take a look in one or two of Liebermann's favorite coffeehouses.

It was not necessary to speak to Liebermann. Yet Rheinhardt had been hoping that his friend might be able to provide him with one last crucial insight. Of course, this was, like pardoning the mouse, another sign of desperation. If Liebermann had anything more to say, he would surely have contacted him. Liebermann was hardly likely to forget the significance of the date. Even so, Rheinhardt was haunted by a curiously persistent need to speak to Liebermann—to go over Olbricht's diary entry just one more time.

There was a knock on the door.

"Come in."

It was Haussmann. "Sorry, sir. No luck."

"Very well," said Rheinhardt. "We had better get going."

85

LIEBERMANN STOOD BESIDE STEFAN Kanner, attempting—somewhat unsuccessfully—to feign familiarity with the ceremony that was taking place. After much deliberation, the venerable had given him special dispensation to attend. But he had stipulated that the outsider should be present only for the initiation, and that he would not be permitted to mingle with any of the brethren prior to the opening of formal proceedings. Moreover, the old man had demanded that Liebermann should take a solemn oath of secrecy. He must never reveal to anyone—especially his associates in the security office—what he was about to see. Consequently, Liebermann had been confined to a small antechamber. While he had been waiting there, Kanner had given him notice of what to expect and had provided him with clothing suitable for the occasion. It was only after the temple was almost full that Kanner guided Liebermann to their designated places among the most junior members of the fraternity.

An introductory ritual was in progress, during which Herr Lösch and his sergeants seemed to be reciting from memory a kind of Masonic catechism. In addition, there was a lot of general activity: the great bronze doors kept opening and closing as high-ranking officials departed and returned.

Herr Lösch was much dignified by his office. He occupied a big wooden throne and wore around his neck a V-shaped collar of red silk. Attached to the bottom of the collar was a large letter G, superimposed upon a circle of radiant gold spokes. A small table covered in scarlet drapery had been erected to the right of the throne, which permitted the venerable to use his gavel. When the venerable spoke, the rich acoustics of the subterranean temple imbued his voice with otherwise absent gravitas.

Liebermann was not registering the words of the introduction. He was still somewhat overwhelmed by the scale and design of Elysium. It reminded him of the Stadttempel—the synagogue where Clara had wanted to be married. (A stab of guilt made his heart palpitate.) The Stadttempel was a secret meeting place, built in less liberal times when laws enacted under Josef II had determined that all synagogues would be hidden from public view. The most striking similarity, though, was the ceiling, which—like the Stadttempel—was blue and studded with gold stars. Masonic symbology seemed to borrow extensively from the rabbinical tradition: an epic mural showed the Ark of the Covenant and Jacob's ladder ascending toward a letter from the Hebrew alphabet. Perhaps this was why Pan-German nationalists were so fond of the slur "Jew Mason."

Although the temple was equipped with gas lamps, none of them had been lit. Instead, light was provided by numerous randomly distributed three-branch candlesticks. Unfortunately, Elysium was too cavernous to be fully illuminated by such modest means and Liebermann was troubled by the abundance of shadowy recesses. Each one could provide Olbricht with ample opportunity for concealment.

The venerable's voice sounded firm and resolute.

"Beloved brethren! The chief purpose of our work today is the reception of the seeker, Prince Nádasdy. He is present in the preparation room. He answered the questions propounded, and I ask the brother secretary to read these answers . . ."

The floor was tiled with slabs of white and black marble, like a chessboard, and in the middle of the nave was a peculiar arrangement of three columns—Ionic, Doric, and Corinthian. A large altar candle had been placed on each of the capitals. Between the columns was a pictorial carpet, embroidered, with an array of mysterious images: pomegranates, a rough stone, the moon and the sun, a square and compasses.

Beyond the pillars, on the other side of the nave, Liebermann examined the congregation of Masons. They were all dressed in tailcoats, top hats, white gloves, and richly embroidered aprons. Some wore sashes, others V-shaped collars like the venerable. Everyone present possessed a sabre. Liebermann had asked Kanner why the brethren took weapons into their temple, and he had discovered that it was a tradition that embodied their egalitarian principles.

Back in the eighteenth century, Max, swords were used to signal nobility. Freemasons wore them to show that they were equals and to proclaim that greatness was a question of deed and character—not of birth.

Liebermann had been given a simple lambskin apron, the bib of which had been raised: a small modification of wardrobe that identified him as a novice. Kanner had made the same adjustment to his own dress.

The venerable was addressing two of his sergeants who had come forward. One of them was carrying a lamp and a large leather-bound volume.

"Brother Master of Ceremonies, you will now repair with the brother orator to the seeker, in order that this brother may make him more fully acquainted with the principles of our craft, and invite him to once again examine himself. If he stands to his decision to enter our craft, then lead him, deprived of his jewelry and outer clothing, according to the ancient usages of Freemasonry, to the gate of the temple."

The two sergeants bowed, turned, and walked toward the bronze doors that swung open to facilitate their passage. Above the entrance the All-Seeing Eye surveyed the throng with transcendent disinterest. As the two men dissolved into the gloom, the sound of a pipe organ filled the air. The combination of stops that the organist had employed created a sound similar to that of a small band of recorders. The chords progressed like a hymn, and the transparent, luminous harmonies, suffused with gentle, compassionate warmth, declared the unmistakable handiwork of Wolfgang Amadeus Mozart. The company began to sing:

"Lasst uns mit geschlungnen Händen, Brüder, diese Arbeit enden . . ."
With clasped hands, brethren, let us end this work . . .

Liebermann was not familiar with the melody and wondered whether it belonged to some obscure body of work jealously guarded by the Masons.

May this bond tightly embrace the entire globe,
As it does this holy place . . .

As the music continued, Liebermann scanned the faces of those standing opposite. There were so many of them, and what with their hats and the gloomy light, the task of trying to identify Olbricht among such a large gathering was beginning to feel like an insurmountable challenge. Moreover, his general view was restricted. He could not see the Masons standing behind him, nor the faces of what appeared to be a secretariat seated at tables below the venerable's throne.

Then not in the east alone will light shine,
Not in the west alone,
But also in the south and in the north.

The organ progressed to a final cadence, and then there was silence.

It was broken by three loud knocks on the door. Each blow boomed like a bass drum.

In the blue-gray misty distance, Liebermann saw a tall, gaunt man raise his hand.

"Venerable Master!" he cried out. "One knocks as a stranger."

"See who knocks," replied the venerable.

The bronze doors were opened again.

"It is Brother Master of Ceremonies and Brother Hänsel, with the seeker."

"Inquire of him if the seeker is a free man who has the good repute of his fellow citizens."

More questions and answers followed, and a request for the sponsor to show himself. A man appeared between the two columns of the doorway and declared, "As far as I know, I believe that the seeker is worthy of my sponsorship, and I hope that he will persevere."

His accent was Hungarian.

The venerable responded, "Now then, you will let the seeker enter." He gave a single rap with his gavel and continued. "To order, my brethren."

Again, the sound of the pipe organ filled the air, and a tenor voice began to sing a familiar refrain.

"*O heiliges Band der Freundschaft treuer Bruder . . .*"
Oh, holy Bond of the Friendship of true Brothers . . .

Liebermann recognized it immediately. It was the song that Kanner had been singing in the private dining room.

A young man with long black hair had been marched to the threshold of the temple. He was blindfolded and his shirt—the cut of which suggested the eighteenth rather than the twentieth century—flapped open at the neck and hung loosely from his shoulders. This, then, was the seeker: Prince Ambrus Nádasdy. Now that both the venerable and the prince were in the same room, Liebermann tensed.

Where is he?

The question made him peer into the darkened corners of the temple in trepidation.

As the music faded, the prince's guide proclaimed, "Up to now I have led you safely. Now I must turn you over to another conductor. Trust in his guidance."

The guide presented the young man to the gaunt Mason.

"My Lord!" cried the venerable. "No mortal eye can gaze into the heart. If you were led here by some selfish motive, or if you had the hope of discovering supernatural information and hidden knowledge through us, which was unobtainable outside of our tie, then you would see deceptions in your expectations. Our craft is devoted to humanity. Our closest task is to cultivate the pure nature of man within us with a united effort. If you are determined to unite with us in the noble work of humanity, you will affirm it according to your conscience and on your honor by a distinct *Yes*."

The prince responded as instructed: "Yes."

"Will you submit yourself to our guidance?" asked the venerable. "Do you trust us?

Again, the decisive affirmative: "Yes!"

"Man alone," continued the venerable, "among all terrestrial creations is capable and called upon to work on his self-improvement. Man is destined to a higher perfection. But the way thereto is difficult to find and beset with dangers. Brother Junior Warden, let the seeker try his strengths upon the travels he now enters upon."

Kanner tugged Liebermann's sleeve. At once, all the Masons sat down.

The gaunt, willowy Mason addressed the prince—but in tones that could be heard by all of the assembly.

"In the ancient mysteries, allegorical journeys and tests were arranged for those who were to be admitted. Accordingly, we have retained these forms of the tradition. The journeys that you will undertake are representative of life. Masonry educates its youths by imprinting their lives through symbolic acts."

Liebermann felt uneasy. Although nothing material had changed, he felt a disturbing prickling at the back of his neck—like the prescient discomfort that precedes turning around to discover that one is being stared at.

"Pay sharp attention," intoned the junior warden, "and keep true in mind the admonitions that will be given to you on these journeys. Whoever travels in darkness to unfamiliar places, as you do, requires a conductor. Fortunate is he who finds in the darkness an honest friend as a skillful guide. Follow me, I will lead you safely."

The gaunt Mason took the prince's left hand and walked him into the body of the temple. When they reached the three columns, the pair began a slow, stately circumnavigation of the carpet.

"The life of man moves in a circular fashion," the guide continued. "But the eternal center of these circuits is the one God that Freemasons worship under the designation of the Great Architect of the World. Freemasons are worshippers of God, however different your conception of God may be."

Since the brethren had sat down, Liebermann had been afforded a better view of the desks that flanked the venerable's throne. He scrutinized the seated figures. Then Kanner nudged him in the ribs to draw his attention back to the central drama. Clearly, something significant was about to happen.

The junior warden suddenly pulled the prince back a step. "Deprived of your eyesight," he taunted, "you would fall into the abyss before your feet if the hand of a friend did not hold you back. The blindfold over your eyes is a representation of your ignorance, which does not know the dangers that threaten the paths of life."

Liebermann returned his gaze to the desks.

One of the secretaries was not looking up.

His head was bowed and there was something odd about his position. He looked uncomfortable, awkward, angular. Liebermann realized why. The secretary's right arm was pulled back and his hand was gripping the hilt of his sabre.

Could it possibly be . . .

Liebermann's instinct was to act, but the formality of the initiation ceremony demanded caution, respect.

Olbricht? A Mason?

Liebermann felt bound, inhibited—unable to raise an alarm. What if he was wrong?

And yet . . .

The gaunt Mason was leading his royal ward up through the nave, toward the venerable's throne. They were drawing closer together. If it *was* Olbricht, then the venerable and the prince would very soon be in striking distance.

Sarastro and Tamino.

It must be him.

The suspect Mason raised his head a little, but the brim of his hat was wide, leaving most of his face in shadow. A candle flared—and for the briefest moment his mouth and chin were illuminated in sharp relief. Liebermann registered the wideness of the lips and the deep, distinctive creases.

"Bow yourself!" commanded the gaunt Mason. "Here is the seat for one who has obtained our free election to have administered the laws of the craft."

The prince lowered his head.

Liebermann could delay no longer. He leaped up and propelled his body forward, interposing himself between the prince and the secretariat.

"Olbricht!"

His interruption caused an immediate furor. There were gasps and cries of dismay. The gaunt Mason advanced after glancing at the venerable, who responded by raising a hand, urging moderation. Olbricht, though, was sprinting down the nave and heading for the bronze doors—his hat tracing a wide arc around the three pillars in his wake.

86

LIEBERMANN RACED DOWN THE avenue of shocked faces.

"Stop him!" cried the venerable over the ensuing uproar. "Brother Diethelm! Stop him!"

Liebermann registered the name.

Brother Diethelm?

It seemed that the venerable was referring to Olbricht rather than commanding someone called Diethelm to intervene.

Two Masons who seemed to be acting as a ceremonial guard at the entrance of the temple jumped forward, their arms outstretched. Olbricht lowered his head and charged through their feeble blockade, knocking both men sprawling across the floor. His escape took him between the great Corinthian pillars and into the darkness beyond.

Liebermann ran faster, the soles of his shoes pounding the black and white tiles as he pursued his quarry. He was unable to stop himself in the vestibule and skidded to a painful collision with the central stone column of the stairwell. The impact left him breathless and brought him to a jarring halt. From below came the fading diminuendo of receding footsteps. A question, barely articulated, flashed into Liebermann's mind: *Why didn't he go up?* It was accompanied by a shiver of unease. He dismissed this odd presentiment and hurled himself into a stumbling descent, his top hat flying from his head in the process. He thundered down the stairs, made dizzy by the tight curves of the spiral. Down, down—deeper and deeper into the earth until the stone wedges vanished and momentum carried him forward, through an open door.

Suddenly he found himself in the middle of a library.

There was no other exit through which Olbricht might have made an escape. Bookshelves lined the walls on either side. Directly ahead was a painted escutcheon, showing the sun and moon personified by the superimposition of sinister faces. Liebermann swung around, just in time to see Olbricht slam the door and turn a key.

The two men froze as if they had both come into the purview of a petrifying Gorgon.

Liebermann swallowed. A sequence of images flashed into his mind, each one jolted into consciousness by a ruthless magnesium light. Mutilated flesh, lakes of blood, exposed viscera—the corpse of Ra'ad, laid out on the table like some sacrificial offering to a perverse and cruel god.

Liebermann swallowed again. But this time there was no saliva in his mouth. He had become desiccated by terror, a chill, sickly, enervating terror that sucked the marrow from his bones and made his legs untrustworthy.

Someone was thumping a clenched fist against the door.

Three strikes.

Pause.

Four strikes.

Then a muffled voice: "Open up, open up!"

Olbricht was preternaturally still—just as he had been in the sewers when, from his elevated vantage point, he had calmly studied his pursuers. He seemed oblivious to the noise outside.

Quite suddenly he raised his right hand, creating an angle with his extended forefinger and thumb. For a brief moment he closed one eye and assumed the traditional stance of a portraitist mentally "framing" his subject.

"Herr Olbricht . . ." The name escaped from Liebermann's lips like an involuntary sigh. But nothing followed. What could he say to such a creature? What appeal could he make? Begging Olbricht to be rational, merciful, or prudent would be as pointless as reciting a Goethe poem to him.

The thumping at the door had become an incessant drumming, like heavy rainfall.

"Open up!" The muffled voice had been joined by others.

Olbricht's right hand dropped to his weapon's hilt. There was a harsh ringing metallic scrape, and a moment later he was holding his sabre above his head.

Whoosh, whoosh, whoosh.

Olbricht sliced the air with a showy display of swordsmanship. After a ferocious burst of activity he tossed his sabre into the air, where it seemed to remain suspended, in defiance of gravity. The revolving blade flashed flecks of lamplight around the room until Olbricht reclaimed it with a swift snatching action. Although such bravura might represent little more than burlesque villainy, empty fanfaronade, Liebermann instinctively understood that this was not the case. He was in the presence of a confident, assertive swordsman.

The artist strode forward.

With great reluctance, Liebermann drew his own sabre, wishing as he did so that he had been very much more attentive during Signore Barbasetti's fencing lessons. Why had he spent so much of that precious time thinking about pastries instead of technique?

Liebermann braced himself for a wild, slashing attack. But he was surprised by Olbricht's approach, which was slow, cautious, and measured. Their swords drew closer together but did not touch. Instead, the blades made minute movements—tiny provocations and withdrawals. It seemed that contact was denied by an invisible field of repelling force. Eventually the mysterious prohibition was broken, and they crossed swords for the first time with a gentle tap that produced a soft ringing sound.

Olbricht tested his opponent with a feint, which Liebermann replied to calmly, maintaining a considerable distance. The young doctor was mindful of Olbricht's posture. There was something about the buoyancy of his body—and a certain generalized tension—that suggested a readiness to spring.

The thumping on the door stopped and a voice called out, "Open the door or we'll break it down."

Olbricht was completely unperturbed by the threat. He edged forward—choosing, like most accomplished swordsmen, to study his opponent's eyes rather than the position of his opponent's blade.

Liebermann made a half thrust—intending it to be a false attack—before following through with a *passata-sotto*. Olbricht stood firm. Then Liebermann found himself watching the monster's blade arcing past his stomach. He felt something catch. The tip of Olbricht's sabre had sliced through the material of his vest. Too astonished to respond swiftly, Liebermann was driven backward by a powerful lower thrust.

The door frame gave a sharp cracking sound. Unfortunately, like everything in Elysium it had a sturdy well-constructed appearance.

Liebermann essayed another thrust but Olbricht opposed him with a perfect counterparry, circling the young doctor's blade and casually turning it aside. The defense had been cleanly and precisely executed.

"Herr Olbricht," said Liebermann, breathless with exertion, "the door will not hold for much longer."

Olbricht's response was as to the point as his counterparry.

"I know."

Liebermann tried to think of something else to say—something that might engage Olbricht in a few more precious seconds of conversation. It was just a matter of delaying him. But no words came. Liebermann's mind was a white sheet of fear: void, blank, intractable.

Olbricht's brow furrowed with concentration. He lunged, this time with extreme speed and violence, so quick that Liebermann only just managed to interpose his own sabre. Once again the sheer force of the attack pushed him backward.

A regular thudding sound declared that the Masons had adopted a systematic strategy for breaking down the door. Liebermann imagined them inefficiently pushing against the panels with their shoulders.

"Kick it! Kick it down, for pity's sake!" he shouted in desperation. "Kick it by the lock."

Before he had finished the sentence, Olbricht was upon him and they were locked in combat. The confined space reverberated with the harsh clash of steel.

Parry, parry, parry.

The onslaught forced Liebermann into continuous retreat. He lost ground and Olbricht came forward. Again he lost ground—and Olbricht's attack became more frenzied.

Parry, parry, parry.

Liebermann sensed an object behind him—a desk, perhaps? Very soon he would be trapped. His mind was seized by an uncontrollable panic. Without thinking, he ran off to the side, exposing his back. It was utter stupidity. Suicide. He expected to feel the force of Olbricht's fatal lunge at any moment, the sabre penetrating his flesh and skewering his liver—but it never came. It was then that Liebermann realized the true nature of their conflict. Olbricht was simply playing with him, teasing out new registers of fear for his own deranged pleasure.

The young doctor's awkward escape ended as he tripped clumsily. He turned to face Olbricht and tried to discipline his panic.

He is only human, only human.

Liebermann repeated these words to himself like a litany.

Only human, only human.

The hysterical terror began to subside.

Lieberman thought of Signore Barbasetti. He remembered how his fencing master would often express displeasure by tapping his temple to emphasize a favorite injunction: *Think, Herr Doctor! If you do not think, all is lost.*

Again, their weapons connected.

Parry, thrust, parry, coupé, parry, thrust.

Liebermann was surprised to discover that he was able to hold off Olbricht's attack somewhat better than before. The artist's movements were not so swift. Perhaps he was becoming complacent. Or, even better, perhaps he was tiring.

Encouraged, Liebermann lunged. Olbricht deflected the attack but failed to resume his guard. The artist's chest was exposed. He could do it—he *would* do it! Liebermann raised his sabre but found that he was unable to deliver the fatal blow.

If only he had been more attentive in Barbasetti's lessons!

How often had the Italian demonstrated the very same maneuver? A line intentionally left open to invite an impetuous attack.

Liebermann held his breath. He was utterly paralyzed by the pricking sensation over his heart. With consummate skill, Olbricht had halted the blade at the point of penetration. Liebermann dared not move. If his own sabre so much as trembled, Olbricht would strike. Liebermann closed his eyes—and waited. The door frame groaned.

Even as he resigned himself to oblivion, Liebermann could not help making one final clinical observation.

He is feasting on my terror, savoring my despair. He cannot plunge the blade between my ribs until his sadistic appetites have been fully satisfied.

Liebermann opened his eyes. He did not wish to die a coward. He wanted to meet his end defiantly.

Olbricht was craning forward, tilting his head to one side, making a close examination of Liebermann's features. The young doctor stared into the widely spaced eyes—and noticed for the first time that they only appeared to be set so widely apart because the bridge of Olbricht's nose had sunk. The deep creases around Olbricht's mouth compressed and his lips parted. He was smiling—and in doing so he was exhibiting two rows of peculiarly stunted teeth, the ends of which were rough and uneven. Liebermann had never been this close to Olbricht before, had never had the opportunity to study the peculiarities of his physiognomy.

Think, Herr Doctor! If you do not think, all is lost.

Signor Barbasetti's injunction returned with haunting persistence.

Yes, of course!

Olbricht's irregular lineaments were not merely the result of his parental legacy—the germ plasm of his mother and father—but of some other process: a pathological process. The young doctor made his diagnosis, from which a series of bold inferences followed.

"Your mother," Liebermann began. "You loved her, didn't you? But she never returned your love. She never had the time. Always busy entertaining gentlemen. Foreigners. Hungarians, Czechs, Croats . . . Jews?"

Olbricht looked startled. His eyes widened.

"And you had dreams," Liebermann continued, gaining confidence. "Terrible dreams. Nightmares. About animals: wolves, dogs. . . . You still get them, don't you?" The words tumbled out, hurried, frantic. "And then there was the music! You lived behind a theater—a small folk theater. When your mother was entertaining her gentleman friends, you could hear music. Operettas, popular songs. But the most unforgettable melodies, the ones that lodged in your mind and wouldn't go away, were from an opera by Mozart: *The Magic Flute.*"

Olbricht's expression changed. He looked bemused, almost frightened. Childlike.

"What are you?" His voice sounded hoarse, as though he had suddenly been confronted by a supernatural intelligence.

"I am a doctor—I can help you."

But Liebermann had miscalculated. Olbricht did not want to be *helped*. The fearful expression on the artist's face was fading. Liebermann edged gently backward. In doing so, he created just enough space between Olbricht's blade and his chest to risk a single swift emancipating movement. He knocked Olbricht's sabre aside with the flat of his free gloved hand—and ran . . .

When Liebermann turned, he found himself backed up against a wall, facing an attack of demonic intensity. Blow followed blow. They rained down upon him: heavy, insistent, and deadly. Although Olbricht's attack was no longer controlled, Liebermann knew that he could hold off such a brutal assault for only a matter of seconds. His arm ached, weakened by each shocking impact.

Liebermann fell down on one knee. His weapon felt heavy and it began to slip from his hand. Drawing on some hidden vital reserve of energy, he held his sabre aloft horizontally, like a shield. The relentless pounding continued, powered by an inexhaustible fury. Liebermann was dimly aware of a loud crashing sound—and suddenly, miraculously, he was no longer alone. A sea of faces had appeared behind Olbricht, and a moment later Kanner was by Liebermann's side, deflecting Olbricht's hammer blows.

Exhausted and close to collapse, Liebermann watched the artist retreating, surrounded by a host of fresh, energetic adversaries. Olbricht wheeled around like a deadly dervish, his glinting blade creating a scintillating protective aura.

Kanner knelt beside Liebermann, placing a solicitous arm around his shoulders. "Are you all right?"

Liebermann nodded.

The crowd had closed around Olbricht, obscuring him from view, but Liebermann could still hear the chilling shriek of the artist's scything blade. Eventually the pitch of the screaming of metal through air dropped and the rhythm of more conventional engagement resumed, eventually slackening off to the rattle of intermittent, irregular contacts.

A powerful voice rose above the melee: "Brother Diethelm, I command you to drop your sword."

The clattering stopped and an eerie silence prevailed.

"You are vastly outnumbered. I repeat: drop your sword."

A pendulum clock sounded a hollow beat. Each percussive swing seemed to ratchet the tension up by degrees.

"Brother Diethelm?"

A thud followed by a metallic ringing was accompanied by a collective groan of relief.

Through a gap in the crowd, Liebermann briefly glimpsed the defeated artist. He was standing, arms outstretched, like Christ crucified, his head thrown back. A sob convulsed his chest.

"It is over," Olbricht cried. "I can do no more."

In his eyes, Liebermann recognized the light of Valhalla burning.

87

RHEINHARDT PRESSED HIS KNUCKLES against his eyes and after releasing them looked steadily at the wall clock. At first he could see nothing but a kaleidoscopic arrangement of luminous blotches. Then, slowly, his vision began to clear, and the hands came into sharp focus: a quarter past one. It had been a long, tiring day.

On returning home he had been unable to sleep. He had sat on a chair next to the telephone, dreading its fateful ring followed by the crackling connection and the voice of the Schottenring sergeant regretfully informing him of the discovery of two bodies. Rheinhardt had fallen into a fitful half sleep and when—as expected—the bell had sounded, he had lifted the receiver in a confused, fearful state. He had listened to the sergeant's report, but could not quite believe what he was hearing. He had asked the man to repeat himself. The officer politely obliged, prompting Rheinhardt to pinch his thigh to establish whether or not he was dreaming.

The long hand of the clock jumped forward and Rheinhardt lowered his gaze. Liebermann was fussing with some lint on his trousers, tutting impatiently at its obstinacy.

"So," said Rheinhardt, "you arrive at the Schottenring station dressed in a top hat, white gloves, and tailcoat—which, if I am not mistaken, has been cut in two places by a sabre blade. In your custody—bound and gagged—is the monster, Andreas Olbricht! The duty officer requests, very reasonably, that you give an account of yourself. You choose, however, to respond in the vaguest possible terms, suggesting that you managed to find and capture him with the help of some Freemasons. . . . Now, my dear friend, although I am accustomed to your predilection for evasive answers and your often quite taxing insistence on dramatic subterfuge, it seems to me that tonight you have excelled yourself."

During his speech, the inspector's voice had risen in pitch and his eyes had acquired a menacing shine.

The young doctor gave up trying to remove the intransigent lint from his trousers and, chastened, straightened his back.

"I may not possess the most incisive mind," continued the inspector, attempting to calm himself by spreading his hands out flat on the table. "But one doesn't need to be so very clever to guess how you came to deliver Olbricht earlier this evening—or, more correctly, yesterday evening." His finger flicked up toward the wall clock. "You infiltrated a clandestine Masonic gathering, where you discovered Olbricht preparing to murder persons corresponding with the figures of Sarastro and Prince Tamino. You challenged Olbricht, fought with him, and finally, with the assistance of those present, overpowered him."

Liebermann nodded. "Yes, broadly speaking, that is correct."

"Now, I am bound to ask you a very obvious question: Did you not think to inform the security office?"

"Of course I thought to inform the security office—it just wasn't possible."

Rheinhardt picked up his pen and dated the official notepaper that he had laid out on his desk.

"Oskar," said Liebermann, "before we proceed, you must promise me something."

"What?"

"That the security office will not investigate or hound the Masons."

"I am very happy to leave the Masons to their own devices. But Commissioner Brügel may take a different view."

"Then you must persuade him otherwise."

"Commissioner Brügel is nothing if not opinionated. I fear he will take his own view, whatever I say."

"Come now, Oskar, a man possessed of your quite considerable eloquence and charm should—" Rheinhardt raised a cautionary finger. Liebermann acknowledged the transparency of his flattery with a wry smile and chose a different approach. "At the very beginning of this investigation you likened Olbricht to the infamous Ripper of London. Well, unlike Scotland Yard we have actually caught our 'Ripper.' This will no doubt raise the international standing of the Viennese security office. It is even conceivable that your superior—having presided over such a coup—might expect to receive some token of recognition from the Hofburg." Liebermann assumed an expression of cherubic innocence. "I do not wish to interfere with your dealings with the good commissioner, but I am convinced that touching upon the subject of honors will be . . . expedient. Once he is preoccupied with dreams of the emperor pinning a ribbon on his chest, Brügel will be much less inclined to rake over the minor details of your report."

Rheinhardt sighed. "We shall see."

"Thank you, Oskar."

"Be that as it may, I *must* press you for more information." Rheinhardt underlined the date and looked up at his friend. "Commissioner Brügel will expect more than a few opaque lines—and, needless to say, I have some questions of my own." Liebermann leaned back in his chair and gestured for Rheinhardt to continue. "First, how on earth did you manage to get yourself into a secret Masonic meeting?"

"On Saturday I was taking dinner with a trusted friend, with whom I sometimes discuss my involvement with the security office. I told him of the discovery of Olbricht's diary and of our fear that Olbricht might attempt to kill a member of the royal family and a high-ranking Mason the following day. To my great surprise my friend revealed that he was a Mason. Moreover, he informed me that Sunday the twelfth of December was, for him and his brethren, a date of great significance. A foreign prince was to be initiated at a secret location in Vienna on that very day. I was given permission to attend the ritual, providing that I gave my solemn word not to disclose anything of what I saw to anyone, and in particular"—Liebermann tapped Rheinhardt's desk twice—"a certain detective inspector with whom my name has become recently associated."

Rheinhardt grunted dismissively and began writing. "Who was this foreign prince?"

"I am afraid I cannot say—I gave my word."

"Very well. What is your friend's name?"

"I am afraid I cannot say."

"All right. Did you encounter a man with a Vandyke beard?"

"I saw many men with Vandyke beards."

"A man called Lösch?"

Liebermann shrugged.

The inspector raised his head slowly, revealing a pained countenance.

"Oskar, I have already broken one promise this year," said Liebermann gravely. "I do not intend to break another."

The inspector gave a colossal sigh, and with exaggerated movements made a show of putting his pen down. He then opened the drawer of his desk and removed a small bottle of slivovitz and two glasses. He filled the glasses to the brim and then offered Liebermann a marzipan mouse, which the young doctor observed for a few moments before politely refusing. Rheinhardt sat back in his chair and said resignedly, "Very well. You will please proceed."

Liebermann, looking much relieved, continued his story. "I was taken to the secret location yesterday."

"I don't suppose there is any point in my asking—"

"No," Liebermann interrupted. "There isn't. Not because I *won't* tell you, this time—but because I *can't*. I have no idea where it is. I was blindfolded. And on my return with Olbricht, I was blindfolded again."

"How long did the journey take?"

Liebermann shrugged.

Rheinhardt smiled, sipped his slivovitz, and urged his friend to continue.

"I attended the initiation rite—"

"About which you can say nothing," Rheinhardt cut in.

"And in due course I observed a gentleman whom I supposed to be Olbricht."

"Supposed?"

"It was quite dark. The Masonic temple was large and inadequately illuminated by candles."

"I see."

"When Olbricht was in striking distance of both the principal Mason and the prince—"

"Sarastro and Tamino."

"I noticed that his fingers had closed around the hilt of his sabre."

"He was wearing a sabre?" Rheinhardt cut in again.

"I hope that I am not betraying the trust invested in me by the Masons—"

"Heaven forfend!"

"If I disclose to you that they were *all* wearing sabres."

"Were they indeed," said Rheinhardt, nodding with interest.

"At which point . . ."

The inspector lifted his hand.

"One moment, please! What was Olbricht doing at this secret meeting? How did *he* get in?"

"Isn't it obvious?"

Rheinhardt's eyebrows knitted together. "Surely not . . ."

Liebermann pressed his lips together and jerked his head forward.

"He is a Mason. And not only that, he is a librarian! He has been engaged for many months in the arduous task of cataloguing a vast collection of Masonic literature. Several of the books he has handled are very ancient in origin—guides to arcane rites and rituals."

"So Miss Lydgate was right after all."

"Of course—she is a remarkable woman." Liebermann paused for a moment.

"Max?"

Liebermann coughed, a little embarrassed by his momentary lapse of concentration.

"I am of the opinion that Olbricht entered the craft as a kind of spy. One can imagine such an infantile act of daring, such a caper, earning him the respect of his friends at the Eddic Literary Association. As you know, nationalists despise Masons. In my ignorance I have often wondered why. I had attributed their hostility to some species of paranoia; however, the answer is very simple. At the heart of Masonry is a belief in universal fraternity and equality—a belief that stands in stark opposition to the exclusive, supremacist philosophy of Guido List. As a Mason, Olbricht was known as Brother Diethelm. Gunther Diethelm. Interesting, don't you think, that he should choose that as his nom de guerre?"

Rheinhardt looked puzzled.

"Gunther," Liebermann continued, "means 'warrior' and Diethelm means 'protector of the folk or people.' All of which suggests to me a powerful identification with the legendary *Unbesiegbare*—The Invincible, or strong one from above, the Teutonic savior."

Rheinhardt sipped his slivovitz.

"He played a perilous game. What if a Mason with whom he was acquainted had come to one of his exhibitions? His masquerade would have been discovered immediately."

"It wasn't such a risk. First, Olbricht rarely had his work shown in galleries. He was never good enough, and without Von Rautenberg's patronage he would never have exhibited at all. Second, German nationalists and Freemasons occupy very different worlds and those worlds rarely touch. It is a peculiarity of our city that different peoples can coexist and live in close proximity but never meet."

Rheinhardt grumbled his assent. The memory of the sewer people was all too vivid.

"I do not imagine," Liebermann continued, "that Olbricht joined the Masons intending to murder any of their number. Rather, the possibility presented itself as his curious program for murder—and the disease process—progressed."

"Disease process?"

"Forgive me—I am racing ahead of myself." Liebermann tasted his slivovitz and looked mildly startled by its potency. "Where on earth did you get this from?"

"A Croatian scissors-grinder."

"That doesn't surprise me. Now, where was I?"

"You saw Olbricht's hand on his hilt."

"Ah yes." Liebermann disdainfully placed the glass back on Rheinhardt's desk and leaned back in his chair. "I challenged him, and he immediately made a dash for the door, escaped from the temple, and made his way to the library, which was situated at a lower level. I can remember feeling uneasy. Clearly, someone meaning to escape would have run *up* the stairs, not down; however, somewhat overexcited by the chase, I pursued Olbricht without thinking and so fell into his trap."

"Trap?"

"He had concealed himself behind the library door and, after locking us both in, drew his sabre. From the moment our blades touched it was obvious that he was the superior swordsman. My only chance of survival was to ward him off until the Masons broke the door down and came to my rescue."

Rheinhardt peered at the slashed material over Liebermann's heart.

"Looks like he almost killed you."

"He almost did. He had me pinned to the wall. All he had to do was push."

"What stopped him?"

"I surprised him—shocked him, even—by making some observations which, given his reaction, I have every reason to believe were correct: and while he was distracted, I made my escape."

Rheinhardt leaned forward. "Observations? What observations?"

"That his mother was a prostitute who entertained men of many different nationalities, that they had a room close to a folk theater where *The Magic Flute* was often performed, and that Olbricht has always been—and continues to be—tormented by dreams of animals."

Rheinhardt shook his head. "But how could you possibly . . ."

"Know? I didn't. I was simply making some educated guesses."

"On what basis?"

"His appearance."

"But you have always told me never to judge a man by his appearance."

"That is true. And in almost all cases nothing can be deduced from the shape of someone's nose, the slope of his forehead, or the thickness of his lips!"

"So what was it about Olbricht's appearance that permitted you to make such bold and seemingly accurate assertions?"

Liebermann placed his long fingers together.

"His face, his distinctive features. They are a form of stigmata . . . but stigmata that have nothing whatsoever to do with Lombroso's speculations about the relationship between physiognomy and criminality."

Rheinhardt was beginning to lose patience again. "Max, I haven't a clue what you're talking about. Please speak plainly."

"The sunken bridge of his nose, the creases around his mouth, his odd teeth. It was only when I was up close that I realized their significance. They are all symptoms. Herr Olbricht has congenital syphilis."

Liebermann paused, allowing Rheinhardt to absorb his revelation.

"What? He was born . . . syphilitic?"

"Indeed, and once I had established this fact, I immediately grasped the nature of his history. What kind of mother might have syphilis? A prostitute! Why might Olbricht despise other nationalities so much? Because these were her clientele: down-at-heel Hungarians, Poles, Czechs, and Jews, newly arrived in Vienna. These were the men who took her away from him. Why had *The Magic Flute* acquired such special significance for Olbricht? He had heard it being sung incessantly as a child—how could anyone forget those glorious melodies? And how might the son of a prostitute get to hear opera? His mother must have rented a room next to a folk theater. The German nationalist doctrine of race hate provided the adult Olbricht with a rationale for many of his attacks, but his real motivation was much deeper. An angry, jealous child was still raging silently in the darkest recesses of his psyche."

Rheinhardt twirled his mustache. "All of this suggests that he loved his mother. Yet he chose to attack women who suffered the same fate, those poor Galician girls."

"Ambivalence, Oskar! Professor Freud has taught us that the roots of motivation are profoundly deep and hopelessly tangled. In the unconscious, love and hate coexist, as comfortably as sewer people and archdukes in our beloved city! Olbricht loved his mother—but hated her at the same time. Hated her for being a prostitute, hated her for neglecting him . . . and most of all, I suspect, hated her for not being Aryan. It would not surprise me in the least if in due course we discovered that Olbricht's mother was Galician herself! Maybe even a Galician Jew."

Rheinhardt puffed out his cheeks and let the air escape slowly.

"Congenital syphilis," Liebermann continued, "also explains Olbricht's ghastly predilection for genital mutilation. In a way, he was attacking the very source of his infantile anguish."

"And his dreams? How did you know he was tormented by dreams of animals?"

"The infant Olbricht must have occasionally awoken to see his mother practicing the . . ." Liebermann hesitated before selecting a euphemism. "*Requirements* of her profession. Clearly, this would have been a highly disturbing experience. I have good reason to believe that such traumatic memories are transformed in dreams. Defensive mechanisms come into play, turning people into animals. In particular, dogs and wolves."

Rheinhardt raised his eyebrows. "I have dreamed of dogs on many occasions, and I am certain that I—"

Liebermann shook his head. "I wasn't suggesting that all dreams featuring dogs disguise a traumatic memory of this kind! Sometimes a dog is just a dog!"

"I am much relieved to hear that," said Rheinhardt, fidgeting uncomfortably. "Please continue."

"Congenital syphilis can remain latent for decades but typically, at some point, it will attack the central nervous system. The brain tissue softens, causing either progressive paralysis, insanity, or both. Grandiosity and irrational rage are very typical of syphilitic insanity. As Olbricht gradually lost touch with reality—and learned more from List's writings—the delusional belief that he was the Teutonic Messiah may have become more established." Liebermann picked up his glass of slivovitz and turned it in his hand. "Moreover, as his inner world became more and more chaotic, The Magic Flute would have acquired increasing significance as an organizing principle for the expression of his violent emotions, which had become directed—again under List's influence—toward anything un-Germanic. I am also of the opinion that after his execrable exhibition attracted the critical scorn it deserved—"

"You know," Rheinhardt interrupted, "I really didn't think some of his paintings were all that bad."

Liebermann ignored his friend's comment and continued. "His creative urge became—as it were—redirected. The opportunistic murder of Sarastro and Tamino would have completed a kind of grim masterwork. Among Nationalists, his name would have passed into legend."

Liebermann sipped his slivovitz and his face clouded with dissatisfaction. "What troubles me, however, is that I cannot explain why he chose to initiate his campaign when he did. Something must have acted as a trigger, but I cannot say what. I strongly suspect that the answer may be connected with the location of the Eddic Literary Association: Mozartgasse. One day, I hope, the answer will present itself, and we shall be able to add a little footnote of explanation to this most interesting case."

The two men shared a moment of silence before Rheinhardt said, "You have yet to finish your story."

"There is little more to tell. I managed to hold off Olbricht's final attack until the door was broken down and I was saved by my friend and his Masonic brothers. Had my rescue been delayed a moment longer . . ." Liebermann smiled. "Well, perhaps it is best not to dwell on such things."

Rheinhardt shook his head and the rings under his eyes seemed deeper, darker, and heavier. The simple gesture communicated much: reprimand, disapproval, admiration, and concern. There was something distinctly parental about Rheinhardt's mien. The sad resignation of fathers who—motivated by love—must admonish their foolish, headstrong, exuberant sons, and who know, at the very same time, that their words are wasted, having been young once themselves.

"I trust that you now have enough for your report," said Liebermann.

Rheinhardt looked mournfully at his blank sheet of paper.

"I daresay that I shall be able to produce something by the time Commissioner Brügel arrives."

"And I sincerely hope you will respect my wishes concerning my promise to the Masons."

Rheinhardt nodded.

Looking up at the clock, Liebermann added, "I am expected at the hospital at eight o'clock and would very much like to go home. I must change out of these ridiculous clothes and get a few hours' sleep."

"You are free to leave, Herr Doctor."

Liebermann placed his unfinished glass of slivovitz on Rheinhardt's desk, stood up, and walked to the door.

"Oh, I forgot to mention," he said as he took his top hat from the stand. "Some time ago I ordered several volumes of Russian songs from a publisher in Moscow. They never came, and to tell the truth, I'd quite forgotten about it. Well, that is, until last week, when they actually arrived."

"My Russian isn't very good."

"Nonsense. When we performed those Tchaikovsky romances, I thought that Fyodor Chaliapin himself had stolen into the room! Perhaps your dear wife would be willing to forgo your company tomorrow evening?"

"With respect to tolerating my absences, she is nothing less than a saint."

"Good. Tuesday, then."

Before Liebermann could close the door, Rheinhardt called out, "Oh, and Max." Liebermann halted, expecting the inevitable debt of gratitude. "If you ever act on your own like this again, so help me God, I'll . . ." The inspector mimed the violent strangulation of a young doctor, his jowls wobbling as he throttled the column of air beneath his desk lamp, creating a whirlpool of starry motes.

Liebermann feigned indignation and, placing the top hat on his head at a decidedly impudent angle, made a swift exit.

88

LIEBERMANN FOUND HIS MIND occupied by thoughts of Miss Lydgate. The image of her seated, reading her book in the Natural History Museum, returned to interrupt his concentration throughout the day: a vaporous impression of her flame hair, burning like a beacon. While undertaking his medical duties, he had silently acknowledged his need to see her, and resolved to visit the university. He suspected that he was more likely to find her there than at home. His decision to see her was not without a convenient justification.

I must tell her that her microscopy results were correct. Yes, it is only right that she should know.

But even as the justification presented itself, Liebermann found it unconvincing. The words were hollow and the sentiment disingenuous. The undercurrent of desire was too strong to ignore. It flowed through his being like an electric charge, thrilling his nerves and heightening his senses.

The memory of Olbricht's blade still exerted a ghostly pressure over his heart, reminding him that nothing in life should be taken for granted and no opportunity should be ignored. It would be unforgivable, he mused, to die harboring regrets.

Liebermann promptly placed his case files in his drawer, turned the key, and left the hospital.

The föhn was still having its curious effect on the climate. It wasn't like a winter's evening at all. Indeed, it was more like early spring.

Chairs and tables had been put out in front of the coffeehouses, most of which were already decked with seasonal lights and decorations. The streets vibrated with laughter and conversation. On Alserstrasse a group of singers were caroling, accompanied by cymbolom and a rustic violin. The air was fragrant with an intoxicating heady mixture of roast chestnuts, honey, and cigar smoke. The whole city seemed to be in a festive mood: middle-aged men with short gray beards, women in long dresses and feathered hats, soldiers, street vendors, artists—fashionably wearing their coats loosely draped over their shoulders—students, businessmen, bohemians—with thick hair and purposeful, glowing eyes—light-footed teachers from the dancing academy, priests, lawyers, and chorus girls. Liebermann inhaled the air and felt a thrill of excitement. It was wonderful to be alive.

Outside the university he stopped under a streetlamp and waited. As the students began to spill out beneath the massive triple-arched entrance and descend the wide stone stairs, he willed Miss Lydgate to be among them. She would be easy to identify—a woman, among so many men.

The streetcar to the Kahlenberg was pulling away, its overhead cables flashing like lightning. When it had passed, he could see Miss Lydgate standing beneath the central arch, investigating the contents of her reticule. It seemed to Liebermann that although she was surrounded by people, she was somehow alone. A hazy light seemed to collect around her, making her stand out from the crowd.

"Miss Lydgate!"

The Englishwoman raised her head and peered down the stairs. Something of the cable flashes seemed to have inexplicably remained in her eyes. It made her look wild, elemental—almost mythic. For a moment she showed no sign of recognition, but then, quite suddenly, her features softened, and she smiled.

Acknowledgments and Sources

I WOULD LIKE TO THANK Hannah Black and Oliver Johnson, and my agent, Clare Alexander, for their editorial comments, interest, and enthusiasm; Nick Austin for a thoughtful copyedit; Paul Taunton, Jennifer Rodriguez, and Bara MacNeill for their assistance in preparing the U.S. edition. Steve Mathews for the loan of his invaluable critical faculties; and Raymond Coffer for pointing me in the right direction with respect to numerous obscure issues pertinent for my research. Martin Cherry of the Library and Museum of Freemasonry, London, for being so very helpful with respect to my questions concerning the history of Freemasonry and Masonic symbols, and Dr. Otto Fritsch of the Grand Lodge of Austria for his scholarly letter concerning the practice of Freemasonry in the Austro-Hungarian Empire. Helmut Portele of the Tram Museum, for answers to questions concerning the electrification of the Viennese streetcar system, Frauke Kreutzler of the Wien Museum for finding out where the Mozart monument was in 1902, and Mirko Herzog of the Technisches Museum for alerting me to the existence of the *Illustrierte Kronen-Zeitung*. Nathalie Ferrier and Luitgard Hammerer for invaluable help with translations (and Bernardo for being patient while said translations were being undertaken). Clive Baldwin, for being generally knowledgeable on all things Austro-Hungarian, Dr. Julie Fox for advising me on the precipitin test and the symptoms and course of congenital syphilis.

{ 475 }

Finally, Nicola Fox, for accommodating Max into our lives since 2003—and for so much more.

I quote directly from Charles Darwin's *The Descent of Man, and Selection in Relation to Sex* (1871) and an article from *The Lancet* written in 1886. Foch's open letter to the *Zeitung* is a bowdlerization of *Science Proves Women Inferior* by Dr. Charles H. Heydemann, from *Ives Scrapbook*. All of these can be found in the excellent anthology 1900 (edited by Mike Jay and Michael Neve), published by Penguin in 1999. I also quote directly from *Rituals of the Masonic Grand Lodge of the Sun, Bayreuth*, translated from the German by Art deHoyos. All of Guido (von) List's works are real, with the exception of the pamphlet *On the Secret of the Runes—A Preliminary Communication*, which is loosely based on his book *The Secret of the Runes* (1907/1908).

Frank Tallis
London, December 2005

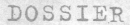

DOSSIER

Vienna Blood

FRANK TALLIS

The Secret Societies of Vienna
Freud, Repression, and the Dark Beginnings of National Socialism

FREUD WAS RATHER FOND OF SPHINXES. He was an avid collector of antiquities, and his rooms were crammed with statuettes, steles, and artifacts. Among this vast collection were numerous representations of Sphinxes: a seated Sphinx on a fragment of first-century Roman wall painting; another on a Greek water jar from the classical period; another in the form of a terra-cotta figurine; another in the form of a faience amulet. Hanging on the wall was a reproduction of a painting, *Oedipus and the Sphinx*, by Ingres. Freud's apartment was not the only place in Vienna you could find a Sphinx.

Vienna is full of Sphinxes: you can find them in the art history museum, in the public gardens of the Belvedere Palace, or more subtly, as molded cast-iron supports at the foot of streetlamps. Their presence suggests that Vienna is a city of secrets—a haven for conspirators, cabals, and secret societies.

Freud's psychoanalytic movement started as a kind of secret society. He gathered around himself a small number of followers who would meet every Wednesday evening in the waiting room of his apartment, Bergasse 19. Beneath banks of cigar smoke, under the watchful, silent stare of his statuettes, they would discuss dreams and the mysterious workings of the human mind.

Max Graf, one of Freud's early acolytes, provides us with the following firsthand description:

The gatherings followed a definite ritual. First, one of the members would present a paper.... After a social quarter of an hour, the discussion would begin. The last and decisive word was always spoken by Freud himself. There was an atmosphere of the foundation of a religion in that room. Freud himself was its new prophet who made the heretofore prevailing methods of psychological investigation appear superficial. . . . Freud's pupils—he was always addressed as "The Professor"—were his apostles....

At first, Freud's secret society had only a few members: himself, Alfred Adler, Max Kahane, Rudolf Reitler, and Wilhelm Stekel. However, over the next few years, the circle grew—welcoming names such as Otto Rank (in 1906) and Sándor Ferenczi and Viktor Tausk (in 1908). Among the early "guests" of the society were C. G. Jung and L. Binswanger, 6 April 1907; Karl Abraham, 8 December 1907; A. A. Brill (an Austrian émigré to the United States from the age of thirteen) and Ernest Jones, 6 May 1908; and M. Karpas of New York, 4 April 1909.

In the spring of 1908, the burgeoning psychoanalytic society had begun to assemble a library. This had grown, Ernest Jones tells us, "to impressive proportions" by 1938. Unfortunately, the early arcana of the psychoanalytic movement did not survive that year, which marked the arrival of the Nazis and the library's subsequent destruction.

The description that Graf gives us of the gatherings at Bergasse 19 (with their sacramental atmosphere) is usually taken out of context, particularly by critics of Freud, who use it to create an impression that psychoanalysis is—and always has been—a pseudoreligion rather than a scientific project. However, in Freud's Vienna, secret gatherings were thick on the ground. There was nothing unusual about Freud's group. Behind closed doors, the city was overburdened with earnest men, hunched around tables beneath flickering gaslights, united by common beliefs and convinced that they might change the world. Unfortunately, not all of these societies were benign.

From about 1900, a number of secret societies began to coalesce around the sinister figure of Guido von List—a successful journalist and writer, beloved of the German literati. Eventually these disparate societies united under the banner of a single mystical association: Armanenschaft. The term *Arman* refers to a mythical tribe of pre-Christian nobles.

The Arman fraternities used a special sign by which they could recognize one another: the eighteenth rune, the *fyrfos*, or hooked cross. We would all know it by its other name: the swastika. Von List was obsessed with the superiority of the German-speaking peoples and preserving the purity of German bloodlines. He divided humanity into two groups: the Aryan masters, and the "herd people," by which he mostly meant the Jews and southern races. He wrote of the coming of a German Messiah—The Invincible, the strong one from above, a Wagnerian hero, who would establish a great northern alliance and reign as a god-man, subject to no law but his own.

It is noteworthy that the writings of Von List and his disciples are rarely referenced in twentieth-century histories. When they are referred to, they are usually dismissed as something of a joke, with accompanying remarks to the effect that Von List was not taken very seriously by his contemporaries.

Although we can be fairly sure that the liberal patrons of Vienna's coffeehouses—the likes of Schnitzler, Mahler, Klimt, or Freud—would have had little time for Von List's posturing, we can be absolutely certain that one person at least took Von List's writings very seriously indeed.

Little of Hitler's personal library remains, but some fragments and books have survived. One of these, a book on nationalism, contains a longhand dedication:

To Mr. Adolf Hitler, my dear Arman brother, B. Steininger.

The word *Arman* might have been employed here as a term of respect or honor, but it's far more likely that Hitler was associated with Von List's Armanenschaft—or a related organization called the High Armanic Order. Hitler would have first encountered Von List's ideas when he was a poverty-stricken artist in Vienna. We know that these ideas made a deep impression on him, because after his rise to power, Hitler incorporated whole passages of Von List's writings into his speeches.

Von List's closest disciple was Josef Adolf Lanz—now better known as Lanz von Liebenfels (a completely fabricated identity that allowed him to claim noble descent). Von Liebenfels proposed the revival of the Knights Templar as an Aryan order, and on Christmas day 1907, he unfurled a flag bearing the swastika on the summit of Burg Werfenstein—their intended seat of power. Liebenfels's most famous work, rejoicing in the extraordinary title *Theozoology, or the News about the Little Sodom Monkeys and the Gods' Electron*, envisaged a future society guided by Von List—inspired ideals of racial purity. Liebenfels insisted that a blond heroic race should be raised in secret cloisters, and that Aryans should be trained to exterminate "impure races" by castration and sterilization.

Like Von List's Armanenschaft, Von Liebenfels's cult has always been regarded as something of a joke. Contemporary intellectuals were convinced that he and his followers posed no threat to the established order; however, once again, twentieth-century history reminds us that one can never be too complacent when it comes to secret societies and prophetic visionaries.

Between 1905 and 1931, Von Liebenfels published a journal in Vienna called *Ostara* (the German goddess of dawn). One of his readers was so keen that he visited Von Liebenfels in 1909 to collect some back issues. In 1951, the aged Von Liebenfels remembered the enthusiastic nineteen-year-old fondly. Indeed, he was pleased to give Hitler the copies he wanted, and because the young man looked "quite poor," he was moved to give him two kronen to help him get back home in comfort.

The influence of Von Liebenfels on Hitler was not merely ideological (although that would have been bad enough). Of all the Pan-German writers and race theorists around at the time, Von Liebenfels was the most florid. His language was fierce and garish— febrile with maniacal evangelism. Experts claim that Von Liebenfels's cadences are clearly evident in Hitler's *Mein Kampf*:

> With satanic joy on his face, the black-haired Jewish youth lurks in wait for the unsuspecting girl whom he defiles with his blood, thus stealing her from her people. With every means he tries to destroy the racial foundations of the people he has set out to subjugate.

All of the above begs the question: Why were there so many secret societies and cults in Vienna around 1900? Vienna was the most civilized city in Europe, enjoying a cultural renaissance and producing unprecedented advances in the arts, science, and philosophy. The alarming answer might be a simple piece of legislation: article 18 of the postrevolutionary "Law on Associations" of 1867.

In a sense, the city was dramatizing the principles of Freudian repression. Essentially, psychoanalysis tells us that if you push something down (for example, a memory), it'll pop up somewhere else (perhaps as a symptom). Article 18 of the "Law on Associations" was all about pushing things down.

The Austro-Hungarian Empire was undoubtedly repressive with respect to the formation of societies and associations. A license to convene was required and this was granted only by a specially appointed commissioner. These licenses were not easily obtained and were often given with strings attached. The Freemasons, for example, could meet in Vienna under the auspices of a friendly society—but they were forbidden to work their rituals. The "Law on Associations" was extremely counterproductive, driving subversives underground and "infecting" the body politic in the process. One could argue— perhaps controversially—that the social illness that eventually emerged was National Socialism, and so virulent was this illness, it took a world war to treat it.

In these troubled times, there is still much to learn from events in Vienna in 1900 and the principles of psychoanalysis. Freedom of speech is sacred and should never be compromised. When we consign demons to the unconscious, they do not go away, they simply become more powerful.

Frank Tallis
London 2007

Sources

Gamwell, Lynn and Richard Wells, eds. *Sigmund Freud and Art: His Personal Collection of Antiquities.* New York: Harry N. Abrams, Inc., 1989.

Graf, Max. "Reminiscences of Professor Sigmund Freud." *The Psychoanalytic Quarterly* 11, 1942.

Hamann, Brigitte. *Hitler's Vienna: a Dictator's Apprenticeship.* Oxford: Oxford University Press, 1999.

Jones, Ernest. *The Life and Work of Sigmund Freud.* Penguin Books Ltd., UK, 1964.

Personal communication to the author concerning the practice of Freemasonry in Habsburg, Vienna, from Dr. Otto Fritsch of the Grand Lodge of Austria, 2004.

FRANK TALLIS is a practical clinical psychologist and an expert in obsessional states. He is the author of *A Death in Vienna* and *Vienna Blood*, as well as seven nonfiction books on psychology. He is the recipient of a writers' award from the Arts Council of Great Britain and the New London Writers Award from the London Arts Board. *A Death in Vienna* was short-listed for the 2005 Crime Writers' Association Ellis Peters Historical Dagger Award. Tallis lives in London.